The King
of Babylon
Shall Not
Come
Against You

Other Books by George Garrett

George Garrett

(((((((((((((((

The King of Babylon Shall Not Come Against You

Harcourt Brace & Company
New York   San Diego   London

Library of Congress Cataloging-in-Publication Data
Garrett, George P., 1929–
The King of Babylon shall not come against
you/George Garrett.—1st Harvest ed.
p.   cm.
ISBN 0-15-157554-1
1. King, Martin Luther, Jr., 1929–1968—Assassination—Fiction.
2. City and town life—Florida—Fiction.
3. Journalists—Florida—Fiction.   I. Title.
PS3557.A72K5   1996
813'.54—dc20   95–45188

Text set in Galliard
Designed by Camilla Filancia
Printed in the United States of America
First Harvest edition
E D C B A

For JANE GELFMAN *and for* CORK SMITH
With gratitude for many things and,
of course, with love and squalor . . .

Where are now your prophets which prophesied unto you,
saying: The King of Babylon shall not come against you
nor against this land?

—JEREMIAH 37:19

Throughout more than four centuries,
from Ponce de Leon in his caravels
to the latest Pennsylvanian in his Buick,
Florida has been invaded by seekers of gold
or of sunshine; yet it has retained an identity
and a character distinctive to itself. The result of all this
is a material and immaterial pattern of infinite variety,
replete with contrasts, paradoxes, confusions
and inconsistencies.

> —*Florida: A Guide to the Southernmost State,*
> Federal Writers' Project
> of the Work Projects Administration

Act so that there is no use in a centre.

> —GERTRUDE STEIN, *Tender Buttons*

*The King
of Babylon
Shall Not
Come
Against You*

Then and There

ALPHA WEATHERBY

Be with me. . . .

He will cut off my hair. He is going to cut it all away. Scissors flash bright and then go click-click in empty air. His fingers grasp and twine handfuls of hair. Snip-snip-snip go the scissors but I won't look.

Be with me, merciful angels.

I close my eyes and feel now a new lightness as hunks of hair fall away. When he has finished with the scissors he will next shave my skull smooth and clean. Like (they say) the women collaborators after the war. Like his own clean-shaven skull.

Be with me, merciful angels, now and forever.

Here and Now

THE QUINCY COUNTY LIBRARY

The young librarian reminds him of Judy Davis in *Barton Fink*—thin, nervous, intense, vaguely unhealthy and oddly dangerous. Therefore oddly exciting. To him, anyway. The librarian, whose name is Eleanor, has taken him back to her office so she can smoke a cigarette.

"Do you mind?" she says, lighting her filter-tipped cigarette.

"I used to smoke a lot, three packs a day, actually," he says. "But I finally quit."

"Oh . . ."

"Doesn't bother me. I like to smell it. And I just can't bring myself to believe all that stuff about secondhand smoke."

You may not believe this, either—he doesn't—but here she

is blowing smoke rings, one neatly inside the other. She seems to be good at it.

He has recently signed a contract to do a nonfiction book about some things that happened years ago, in 1968, in and around the growing city of Paradise Springs, located in central Florida, north of Orlando and south of Gainesville. With the advance he paid off some of his most urgently pressing debts and bills. Dodged others. Flew down from New York to Jacksonville, where he rented a car, a nondescript blue Taurus. Then drove on to Paradise Springs and checked in at the Ramada Inn. Which, of course, wasn't there in 1968. There are all kinds of things which weren't there in 1968.

Strangely enough, he is not one of them. Happens that he was there, in person, during at least some of the events of the first week of April 1968, and he is still possessed of some vague and confusing memories of what was happening then and there. He has never told anyone about his own part in any of it.

He has come here, briefly to be sure, to do a little "on-site research" and maybe to refresh and clarify his memories. He has come here to the library because that is a good place to begin.

"Mr. Tone?"

"Call me Billy."

"I know who you are. I have even read some of your work, including that Hollywood thing."

"I guess I'll never live that one down."

"It wasn't so bad."

"Thanks."

"Nothing to be ashamed of."

Yes, very much like Judy Davis in *Barton Fink*. Thin and nervous in her light flowery dress, her sensible shoes. Good legs.

"This doesn't really seem like your kind of subject," she says.

"How can I lose?" He smiles. "It's got two murders, a robbery, a suicide, a grotesque kidnapping, a deliberately set fire in a very crowded place. All kinds of unusual, not to say totally bizarre occurrences."

"Classic Southern Gothic."

"I'm aiming for a little bit more than that."

"I should hope so."

She stubs out her cigarette and lights a fresh one.

"You've been here before, haven't you?"

"I grew up in Florida. I have kinfolk here. I'm related to the Singletrees and the Royles. I used to visit here. I remember the old library."

This one is new and shiny, concrete and glass, all air-conditioned. Computers and videos and audiotapes and good lighting. Not enough books. The old library was crumbling brick and high-ceilinged with lazy overhead fans. Stacks were crowded and badly lit, kind of furtive. All the women who worked there were ancient. Frail and dyspeptic. Constantly on the lookout for sneaky teenage boys like himself who might try to find and check out a dirty book or tear a picture out of a magazine.

"That's not what I meant," she says, narrowing her pale blue eyes. Nice natural lashes. Very light touch of eyeliner. "I mean, is there something personal about this story?"

"Even if there was, it wouldn't change anything. I try my best to keep out of my work. I look, I listen, I ask questions, that's all."

"I am a camera."

"More like I am a camcorder."

"You know what happened at exactly the same time, don't you?"

"What?"

"Thursday, April fourth, same day as the murders here, Martin Luther King, Jr., was killed in Memphis."

"Is there any kind of connection?"

"I doubt it. But I don't see how you can ignore it completely."

Then, after a pause, she continues. "There's a man here, a poet, who's trying to write a novel about King."

"White man?"

"Yes."

"Lots of luck."

She puts out the second cigarette.

"Well, let's go take a look at some old newspapers."

He follows her into a room with a row of microfilm machines. She looks just fine from behind. Urgently thin, but well shaped, well rounded anyway. There's a hint of the scent of a very nice, not cheap perfume. It is suddenly important to him to find out the name of it.

"Did you ever see *Barton Fink?*" he asks.

She laughs. Good straight teeth, though a little tobacco stained. Can you get secondhand smoke from a kiss?

"Judy Davis was wonderful," she says.

"Simply marvelous," he says, trying to imitate Billy Crystal.

Then and There

DUDLEY HAGOOD, EDITOR
OF THE *Paradise Springs Trumpet*,
SPEAKS HIS PIECE

When everything is at best debatable and always doubtful, I can't see any sense whatsoever in choosing to ignore the simple facts. So here are some of the relevant facts. Such as they are:

1. It is a fact that the various incidents herein recounted and recorded and speculated upon did take place in and about the town of Paradise Springs, county of Quincy, state of Florida. What people would once have called a "typical small town" is now a type only of the dead and wilting stalks left on the vast cornfield which was once America. The said field is scheduled soon to vanish forever, probably to be covered up with asphalt, and the asphalt covered with painted arrows and parking slots, all aiming to become the biggest continuous shopping center in the history of the world. That is, unless

they succeed in blowing it all up first. In which case, friends, it will be the biggest desert we have yet seen, making the Gobi and the Sahara and so forth look like piddling sandpiles.

2. It is a fact that there was, indeed, a double murder, the victims being one Alpha Weatherby, a native of Paradise Springs, born and raised here, aged twenty; and Dan Lee Smithers, also known as Little David, an itinerant revivalist preacher, estimated to be in his late thirties or early forties, but so small and delicate of bone and stature, so pure and high in speaking and singing voice, so unlined and unblemished of skin and complexion, that (with the aid of the proper cosmetics and costume and a gold curly wig) he could pass for a child, a prodigy chosen by the Lord to be blessed with the gift of tongues and a healing touch.

3. It's a fact that two people were accused of, and have been subsequently tried for and convicted of, the crime of first-degree murder, involving conspiracy to commit a felony, to wit: to rob or steal from the aforesaid Alpha Weatherby the sum of $1,547.88, a sum which (for reasons that are not clear and not likely ever to be) she herself took from the People's Bank and Trust Company, where she was employed as a teller.

4. It is also a fact that these two convicted criminals are presently in custody and awaiting the eventual disposition of their cases and the outcome of separate and sundry appeals filed against the decision and verdict of the jury and the sentence of the lower court. They are: (a) Billy Papp, alias "Billygoat" and "Goathead," born twenty-some years ago in Bessemer, Alabama, and in recent years variously employed as a short-order cook, an undertaker's assistant, a used-car salesman, a carnival barker, and, at the time of his crime and apprehension, as the general business and promotion manager for Little David Enterprises, Inc.

The other (b) is Geneva Lasoeur, born Mary Lou Frond, aged thirty-nine. Born in Big Spring, Texas, but raised and educated into maturity in a house of ill repute in Galveston. She later enjoyed a period of prosperity and even some notoriety as a specialty dancer in various places such as New Orleans, Newark, Phoenix City, and Tijuana, Mexico. This period ended when, as a result of some glandular irregularity or radical change in body chemistry, she began to gain an inordinate amount of weight, fat which, evidently, no treatment or weeping, praying and fasting could control or shed from her weary frame of bones. She is said to have been the common-law wife of the aforesaid Little David. This cannot, however, be established as true or false and in any case taxes ordinary credulity, if not the capacity of fantasy; for Geneva stands well over six feet barefooted and weighs easily as much as many professional football players.

5. It is a fact that no trace of the missing money has been found yet.

6. Also, no one has been able to offer a satisfactory and rational explanation of why the victim, the aforesaid Alpha Weatherby, was both as nude as and as bald as an apple at the instant of her unfortunate demise.

7. It is a fact that following the trial and the brief and prosperous invasion of our community by reporters, cameramen and crowds of curious tourists, life again now goes on in Paradise Springs very much as it did before any of these unhappy events took place. Indeed, even gossip and speculation have faded away now, the faint echo of human voices drowned out and lost against the rising volume of noise and news of the moment. That clamor is all there is. The rest is history.

Then and Now

THE PLACE

Quincy County is long and narrow and flat as can be. The northern part is much more like south Georgia or Alabama than the name and image of Florida might invoke. Wide acres of green and shadowy pine woods (with, here and there, some live oaks and post oaks and blackjack oaks with their beards and wigs of Spanish moss), woods orchestrated by insects, haunted by birdsong, brooded over by buzzards searching and circling in their lazy, smudged circles, a fingerprint against the blue-and-white, sun-drenched sky, for something dead or dying. To the hunter's joy this is a home for the quick, small, apparitional white-tailed deer, the sometimes heard and more rarely seen wild turkey. And some of the oldest among the living will surely claim to have heard or even to have seen, in long-gone days, the last of the Florida panthers there; with, once in a while, a claimed hearing or sighting, even here or now, by some barely credible witness.

Wide acres of shadowy green pine woods broken by small farms and pastures. These woods were, once upon their time and not so long ago, the chief source of industry and wealth in the county, with mills and turpentine camps producing the products they called naval stores. And at the farthest edge to the north of the county there were some few ambitious souls who seriously tried to grow some cotton and, sooner or later, seriously failed. Their large fields are mostly woods again.

In the southern half of the county, below the town which sits in the middle, there are wetlands and hammocks, palmetto and cypress, home for the gator and the slithering moccasin, for bass and bream and catfish. And a sandy soil that more than once has tempted the folly of trying to plant and to grow oranges this far north. This part of the county is, then, threaded and crisscrossed by a network of dark, slow streams, moving eastward, uncoiling as lazy as snakes in dog days, toward the St. Johns River.

Quincy is too far south for a true winter season, though there are sudden cold snaps and even, like the cry of the panther in deep wooded places, historical memories and rumors of some dusting of snow—at least of snowflakes seen in the air.

A long hot summer and not much winter, true, but there are nonetheless palpable, if subtle, seasons. Sometimes in early springtime, time for the redbud and dogwood to bloom, time when the woods are bright with sudden birdsong and all the new-minted opulence of every kind of blooming and budding and flowering and the air is as clear and sweet as the vanished springs that gave the town its name, there comes a time when it seems entirely possible that all the lost ghosts of childhood will gather together again in a ring, joining hands to dance and to sing in high, sweet, happy voices to celebrate the birthday party of the world. Then sometimes the deep-dreaming creeks and streams wake up in the rain and uncoil, lash out, strike and gnaw at the land, biting away huge cakes and chunks of it. In the old days, still vaguely remembered, the low-lying farms drowned, and the lightweight, transient shacks of squatters and trappers and lonely fishermen bobbed and floated away in the floods like little arks.

And then comes the long session of summer. The old sun shouts and trumpets over a stricken land. Raises bruised and black thunderheads which, daily, will explode into showers in the late afternoon. Meanwhile all day long the dust rises in response to the least hint or promise of a breeze and dances wildly in the tepid air, abandoned and careless. Leaves on the trees are brittle as tinfoil. Time of and for insects, crawlers and creepers, brooders with dry wings, sudden swells and diminishment of insect sounds like a demonic orchestra of distant, dissonant strings. And in this season people begin to speak softly to each other as if they were all involved in a conspiracy. And they move slowly, when they move at all, like awkward, old-fashioned, heavy-booted divers at the bottom of the sea.

It seems then, during summer, that the brief, flaring days of autumn, when the stars are all brighter and nearer and the old moon grins like a man to be reckoned with; and the cold and wince of the winter, like the sudden pain of something too sweet for the teeth; and the pastels and watercolors of the sweet springtime: all these things are only the broken shards of a summer dream.

Here and Now

BILLY TONE: PRELIMINARY INTERVIEWS WITH THREE PRINCIPALS

PENROSE WEATHERBY, *Developer and Entrepreneur*

He drives a Jeep Cherokee. Lusts for a Range Rover. Takes me to his office. New and shiny in the new and shiny and tallest building in town—Central Florida Bank and Trust Co. Directly to lunch at Palmetto Club on top floor: deep carpets, innocuous art, muted place (cutlery noise sounds loud), soft-footed, white-haired black waiters (must have been lured away from old Seminole Springs Country Club). Nice view of downtown if that's your pleasure. Half-decent if pretentious menu.

PW wearing dark trousers (knife-edge crease), silk jacket, short-sleeve button-down shirt. Cute tie—red, sheep on it, one of them a black sheep.

Good-looking fellow. Middle or late thirties (check that). Tan, fit, good teeth and smile. Blue Paul Newman eyes. Put on reading half-glasses for menu.

His joke: If Dan Quayle and Packwood and Teddy Kennedy all got into a spelling bee, who would win? Answer: Quayle. He's the only one who knows that harass is one word.

Orders a Bloody Mary.

He says things have changed a whole lot around here since the '60s. Lately he has had a little something to do with changing them. Voted for Bush out of reflex, but sees need for, likes idea of change. Change comes anyway like it or not, right? Might as well embrace change and try to control it.

Clinton may very well be your classic bubba, he goes on, but then, so am I. I understand him. Which isn't the same thing as *trusting* him. I'm sympathetic but not crazy. Not yet.

All this Whitewater stuff, small-time as it is, has been a big relief to me, he says. I was starting to believe the moral-superiority crap he and his gang have been putting out. So? He's just another one of the good old boys.

JOKE: Clinton exits White House carrying a pink pig with a ribbon around its neck. Marine guard says: "Nice pig, sir." CLINTON: "Yes. I got it for Hillary." MARINE: "Good trade, sir."

Orders second Bloody Mary.

Weatherby made good money in the '80s. Right place at right time, don't you know? After sleepy years this area, and especially Paradise Springs, caught on. Location good. An hour from either coast. Pleasant climate and surroundings. Permanent population has increased by at least five times since the 1960s and still growing fast. He and his partners put up the first shopping malls. Downtown promptly died. Then, after a while, rose from the dead. He and his partners plugged into downtown resurrection. Then he took a big jump on his own. Developed the DeLeon Lake area east of town. High-priced houses with a very nice lake view. New golf and tennis club. Airstrip. Security.

All in all has done very nicely, thank you very much. Sometimes American dream comes true. Grateful. He wants to give something back.

Latest project is low-cost and middle-class suburban housing for African-American community. Adequate and decent at an affordable price. Out there in Seminole Springs area, near defunct country club. Plans to revive the club for his new clients when possible.

Times change. Twenty years ago he probably would have called them "niggers" like everybody else. Live and learn. Now he calls them clients and customers and whatever else their latest socially acceptable name may be. At first people around here kidded him about "Penrose's Lumumba Gardens" and the "Idi Amin Theme Park." Well, joke's on them. He's meeting a real need and making a few bucks at the same time. What could be better or more honorable?

Another Bloody Mary and orders the tuna salad plate.

I have to watch my weight all the time, he says. Clients don't trust fat people.

He continues:

Now I know and you know, too, that the environment is a whole big thing these days. Twenty years ago all you had to do down here was to find yourself an old cypress hammock or some big old piece of swamp, damn near worthless. Slash and burn, drain off the water and lay in some landfill and a little coat of topsoil. And you would be in business. Those old boys only had to worry about two things—the market and the limits of their own vision. They really opened things up in this state for the first time since the boom in the twenties.

Comes my turn at the trough and we got a whole lot more to think about. We got to be environmentally sensitive, don't you know. Which basically means that some half-assed, four-eyed, pissant bureaucrat, the kind of a man who's been feeding at the public trough all his life long and just can't wait to retire on a big fat pension that none of us could afford, some sorry-ass shitbird can come along and tell you what you can and can't do with your own property.

You will say they've got a point. We are running out of water in this state. People keep coming and building and living here and pretty soon Florida will be nothing but one big toxic sand-pile. Sure we have got problems, but you can't blame them all on the developers.

Anyway it has not been easy meeting all the regulations and

requirements, trying to create a worthwhile product at an acceptable price and still make a little profit. And I'm kind of proud that I have done just that.

I'm not asking for no Hillary Clinton fun and games. Put in a thousand of your own and take out a hundred thou of everybody else's. And doing it all the while bad-mouthing everybody else about being selfish and greedy. Politics of virtue! Virtue my ass!

But don't get me going on that. It's bad for my blood pressure.

Some people say, and you may hear it yourself, that on top of being a hard-hearted, mean-spirited developer, I am a world-class racist, too. Well, maybe I was at one time. So was everybody else. You read the Kerner Commission report, didn't you? He said everybody, *all* white people are racist whether they know it or not. And that was back in 1968. Of course, you know what happened to old Kerner, don't you?

Maybe as a kid growing up in a different world I would have fit into the general category of racist. But who was it around here that took the risk and put in the first suburban development for black people? Who is investing in low-cost housing for the poor?

You won't catch any niggers investing *their* money in stuff like that. And you won't catch very many of these white liberals, either, the ones we used to call "nigger lovers," if you'll pardon the expression, taking a serious chance on their fellow man. They will raise all kinds of holy hell about South Africa or affirmative action at the Ivy Leagues. But see how far you will get depending on them for support of minority housing in central Florida.

So I don't care what the assholes call me. All I got to say is look who's laughing now.

Wants me to be sure to come and look at—hell, *inspect*—the new Booker T. Washington housing development. Something he is honestly and genuinely proud of. Quality construction. These days "colored people" have money like everybody else and deserve opportunity to spend it on things better than fast cars, expensive threads and crack cocaine.

Yes, dope problem has reached even here, little old Paradise Springs. But mostly more or less under control. Good new chief of police. Yankee from New Jersey or somewhere. Knows how to talk all that liberal talk, that sociological bullshit, in public and then kicks ass when he has to. Smart. Works well with county sheriff, who is local but not dumb, either. Local Negroes are law-abiding and well behaved. Mostly it's the outsiders, dope dealers and that ilk, people from large urban ghettos who cause all the trouble.

Speaking of trouble . . .

Says he knows a little bit, but not a whole lot about the events of spring 1968. After all was only a kid then. Doesn't remember much. Maybe could answer some specific questions. If he doesn't know, he can steer me to somebody who does. Mostly he believes in letting the past alone. Let the dead bury the dead. Don't look back. A waste of time and energy. And it can be dangerous. Remember what Satchel Paige said: "Never look back. Something may be gaining on you."

Nevertheless, glad to help me in any way he can. Anytime I'm ready, glad to meet with me again. Maybe come to dinner at his house and meet the wife and kids. Recommends I should also talk to Dave Prince, who was sheriff in 1968. Still alive and still got most of his marbles. Short-term memory a little foggy, but good on the old stuff.

"Say," he allows as we are waiting for the elevator, "I hear you took Eleanor Lealand to dinner at the Ramada."

"The librarian?"

"You can do better than that. The place, I mean. I'll arrange for you to have a guest membership here at the Palmetto. It's kind of nice in the evening when all the lights come on. Then you can bring anybody you want. It beats honky-tonking."

Then: "Don't look surprised. We have grown a lot and are still growing. But basically Paradise Springs is nothing but a small town."

W. E. GARY, *Attorney-at-Law*

Same building. Better and grander office. All of a floor for the law firm—Thornton, Grove, Gary and Chappell. Usual and impressive paneled grandeur, extravagant space. Usual sense of muted panic.

Gary looks like a slightly thinner and lighter-skinned version of Danny Glover. Talks and acts like smooth, successful corporate lawyer of any color. Except when he wants to talk black. Why not? Magna cum laude graduate of Princeton. Then Harvard Law School. Probably on law review. Don't feel like asking.

In another league than hard-grabbing Penrose. Gary's got on a four-button linen Calvin Klein suit, worth maybe a cool thou, give or take five bucks. Nice silk tie, too, and not cheap.

Lays on some very good coffee served in very good china.

Owes it all to the old Judge, he says. Judge Singletree. Some people called him The Colonel and others the Judge, though in fact he was neither one. Helluva lawyer, though. Maybe a great one for his time. Not precisely a role model.

He settles into his story: As you may already know or will hear soon enough, the old Judge left me a chunk of money, a good deal of money, really, enough to pay for my education and to get me well started.

Nowadays all you need is a black skin and the ability to recite your ABCs without making too many mistakes to get a shot at the major universities. What I am saying, what I am proud to say, is I had to earn my own way, the hard way. Judge's money made it possible, but the rest was up to me. No affirmative action admission or degree.

But more than that. More than money. He also left me a legacy of good will in this community. I might as well have been his own son, his only living son. I took the place of Richard, who was killed in Italy in the war. He also took care of his nephew, Jojo. But that's another story.

Jojo is still alive and living in the Judge's old house. Talk to him. No telling what he can remember.

How did it happen for me? Well, you know, my mama, Hattie, worked for those Singletrees all her life. Cooking, cleaning, running the house, everything. When I was real little she used to bring me to be with her. Later when I was a little older, she fixed it up for me to work there, too, after school, with Ike, the gardener and yard man.

I was just finishing up high school when the Judge had his first stroke. Crippled him up pretty good, but he didn't lose his speech. That came a good deal later. Anyway, he needed somebody to help him get dressed and in and out of his bed and his wheelchair and to drive him around. Somebody to talk to and to yell at.

My mama volunteered me. She told me: "The Judge is mostly a good man. Hard and hard-edged, sometimes as mean as a moccasin. But mainly a good and generous man. He will try you and test you, boy. Don't you bend and break. If you prove you can take it all, the bitter and the sweet, if you do right, then he will do right by you. Believe me."

Turned out to be true. He surely tried and tested me to the quick. To the limit. I would rather not talk about it now. But many a day I went home in tears. Many a time I told my mama I couldn't take it anymore. "Go ahead and quit, then," she would tell me. "Go ahead and be a no-account nigger for the rest of your days." Now she has gone to her glory, and the Judge has gone to his reward—whatever it may be. And thanks to the both of them, here am I, a full partner in the best firm in this whole part of the state—maybe better than that. Doing just fine and dandy, thank you kindly. Shit, I may even bring myself to vote Republican in the next election. I have managed to accumulate a few nice things, and it looks like this bunch of crackers in the White House has plans to take it all away from me.

Don't be fooled. I'm not. Paradise Springs is a long way away from being heaven on earth. But, my Lord, how far it has come and changed in so little time, *my* time. I am not stupid enough to pretend or to imagine I'm not living in a racist society. How could it be any other way? And I'm not fool enough to think it will all go away in a big puff of smoke, either. But you have caught me at a time when I am feeling a lot more happy than otherwise, more satisfied than discontented. And not so many folks of any race or color or (spare us) sexual preference, can honestly say that. On a good day, like today, I feel inclined to be grateful for my blessings.

If you want to see me doing my bad-nigger number, you will have to catch me when I've got a bad hangover and a world-class headache.

You may be wondering—if you are any good at this stuff, then you surely are wondering—why I came back here when I could have found a place in the government or in the best law firms anywhere. Two reasons. One—the legacy. I like being the Judge's heir. I like to watch them wonder if maybe I am more than that. Like maybe I am really the Judge's own son. It's not exactly big frog in little pond. It's that this frog likes it, feels good in this pond.

And, believe it or not, I have the time and occasion to do some pro bono work for my own people. And I do that whenever I can. Because it makes me feel a whole lot better about myself and my good luck.

Know what I mean?

One thing more. I'll be up-front about it. We had a black middle class, very small and very proud, a bunch of snobs really, the whole time I was growing up. People who profited directly from segregation—lawyers, doctors, dentists, preachers, under-takers (oh my yes) and so forth. They had a monopoly on services for black folk. And naturally they lorded it over me and my kind. Well now. I would be lying if I didn't admit it gives me great pleasure to have left them in my dust. I like it when they come to me, hat in hand, with their piddling problems.

Another good reason I came back here to practice law is this. I am thinking about going into politics one of these days when the time is right and the right occasion comes along. I'm serious about that.

Way back then, when I was pushing the Judge's wheelchair,

he would say to me: "Willie, one of these days, sooner or later, if you don't fuck up, you are going to have a chance to run for public office and maybe even win. It's going to happen. You are pretty smart and you have a decent appearance. And if you can get yourself some education along the way, you might well make it.

"So, Willie, I have a little advice for you. Which is: Don't ever forget your constituency. By which I do not mean the Negro voting block that will automatically, reflexively, thoughtlessly vote for anybody with a black face—if one happens to be running. And with this new Lyndon Johnson civil rights bill more and more Negroes"—the Judge, being a gentleman, would never use the word "nigger" unless he was trying to shock me or to test me—"more and more Negroes are going to be running for office. And the political manipulators will be constantly on the lookout for presentable Negro candidates.

"But there's more to it. To win any office that's worth the trouble and effort, anything that's worthwhile, you will have to carry more than the Negro vote. Your constituency will have to include, most of the time in most places, about twenty percent or more, ideally more, of the white vote.

"Now that won't be as difficult or far-fetched as it may seem to you. The reason this whole movement for civil rights has been working at all is that there is a white constituency for it, I mean locally as well as nationally. A very considerable number of white people—I would argue a majority, though it hasn't been seriously tested yet—is at least not *against* civil rights. You are succeeding because you have the tacit support of the majority. And I don't believe for a minute that they are acting out of fear alone or guilt alone. They are not against you because they think you are right.

"Some people seem to understand this. King does. Malcolm X, Rap Brown, all that crowd, don't understand where they have to get support if they are going to win.

"It's pretty simple, Willie. It's numbers, arithmetic. *Hang on to your constituency.*"

You know, I think the Judge was mostly right about all that—at least in an abstract way.

Very deftly, gracefully, he glances at his wristwatch. It's a Piaget. I've seen it advertised in *The New Yorker* and *Vanity Fair*.

Anyway, to the point and purpose. I do indeed remember many of the events of 1968 that you are concerned with. I remember that lots of shit hit a lot of fans around here. And elsewhere. Over there in Memphis, somebody killed Brother Martin and then black folks went on a predictable rampage and tried (in vain as usual) to burn up half the big cities in America.

I spent the whole time of it at the Judge's house. At that point there wasn't anybody home, nobody but Mama and me, to look after him. Jojo went bananas and ended up in the hospital. He didn't come home for a week or two. We just hunkered down at the Judge's watching and listening to the news, and we just waited. We didn't know what would happen next. In that sense you could say we weren't directly involved.

Later on that year I took the Judge in his wheelchair to the trial. (By the way, I can help you on that with a transcript and some documents.) He sat there watching the proceedings, groaning and drooling a little—I was still young enough to be embarrassed by that. Just watching things happen. I could tell he was really unhappy. But he didn't say or do anything until all of a sudden he took his gold-headed cane (he didn't need that cane with me and the wheelchair, but he always carried it anyway), took his cane and pounded on the floor. The whole courtroom shut up and everybody looked at him, at us.

You have to bear in mind that in those days the Judge was without doubt the most prominent person, the closest thing we had to a really famous man, hereabouts anyway, a genuine homegrown celebrity.

Well, it got really quiet. You could hear the old overhead fans squeaking a little as they turned. It was like everybody was waiting for him to pass judgment. And pass judgment he did:

"Cooke! Rivers!" he hollered. "You goddamn fools! Don't

you realize this is a capital case? You ought to be ashamed of yourselves. What do you think this is, *Perry Mason* or something? And as for you, Spence. I don't know where you studied the law, but it must have been a sorry-ass place because you are some sorry excuse for a trial judge. Shame on you! Shame on all of you!"

Squeak-squawk of the ceiling fans. Stink of the sweat and tears of many years. Light gleaming on bald heads. Then somebody accidentally dropped keys and a bunch of change on the courthouse floor. Coins rolling in different directions. People jumped like a bomb had gone off.

"Take me home, Willie," the Judge said to me in the same loud voice. "Take me home right now."

MOSES KATZ, *Professor Emeritus of English,*
Central Florida Baptist College

A dumpling of a man. A white-haired muffin. Small and plump and quite cheerful and lively when he is not busy being curmudgeonly. Nevertheless frail. Suffers from arthritis, emphysema, hypertension, diabetes and God knows what else. Complains of vision problems, deafness, ingrown toenails, etc. Announces his days are numbered.

So? So are yours and mine, my friend.

I can't complain too much, he says. As long as I've got my health. . . .

This sets him to laughing and coughing. And Ruthe-Ann has to hurry with the oxygen.

Katz lives in a mobile home that has seen a lot of better days. It sits uneasily atop cinder blocks in Half Moon Trailer Camp, maybe a mile north of town and not far from the arched brick gate to the college. Lives, as he has for the past twenty-five years, with a younger woman. She must be around fifty now, plus or minus. Maybe she's his lawful wedded wife. Works as a waitress at a place, Pete and George's Gourmet Restaurant, locally known as the P & G, out on "the strip," within walking and easy biking distance. They own an old gas-guzzling Plymouth but it has recently died on them. A locked three-speed bike (a boy's bike) leans against steps to trailer. She is getting ready to go to work, wearing her clean yellow uniform but no shoes yet, when I arrive.

He is wearing bib overalls and a sleeveless undershirt.

Place is a general clutter. Books and papers everywhere. Dirty glasses and dishes and clothes. TV set, a good-size, fairly new Sony, is on. She is watching some kind of a game show with the sound off. She tells me that he likes to keep the sound off except for the news and his favorite soap operas and the talk shows. He is not that much of a fan of the news (except *MacNeil-Lehrer*), but he likes to yell back at anchorpeople.

Ruthe-Ann has the remains of an accent that is not at all local. Generally Appalachian. Maybe western Carolina or east Tennessee.

They have a VCR setup and they watch a lot of videos. She will often rent a couple of movies at Blockbuster on the way home from work. And they buy travel videos at a store in the nearby shopping mall.

"On his pension and the social security, we sure ain't fixing to go anywhere else," she says. "So we watch a lot of places and pretend like we did."

Lately we have been touring Scandinavia, he adds.

Oddly, there are stacks and stacks of old and new fashion magazines—*Elle, Glamour, Mademoiselle, Vogue, Harper's Bazaar, Mirabella, W, Allure* . . .

His or hers?

Both of us, he says. She likes to look at the clothes and I like to look at the girls. The girls look better nowadays than they ever used to.

"Thinner and meaner," Ruthe-Ann says. "He likes them thin and mean like that."

There are cutout pictures of various and sundry supermodels Scotch taped to walls and surfaces—Claudia Schiffer, Cindy Crawford, Christy Turlington, Linda Evangelista, etc. And there is a large lamp shade completely covered with photos of Kate

Moss. As far as I can tell the only photograph not of this kind is a matted print of the famous photo of a small, frightened Jewish boy in a flat cap, hands raised in surrender to German soldiers.

There was once a great modern poet named Cavafy, Katz says. For your information he was a Greek from Alexandria. Just in case you never heard of him, Billy. If you want to know more, ask Eleanor. Whenever someone truly beautiful, male or female—in *fact*, Cavafy was a flaming faggot—crossed the threshold of his apartment, he ceremoniously lit a candle to celebrate and honor the moment. I think about that a lot. Beauty is so rare, so brief and fragile. Brief as any candle. Fragile as a candle flame in the wind. An apt image and gesture, then, right? And of course all those who have been beautiful are touched (wounded) by the fire and scarred by the experience. For a while the world comes to them. The world brings burnt offerings. And they, too, the beautiful ones, become burnt offerings, forever possessed and offered up in the thoughts and dreams of their envious beholders. The truly beautiful are parceled out to live in a multitude of fantasies, the fantasies of strangers, even as their own ashes are scattered by the restless and unforgiving wind.

Lacking the gifts of the poet and in the absence of an apartment in Alexandria, I must invite beautiful people to come and to step over the threshold of my mind.

At any given moment, I confess, my brain has more lit candles than a great cathedral on a feast day.

I read that Hollywood thing you did, he says. Not bad. Not really good, either.

"Well, sir, that makes us even. I read your book on the rhetoric of pornography."

"He was nothing but truly horny back in those days," Ruthe-Ann says over her shoulder, still concentrating on the silent game show. "He would wear a body out."

Now it's more of an aesthetic thing, he says. You may well wonder if at my age the rage of desire still persists. Does it go on? Are you ever free of all that fire and ice, the sudden surges and hungers? Very well. All that happens is that your expectations are somewhat modified so as to conform with your abilities. The fires that nearly burned you to a crisp like bacon throughout adolescence and the prime of your adult life ease off, cool off a little. But not much.

And that's the good news.

"Quit complaining," Ruthe-Ann says. "Nobody likes a whiner."

All those books and papers.

"What are you working on these days?" I ask him.

Reading. I'm reading everything I can find about the Weimar Republic.

It was supposed to be the beginning of something. Once I understood what had happened I would go on from there. But there are still so many problems, so many questions. Not enough answers.

"Where are you headed?"

What?

"What is your larger subject? Where are you going after the Weimar Republic?"

The Jews, of course.

"The Holocaust?"

Not exactly. We know that it happened. We even know how it happened. In detail. I want to know *why* it happened. No, I want to know how and why it could happen. I am trying to understand what they—the Nazis, the Germans, and all the others—what they thought they were doing and why they did it.

It's too easy to say that the Jews were simply available scapegoats or that it was an act of collective insanity. Both of which are probably true. But . . .

"You are looking for some reason."

What I want is to know what kinds of thoughts and feelings permitted them to do what they did. I want to know by what right they imagined they could justify killing my people, and millions of others of all kinds, too, men and women and children!

"Honey," Ruthe-Ann says. "He don't want to hear all that ancient-history stuff. He came all the way here to talk to you about the crazy time in 1968."

If he has heard her, he ignores her. His voice rises. His face is flushed and sweaty.

We know from all history—actually, we only need the history of this century, this bloody and murderous century, to prove it—we know for certain that there are no limits to human cruelty. No limits to folly. No limits to hatred once it has been summoned up and set free. There is no news there. But what I really want to know is how the survivors (survivors on all sides, never mind which sides) have been able to go on living without shame. While I am at it I want to know why *I* am not ashamed.

Here a great fit of gasping and coughing brings Ruthe-Ann and the oxygen.

"He gets himself all worked up when he gets to talking about that stuff. It's going to kill him one of these days. You want a can of beer?"

"Maybe I should just go along and come back some other time."

"Suit yourself," she says. "But he'll be just fine now. It's not as bad as it looks and he's not as bad off as it seems like."

While he breathes the oxygen she puts on her shoes and fixes him a glass of iced tea. She takes a quick look at herself in a mirror. Not a bad-looking woman. Blond and rangy. Kind of like Laura Dern with a good deal more mileage on her. Then sets off to work at the restaurant.

After a while, calmer now, Professor Katz has some pedagogical thoughts about my method and process:

Try your damnedest not to let what you know get in the way of the steady revelation of things as they happened. To do it right, to get at or near the truth, you are going to have to get the context right. And you are going to have to unlearn and forget all about the consequences—the way things turned out.

Not an easy thing to do. Not as easy as you may think. You

can't even let your memory guide and deceive you. Even though memory is, in fact, all you have to start with and to go by.

Consider the broad outlines. In February we had the Tet offensive in Vietnam. A shattering experience as witnessed on the boob tube. Presented to us by the press, the—pardon the expression—media, as a catastrophic defeat. Cronkite, himself, turned against the war. It was only much later, with the war more or less behind us, that we learned it was also a major military victory for us, so successful that it almost ended the war then and there.

So, anyway, whatever you think, you will have to allow that we were, all of us, profoundly confused about that war. All that coverage. All that evening television.

Then, before the end of March you have the New Hampshire primary with Clean Gene McCarthy running strong enough—at least in the eyes of the media—to trouble President Johnson. And Bobby Kennedy jumps into the race. And Martin Luther King busy planning and promoting the Poor People's Campaign he was going to unleash on Washington, D.C. Then at the end of March LBJ suddenly pulls out of the presidential campaign before it even got started. Leaving McCarthy and Humphrey and RFK to fight each other for the nomination like a pack of dogs over a bitch in heat.

Talk about chaos and confusion!

And wait a minute. Don't forget the immediate past, 1967, still fresh in mind: the Six-Day War, huge Israeli victory, recapture of Jerusalem; the Detroit race riots and riots in maybe fifty other major cities; the march on the Pentagon, protest being already fashionable enough and safe enough (good career move) to have attracted the likes of Norman Mailer to the ranks.

And then there is the future. In early spring of '68, nobody, not even a psychic or a bona fide prophet, could conceivably have imagined the things already coming at us in the near term. Here at home and in the rest of the world: the murder of King, the murder of RFK, the anarchy of the Democratic Convention in Chicago, then the election itself, which finally put Tricky Dick Nixon in power.

And meanwhile we had all the usual wars and rumors of war and the Cold War as well as the Soviet invasion of Czechoslovakia, the riots in Paris and West Germany, the North Koreans grabbing and then keeping the *Pueblo* . . .

I mean, shit would soon be falling like rain out of the sky.

What you have, then, is a block of time, a year (and never mind the even wilder years that followed) that was unimagined and, indeed, unimaginable to the people living in the big middle of it, then and there. Not only out of control but clearly uncontrollable. A paradigm of social insanity.

Crazy? I'll give you crazy. One of the big best-selling books of 1968 (I forget the author's name; ask Eleanor) was *Chariots of the Gods,* all about the existence of ancient astronauts and prehistoric space travel. Perfectly ordinary, decent people believed that shit.

Now then. Right in the middle of all of that we had our own little season of local madness here in Paradise Springs. A madness during which I had a small, modest part to play. And now here you are, years and miles later, long after everything has faded away from fickle public memory and is no more than a vague bad dream to those few who actually have any memory of it.

I wish you good luck, young man, he says. And I'll do what I can to help you. But I have my doubts about it.

"So do I, Professor."

Good, he says. Doubt is the beginning of wisdom—sometimes.

Another thing. Don't you forget that for a lot of people—most of them, maybe—none of it registered or had any meaning beyond a brief jolt, a nod or shake of the head, a raised eyebrow, and then back to their own profound and pressing concerns. Never mind how trivial. Not trivial to them.

How do you think we survive and endure with all this stuff thrown at us night and day by day by day? We can't escape it.

No way to do so. But we can eliminate it, excrete it almost instantly.

Suppose your book was all about here and now, April 1994. What would the context be—Lorena Bobbitt, Tonya and Nancy, Whitewater? By the time you type the words—or do you use a computer?—the names and the things would already be fading. By the time your book came out you would have to have footnotes.

I'll tell you the truth. To be accurate, to be authentic you would have to present most of us not as empty-headed, not grinning Halloween pumpkins. Not exactly. But rather with our heads stuffed and filled and troubled by a multitude of private things. Truth is, there is no public life.

But how can you tell a story, true or false, based on that premise?

I don't envy you.

The other day Betty Furness died and it was front-page news in big papers (I read the *New York Times* every day). Wonder how many of our large and sprawling, seething population have the slightest idea who Betty Furness is or was? Of those who know, how many seriously care if she is dead or alive? And why should they care?

I am thinking we are building up to yet another coughing fit and maybe some more oxygen. He pauses long enough to catch his breath.

"Have you seen *Schindler's List?*" I ask him.

Not yet. I can't go to the theater anymore. We just have to wait for things to come out in video.

He removes his greasy glasses and wipes them on his shirt. His eyes, dark in their net of wrinkles, are watery.

One thing more, kiddo. Maybe the most important thing to bear in mind. You and I, each in our own way, are looking for something that isn't really there. We're looking for connections that may or may not be there and, finally, if we are lucky, we are looking to find a pattern in the shape of events. Well, sir, the more I study this cruel and crazy century, the more I am haunted—not *convinced*, mind you, but anyway deeply haunted—by the prospect that there may not be any pattern. That the only pattern, the one constant in a world of accidents and variables, is our wish for one, our hopeless, feckless desire to find one.

Take the assassinations. Take Martin Luther King. Take the Kennedys. Those things could just as well have *not* happened. About as much cause and effect as flipping a coin. Bobby Kennedy could just as well have *not* gone out through the hotel kitchen when he did. It wasn't planned that way. It just happened. Same thing with King. Truth is, at the moment of his murder, he was about as well protected as anyone could possibly be. But he happened to come out, just when he did, and pause there. And somebody—maybe it was really James Earl Ray and maybe it wasn't; chances are we'll never know—shot and killed him. And Jack Kennedy, himself, made the decisive last-minute, unanticipated decision not to use the bullet-proof bubble on his car. Oswald couldn't have known that until it happened, couldn't even have imagined it, let alone planned on it. And so forth and so on. The Oliver Stone stuff is unacceptable not just because it is implausible and improbable (though it certainly is both). It's dead wrong because it depends on a pattern that is not there.

From our point of view—and what else do we honestly have to work with?—things happen. Things happen arbitrarily, randomly. We come up with rhymes and reasons, but they don't mean anything.

"That's a pretty scary idea, Professor."

The really scary idea is that I may be wrong. That there *is* a pattern in events, in history, and it's beyond us. Beyond our capacity even to consider, let alone to comprehend. And all we can do is hope and pray it isn't so.

Then, after a moment: Would you mind turning up the sound on the TV, son? It's almost time for Oprah.

Then and There

ALPHA: SIGNS AND WONDERS

On the way to work one morning, the morning after she had been pestered by troubling dreams, Alpha stopped to look carefully at one of the posters, bright red, scattered all over the place, on telephone poles and bulletin boards and in store windows. Right at the bottom of the poster, which announced the HOT GOSPEL SHOW and further advertised MAGIC TRICKS AND ILLUSIONS / SECRETS FROM THE ANCIENT WORLD / FUN FOR THE WHOLE FAMILY, etc., there was a photograph of Little David in person. He was wearing short pants and kneesocks. He had on a loose white shirt with a wide, open collar. And he had what looked like long and curly golden hair, as long and beautiful as any girl's. His bright eyes were staring out into the camera. He was holding a guitar in his hands. He could have been any age at all, young or old, except that in this particular picture he looked to be about the same age as her brother, Penrose. Except, too, Penrose wouldn't be caught dead wearing an outfit like that.

Little David had the power, great powers, and no doubt about it. But, she realized, she had power, too. With all his clever tricks and illusions, with his powers of healing, he might be able to change Paradise Springs into something new and strange. Briefly that would seem to be a blessing. Like a magician with his rabbits and doves, flashes of fire and puffs of smoke, he could dazzle them out of their suffering skin and bones and leave them (briefly) empty and contented. And then he would be gone, maybe for good, forever, leaving them behind, slowly rejoining their company of ghosts and sorrows, only the worse for wear now. For they would have been given a vision of something else, just enough to leave them ever after unsatisfied. Now they would starve with a new hunger. The whole of God's created world (and all the creatures in it) would blur and fade like an old photograph. And thus, in the end, their suffering would be compounded, forever accompanied by the steady sounds of lewd and demonic laughter.

It was within her power to stop all that from happening. It was within her power to change everything, too, so that the scales of their eyes would fall away and suddenly they would be able to see the world (Paradise Springs) as it really and truly was and is and ever shall be—marvelous, strange and beautiful, world without end.

Just about the time she was thinking these things, a small boy on the way to school paused long enough to draw a big mustache with a black crayon on the poster picture of Little David. They will do it every time. They will spoil everything if they can. Only he was too late to spoil things this time; for she already had more than a glimpse of her secret power and her bounden duty.

"That Little David is nothing but an overgrown midget, a dwarf or something," her friend Darlene Blaze said when they had a chance to talk about it later.

"I don't care."

"Well, me either, honey. I am just stating a fact. You know me. I like men in all different sizes."

Alpha kept on thinking about the face in the photograph. Trying to know it by heart so that she could, any time she wanted to, close her eyes and concentrate and see it clearly. A face at once hurt and cruel. A face as hard and composed as the face of a ventriloquist's dummy. And yet without words and without facial expression, without the least kind of gesture, saying: *I know all about hell. I have been there and seen hell and I can see it now and always. It is here and it is everywhere.*

It was that last part that worried her the most. It was that last part that was the biggest lie. She had seen hell, too. She knew the truth of it.

And so she continued to go to work at the bank, wearing a blank wooden mask of a face herself, as always, and doing the things she was supposed to do, mechanically and efficiently and without one slipup or error. She was extra careful. On the way home from work she would pause to refresh her sense of purpose by looking at the poster, mustache or no. Not planning anything yet (something would come to her), just waiting patiently and meantime continuing to confirm herself in her duty. With the same kind of inexorable patience and humble tact she managed to deceive her parents too. Her father with his one leg, hobbling ever since the Korean War, his big fist shaking in the face of a world composed of fools and knaves and niggers. Not religious himself, he ridiculed the God that the knaves and fools had first of all invented, then killed, then dispossessed of His own by sending Him off to live in the blue sky, somewhere else, lonesome and far from His riotous creation. You could see John Weatherby limping to and from the post office to pick up his V.A. disability check. Or in the park on a park bench near the World War I seventy-five-millimeter howitzer or the World War II tank. The rest of the time (it seemed) sitting, grim and comfortable, in a high-backed rocker on the front porch, watching the fools and the knaves hurrying to and from their separate and shabby little dooms. Or maybe at his kitchen table in another kind of mood, cleaning and oiling his rifles, pistols and shotguns and muttering to himself as he prepared, not grimly but gaily now, for the inevitable coming day when the U.N. and the Supreme Court would openly and shamelessly fly the hammer and sickle, and the Combined Operational Forces of the niggers, the commies and the Jews would try to take over the U.S.A. Which, he figures, they will accomplish swiftly and easily enough. Except for one small surprise. Except for one small, tidy frame house with its shady patch of yard, fore and aft, a house in need of some new paint, yet gracefully concealed by a high growth of shrubs, a small house on a side street in Paradise Springs, Florida, where a lone veteran with one leg would be waiting there to make them at least pay in blood for his living space.

Also her mother. Her mother who, in spite of or maybe *to*

spite (who knew?), kept her mouth zipped shut, her lips like a thin scar, going regularly, faithfully to the Primitive Church of Jesus Christ out on the far outskirts of town, walking to and from that plain and shabby temple by herself. Otherwise spending most of her waking hours hunched over her old-fashioned Singer sewing machine in the front room, the living room, bending and staring, squinting as the machine buzzed and the bright little needle blurred up and down, making fine clothes with a fine fit out of good materials and at half the price of the stores downtown. Made bridal gowns and widows' weeds. Made dresses for baptism, confirmations and first communions. Or, with the same extraordinary skill and without a change of expression, making clothes like Darlene's, things designed to fit the form hand in glove, and to catch the eye and to arouse and incite the glands of any man old enough or young enough to be ruled by his hormones.

They agreed that Alpha could go to the revival meeting provided that Penrose went along also. Penrose, her little brother, a crazy nut and practically a sex maniac, with his collection of nudist magazines and all that, keeping a straight, sincere, poker-and-choirboy face, assured them that he would be happy to accompany Darlene and Alpha and to make sure the girls got home safe and sound.

By Thursday morning everything was set and ready and all she had to do was to wait for the sign. It came to her in the afternoon, praise the Lord. She was counting the money in her drawer, counting it very carefully, when she heard a kind of soft noise in her hands. And when she looked around for the source of the sound, she saw that the green dollar bills had been transformed into a nest of little green snakes. They writhed and hissed in her hands and were cold and slimy to touch. At first she was going to drop them and run out and away, but she knew it was a sign and a test, so she gripped them so tightly that her fingers turned white and cold. Then the snakes stopped moving and turned back into paper money again.

She smiled and began counting again, light-headed,

lighthearted and greatly relieved. When she finished and was sure that the count tallied, she took a slip of paper and wrote the date, April 4, 1968, on it. Then she wrote, carefully and neatly in her tiny hand: "I, Alpha Weatherby, 471 Garden Road, City, do hereby freely declare that I owe the State Bank and Trust Company one thousand, five hundred and forty-seven dollars and eighty-eight cents ($1,547.88), this same sum of which I am now going to offer up in sacrifice, to lay upon the altar of Jesus Christ for the purpose of doing His work and His bidding in this wicked world. And I hereby affirm my intention and promise to repay this borrowed sum at standard rates of interest at some later date to be mutually agreed upon." She signed the note. Then she put it in the money bag, which she stuffed with Kleenex so it wouldn't look suspicious, and she put the bag in the place in the vault where it belonged. They would, of course, find out by the middle of tomorrow morning. But by that time she would have done what she had to do.

At home she pondered what she should wear for the occasion. It was a difficult choice, and she might not ever have decided except that she was suddenly, blithely aware that her anxiety was, itself, another sign, a definite answer to her dilemma. She would slip on her black raincoat over nothing at all. That's how simple and easy it would be.

So she did that. And she stuffed the money in one pocket and one of her father's pistols, a short-barreled, .38 caliber revolver, in the other.

Here and Now

PRELIMINARY INTERVIEW WITH **STANLEY RUBIN,**
CHIEF OF POLICE

He's a medium-size guy (slightly better looking version of Al Pacino) who looks a little rumpled and uneasy in the light blue, white-shirted uniform. Local cops, these days, wear an

American flag patch on the right shoulder of the shirt. He tells me that when he came here (from Plainfield, New Jersey) a few years ago, the police were wearing a Confederate battle flag patch on the left shoulder.

Figured I had sure better do something or other about that, one way or the other, he says. Either go with it proudly or get rid of it. Figured, at the risk of being taken for a world-class damn Yankee, I had better get rid of it.

Sure some of the old-timers, the diehards, hated to lose it. But, lucky for me, mostly they don't give a shit. Anyway one of the main reasons they hired me here was that I had taken some sensitivity training.

"Did you learn anything?"

Hey, I got sensitive enough to aim for the South like a fuckin' migratory bird. It's a lot easier to be sensitive around here than it is in Plainfield. You get too sensitive up there and the boogies will cook you and eat you.

I'll tell you this, though. It's busier down here than I thought it would be. We got some of the same problems. Keeps me wide-awake trying to keep up with things.

Now then, Mr. Tone, I have to tell you that you are wasting your own time as well as mine on this thing. I don't know did-dley squat about it. Neither does anybody else in the Department. What happened here in 1968 might as well have happened on the moon or Mars. I will read your book and find out all about it. We don't have any files here going that far back. I'm sure there are *some* files and records somewhere, but you'll have better luck with your friend the librarian than with me.

I wish I could help you, but I can't. Not exactly anyway.

"What do you mean—*not exactly*?"

Just what I said. Listen. I don't know how much you know about this place. More than I do, I would guess. I didn't even know where it was on the map when I came down to interview for the job. Anyway, you know, and so do I now, what these people do when they want to tell you something.

"They tell you a story."

Right you are, my good man. And, in keeping with the local habit and custom, Stan Rubin is now going to tell you a story about law enforcement in Paradise Springs that means a good deal to me. It isn't like, you know, *pertinent* to your subject. It's just a matter of ambiance.

Anyway. Way back in the deep Depression, Paradise Springs couldn't afford to have a real police force. They got down to a single constable. Then they tried to make do with what they called (in those lost days) a day marshal, a guy who was on duty only during daylight hours. After sunset, it was anything goes. At least in town. They still had an honest-to-God county sheriff, of course.

Pretty soon they couldn't even afford to pay the salary of a day marshal.

What to do?

There were some who thought maybe there would be a future for the place as a sort of sanctuary or free city for criminals. Like some of those pirate communities in the Caribbean, way back when. But, you know, what self-respecting, moderately successful criminal would want to come and live here?

Well, in the end they decided to keep the day marshal job but to ratchet down the requirements and the pecuniary rewards and fringe benefits. They located and hired an eighty-five-year-old gentleman, a retired Texas sheriff from the Wild West days. A man who liked the climate here because he thought it helped his arthritis—his "misery," as he called it.

Old fellow tottered around town in a broad-brim cowboy hat and a nice khaki uniform with a big shiny star badge. And he strapped on an antique single-action black-powder pistol, a big old .44 that looked too heavy for him to lift, let alone to shoot something with.

Everybody liked the old gent, they really did. And mostly they behaved themselves, because they didn't want to cause him trouble or aggravation. And the town elders were absolutely dead certain they could never hire any kind of a living lawman cheaper than that.

Well, sir. One fine day, it being the season of such things, a gang of bank robbers came to town in a souped-up four-door Ford that would have outrun anything. Assuming anyone would want to chase after them. Parked on the corner next to the old Sunshine Bank. (Only bank in town those days.) One sat at the wheel and the other three went in and robbed the Sunshine Bank.

So they are right in the middle of robbing it when along comes our day marshal, Texas Pete or whatever his name was, stumbling along the sidewalk headed in the general direction of the bank, aiming (if he don't forget) to cash his pitiful monthly check. He is about fifty yards away when all of a sudden the outside alarm goes off. *Clang! Clang! Clang!*

He stops on the sidewalk and peers from under the shade of his hat brim and sees, sure enough, the three guys, guns in hand, come backing out of the bank. He raises his left hand, in admonition as they say, and is tugging at the pistol with his right.

"Halt in the name of the Law," he says in a quivery but clearly audible voice. Like it's something he has said before in dim days beyond recall. Like, quivery or not, it has some authority to it.

The bad guys think this is funny as hell and they start laughing and shooting at him as fast as they can. Bullets are zinging and ricocheting all around him while he tugs at that old pistol. He finally gets it free of the holster, cocks it (you have to cock those things for each shot) and takes it in both hands and aims, very carefully, and pulls the trigger.

Whamo! There is a tremendous explosion and a cloud of smoke around him. And one of the bad guys is down and dead. Shot right between the eyes.

By the time this dawns on the perpetrators, he has already managed to cock the pistol and kill another one. With one shot right between the eyes. Hands up and we surrender from the last two, the driver and the other one. They can't quit quick enough.

Day marshal deputizes a few men on the spot and they take

the two off to the pokey. Which hasn't been used in so long that they have to get the lights and the water turned on.

Never mind. The word goes out like wildfire to the criminal world: *Stay the fuck out of Paradise Springs. They got some kind of a Hoot Gibson policeman there that can blow your fuckin' head off at fifty yards. And he will do it, too. I mean to tell you, this fella is a pure killing machine. You want to die? You want to do yourself in? Just go over to Paradise Springs and try to pull a stickup job.*

And the beauty of it is that there was never another bank robbery in this town. Banks all over the South were being held up and robbed. But not here. Not as long as he lived.

Sometimes I wish the old fart was still alive. I could use him.

That's all I got for you. Do what you will with it.

What I don't tell Chief Rubin (and why should I?) is that I first heard that story in a barbershop here when I was about ten years old. A few details different, but basically the same.

From Wild West to sensitivity training. From pioneers to pansies, as the Judge used to say.

I could have told him how it ended if I had the time and felt like it. How Texas Pete put in for reimbursement for the two bullets he fired. And how the town turned him down on that, arguing that the gun and the bullets were not public property and were, in fact, just decoration.

Then and There

DARLENE BLAZE

"Does he really have snakes? I'm not going if he don't have no snakes."

"Then don't!" I said.

"Watch your grammar, Penrose," Alpha said. "You know better than that."

I tell you I was weary to death of the both of them. I was sick of his silly smirk and his smart-ass attitude. Skinny and freckled and all jerky and nervous like one of those little toys that you used to wind up with a key. And he always made me feel so heavy. He could make you feel embarrassed about your good health.

"I bet he's got plenty of snakes," Alpha said. "All kinds of snakes."

But Penrose was already running away across the park, once around the bases of the softball diamond, down in and then through and then out again from the empty public swimming pool (that they closed when the court said they had to let the colored people swim there too), across the tennis court (where there was a mixed-doubles game in progress), jumping the net and ignoring the curses of the players, and off toward the green, jungly clump of shrubs and trees at the far end.

"Catch me if you can," he hollered back at us, his hair on fire from the blaze of the late-afternoon sun.

"Now we have gone and done it," I said.

Alpha sat herself down in one of the children's swings. She was a tall girl with the same kind of red hair as Penrose. She was light-boned and thin enough to sit comfortably in a child's swing. Which is sure enough one thing I'll never be able to do again. I gave her a little push and then another one a little harder and in a minute or two Alpha was all smiles. She stood up and started pumping, holding her head up high, looking into the heart of the sky. Her hair blew free in the breeze she was making and it flared the edges of the black raincoat she was wearing. She kept on pumping higher and higher until it seemed like any minute she would go up and over, loop the loop, and come crashing down on her head.

"I'm ashamed of you," I told her.

"Why?"

"You don't have any underpants on."

She caught the ropes and checked her swing. She let the swing slow down and then dropped off.

"That's not all of it," she said. "The truth is I don't have on stitch one underneath this raincoat."

She smoothed the coat and pulled the belt tight at the middle like a sash.

"I guess nobody else will ever know," I said.

"Well, I couldn't care less if they do or if they don't," she said.

"Sometimes I have real trouble trying to understand you."

"It doesn't matter, anyway," Alpha said. "Because I am a virgin."

What could I say to that? Nothing. I would never in this world dare to do a thing like that, though. I mean go around naked underneath a raincoat. I would do just what I was doing—wear a tight-fitting, bright-colored dress. I would have on a hat and gloves and carry a purse. I would be all nicely made up fit to kill and drenched in my favorite perfume. Not that I felt superior to Alpha or anything like that. How could I when half the men in Quincy County, all the ones between puberty and senility, had learned by heart, by daylight, lamplight, moonlight, headlights and flashlights and by Braille in the dark, every line and contour of myself? Not morally superior. Not inferior either. Just that I was curious. Fascinated by Alpha, my unpredictable friend, my best friend in the world. Whose half-formed body was more like a boy's. Who was all gangling and shifting of weight from one side and one leg to another like a boy. I liked clothes and the more the merrier. All wrapped up in a network of buttons and hooks, elastic straps and zippers, I could laugh out loud and without hard feelings at the fumble and tremble of men's clumsy, impatient fingers.

"Well, I reckon you will be cool, anyway," I said to Alpha. "It's going to be hotter than the hinges of hell inside of that tent. Unless they have some kind of air-conditioning. Which I personally doubt."

Here and Now

PRELIMINARY INTERVIEW WITH
FORMER SHERIFF **DAVE PRINCE**
PLACE: CANTERBURY RETIREMENT COMMUNITY

Prince, though in frail health, is not completely bedridden. Has half-decent room in Assisted Living section. Eats in small dining room with other more or less mobile patients. Place fairly clean, as these places go. Complains that he can't hunt and fish anymore ("I expect that I have hunted and fished over every inch of Quincy County in my time"), but there is an adequate library and a good collection of videos. He watches old movies as much as he can.

We talked small talk for a while before we got down to business.

PRINCE says:

This whole thing is now a matter of public record. You can read the various reports and other documents in the files. You can read the trial transcript. When things actually were taking place was the same time as the murder of Martin Luther King in Memphis; and then there were all the riots and looting and burning, the usual 1960s Negro reaction to anything; so almost all the newspaper and the TV people, what we now call the "media," were busy elsewhere during the trial. I gave some interviews and stuff to reporters, though I had best, here and now, disclaim any responsibility for what they actually printed or said about me.

In the first place, I haven't got any use for the way they come down on places and people like a flock of buzzards. Just adding to the trouble. They feed on dead flesh. Only a buzzard or a maggot, say, performs a real service. These newspeople are worse than maggots or buzzards.

You aren't a reporter, are you?

By the way, I read in the paper the other day how last winter in northern Virginia the buzzards became predators and attacked living creatures—calves, lambs, pets, even babies. Maybe that's more like it. These newspeople are like crazed, predatory buzzards.

And in the second place, you can't pay any attention to what they put in the papers anyway (TV is even worse), because they don't put down what you say in the same words and in the same way that you say them.

If you want the facts, I suggest you check out everything and see what you can make out of it.

If it is my opinion, my impressions you are interested in, for whatever they may be worth, I will have to begin by telling you a funny thing. At this point in my life my most vivid memory of the whole thing is, strange as it may seem, the very beginning. At least the beginning as far as I was concerned.

How it happened. I was sitting there in my office playing a game of gin rummy with a Mr. Irving Feldman, a fine Jewish gentleman from New York City who we happened to be holding on a federal warrant for alleged mail fraud.

You know those guys they put up on the post office bulletin board? Well, Mr. Feldman was the first one I ever saw and ever expect to see in the flesh. And where do you think I picked him up? At the P.O., naturally. I went down there to pick up my mail and see what the gossip was. And I saw this little crowd of the usual loafers who hang around there gathered next to the bulletin board and all buzzing like a hive of bees. So of course I walked over to see what in the world it was that had stopped them from chewing and whittling and aroused them to get up off of their various and sundry dead asses and stand up to look. Right in the middle there was this stranger laughing and shaking his head, saying, "It doesn't look like me at all. Not at all. That bitch, my wife, she had to hunt high and low to find a picture of me that looks that bad. See, I actually look like a criminal type."

Everybody else seemed to be in agreement that it was a sad thing and that the picture didn't begin to do him justice. And it was the truth. I almost didn't have the heart to arrest him. Later on, after we got to be friends, I asked him why he allowed himself to get caught like that. "Sheriff," he said, "I imagine you are thinking that I intended to be caught. That it was deliberate." "The thought crossed my mind, I'll admit it," I said. "Nothing could be further from the truth," he said. "It was a lot more simple than that, I assure you. You have my word of honor that I had no intention of being caught and that, in a very real sense, being caught and arrested and now having to face the dismal prospect of a criminal trial and maybe even a jail sentence, amounts to a kind of personal calamity. No, sir, I was motivated by vanity and curiosity, pure and simple. And you might say that I was rewarded in kind for both. My curiosity has resulted in my apprehension and incarceration. My vanity was all but quelled by the idea that, with my picture prominently displayed in post offices across the length and breadth of the land, it had to be that unflattering photograph."

"I am glad you can be so philosophical about it," I said.

He shrugged eloquently. "Perhaps I should have been a philosopher. Pure animal lust betrayed me into an unfortunate marriage. Which, in itself, led me into folly and greed. For my lust was gratified in direct ratio and proportion according to my ability to earn the resources to make offerings unto her. When I had exhausted myself and the usual channels of free enterprise as well, I was compelled to exercise some ingenuity of a type which is, of course, outlawed. And here I am."

As I understood it, Mr. Feldman was in trouble for selling real estate on the moon. Which seems to me harmless enough, and maybe at another time the Law would have felt that way, too. That was a year before we landed there. The trouble is that the government takes the moon very seriously. "Irony is everything and everything is irony," Mr. Feldman used to say. And he pretty well convinced me of it after I found out more or less what he meant. Here's an irony for you. And I think he would appreciate it. From my point of view you could say that Mr. Feldman's catastrophe was highly beneficial. He gave my education a second wind. And I do wish him well, wherever he may be now.

So, anyway, me and Mr. Irving Feldman were killing some time and exchanging a few pennies on a gin rummy game when Papp and the big woman walked in. Strangers. I had never seen either one of them in my whole life. I was glad of it, too, at first sight. She weighed well over three hundred if she weighed an ounce, and stood more than six feet tall. This fella, Goathead Papp, had a many-times-busted nose and little red-rimmed eyes, eyes like a sick pig's. They might have looked better, more appropriate, on her, those pig eyes. Instead she had big, baby-blue eyes, bright beautiful eyes like a child's. But all lost and wasted in a face with more lines and seams and pockmarks on it than the full moon. Both of them were dressed to kill—their Sunday-go-to-meeting best. But in a funny way those clothes looked like costumes, if you know what I mean.

My first thought was that somebody had sent these two weirdos to pull a joke on me. (Paradise Springs is a great town for practical jokes.) He introduced himself. I can't recall if he introduced her by name at that time or not. I do recall that he said he was the business manager for Little David and that the big woman was Little David's wife. He set right in trying to arrange to stage his revival show in the county.

"What kind of a show is it?" I asked Papp.

"It's kind of hard to describe," he said. "It's religious, of course. But there isn't another one like it that I know of. You might say that it's unique."

"They all are."

"What I mean is, it's religious and highly entertaining, all at the same time."

"I have had some pretty entertaining times at revival meetings," I said.

"I bet you did. Boy, I just bet that you did."

I looked at the big woman to see if I could tell how she

meant that remark. She noticed me looking and she winked at me and laughed. And when she laughed she really let go of herself. She shook all over from head to toe. Like she was having an internal earthquake. Then I noticed that she was almost entirely flesh and fat, because her bones were tiny and delicate. Her feet and her hands were as small as a child's. "We want to get permission," he said. "The only way you can get permission is from the Quincy County Board of Recreation," I said. "And they don't even meet until the middle of next month." "We are, of course, anxious to make some compensation for the privilege," he said.

I looked over at Mr. Irving Feldman. He was concentrating, practicing handling the cards. He never even looked at me. "Do you play cards, Mr. Papp?" he said quietly. "Sometimes." "Bridge?" "I'll tell you what," I said, interrupting a little too soon. "You and the . . . lady draw up a chair and play me and Mr. Irving Feldman a bridge game. If you can beat us, then you can put on your show and it won't cost anything." "And what if we lose?" "Oh, I don't know," I said. "I'll think of something. Maybe I'll have to arrest you for gambling on public property."

That started the big woman to laughing again. Which was exactly what I had had in mind. She laughed so hard that she was coughing, and Papp had to pound her on her huge back to stop her. "Hey, it wasn't that funny," I said. "The only thing is," Papp said, "I don't know how to play bridge." "Where is your sporting blood, Goathead?" she said. "Let's beat the pants off of them."

Damn if they didn't, too. That big woman was a whiz at cards. It was worth it, though, just to see Papp sweat. He must have sweat off five pounds. And he was skinny to start with. And when it was over he still didn't know the first thing about how to play bridge. And that to me is the most important and interesting part of all of it. Not what happened later, but how it all began. With a game of cards. A game of chance. Which, as Mr. Irving Feldman would probably say, is ironic, definitely ironic.

Then and There

CHALLENGE

Penrose is way up a tree. He's up there about as high as he can get among the squirrely top limbs and branches of an old live oak. He is far out on a limb and it bends a little, like a tired springboard, with his weight. He sits astraddle, facing toward the trunk and looking down through leaves, limbs and dangling moss at the two small white ovals—the pale, impassive, upturned faces of Alpha and Darlene. They look to be rooted and growing there like a pair of flowers swaying gently.

Man that is born of woman hath but a short time to live. He cometh up and is cut down like a flower; he fleeth as it were a shadow, and never continueth in one stay.

Penrose loudly clears his throat as if to spit. And they dance back and away, out of range.

They know him of old. He grins to himself. He would pee on them if he thought he could get away with it.

"Penrose," his sister calls sweetly. "Please be good and come on down."

Darlene, who is no kin to him, doesn't feel like fooling around. "Get your bony ass out of that fuckin' tree!" she yells, as coarse and shameless as any crow. "I'm going to count to ten and then I'm coming up to get you."

He cups his hands to holler. "Counting will be a waste of time. Start climbing."

She has already reached five. So she stops and sticks out her tongue at him. Flutters it loud and rude. Then she slips off her high-heeled shoes and puts them neatly on the ground, side by side. She takes off her silly hat and hangs it on an oleander bush alongside her pocketbook. She peels off her white gloves and fixes them on the bush, also, each pulled along the length of a slim green twig. There they hang, limp and slack and funny-sad, like the vague imploring palms of a scarecrow or a baggy clown.

"Unzip me, honey."

She has turned her back to Alpha. Alpha tugs at the zipper, and, with a swish, Darlene slips and steps out of her tight shiny dress. Carefully she folds it over Alpha's arm. Then looks back at Penrose, spits on her palms, rubs them together and sizes up the tree.

It is a pleasure to him and amazing to behold Darlene in her bright red panties and bra.

"What if somebody comes along?" Alpha asks.

"They won't."

"Yeah. Sure. But what if they do?"

Darlene pauses, her hands on her ample hips, to think about that.

"Well, if they do," she says, "You can figure it won't be a woman walking this way. And if it's a man—and he's old enough to notice and not too old to care less—then he has most likely seen a lot more of me than this, one time or another, already. Unless maybe he would be a perfect stranger. And what the hell would a stranger be doing wandering around Paradise Springs? I ask you."

"Beats me."

Darlene restores her attention to Penrose. "Okay, you little son of a bitch," she yells up at him. "Better give your soul to God because your ass is mine!"

She grabs for the lowest-hanging limb. Jumps for it. Catches, swings, pulls herself up. Now, quick as a cat or a monkey, here she comes up the tree after him, never even hesitating. Picking herself a pretty good route, too, though it is not the same way that Penrose took. Maybe he could even learn some tree-climbing tricks if he would seriously study the way she is coming up after him, instead of just sitting there staring, bug-eyed and unblinking, at the contrast of her tan, smooth, rounded, almost perfect skin against the astonishing brightness of her underwear.

He thinks: *Here comes the whore of Babylon if I ever saw one.*

Here and Now

Billy, my lad, I have been, as much as I am able to without neglecting the duties for which they pay me an immodestly inadequate stipend, poring over pictures in the library. Looking for things that might be of some help to you. We have all kinds of videos, of course, for example the whole set of *Eyes on the Prize*. Would you have believed that, twenty or thirty years ago, that a little old Southern public library would, as a matter of course, pay for, preserve and make available a history of the civil rights movement?

Well, anyway we have a gracious plenty of picture books and some pictures of our own that, one way and another, we have acquired from old family albums and attics in Paradise Springs.

Just for the record and because you asked me to, I can report that we have any number of books with a lot of photographs of Martin Luther King, Jr., in them. Except for Presidents and beauty queens (you can include the supermodels for the sake of old Moe Katz), he must have been one of the most photographed Americans of the century. These books show him doing just about everything you can think of except brushing his teeth or sitting on the pot. And probably somewhere there exist photos of him doing that, too. Anyway, his life, his life as a public figure, which began early, really, when he was still a very young man, with his first church and congregation in Montgomery, his life was surprisingly well covered by professional people taking pictures.

There are very, very few photographs (published ones, I mean) that show King smiling. (That's a surprise to me. Most of our public figures smile and smile and smile and are villains.) There are several pictures with King and little children, his own or others, in which there is a very slight smile, tentative as can be, if well-meaning, uneasy. There's a lovely one of Martin and Coretta on the steps of his first church, the Dexter Avenue Baptist Church, and with the Alabama State Capitol filling the wide background. Coretta in hat and light, flowery dress, beaming, as King, impeccable in his tailored dark suit, holds their baby girl, Yolanda Denise. His smile there is slight and slightly nervous, as if he expected the baby to wet him any minute. But you also take notice of that smile, however faint, because there are so few others in which there is even the ghost of a grin. The big exception is the photograph of the moment, on December 10, 1964, when, amid a somewhat dour and mostly Nordic crowd, and with the smiling Coretta beside him, King is shown shaking hands with King Olaf V of Norway, having just received the Nobel Peace Prize. King is simply splendid in his perfectly tailored cutaway and elegant striped ascot. And he is just beaming, brilliant really, as nowhere else that I can find. It's a warm, happy, wonderful smile. A handsome smile. And with that image everything suddenly changes. For me anyway. His round, brown, impassive face in almost all the other photographs, unreadable except for its clear intent of high seriousness, now becomes more of a mask than anything else. All the more so since you now know the animation and, indeed, the charm, the pleasure he was capable of expressing, but held in check. For most of his public life the camera, which was everywhere, always around him, was at once his friend and ally and his mortal enemy. Mostly he turned that face toward the lens like a mask, serious and almost blank except for a subtle tinge or tic of apprehension, and yet that mask seems to have been there for him always, too. One of the earliest *published* photographs of King is a birthday-party picture, himself at age six (not his birthday, by the way) kneeling in the front row of a posed photo. The children are all wearing little paper party hats and dressed appropriately, King in a white short-sleeved shirt and dark shorts. You look at that face which is looking directly at the camera (the camera which will eventually swallow him whole and leave only its multitude of fragmentary images behind all in due time), you look at that face, being at first surprised by the simple youthfulness of it. Surprised that it is, after all, the same smooth brown mask, already in place. Though as a child, he cannot yet quite contain or conceal the child's frightened apprehension.

What I'm saying, Billy, I think, is that the mask he came to wear (at least for the ubiquitous camera that stalked him all of his short life) not only suppressed and concealed his lively emotions, but also held in grip a fear as deep as childhood and as sustained as the ineradicable memory of childhood.

And so we are talking about something remarkable—a public man who was able, by and large, to overcome both his joy and jubilation (which were plentiful) and the sad and fearful apprehension at the very heart of his being. And I reckon that the terrible irony was that his fear of *something* from the age of six until when, in his thirty-ninth year, he came out on the balcony of the Lorraine Motel, intending to go to supper with a few of his old friends, was wholly justified. Something terrible was waiting for him all right, all along.

Then and There

COMPROMISE

Penrose cuts his eyes away from Darlene for a moment. Because from the look in her eyes and the expression on her face she is getting ready to murder him. At the least. Alpha seems to be still worried about the chance of someone coming along and catching Darlene in the act of climbing the tree in nothing but her underwear. Far below him Alpha stands like a dark candle, her bright red hair and her black Navy officer's raincoat in sharp contrast to the pale leaves and the soft, sugary pink of some oleanders. She has gone and lit a cigarette which she cups in the palm of one hand, concealed from anybody. But he can smell it. And cupping his hands to make a pair of lensless binoculars, he stares until he can see the thin dancing ghost of the rising smoke.

"Hey, Alpha?"

"Huh?"

"Will you give me a smoke if I come down?"

"It stunts your growth."

"I don't give a shit."

Just then the limb he is on dips and shudders and he has to grab hold with both hands.

"Like to have broke your fool neck that time," Darlene says, laughing.

"I ain't never fell out of a tree yet."

"There's always a first time."

Close to the trunk still, Darlene has straddled the same limb and faces him. Panting from her climb, she grips the limb and glares at him. Penrose edges back very slowly, farther out on the limb. He stares. To Penrose the size and shape of her boobies, captured in the glorious red bra, are amazing. Truly a marvel. Worth all the trouble. Between the thin, tan, upthrust mounds of perfect flesh there is a flash and glint of silver. She is wearing a tiny cross on a fine chain around her neck. "What do you think you're looking at?"

"You."

"Are you about ready to come down and behave yourself?"

"What'll you give me?"

"I'll give you a quarter when we get down."

" 'When we get down.' *Sure.*"

"Hey, I couldn't climb all the way up here with my purse, could I?"

"I don't guess so."

All of this time he has continued staring, as if hypnotized by the silver cross. And she has been inching along the limb toward him. He moves back with a start, shaking the limb for both of them.

"Don't you trust me?" she says.

"Not specially."

She holds on and hikes her shoulders in a weary shrug. She looks way down at Alpha, who is shading her eyes so she can see them.

"Security," Penrose says. "I gotta have some kind of security."

"People in hell want ice-cream cones, too."

"I'll take that red thing," he says, pointing at her bra. "The top."

"Well, don't that take the cake!" she says. Then yells down to Alpha: "Penrose is dirty."

"Forget it," Alpha answers. "Let's just go home."

"But I thought you wanted to go."

"I do, but . . ."

Clamping her strong thighs tightly around the limb, Darlene bends forward very carefully so she can reach around behind and unhook the snap. She does that and the cups of the bra fall off, freeing an almost blinding surplus of ripeness. He notices, with an almost objective interest, how the nipples seem to firm up and point.

She tosses the bra to him.

"Okay, kiddo," she says. "You have now seen some titty. Let's get down from here."

"Not yet."

"Wait just a big minute. We made a deal. You made me a promise."

He shakes his head. "Things have changed. Now I want to touch them, too."

"Is that all? Do you swear?"

He nods. "Scout's honor."

"Well, then, what are you waiting on?"

He inches toward her, keeping his eyes fixed on hers, not wanting to spoil it by looking now, taking it real slow and careful because his palms are sweaty and he's trembling a little. When he gets close enough, she closes her eyes and hikes back her shoulders. He reaches forward as if he were reaching into a nest of flames. Reaches, gingerly touches, then recoils.

She opens her eyes.

"That's all," she says.

"All right," he says. "Fair enough."

She slides back out of reach and, very businesslike, begins to go down. Holding on to the bra tightly, he watches her climbing down. Then he smiles to no one but himself, loops the thing around the limb, knots it once and climbs down behind her.

"Little old Penrose is growing up," Darlene says, gathering up her clothes. She glances all around, then looks up to see her bra hanging lonely on the limb, fluttering like a red flag.

"I still got a quarter coming to me," Penrose says, dropping down beside them.

"Reach in my purse, honey, and give him a quarter."

He accepts the quarter from Alpha's hand. And with it comes a sight-shattering pinwheeling slap from Darlene, a smart pop right across the face which staggers him and sinks him to his knees as if in instant prayer.

"Snotnose!" She yells.

He kneels there, grinning and trying to shake the cobwebs out of his head.

"It was worth it," he says.

Here and Now

INTERVIEW WITH **LLOYD MACINTYRE**, EDITOR OF *Paradise Springs Trumpet*

He is an outsider. Vaguely Midwestern accent. Iowa? (When I was a kid growing up in Florida, we called all Yankees people from Iowa.) Reminds me of a kind of sawed-off version of Jason Robards. Khaki trousers, running shoes (Nike Air), short-sleeved cotton shirt, stripes. We met at his office and then walked over to the Sanitary Cafe for lunch.

Oldest eating place in town, he tells me. You go to an old Southern town like this and chances are you will find a cafe called "Sanitary" there. From back in the days when the claim of cleanliness was rare enough and important enough to be good advertising.

I nod and say nothing in answer. When I was a teenager visiting here in Paradise Springs, my idea of a good time was to go to the Sanitary Cafe. They had a soda fountain in those days, old-fashioned even then, and they made wonderful malted milks and banana splits. Later I could drink beer there.

A lot of the locals eat here, he continues. Busy people who wouldn't want to be seen coming in or out of the Palmetto Club.

He tells me the soup and the sandwiches are very good, but to stay away from the salads and desserts.

I haven't been here all that long. I never knew Dudley Hagood. After he died, his family sold the paper. Like everywhere else, it's part of a chain these days. I came down here from a job in Pennsylvania—in Lancaster. Before that I was working in Toledo as a reporter. How about you?

I establish my credentials mentioning a couple of half-decent papers and with a few familiar, well-dropped names. I do not mention the fact that I started out in the groves of academe (briefly, briefly). And I skip over the bad times when I was stuck in the heart of West Virginia and drinking much too much most of the time.

Think you will ever come back to it? he asks, ever the inquiring reporter.

"Not if I can help it."

Well, I envy you, he says. But I couldn't stand the insecurity of it. I've got a family, kids getting on to college age. I need health care and at least the prospect of a pension.

He, too, has a Clinton joke. Doesn't everybody? Especially down home, where hopes were so high and people are now embarrassed and feel that they were conned by all the Boy Scout (he and Al Gore as a pair of patrol leaders) sincerity.

Well, it's the season for it, he says. But this one is on his side:

Jesus and Clinton, never mind how and never mind why, are together in a boat on the Sea of Galilee, having a quiet conversation. The wind springs up and blows the hat off of Jesus' head. (Never mind how or why Jesus is wearing a hat or what kind of a hat it is.) The hat skitters and skims over the water. Comes to rest and to float (briefly) some distance away. "Allow me," says Bill Clinton. And he jumps over the side and runs on the water to pick up the hat and bring it back to Jesus.

Guess what the headlines were: CLINTON CAN'T SWIM!

The waitress brings us tall thick glasses of sweetened ice tea.

They don't serve it any other way, he tells me. Then: If I seem nervous, I am. I'm trying to quit smoking.

"Good luck."

We talk awhile about the newspaper business in this age of television.

Hagood was at the tag end of the old days, he says. Television was coming on strong in the news business. Not just reporting the news or even seriously examining it, but *changing* the news right before our eyes. Magic. Houdini stuff.

Way I look at it, the years you are interested in, the sixties, are when it all happened. When public figures began to get the hang of it, how to use it. They could see that in TV, image was far more important than "reality." That shadow had more value than substance. They could understand that it's all smoke and mirrors. What you see is what you get, and what isn't there doesn't exist. They could see—I'm thinking of Johnson, of the Kennedys, hell, everybody in the public light—that you either control it or it controls you. It can make anything happen. It can turn victory into defeat, vice into virtue, cowards into heroes. And most of all it has no memory at all. Now you see it and now you don't. Yesterday's heroes are today's criminals and vice versa.

Maybe the greatest irony is that it is finally impossible to control. You can't really control it, not for long. It cannot be done. Sooner or later it just does what it pleases. Like a wild animal, a wolf, say, that can never be fully domesticated. Whether you worship it or scorn it, no matter, it will eat you alive if it has a mind to.

There must be a lesson there somewhere. Beats me what it is, though. Except it's a sad time to be in the newspaper business. For everybody except the owners.

He gives up and lights himself a filter-tipped cigarette.

Rotten bastards! They claim they are not really addictive.

Then: What is interesting from my point of view, about this book you are writing, is that it comes along almost without benefit of TV. That weekend there were a hundred cities and towns on fire after the King shooting. Nobody had any people or cameras to spare for anything else. Today there would be enough amateurs with camcorders right here in Paradise Springs to give us all the footage and images you could possibly ask for. But then there was only print and Martin Pressy's photographs. Later on, come time for the trial, we had a flicker or two of national coverage. But not much. And here you are, doing a book, not a documentary film.

"More like a documentary without any pictures. A sound-track for an imaginary film. Voices without sources. Ghost noise."

Don't go and get literary on me. He stabs out the butt end of his cigarette in his plate. Then: Let's have a cup of coffee. They have pretty good coffee here.

(They always did have good coffee.)

So. You are welcome to use anything we have. Come and have a look, anytime. Anything else?

"People. A quick take on a few folks I have already interviewed."

PENROSE WEATHERBY: Mr. Slick these days. Don't know anything about his background, really. Looks after his one-legged old father, though. . . .

"The old man is still alive?"

He sends us crackpot racist letters-to-the-editor from time to time. I've even printed a couple of them. Just to see if anybody actually reads the letters. Mostly they don't.

W. E. GARY: Very interesting guy. Very smooth. Damn good lawyer, all around. Seems to have found a place for himself. Local blacks are ambivalent about him. Appreciate his success and accomplishment, but envy his freedom. Flip side is your basic white folks who cherish him as living proof that they don't hold a good man back or down on basis of race. They also see him as proof that his dark-skinned brothers *could have* done a lot better if they had got off their collective black asses and gone to work. He has a good-looking white wife.

"I didn't know that."

FORMER SHERIFF DAVE PRINCE AND DUDLEY HAGOOD: He ran a tight ship. Didn't look the part. Not much like Rod Steiger. Smart fellow, though. Hard as nails when he thought he had to be. Different world then, world in transition. He was the right man for the time, maybe. Nowdays he would be as out of date as the Green Knight. Nowdays he couldn't have gotten himself elected. A killer, too. Killed more than one man in his time.

"You said you never knew Hagood?"

That's right.

"Have you ever looked at his editorials?"

Sure.

"Where did he stand?"

More or less your basic Southern liberal of the era. Poor man's Hodding Carter. Some odd contradictions, though. Did *not* approve of the 1954 decision on integrated education. But for a different reason. He argues that it would be impractical. That it would never really work. Was he wrong? I don't know. Right now the schools are as segregated as they ever were nationwide. It hasn't really worked. What else? Seems to have been an exemplary chap, good citizen. Popular for a newspaperman.

MOSES KATZ: Is he still alive? That's astonishing. A nutcase, but very brainy at times. He's got a lot of theories. Some of them worth considering. You know, we were talking a while ago about the power of television and the image, the *perception* over what we used to call "reality." Moe had a theory about that. He said that the great men of the century—Roosevelt, Churchill, Stalin, Hitler, Mussolini—were creatures of the big screen, the newsreel in the movie theater. They were gigantic, towered and loomed over us. After them came the little box. It favored little people, diminished types like those little bitty people in *Gulliver's Travels.* So you get the ultimate TV man—Nixon. On a big screen he would have driven people howling out of the theater. On the little screen he seemed little himself and harmless. Like a hand puppet. All the same, except for Reagan who could do big screen and the tube both.

Of course, the worst thing is that they always used to manipulate us, but at least had the good manners to deny it. Now they, Clinton's people and the others, too, openly discuss changing and rearranging images and perceptions, all but admit there is no core behind the image.

"How about Harry Truman?"

Ah. There you go! He looks better to me every day. He simply transcended the media by ignoring them.

We come out of the air-conditioning and onto the sunny sidewalk. People nod greetings to MacIntyre.

Anything else? he asks me.

"You," I say. "You haven't given me a take on yourself."

Oh, I already did. Cynical newsman, knows his business and is weary of it. Whore with a heart of gold.

Pauses at his office door.

What kind of a whore are you, Mr. Tone?

"A working one."

Is that good or bad?

"Time will tell."

Then and There

"GOATHEAD" PAPP

I will tell you one damn thing and you better believe it. If I live through this fuckin' town, I am going to get me some other kind of a job. Count on it. I mean it. I will gladly shovel horse-shit in a barnyard before I will go on another tour with Little David and his Hot Gospel Group again.

Money don't have one thing to do with it, if that is what you are thinking. I make out all right around here. I get a reg-ular percentage of everything that comes in—gate offering, col-lection, sales of stuff—against a minimum guarantee. And I get whatever I can steal. Which would be more than plenty if I had the heart to take advantage as much as I could. The one thing he don't seem to care a whole lot about is money. As long as we aren't stone broke, he will take my word for anything. He next to never looks at my books and receipts and stuff like that. Which you might think would be an ideal situation. Except that—don't you see?—it takes most of the pride and the plea-sure out of stealing from him. I am a man who likes to be chal-lenged. But, never-the-fuckin'-less, a man has got to live and to look out for his own self, and I am willing to swallow a little bit of pride if I have to.

Looks like tonight we have got a pretty good crowd, if I do say so. My advance work and public relations paying off. By the time it was dark they had already filled up the big tent. And there is enough of them left over to mill around outside.

Maybe in the good old days, back during the deep Depres-sion, a traveling preacher didn't have any real necessity for fi-nancial management and planning. Those celebrated old-timey birds could just wander all around and acrost the countryside, stopping whenever and wherever the so-called spirit moved them to. They could borrow an old church or throw up a tent.

And hey-ho, away we go! Nowadays, however, there is getting to be just too much competition. It doesn't seem like there is a lonesome, tumbledown old shack out in the swamp that doesn't have its very own TV antenna poking up from the roof. Probably (though not necessarily) got a boob tube inside to go with it, too. And nowadays if you don't come on like Billy Graham or Martin Luther King, Jr., or somebody in a fancy suit and with a good haircut and a college diploma, the local preachers won't even give you the time of day. They are all pretty much like the Episcopalians they would (secretly) like to be. They don't take the Gospel or religion seriously at all. What I mean is those boys are in the business of selling peace and quiet on Sunday morning. Organ music and bunches of pretty flowers from the florist and good air-conditioning that gives you a chance to put on your very best clothes and to show off. It's like they are dispensing spiritual tranquilizers while we are still stuck trying to hustle goofballs and happy pills.

We are nothing but hell-raisers.

"How you going to get to Heaven if you don't even know what Hell is?" That's what Little David always tells them.

Tell the truth, I wouldn't know nothing much about either place. Because I am too busy. I don't have the time to study about all that. I am a salesman and a legitimate businessman. I have got a product to sell. I got to make out right here and now in this world. And, like I said, moneywise it's all right. I may not be getting rich. But it sure beats the hell out of selling Bibles and encyclopedias. Which is what I was most recently up to. And, hard as it is, it's easier than some of the other kinds of selling jobs that I have had. Like trying to move used cars off the lot. Or talking rubes into a carnival sideshow.

I have got a product and I have got a property also. That Little David can preach and pray with the best of them. He can beat and pick a steel string guitar about as good as many of them that are in the music business. And he can sing pretty good, too. He can laugh when it's called for and cry like a little

baby anytime he feels like it. But, chiefly on account of being
so stunted and short that he is practically a midget or a dwarf
and being as ugly as sin without his makeup and his wig on,
I don't think he could make it in any other branch of
show business. He might be good for a record album of gospel
hymns, and I am going to pursue that possibility when I get a
chance to.

Little David doesn't know it and probably never will, but he
owes me just a whole lot. Nobody else I know of would go
ahead like I do and get everything set up for him. I get the
protection of the Law on our side, and very cheap, too. I get
the word out and all over the area. I mingle with influential local
people so that our whole operation can be respectable.

If Little David was strictly on his own, chances are he
wouldn't draw a dozen in this day and age. Most of them would
probably be niggers.

Does he appreciate what I do? Hell no. If I had to depend
on what he actually allows me for the actual business expenses,
I couldn't accomplish anything. As I have said, I don't abuse
my freedom with the money. I take what I need to get the job
done and just enough extra, above and beyond that, to make
doing the job worth my time and my trouble. Just like everybody else in America does. I mean to tell you I am not greedy
or anything like that. As long as the money comes in steady and
regular, that suits me fine. Greed is bad for you. It can help to
get yourself caught.

Anyway, as I was trying to say, I fixed up this arrangement
fine and dandy. I had to make a promise to the sheriff that we
wouldn't be using any snakes. I guess a friend or a relative of
his or something may have gotten bit sometime. If you have
ever seen what happens when somebody gets bitten by a snake,
it will tend to make you kind of spooky and shy of them. I told
the sheriff all about Raphael, the coon that we have got that
looks after them. He milks them down and keeps them about
half-groggy with some kind of chemical or dope so that won't

nobody get hurt playing with them. But the sheriff was bound and determined that we wouldn't use no snakes at all whilst we was in his county. And it is, after all, his county.

"You do it, and I will punch your lights out and jail the whole fuckin' bunch of you. You hear me?"

"Yes, sir, Sheriff, I have received your message."

"I figured you did," he said, laughing, trying to imply in the usual devious way of a fuckin' policeman that, just by the look and the manner of me, he could tell I was more than likely fully familiar with the interior decoration of any number of Southern jailhouses.

So I paid the old bastard fifty bucks. And I hired a couple of his deputies to come and handle the traffic and security for ten dollars apiece. And even though we have got almost a whole truckful of folding chairs of our own, I rented some chairs from the Paradise Springs Women's Club. And I got paper fans from the Raleigh Funeral Parlor.

You get the Law, the Ladies, and one rich undertaker on your side and that is about half of the battle.

Little David, though, naturally, he wasn't too happy about not being able to use our snakes.

"Goddamn you, you fuckin' half-assed idiot!" he said. (That is a typical example of the beginning of a conversation by Little David.) "Don't you know that I am supposed to heal people?"

"Sure, sure, sure," I said. "I'll get the people here and you can do whatever you want to with them. I am absolutely not going to butt in and meddle with your end of the business."

"Don't you know, don't you even know, you lamebrain half-wit, what the Good Book says: *They shall take up serpents; and if they drink any deadly thing, it shall not hurt them; they shall lay hands on the sick, and they shall recover.*"

"So why don't you go get something deadly and drink it?"

That was intended to be a kind of a ironic wisecrack. On account of Little David is capable of putting away enough in the line of alcoholic beverages to kill a full-grown bull or a bull elephant. But I could see that he either didn't get the joke or he wasn't fixing to laugh if he did get it. So I had to settle down and get serious real quick.

"You can prove anything by the Book," I opined. "I should know. I made a very good living hustling them."

"Piss on you, Goathead," he said, as ever resorting to name-calling when he saw that I had the best of the argument. "You never looked at a book in your whole life, unless it was some kind of a funny book."

Boy, that's Little David for you.

Who does he think he is? Who does he think he is fooling?

Then and There

PICTURE

Photograph of Colonel William T. Singletree, C.S.A., taken by unknown itinerant photographer somewhere in Trans-Mississippi, early in 1865. Certainly prior to the surrender of Trans-Mississippi on 26 May 1865. Blank wall forms background for seated figure in full-dress gray uniform, loose-fitting this late in the long war. Oddly, Colonel Singletree is wearing (judging by the sleeve insignia on his right arm) the uniform of a Confederate brigadier general. Perhaps he borrowed the coat from a superior officer.

Or perhaps, in the confusion of the last days, with everything—government, armies, navy, all—east of the Mississippi lost and gone forever, perhaps Singletree took occasion to promote himself to a higher rank for posterity.

Runs in the family, old-timers would and do say. Look at his grandson, the "Judge" who never was one, the "Colonel" who served, not without honor, as a captain in the Great War. This whole business of ranks and titles, these same old-timers will tell you, plagued the South anyway, for two generations. Every man

an officer. Fifty years in which one appropriate form of address
to a decent stranger in civilian clothes was "Captain." Usually
shortened, contracted to "Cap'n."

So the Colonel, photographed as a brigadier somewhere in
Texas at the tag end of things, the nation's worst and bloodiest
war. He wears a clean white collar, like today's clerical collar, a
dark gray waistcoat, a lighter gray coat with double row of round
brass buttons. Shiny. His hair is medium-length and recently
well cut. He has a full mustache and a short, trimmed beard.
His eyebrows are heavy and also look trimmed. Maybe by the
barber who cut his hair and clipped his beard. His pale, firm face
is as unlined as a mask. His attitude is confident, though not,
of course (not in his day and age) smiling. Even in this dark and
fading photograph his eyes are bright. Pale and bright. Pale and
bright and hard and unrevealing. They might as well be glass
eyes.

Hell of a poker player, the old-timers will tell you. He could
bluff you. Indeed, like so many others, he was bluffing then and
there when he sat still for a long time to suit the traveling photographer who hasn't left a name with his picture. The Colonel
is defeated. His country is in ruins. His future and the future of
his place (nation no longer) are beyond imagining. He is far
from home and must wonder if he will ever see home again.
We know all these things now and have to think, also, that he
knew it all when the photograph was taken, *knows* it now in the
photograph which lives on even beyond the memory of him.
But—and here's the point—if he knew it, as he must have, still
he showed none of that in expression, attitude, appearance. You
can read what you want to on the blank wall in the blank face.
But you cannot justly read doubt or fear or sorrow. Merely
blankness. He was bluffing. Is still bluffing.

Sometimes he (they; all of them, only ghosts and old images
now) won and sometimes lost.

Bluffing. It worked well enough some of the time. While the
game lasted.

Here and Now

CONVERSATION AT MIDNIGHT

Smoke rings.
I'm too old for you, he says.
We'll see, she says. Tell me about your wife.
My former wife.
Whatever.
What is there to tell? She was tall, red hair and fair skin, blue-green eyes. Soft voice and a very nice throaty laugh when she felt like laughing. Reminded me a little of Glenn Close. Only prettier.
Was?
Okay, is. Was for me.
Children?
Two.
Who are they?
Kimberly. She's a sophomore at Princeton. Costing us both a bundle to send her there. I have become a great believer in community colleges and state universities.
The other one?
Other what?
Child.
Oh, then there is Andrew, our genius baby. He is at Exeter aiming for the most expensive education in the U.S.
Bennington. Bennington has the highest tuition.
Perfect for him, then. But I still have a chance. Andrew is smart, but he has discipline problems. Chances are he'll be kicked out of Exeter for smoking dope or something. It has happened before.
You don't like him a lot, do you?
Well, I try. Sometimes I really, seriously try.
Where did you go to school?

Hey, this is crazy. You can see that, can't you? Here we are in bed together and you are asking me all about my ex-wife and my family and my education. Next thing you'll want to know about my sex life.

Not a bad idea in this day and age.

I'll tell you this much. You are the first librarian I have ever been to bed with.

Did you plan it this way?

Did you?

I'm serious.

So am I.

I never plan on anything. Or put it another way. I plan for everything and hope for nothing.

How do you explain the underwear?

What about it?

I've never seen anything like it except in the Victoria's Secret catalogue.

What did your wife wear?

Who, Annie? Very plain, very cheap. Chaste and white. It was pretty sexy, actually.

Doesn't that make it nice?

Hey, you asked, so I told you.

I didn't put on my underwear for you. I always wear it. It's my little secret. You know about the Amish and the Mennonites, don't you?

What about them?

They have very strict sumptuary rules. About everything except their underwear. They are allowed to wear anything they want to. And they tend to do so. Wild things!

Is that what librarians do?

I can't speak for other librarians. And neither can you, unless you lied to me.

I wish I had this on tape.

Like that football player at Florida State?

Is this date rape?

Seduction, maybe. Date rape, no.

Seduction?

Look, she says. We had a wonderful dinner and some good wine. We had a lovely walk on the beach in the moonlight. . . .

I'm not responsible for the weather. I didn't plan any of it. I had hopes . . .

Ah!

. . . but I didn't allow myself any plans.

You see, we are more alike than you realize.

I'm too old for you.

We'll see about that.

Now?

Why not?

Here and Now

BILLY TONE WRITES TO FRIEND

Dear Curly,

Here is a token check for some of what I owe you. I haven't forgotten my debt (and gratitude) to you, and I hope in the foreseeable future to be able to pay you in full and with interest. Your patience, support and friendship have meant the world to me.

I don't know when is the last time you have been down home, but I hadn't been here in years. Sure, I flew down for Mother's funeral a few years ago. But there was no real sense of coming *home,* just loss and sad memory. But now I'm in Paradise Springs (my childhood home away from home while Daddy was still alive and kicking . . . and drinking). And it is very strange to be back. Everything is, looks so different. Everything seems, on closer inspection, much the same.

I mean, Curly, all of America looks so much alike these days, so interchangeable, so helplessly and hopelessly *tacky.* It's like the soul has gone out of the body of America. Leaving a corpse that stinks (to high heaven) and shines. But, I don't know, there are people and places that seem to defy the drift of things. Maybe Paradise Springs is one of these places. We'll see. . . .

I won't bore you with the project I'm working on. It's a true crime story that actually happened right here in 1968. But I'm meeting all kinds of people. Including some nice ones. Nicest of the bunch is a young (and very pretty) librarian who, for some reason (God knows) has been kind and friendly and is trying to help on the project, too.

Listen, Curly, if by any chance you should run into Annie anytime in town or in Connecticut (do you still have your place up there?), do me a big favor and don't mention this letter or anything about hearing from me or this project. I am a little behind in what I owe her. I will take care of it just as soon as I am able to. Meanwhile she and the kids are in fine shape, not needy by any definition. And since she finally went and married her shrink, Dr. Smartheim, she's in clover, anyway, and can afford to wait a little while for me to get my life straightened out.

(Ha! you say. That will be a very long wait. And you may be right, Curly. But don't write me off yet. I am giving it the old college try. Something might become of me yet.)

All best to you. I'll be and keep in touch.

Stay well.

Sincerely,
Billy

Here and Now

A LETTER

Martin Pressy Foundation
250 West 57th Street/New York, NY 10107

5 April 1994

Dear Mr. Tone,

I am writing in response to your query letter of March 30, 1994, addressed to Martin Pressy.

Mr. Pressy is at present out of the country and will be un-
available for an interview with you concerning the events of early
April (and months following) of 1968.

However, Mr. Pressy spoke to me on the phone and dictated
the following statement to be passed on to you:

I deeply regret that I cannot be of any assistance to
you in your interesting project about events (hijinks
would be more like it) of April 1968. It is true that I was
resident in Paradise Springs at the time, having returned
home, following the death of my father, to look after the
estate and to handle various business matters for my
mother. Thus I was, indeed, "on the scene," as it were.
And, of course, as events unfolded, ending in the trial
and conviction of two members of an itinerant revival
troupe, I could hardly ignore the gossip and rumor, not
to mention the daily news, that dwelt upon the subject.

Nevertheless I have very few *personal* reflections of the
events in question. What I do clearly remember is my
own rage and frustration when I discovered that my automobile, the first Mercedes in Quincy County, had been
stolen and totaled by vandals.

I was assured at the time by the police—and I have
no reason to doubt it now—that there was no connection, direct or indirect, between the theft and destruction
of my beautiful car and the other events of that April
evening.

To this day it makes me furious to think about all that.
So I assiduously try not to, preferring to concentrate on
cheerful and happy memories.

Sorry I can't help you, because it does seem to me an
interesting subject; and true crime stories are all the rage
these days—not to mention the tedious courtroom dra-
mas which have been turned into instant best-sellers.
Good luck to you. May you have all the success of John
Grisham and people like that.

Mr. Pressy added two remarks. First, he wondered if you are, perhaps, the same Billy Tone who was distantly related to Judge Singletree and spent some summers in Paradise Springs. Secondly, he stated that if you are (as you surely must be) in touch with "the amazing Professor Moses Katz" you are hereby authorized (to quote Mr. Pressy directly) "to give the old fart and fraud a big sloppy kiss on the lips from Brother Martin."

Mr. Pressy also asks to be remembered to Ms. Eleanor Lealand with whom, as he understands it, you have formed a friendship.

With all good wishes.

Yours truly,

Natasha Auerman
Cultural Affairs Director

Then and There

GOATHEAD PAPP

Yes, we have got ourselves a very good crowd this evening. It's a good thing I hired those deputies to handle the traffic and just in case there should be any kind of trouble or rough stuff. Because you never can tell with a big crowd.

The music has started and they are all singing now. The old gospel hymns. I can hear big fat Geneva booming out like an opera singer, louder than all the rest put together. I have done everything I can do, and they don't need me now until it comes time to count up the collection. With a crowd like this, Little David and I will be up half the night counting. I don't mind, though. I don't mind losing a little sleep to count money. So, go right ahead. Pick them as clean as a wishbone, Little David. A crowd like this one just might be the last one for me. Good old Goathead is liable to pick up his marbles and move on. . . .

Got to wait, though. Think I will head on back to the trailer and settle down in privacy with a skin magazine and a pint of vodka that I have got stashed away. Science is wonderful, and I am sure grateful that they have come up with a hard liquor which don't smell on your breath.

"Hey, mister!"

Here is that snotty little kid I saw hanging around the pool-room, among other places. He's got a smirk on his face and a chip on his shoulder. A regular juvenile delinquent type of a kid. It would be pure pleasure to knock some sense and some humility into his head. It would be like doing a civic duty.

"What's the trouble?"

"Gimme my money back."

"Too late for a refund. Service is half over, son."

"I ain't your son and I want my money back or I'm going to call a cop."

What a smart-mouth kid!

"What's wrong with you, boy? Aren't you even a Christian?"

"Don't give me that shit," he says. "I walked all the way out here. And then I find out there aren't going to be any snakes."

"Snakes are against the law."

Now he hawks and spits on the ground right in front of the tips of my shoes.

"Give me fifty cents."

I take a quick look around. It is dark at this distance from the tent and there's nobody else around.

"Okay," I say, fishing in my pocket. "I guess you have got a point."

Nasty little greedy snotnose, he comes closer to me with his hand out and a grin all over his face. So I am compelled to wipe that grin off of him with the back of my left hand. And down and over he goes, ass over teakettle.

"Go peddle your papers," I say.

But he is just laying there, kicking his heels and hollering like a stuck pig. And I figure it is worth something just to shut him up before a cop or somebody comes. I kneel down beside him.

"Shut up," I say, "and I'll give you a quarter."

"Four bits!"

"Okay."

He stops howling and I give him two quarters.

"That was completely accidental," I tell him. "I didn't mean to bust you upside the head like that."

He is grinning again at me now. The little punk!

"Don't flatter yourself," he says. "I've got a sister that can hit harder than you do."

And then he is gone, scuttling away into the dark before I can hit him again.

I know that it takes all kinds, but I swan, I don't know what this younger generation is coming to. They've got no manners and no morals either.

Then and There

ONE GOOD TURN DESERVES ANOTHER

As soon as Penrose Weatherby discovered that, except for the salty taste of a fleck of blood from his split lip, he was all in one piece and none of it suffering beyond his ability to bear the pain, crouched down as he was in the dark and beneath a truck, he smiled to himself. He was thinking that twice now he had been hit hard and each time it had been worth some money and some fun. He was thinking that if he had fifty cents, or even just a quarter, for every time he had earned and received a cuff or a blow in this world where they are as plentiful as grass, he would already be rich. Suppose people were paid compensation for all the blows, wounds, scars they received. This would be one form of justice, at the least a decent equalizer. And in such a world, a fellow like himself, with a proved ability to take and withstand a large number of blows and to bounce back intact and ready for more of the same, not grimly either, but with an ever-defiant grin; a chap who had tested himself thoroughly in the primitive learning period when fists fell on him at random and without apparent reason like bolts of lightning; one who had done so, in fact and precisely in order to test himself as well as the varieties and levels of tolerance of pain—in such a world he could be an important figure, a natural aristocrat, a celebrity, a kind of star. In some large and altogether honorable sense he would be an evolved version of those other little boys, mostly coons to be sure, who, at carnivals, fairs and charity bazaars, gallantly exposed their skulls in various kinds of targets for missiles ranging from eggs and soft, pulpy, stinky rotten vegetables to baseballs.

Penrose had long since decided that the principal business and concern of humankind was twofold: first, to survive as long as possible, toughly as able, the outrageous and indifferent (therefore both impartial and inequitable) blows of nature and likewise to withstand the more purposeful injuries dealt out by one's fellow humans; second, not to remain merely a passive recipient in this condition, but, as in a complex and elaborate game of tag, *to pass it on* with, if anything, increased ferocity, vigor and vehemence to the nearest skin and bones, body and soul at hand. In which case pain and suffering could be considered as a powerful electric current passing through one's body and, so considered, could be borne, not alone with accepting patience, but also with some sense of pleasure in the contemplation of its transfer. It made one part of the grand scheme of things to know this secret, becoming virtually a priest for a God who was not only unknown and unknowable, save as the divine Hand at the switch which turned on the universal current, the grandly democratic shock, and thus not to be known from the shocking sensation any more than, for example, a lightbulb stands as a symbol of and for Boulder Dam, but also probably better off being unknown. That is, Penrose reasoned, the knowledge of the frying, fading, dying lightbulb was gracious plenty.

Who would even want to know any more? He considered this kind of ignorance to be the greatest blessing, more than likely the kindest gift of God to His creatures. It was from this consolation that Penrose derived his ineradicable optimism, based as it was upon the logical supposition that the nature of God was benevolent. If He were malevolent, wouldn't He have revealed Himself more clearly and surely have struck us blind or turned us into stone?

By the active cultivation of his frailties, Penrose familiarized himself with all human frailty; and by the open, overt and sometimes arrogant demonstration of frailty, chiefly in different forms of folly, he permitted (indeed *created*) the requisite catharsis of outrage and punishment, a condition which, like any subtle art, was priceless and yet which in a few hours had earned him seventy-five cents and was likely to earn him more. Cheap at the price, when one thought about it. For if the message had been learned truly, then he could have saved lives (for as long as any life can be saved) and added to salvation a sudden sense of joy.

Penrose was exalted and joyous, feeling a decorous mixture of pity and contempt for all those others who knew no joy, took none in the state and way of the world.

His sister, Alpha, for example, had much to learn about the world, and she would suffer greatly until she learned. Her refusal was signified by her firm and insistent virginity, by which, evidently, she wished to preserve one small (albeit vital) part of herself from the world. Pure and simple folly. How could she ever learn?

Darlene, on the other hand, or so it seemed to him, was so active in spending and giving of herself that she had no time or energy left to receive the world's wounds and blessings. She sought to resist, if not avoid, the pain by offering to others an unearned, unexpected extravagance of pleasure. Alpha was so fearful of pain that she crouched, immobile and almost catatonic, briefly safe but barely alive, a dreamer wishing never to wake since waking is suffering.

So, with the same smile which, by habit and inclination, was more like a taunting smirk than anything else, Penrose, huddled under a dark truck, was able to reassure himself that he was, to be sure, the right and proper guardian for these two poor cripples, and, as well, that it was perfectly natural and appropriate that they should cling to each other. The blind leading the blind.

In all of this, his scheme of things, earned and cherished without these words (and for which Penrose lacked words but considered even this a blessing—for didn't words with their meanings and shadows *come between* the mind and the thought, the soul and its immediate experience?), Penrose was conscious of only one serious flaw: that the circumstances and conditions of existence prohibited the passing on of pain to anyone except those nearest, closest at hand. In a perfectly made universe he would collide loudly and completely like balls on the green baize of a pool table. And then be gone. Imperfection was obvious in the simple fact that, things being as they are, although Penrose was probably a perfect stranger to Goathead Papp, he nevertheless knew Papp well, having studied him for almost a week at (among other places) the Luxury Billiard Parlor, where Papp had whiled away a good deal of time while awaiting the arrival of Little David and his crew in Paradise Springs.

Speculation was all fine and dandy in its place. Which was not now. Penrose's scheme was simplified. It was now his duty to return the blow Papp had delivered twofold or more. Otherwise the stars might veer from their appointed courses and the angels weep. The money was irrelevant or, at most, symbolic.

In the universe of Penrose Weatherby there was only one currency, one true medium of exchange—payment in kind. And then some.

Then and There

State of Florida v. Mary Lou Frond and William Papp
EXCERPT FROM TRIAL TRANSCRIPT

[Statement of defendant, William Papp, before sentence was passed]

JUDGE SPENCE: Mr. Papp, do you have anything you want to say, any statement you may wish to make, before sentence is passed?

WILLIAM PAPP: I do, Your Honor. You better believe I do. But first, before I make any statement, I have got to know one thing.

JUDGE SPENCE: Go on. Speak up.

WILLIAM PAPP: Do you kiss me now or afterward?

JUDGE SPENCE: What? What's that?

WILLIAM PAPP: Your Honor, sir. All my life, my whole crummy life I have been screwed, blued and tattooed. But I swear this is the first and only time that I have ever been fucked without even getting a kiss.

JUDGE SPENCE: Order! Order in the court! Bailiff, remove these rowdies from this room.

Here and Now

A WELL-KEPT SECRET: **MOE KATZ**

The whole thing about teaching in a Baptist college—and this is a fairly well-kept secret—is that at the theological heart of everything, intellectual activities and enterprises are pretty much irrelevant. What I mean is that you can't reason or read or *think* yourself into grace and salvation. And that's all that really matters, right?—being saved. Baptist kids need to go to college to get an education and to get a college degree if they want to compete and survive in the fallen world. But in a deep sense it really doesn't make any difference whatsoever what subjects they study there.

Oh, I suppose in a serious sense they shouldn't waste all their time in intellectual frivolity and studying all kinds of stuff that will only mess up their heads and confuse them. But in the same very real sense, in the context of the Baptist world, all forms of intellectual activity are essentially and equally frivolous. So how much harm can any of it possibly do?

Result of all this, my lad, in the practical world is that Moe Katz got to teach anything he wanted to teach. Long before the others, the more or less progressive schools were offering all kinds of interdisciplinary courses, we were teaching courses that joined together art and music and history and literature and even popular culture. It was fun. It was even exciting and adventurous. Nobody bothered you unless you laced your lectures with strings of obscenities, smoked cigarettes in the classroom or showed up on campus drunk and disorderly. Unlike a lot of more civilized folk, the Baptists weren't (maybe still aren't) afraid of ideas.

How can you be afraid of things that really don't matter, that are harmless?

I liked it here so much—especially after my brief and unhappy season in the Ivy League—that I made up my mind to stay if I could. To be sure, to get tenure in those days I had to be a Baptist. So? So, big deal. I am a Jew, but I don't practice Judaism. Never have. Not since childhood. I don't practice being a Baptist anymore either. I did for a while. I kept sober and sincere in public and showed up at the Orange Avenue Baptist Church with metronomic regularity until I got my promotion and tenure.

Funny. That year, 1968, was the year I got promoted to full professor. Everywhere else the world was going up in flames and riddled with rhetoric and rage. There were wars and rumors of war, prophets and false prophets. Murders and assasinations. Even Paradise Springs had its share of disasters. . . .

You know when that old circus tent at the revival burned up, it is a wonder that a whole lot of people weren't killed. As it was, nobody died in the fire. Nobody was even badly burned. I have often thought it was a piece of the purest luck that the snakes got loose first, before the fire started, and scared everybody shitless.

Anyway it was a wild and woolly time, an amazing year. And I remember thinking by the end of the year, after the election, that nothing any worse could happen to us. But, of course, it did. It got a lot worse before it got any better.

And I was a part of it, to be sure. It changed my life in many ways. But even so, the main thing on my mind, my own principal motivation and goal, was my promotion and tenure. Whose ass did I have to kiss? Who did I have to fuck to get myself promoted?

Which inevitably leads me to another subject: sex. Baptists, as all the world must know, or ought to if they don't, have a very unusual attitude towards sex. Sex outside of marriage is frowned on, to be sure. But not too much. Not as much as smoking and drinking. You know the old joke, don't you? Why do Baptists disapprove of sexual intercourse? Answer: Because it might lead to dancing.

Do you know, they still didn't allow what they called "mixed dancing" at Baptist College in 1968. Boys could dance with boys and girls with girls. But boys and girls together? Forget it! At the proms they would hire an expensive band and the band would play dance music and nobody would dance. They would just promenade, walking slowly around the dance floor, arm in arm or hand in hand, but not dancing.

That's all changed now. More or less. You still have to be a little bit careful about what the kids call "touch dancing."

———

Talk, talk, talk. Well, who could blame him, stuck in retirement in that beat-up mobile home? Nobody to talk to a lot of the time.

Billy Tone came and took him—wheelchair, oxygen and all—over to the college so that Moe could turn in a bunch of books at the library and check out a bunch more. It was a nice, comfortable little college—brick buildings, clipped lawns, some heavy live oaks and tall, shady water oaks. Quiet enough so that the sound of a power mower was like the buzz of a bumblebee.

One of the college librarians, a woman who put Tone in mind of Joan Blondell in midcareer, made a considerable fuss over Moe Katz.

"Oh, Professor," she said. "We are so glad to see you again. It's been a while. It's been too long. It just doesn't seem right around here without you. How are you feeling? You're certainly looking better all the time. I bet somebody is taking real good care of you."

Christ, another talker. This town was full of talkers.

"And you, Mr. Tone. It's a great pleasure to meet you. We have heard all about you—now don't you make a face. We are nothing but an overgrown small town and we just love to hear about everything that happens. We gossip more that we ought to. Anyway, Eleanor Lealand is a dear, dear friend of mine. So we feel like we know you already. . . ."

Who is this "we"—the United Librarians of Paradise Springs?

"And, of course, everybody in town is wondering what fascinating things you are finding out about the events of April 1968 to put in your book. Some people that I know of are more than a little bit nervous about what you might dig up after all these years and put in print for the whole world to read and talk about. I'm telling you, Mr. Tone, there are some people around here who would be just a whole lot happier if you were writing some other kind of a book."

"Like what?"

"You know, like that Hollywood thing that you did. We've

got a copy of it right here in the library. I wonder if I could prevail upon you to inscribe it for us. And Professor Katz. We have a couple of things for you to sign too, if you will. We have been trying to get a hold of these for some time now. And we finally found a collector in Bridgehampton, New York, who was willing to sell them to us. We keep them in the Rare Book Room. Not so much because they are rare—though they really are kind of rare—but to keep them out of the hands of the young students."

"It stunts the growth," Katz said.

"Whatever," she said.

Then to Billy Tone: "These are some books I bet you didn't know about, Mr. Tone. I mean, everybody (I guess) knows about Professor Katz's scholarly reputation. But not many know about the books he wrote—novels, naughty ones, too—back in the 1960s under the nom de plume of Harry Diadem. I haven't had a chance to read them yet, myself. But they have these delightfully lurid covers and very suggestive titles. Have you ever written anything under a pseudonym, Mr. Tone?"

"Less Than Zero."

"Oh, you are teasing me." She to Katz: "He is a sketch, isn't he?"

Then to Tone: "I was hoping when I first heard about your project that you would come and interview me. I was a student right here in 1968. I thought maybe you would want to know what the young people at the college were thinking about and doing."

"Well, I would like to talk to you, if I can."

"Not about that, though. I would bore you to tears. Because the plain truth is that I just went about my daily life—classes and extracurricular activities—without as much as a thought about what was happening in the big world or even in downtown Paradise Springs. I didn't know anything more than what was in the newspaper and on TV. None of it seemed very real to me. Do you know what was the absolutely most important thing in my life at that time? If he can still remember, Professor

Katz can be my witness on this. The most important thing on my mind in spring semester 1968 (it was my junior year) was how to raise my grade and get an A in Professor Katz's course. It seemed like a matter of life and death to me at the time. I was totally involved. It looked like I had a shot at making Phi Beta Kappa if I could get an A from Katz. And that's the only thing that mattered to me.

"And I did it, too, didn't I, Professor? By the end of the semester I came all the way up to an A."

"A-minus, actually," Katz said. "That's the best I could do for you. But you earned it. You earned it all right and all on your own."

To Tone: "Isn't he the sweetest thing?"

To the two: "Well, it has been wonderful seeing you-all and having a little visit. But now I have to go back to work. Just make yourselves at home here. And if you need anything just give me a holler."

Then a quick, dry peck of a kiss on the moony cheek of Moe Katz. "It's been so nice to see you again, Professor Katz. We don't see nearly enough of you anymore. Come back soon, won't you? Don't just sit there in your trailer moping and brooding. You have a whole lot of friends here at the college and you will always be welcome."

Katz began to wheeze a little.

"I hope somebody is looking after you these days, Professor Katz?" she continued. "Is that sweet little cracker girl, the waitress, still helping out? I surely hope so. She was such a dear. . . ."

Tote bag bulging with books, wheelchair humming and groaning with the weight and bulk of old Katz, they headed back across the campus to the parking lot, passing under the dappled shade of the old trees, smelling the sweetness of the freshly mowed grass. Students (fugitives from an updated Norman Rockwell painting), snug in their jeans or shorts (the boys' baggy, the girls' white and tight), each with his/her backpack, suntanned, clean-looking, smiling with good teeth, passed to and from the handsome buildings.

"That bitch!" Katz said. "I fucked her brains out in 1968. Do you believe that?"

"Why not? If you say so."

"You know, I probably could have married her, too. In spite of—maybe because of—the age difference. Some of these girls have a serious thing about making it with a surrogate daddy. Incest without serious consequences."

"Would you have been happy?"

"How the hell would I know? No. Not happy. Not happy at all. Just maybe a lot more comfortable. The bitch is rich."

"That's always nice."

"Great tits, too," Katz said. Then: "What a waste!"

"Maybe not. You still have memories."

"Memory, like déjà vu, ain't what it used to be."

Then and There

DRAFT OF PREFACE BY PROFESSOR **MOSES KATZ**
TO *The Magic Book of Woman* BY MARTIN PRESSY,
PUBLISHED 1969

This gathering of extraordinary photographs of the female nude is something more than it seems. That is, it is not merely another exercise in depicting and expressing the aesthetic qualities, the "beauty," of the female form, even though many of the individual photographs are, in and of themselves, "beautiful." Nor are the bodies of these young women, captured and exposed here by a gifted artist, displayed for any rhetorical purpose, for *effect*. It is true that many of the individual pictures are highly sensual and do indeed celebrate the subjects as objects of desire. But Pressy does not intend to use or exploit his subjects in this common sense. He is certainly not interested in depicting woman as "a sex object."

Representation of reality is not his aim at all. Rather, this gathering is a carefully structured exploration, the record of a spiritual odyssey. The physical is not so much used as released and freed to express the spiritual essence of eternal and ineffable Woman. The Artist, a secret sharer of profound mysteries, the magic of the female, himself a creature of intuition and dark impulse, is the proper figure to explore the dark continent which is Woman. Now that we have learned, by heart and through wounds and scars beyond counting, the follies and horrors of Western rationalism, the terrors of technology and the frigid agonies of science, now that we have come at last to realize the morbid bankruptcy of the Judeo-Christian heritage (and, as well, of the inadequate Apollonian ideals), now that we have reached the end of an historical era of blindness, it is the magicians and artists who are leading us forward into the new, uncharted territories of the human spirit, a spirit which has been dreaming all the while Man slept and believed his own nightmares were true.

Child of the moon, daughter of the tides, preserver of the dark and hidden gods of body and blood, it is Woman who can lead us to the full recovery of ourselves. And here, in this artist's *Magic Book,* we can glimpse her, nymph or fury seen in a flash of sunlight and leaves, a view like that of Orpheus when he turned back and for one blazing moment saw Eurydice once and for all.

The Magic Book is, then, at once a prophecy and a new testament, an important evidentiary document for the future. It is beyond good and evil; it is at once tragic and affirmative. Silently, these naked shapes sing the oldest songs of Eden. Motionless, in the frozen moment of the photograph, they dance on and on into the future of our deepest dreams.

These are not "models," they are priestesses celebrating the mysteries of themselves in joyous self-abandonment. Indeed, in a *literal* sense none of the young women who participated with the artist in creating this masterpiece are "models" at all. They are real and fully dimensional people. And they are and become utterly anonymous as they blend together in light and shadow, in old song and young dance, to become the One, Eternal Woman, forever freed from the ravages of time.

Martin Pressy is a poet and a prophet. In the end, he, too, vanishes like the photographer in *Blow-Up*. And even his art is a splendid sacrifice to these dancers out of the darkness. But *The Magic Book* remains, brimming with light and with secret laughter, a sacred celebration of all that is true of the self.

Even as I shudder at his fate, I salute Martin Pressy, who has courageously created this work of art.

Cut that last sentence. It's a clinker. Otherwise it suits me fine.
Martin P.

Then and There

MLK PICTURE

Black-and-white photo credited to Bob Fitch, identified as taken in Mississippi in June of 1966. A small, closely grouped gathering of people marching toward the camera. Moving up the middle of what seems to be a country highway at the edge of town. (Philadelphia, Mississippi?) Tall frail telephone poles and light poles march off in the opposite direction toward the flat horizon behind them. A bouquet of black faces, most wearing straw hats against the Mississippi summer sun. Mostly black faces. Look very closely in the middle and you will see, here and there, white faces, hatless. In the front row of the marchers Ralph Abernathy, Coretta King (a rare public appearance), MLK, CORE's Floyd McKissick, Stokely Carmichael and an unidentified, light-skinned young woman close by Carmichael.

Marching.

Marching in this case as a public gesture to finish the private march begun by James Meredith and ended when he was superficially wounded by birdshot near Hernando, Mississippi.

Marching.

How much time was spent by these men, the leaders, marching on foot at the head of crowds to make and prove their points? They would fly in, march a while, then go on to the next place, the next photo opportunity.

They, the leaders, have done this so many times before. They know how to do it, what to wear. King and Abernathy look fit, almost lean, never better. Both wear jaunty straw hats, white, short-sleeved polo shirts, creased and clean khaki trousers (each with a slender, dark leather belt), and comfortable walking shoes. Each has a large shiny wristwatch. King wears sunglasses. So does Coretta King, who is holding hands with MLK. She has hair up, earrings, large purse and a sleeveless, tailored summer dress, hemline at the knees. She might be going to church (except that she wears no hat) or anyway some social event. Except for her dark sneakers with white laces.

In the front row only Stokely Carmichael looks different from the others—no hat, wearing a long-sleeved white shirt, bib overalls and what may be boots, not walking shoes. No one will mistake him for a servant or an ally of "de Lawd." Carmichael is tall and thin, close-cropped, dark-skinned. He looks to be no tribal kin to any of the others. You can read his expression (his mouth with bright teeth is open wide, chanting or singing something) as mischievous if you want to.

In the background, in the crowd, some marchers are carrying large American flags. The flags are upside down in the symbol of distress.

Marching. Coming forward. Coming at you. Indefatigable. Silent (in the photograph) and implacable. Picking them up and putting them down.

Marching.

Here and Now

DOING THE LITERARY

"So you are going to talk to the Poet. Well, all things considered, it's high time."

That, of course, will be Moe Katz talking to Billy Tone. And Billy, by this time, can guess correctly what happens next.

"I'll bet he has a story and that you're going to tell it to me."

"We all have our story. Just like a squirrel has a tail." And Katz tells it:

Poet . . . that's what we call him, to each other and by now even to his face, even though he does have a real name—Benjamin Somethingorother. Poet came here from away. From Ann Arbor, the University of Michigan, where he had a job but didn't make the cut for tenure. Before that was born and raised and went to school in the Detroit area. Claims downtown Detroit, anyway, though I kind of doubt it. Big tall skinny fella with curly black hair and a scruffy beard and bad teeth.

If you kept up with poetry and such at all (which I seriously doubt you do and for which I seriously give you credit) you would at least know of his book *Assembly Line* from maybe ten years ago. Book was nominated for the National Book Award. Short-listed, but didn't make it. Not a whole lot heard about or from him since then. Except that he plugged into the college reading circuit. And gossip (gossip being one of the bodily fluids of the poetry world), gossip had it that he turned into some kind of a superstud in literary circles and among literary groupies. Even outclassing some of our other mythical figures like Dickey and Merwin and Plumly and old Galway Kinnell. I like that part of his story, apocryphal or not.

And what on earth is he doing here in Paradise Springs? I thought you would never ask.

You may or may not know about the Pressy Foundation. Dear old Missy Prissy is long gone—gone to glory, to New York City, to foreign and exotic places. Though once in a while he still comes home for a brief visit, if only to see how things are going around here. How things have changed for the worse. By the way, you may not know that the house you are living in with Eleanor Lealand—come, come, don't be coy, *her* house now because she owns it—was the old Pressy place. Martin sold it to her for a song. Because he likes her.

Anyway. Pressy has created this little foundation. Probably as much of a tax dodge as anything else. But, in any case, it actually and legally exists and from time to time actually gives out grants and awards of various kinds to institutions and to individuals. He gave us—Baptist College, I mean—the money to hire a writer, preferably a poet, to come and to be here for a couple of years. With a possibility of renewal if we really liked the poet. For the Pressy Foundation (read "Martin," because his board is, in fact, a carefully selected bunch of rubber-stamping yes-persons) picks the poet. Then we take or leave the poet.

So. Maybe four or five years ago down comes this person from Michigan, the Poet, to be among us.

He got off to a bumpy start on this turf. He spurned the accommodations the college had arranged for him—a nice little frame house with, admittedly, a big, busy parking lot on three sides. But his objections were not exactly aesthetic. He wanted to be where the action was. At least as he conceived it. So he put on his gray work shirt and his faded jeans and his Nikes and he moved into a raggedy-ass shack in the big middle of Black Bottom. Where he proceeded to get on everybody else's nerves, playing soul music on his stereo loud enough to rattle windows and oouch coffee cups off the shelf. And he became a fixture at the Dead Mule ("No loafing/no loitering/no hanging around"), a black bar and poolroom. They just figured he was some kind of a crazy nigger-lover (a type not unknown) and they left him alone. But Poet just wouldn't have it that way. He had to try to out-nigger them to death with endless stories about exciting life in the big city of Detroit.

Finally somebody beat the living shit out of him. Which sent the Poet to Quincy Community Hospital for a while. And while he was there, some other characters set out to encourage him to move out of their community by ripping off everything he owned and had stashed in his shack. Even the little skinny poetry books. Everything, in fact, except his clothes. Which no self-respecting African-American would ever wear except under the threat of death if he didn't.

Sadder and maybe wiser, and sure enough a little bit uglier to look at, the Poet moved back to the college house by the parking lot. He stays mostly in and around the college these days. Where the women all love him for his rough-hewn, Yan-kee, Jewish, proletarian ways and his titillating reputation.

Hey, I'm not putting him down or bad-mouthing his shtick. It was pretty much the same thing with me way back in the days beyond recall.

Anyway.

Long story short. They have continued renewing the ar-rangement, and that, evidently, suits Pressy and his foundation just fine. The Poet has been here a while and will be coming up for tenure next year. Which is why, I would surmise, he is trying to get his new poems published and also trying to write this book—I don't honestly know if it is fiction or nonfiction—about Martin Luther King.

Let us not worry ourselves too much about other people's artistic and literary motivations. People do all kinds of things—good and bad and indifferent—for all kinds of simple and selfish motivations. As you may sometimes have noticed.

My favorite example is Shakespeare. Of course, in his case there is a certain amount of pure and unsupported speculation. But anyway. Sometime in the 1590s (check it out) he had made a goodly pile of money as a shareholder in his theater company. He was a solid citizen and had a coat of arms and was officially a gentleman. So he moves back to Stratford. He buys the biggest and finest house in town, New Place, and is already at last ready to settle down and live in his hometown with his wife and family. Just gets settled in good and comfortable when he has to pack up and go on back to London (where he always lived an austere and frugal life) to get busy writing more plays to make enough money to support his new lifestyle. And this time around he writes almost all of the great tragedies and most of his finest work.

Why did he have to go back to the city and get to work? Well, nobody knows *all* the reasons for sure. But one very clear and simple one was that they came up with a new tax—a "hearth" tax, based on how many fireplaces you had in your house. New place had ten fireplaces. Nice warm house. Expensive house to maintain. So, back to the old drawing board. There's motivation for you. Motivation for creating some of the greatest works in our language.

So. The way I look at it (with prejudice to be sure), if the Poet comes up with a half-decent book in his relentless drive for tenure at Central Florida Baptist College, let it be.

May the Force be with him.

Another reason I would like to see him make it and be around here for a while longer is that every day he makes me look a little better. Retroactively, to be sure. Any old fart, feeling the chilly breath of mortality on the back of his neck, will jump at the chance to improve on his reputation. I never thought I would have the chance. Then the Poet came along. His abrasive style and nose-picking manners make me (in memory) seem like an old-fashioned Southern gentleman. His insatiable skirt-chasing (O, how he loves those little quimmy, flat-tummied coeds!) makes me look positively ascetic. Now if we both can live long enough, I may end up with a decent crowd at my funeral and maybe a column or half a page in the obituary section of the *Trumpet*.

INTERVIEW WITH THE POET ("CALL ME BEN"): Takes place in the living room of his little faculty house. Air conditioner (window unit) pumping and gulping even though it is a mild spring day outside.

I like air-conditioning, he tells me. I like the air clean and cool. And Debby feels the same way I do.

Debby is Ms. Langley from the library. Who seems to be his current roommate and caretaker. After a while she comes home from the library and fixes tea for us.

Earlier he'd told me: I was a drunk, an alcoholic, for some years. Debby has been a big help to me that way. Among others.

She is close to my age. So I would guess she is some years older than the Poet, though it's hard to tell. He reminds me a little of Willem Dafoe and wears a black patch over his left eye. He has a little gray in his hair but his skin looks young and he is fit. Runs three and a half or four miles a day. Every day, rain or shine. He may have changed his life but not his style. He meets me wearing faded jeans, gray work shirt, Nike running shoes. Impressive belt buckle, shining silver and turquoise. (Debby brought it back from a conference in New Mexico, he tells me when he catches me staring at it. It's worth about a month's salary. My salary, anyway.)

We get right down to business after next to no small talk.

Yes (he says), I am working on a book about Martin Luther King, Jr. Not a biography. It seems to me the biographies, so far, are first-rate. They really do the job, both the popular ones and the scholarly ones. The facts are all there, in order, and the archives and papers are gradually coming along. I can't imagine that a new biography could add anything much unless somebody could determine who paid for and arranged to have King killed in Memphis.

There are all kinds of problems and unanswered, maybe unanswerable questions. But there always are in every assassination we know anything about—Lincoln, both Kennedys, Malcolm X, even George Lincoln Rockwell. And so far nobody has been able to come up with anything plausible or probable about the King murder. Maybe someday they will. But not yet.

"So, if not a biography, then what?"

Well, from the beginning I have been thinking fiction—
a novel. So have some other people. Julius Lester has a new
novel about King. And Charles Johnson has one coming soon.
They have one big advantage over me. They are both African-
American novelists. I'm a white poet who hasn't published a
book in eight years and has never published any fiction before.

"Do you have a publisher?"

Not yet. I haven't tried anybody yet.

Anyway, I don't see any way to compete with Lester or Johnson. That would be arrogant and foolish. I can never know what
a black man knows or feel what a black man feels. I am stuck
inside my white skin with nothing but a paternalistic, Eurocen-
tric imagination to lead me out of the labyrinth.

"Excuse me, but you don't really believe that shit, do you?"

I'm not sure what I believe. Except I know that I'm a white
man and I can't think or write any differently than I do. And
to pretend otherwise would be self-defeating as well as painfully
obvious. And besides that, the critics and reviewers would dump
all over me no matter how I did or what my take on things was.

So what I'm saying is that, one way or the other, this story
of King, his life and death, has got to come through to us from
the point of view of a white man. A white man has to be my
narrator.

"Like who do you have in mind?"

I don't know for sure, not yet. I have thought of doing it
from the point of view of the assassin. And calling him that—
just the assassin. It could be a kind of a shadowy fictional version
or distorted mirror image of James Earl Ray. Except he has already done his book and his version of things. I would have to
change his life. It's such a banal life; he's such a small-time loser,
in and out of jail for stupid crimes, that, given a choice, I would
prefer someone a bit more worthy, if you know what I mean.

"God had something else in mind."

That's not funny. Maybe you think it is. But there is some
kind of a great truth there. I don't want to deal with it right
this minute. But at least consider that from King's point of view,

from his religious beliefs, he was picked out, selected and chosen, by God Almighty, like it or not, to go up on the mountaintop and to see the Promised Land and to lead his people
towards it. He didn't ask to be chosen. He didn't think he was
worthy to be chosen in any case. But he was. From exactly the
same point of view, the same theology, you would have to believe that the assassin (James Earl Ray or whoever) was part of
the same providential equation. He didn't ask to be chosen either, but was elected to terminate the ministry of Martin Luther
King, Jr. and to transform him into a saint.

One shot. One pull of the trigger and (if you take that view)
God's will was done.

"You take him to be like Judas?"

Why not? Anyway, that's one way I could go with the story,
telling it all from the point of view of the *other* chosen man. Or,
anyway, the other man who believed, as King did, that he was
chosen to do what he did.

The assassin, like Ray, would by now have had years and
years to think about it and to replay everything in his mind, his
dreams. He could skip over the flow of time like a flat stone
skimming the surface of a brook. He would have nothing but
memories.

Or there are other possibilities. For instance, throughout
most of his public career King had a couple urban, Jewish, left-
wing advisers who (if the biographers are accurate) talked to him
almost daily and counseled and advised him and even wrote and
edited stuff for him. Well, I am urban and Jewish and left-wing
(I think) and I could lead from strength from this point of view.
Also, from having lived and worked down here for some years,
I not only know the South better than they did or could, but
also I know, better than they did or could have, how people
here would react, what would work and wouldn't. They made
their share of mistakes, you know, his advisers.

Another possibility. A young white man, no more than a
boy, really, an idealist who catches fire hearing some of MLK's
sermons. A believer who finds his beliefs confirmed in the words

and deeds of MLK. His inevitable path would be towards disillusion. For his saint would soon enough prove to have clay feet. The closer he got the more he would learn, things which, measured against the innocence of his idealism, his hopes and wishes set against the hard facts, would lead him towards despair. From which he would be spared if not completely saved because of the murder in Memphis which erased the negative text. MLK is born again in his own blood, renewed and resurrected. All that needed to be forgiven and seemed unforgivable becoming instantly irrelevant. Even all the riots and burnings and killings which followed his death, ironically making a mockery out of all he stood for and at the expense of more money (gone up in smoke) than MLK had ever hoped to be able to raise for the desperate needs of the poor and the oppressed.

"This last one, the idealistic kid, sounds a lot like you."

Not really. I am more like maybe Mickey Schwerner or Andrew Goodman. Except I am luckier and don't have the guts they did. This kid would have to be a Christian. He would have to see and experience MLK as a Christian. He would probably have to be a Southern kid, too. Something of a shared background. And maybe I would need to balance that point of view with one black one—the view of a young and passionate black activist like some of the ones in SNCC who were so impatient with MLK and called him "de Lawd" behind his back and came to believe in the Black Power slogans.

"He sounds a lot like you, too."

One way or another they all do. They are all parts of myself.

"Even the killer?"

Maybe the killer most of all. That was the first scene I wrote. It will haunt the whole story. But I would be lying if I didn't admit that the idea of it, of squeezing a trigger once and blowing MLK's life away, didn't give me a strange satisfaction. Have you looked at my face? Take a good look in the light and see what those black bastards did to me at the Dead Mule.

With a kind of brusque defiance, the Poet puts his face next to a lamp, directly in the light. Then removes the black patch over his left eye, revealing a red and puckered place, a scar where the eye was, daring me to look at it and not to flinch.

"Okay. Except for the missing eye, you have a couple or three bad scars showing. Like maybe you were in a car accident or something."

I know. I know. I *know*. And it was all my own fault, anyway. I believed all that bullshit about brotherhood and the family of man. I didn't understand how things really are. Or, to be honest, I did understand in most things. But not race.

"Listen. I've got no business making any suggestions to you. I don't know the first thing about writing a novel and I'm not even sure that I want to. I have trouble enough with my own kind of words. But, anyway, it seems to me that one answer to your problem is not to choose. Why not put King at the center and then tell the story from all three points of view—the assassin, the advisers, the disciple?"

Maybe. Maybe that would work.

"Three versions, three visions. Like in *Rashomon*."

What's your interest in MLK?

"Only this. I'm trying to write a true crime thing about Paradise Springs that same weekend. I'm looking for connections."

There aren't any.

"Maybe not."

Listen. I need your help. I could use your help in one thing. I hate to ask but I have to.

"What is it?"

Can you help me get an agent?

"Well . . . I can try. I can't guarantee anything at all. But I can try."

Here and Now

INTERVIEW WITH THE
REVEREND PETER WHEELRIGHT,
RECTOR OF ST. PAUL'S EPISCOPAL CHURCH

Of course, I wasn't even born then and haven't got the slightest idea how Father Claxton would have come down on the issues and problems that confront the Church these days. So many things are so different. I mean, we still had the old 1928 prayer book in those days, although its days were already numbered. The writing was on the wall. We were not going to keep on saying that "there is no health in us" very much longer. That kind of talk, prayer if you will, didn't allow much slack for self-esteem.

And there are all the other contemporary preoccupations like the ordination of women, the sacrament of homosexual marriage, the validity of abortion—I mean *Roe v. Wade* hadn't come to pass yet. We had not yet looked into an unflattering mirror and seen what a sexist, racist, oppressive culture we really are. We hadn't yet learned to be guilty and ashamed of a large part of our history. . . .

I can't tell whether this cat is serious or not. I mean, he has a serious expression on his face when he says this stuff. But, then, so do a whole lot of our best comics.

Nice-looking fella, though. Looks a little bit like Roddy McDowall on a bad day. Very trim and fit. Jogs three or four miles three or four times a week. I had to go jogging with him, myself, a couple of times—damn near killed me—to get a real, sit-down interview with him. He loaned me a purple-and-white Sewanee sweatshirt. Every step I took, puffing and blowing like a walrus, I wondered if it was worth it. I mean, he's a good deal younger than I am. What can he tell me?

But I went to a couple of early services, 8:00 A.M., hungover and full of flannel-mouth contrition and suppressed rage (mostly at myself and my mostly wasted life). Prayed the old prayers, what's left of them, anyway, in *The Book of Common Prayer*. Shook hands and even hugged a few old folks during the Peace. Put up with all of it just to get a shot at Wheelwright.

The church, itself, is much as it was in 1968, though there's a new choir screen (some old-timer out in the county is a pretty good wood-carver), some new banners and some nicely worked kneeling cushions at the altar rail, a couple of half-decent contemporary paintings and a handsome stained-glass window depicting the miracle at the wedding in Cana, gift of Martin Pressy in memory of his beloved mother. Better electrical system, too. Good lighting and an adequate sound system. Wheelwright told me that he tapes all his sermons.

Rectory looks pretty much the same—deftly added on to, but still a large and handsome old Florida house, a smaller version of the Pressy place or the crumbling Singletree house. Outside much the same. Inside very different. Gutted and radically changed. Modernized. Martin Pressy evidently paid for that, too; and they hired a young friend of his from New York, a decorator, to come and fix it up in a kind of black-and-white, artsy-smartsy mid-1970s manner.

Wheelright goes on:

It's like living in the big middle of a glossy Martin Pressy photograph. Of course they had to do something after the tragedy. Some major change was in order. Otherwise the place would have been spooked, haunted.

The only messy part, they say, was the attic. And even that was quickly and easily cleaned up. Turns out—I wonder if you knew this, Mr. Tone—there was a firm even then, Jimmy's Reliable Cleaning Service, up in Jacksonville, that cleaned up after bloody murders and suicides and all that sort of thing. All over north and central Florida. Pretty good business, I would imagine. Better now than then. They're still around. I had to call on them not so long ago in the case of an old parishioner who took his head off with a double-barreled shotgun.

"Do you think Father Claxton really killed himself?"

That was the official conclusion. That's how they disposed of it, wasn't it? I really don't know that much about it, though I've only been here for three years. Of course, one *hears* things. Some of the old parishioners talk about it, and him, too. He seems to have been very well liked around here. For what that's worth.

He wasn't much of a boat-rocker or whistle-blower, as I understand it. About the only unusual thing (for the times) that he did was to preach a few times for racial tolerance. In general. And somebody remembers he had a cutout magazine photograph of Martin Luther King—maybe it was the cover of *Time* magazine—framed and hanging on his office wall. That pissed off a number of the more conservative members of the congregation. But my understanding is that they mostly ignored it or treated it as a harmless eccentricity. Some people have told me he was very good at counseling—though they didn't call it that then. A retired nurse told me that Claxton was a wonder at the bedside of dying patients. He was so good at it, this terminal bedside manner, that people from other denominations used to ask especially for him to come and be with them at the last.

It's a gift. I don't have it. I *hate* hospitals, the stink and the sorrow of them. But I go. I do my rounds. It goes with the territory.

"Is there anything of his left around here?"

Not that I know of, really. Nothing personal. Maybe some of the vestments, though I doubt it. It's been a very long time. Some of his family came and got most of his things and disposed of the others. At least so I heard. In the supply closet there is an old reel-to-reel tape recorder, broken, that he may have used to practice his sermons and such. No tapes for it.

You know, there *is* something that just might have been his. There's a fat little pocket King James Bible that is all marked up with a red pencil. Somebody, maybe it was Claxton—it *could* have been—underlined a lot of passages. You can have that if you want.

Wheelwright keeps a very neat office. I am compelled to consider this while he disappears for a few minutes to find the Bible. A shiny desk, mostly bare. A cup full of keenly sharpened pencils. A silver-framed picture of his family—smiling wife, sort of on the Meryl Streep model. Pretty blond children, three of them.

Here we are.

I open it at random (an old habit, an old superstition) and read the first marked lines I find: *For Zion's sake will I not hold my peace, and for Jerusalem's sake I will not rest until the righteousness thereof go forth as brightness, and the salvation thereof as a lamp that burneth.*

You knew him, didn't you? Wheelwright asks me.

"Who?"

Claxton.

"I knew his daughter. I used to go out with her sometimes. And sometimes I came here to church. Mostly to see her."

Why do you suppose he did it?

"God knows. I don't have the slightest idea."

Then and There

EXCERPT FROM DEPOSITION, DULY SWORN, OF
LEON ("LITTLE BIRD") WADDELL

I would just as soon not talk about it. I would rather not even think about it. But I might as well tell you what I know. Which ain't very much. I mean, I don't have a thing to hide. I did what I did, and I'll admit to it. But that's all I did. I did not have one solitary thing to do with all that other bad stuff, and I don't have a clue what happened or why. And I couldn't care less, either, thank you very much.

The only one of the real criminals that I seen at all was that fellow that called himself Papp. He came hanging around the carnival. He came over to us and hung around because he had some kind of a wild, crazy-ass idea about how our little carnival and his tent revival show could maybe team up. Merge, don't you know.

"If we could just get together like this, only on purpose," he would say (or words to that effect, to the best of my recollection), "then we could really clean up good in a lot of these little old half-ass dying Florida towns."

And it may be that he had a point there, too. Only he was as crazy as a horsefly on a hot frying pan. As all the world knows well now. It's a matter of record.

So, yes, I listened to him, like some of the other guys, and I bummed a few cigarettes off of him. But his high-flying schemes did not mean a thing to me. I forgot him completely the minute he walked away out of my sight. And I would have forgot him for good and forever if he had not become practically a celebrity by the middle of the next morning.

As for the rest of them, I never saw any of them, nor did I know anything about them. Except if you include that little shit they call Penrose. And the less said about him the better.

What really did happen and, really and truly, the only part that I was involved in, so to speak, is that I did one small favor for a nice young lady. I never should have done it. But I did it because I got fooled and faked out. It could have happened to anybody. I mean, you work odd jobs around a carnival like I do, and then a nice and respectable young lady (pretty too, and built like a brick you-know-what) comes along and asks you personally to do her a gentlemanly favor and makes it worth your while to do it, why you don't just stand there and decline the opportunity.

Somebody comes along and gives you a ten-dollar bill and a pint of good whiskey, not cheap either, *just to talk to you*, well now, you might perk up your ears and listen a little. Especially if your name just happens to be Little Bird Waddell and, due to a little bit of misfortune, you don't have enough money to your name to buy a first-class postage stamp.

So the lady gave me a ten-dollar bill and a pint of whiskey.

So I said to myself, Why not.

Now then. What she told me made pretty good sense. She explained and stated to me that there was this person—I guess you might call him some kind of a stud or maybe a sex fiend—who had been playing the hanky-panky with some of her best friends in the world, young ladies who it was her duty and her honor to be representing in this matter.

She said that she and her friends would like to teach this person a lesson. More in the nature of some kind of a trick or a big gross-out, no real or permanent harm done. Something that might serve to horrify him and to shape him up, but not such of a thing as would really hurt him.

"And just what do you have in mind?" I asked her.

And thereupon, without any kind of blushing or stammering, that sweet nice girl just stood right there looking in my eyes and told me more or less what she had in mind for the fellow.

So I took a good swallow from my whiskey bottle and I give it some thought. If that was her idea of a joke and a moral lesson, then who was I to speak out against it?

"What is in it for me?" I asked her politely.

"I will give you one hundred dollars right here and now," she said, "and another hundred tomorrow morning if you successfully accomplish it."

Now then. Some people will no doubt tell you a great long list of things that I would cheerfully do for two hundred dollars. And they will be exaggerating. There are any number of things that I would never do for two hundred dollars or for all the money in the world. But when a nice young lady offers you something to do her a favor in a matter of honor, I can't say I am the kind to ignore her idea. Even if and though her idea was kind of crazy. A crazy sort of a practical joke. I did not know her from Eve. Or the character they were fixing to fun from old Adam himself. Be that as it may, I knew better than to ask her a whole lot of questions and to get her case history. There were a couple of questions I did ask her, though.

"Are you sure that he ain't going to give us, me and my comrades, any real trouble?"

"He couldn't hurt a flea," she said, smiling. "And, besides, he will probably be drunk as a hoot owl."

"How about the Law? I can't afford trouble with the Law, ma'am. I have had a few misunderstandings already."

"Don't you worry," she told me.

I took another taste of that good sipping whiskey and pondered things.

"One little thing worries me," I said.

"What would that be?"

"The way you have planned this, the way you have got it set up, there is no real finger on the guy."

"Finger?"

"I mean, what if we was to pull the joke on the wrong guy?"

"That can't happen. He will be alone in his car. It is the only Mercedes in the whole county. It is impossible to make a mistake."

"And what if he don't show up at all?"

"Oh, but he will. Believe me, he will. But just in case he doesn't, you will still get the rest of your money. If that's what is worrying you."

"It ain't exactly worrying me, ma'am. But I have to admit that the thought did cross my mind."

"Well?" .

"Well," I said. "I guess you have got yourself a deal."

Cool as you pretty please, she opened her purse and got out her wallet and give me five twenty-dollar bills.

"You get the rest of it tomorrow morning."

Nice-looking young lady. Decent. You would not think to look at her, so clean and neat, that she could even think up a joke like that. Maybe somebody else told her or something. I give up trying to second-guess women a long, long time ago. And I am here to tell you they can fool you any time they want to.

Well now. It wasn't too hard to get two of the carnival girls to go along with me. Faye, who is definitely the old bag of the bunch, will do almost anything in the world for ten dollars. (She will do a good many things for five.) I mean, you get to be her age and shape with the mileage printed all over you like a road map, and your days as an exotic dancer are numbered, and you can't afford to be real choosy.

Who would be the other girl was a problem. The lady who hired me had figured on two women to do the job and with myself to be the muscle in case any brute force was indicated. Even if this fella couldn't and wouldn't hurt a flea (something I doubted enough to carry along a baseball bat just in case), it would still take two of them to do it right. But which one. The other three dancers are pretty young and ignorant still. Which is why we have a good show and always draw a pretty good crowd. Lurleen is the truly classy one. But she is a real cool one, also, and she don't mess around. She has still got ambitions. Oh sure, she will learn her hard lessons, too, and she will figure out the score one of these days. But not just yet. Donna is just the opposite. She will do almost anything, even more so than Faye, and she does it, too. She has got no fear and no shame, either. But she is pretty enough (at the present time) to put a high price tag on her time and her services. I can't say that I blame her. But I didn't want to cut into my hundred any more than I might have to.

So Cindy was my best bet. Because she hates all men. Or seems to, anyway. She hates me—or acts like it—that's for damn sure. Probably a story goes with it. How she ended up dancing in a carnival and all. I don't know her story and she's not talking. She hates and despises the men who come and pay to watch her. Or so she says. I don't know what to think. Because when she is actually performing in there, she is far and away the wildest dancer and the biggest tease of the bunch. Her whole face lights up like she had a couple of small bulbs just behind her cheekbones. And she really gets with it. She gets so wild sometimes that we have to be careful. She could get us closed down or maybe even busted sometime. But she is the one they really want to see once the word gets around.

I went and put the proposition to her straightaway, figuring that since I couldn't guess what she would say, I might as well get the benefit of a quick yes-or-no answer. She was in the trailer, dressed in her terry-cloth wrapper, looking at herself in the mirror, plucking at her eyebrows. I said my say, but for a minute I didn't know whether she had heard me or not.

"There might even be a few bucks in it," I said.

She never looked at me. She just continued to look at herself. But she smiled a beautiful smile.

"Little Bird, you are so mercenary," she said. "Don't you know that I would want to come along just for the fun of it? We are going to fix that dirty-minded son of a bitch once and for all."

"Now wait a minute, Cindy. No real rough stuff. I mean, it's only a joke."

"Sure, sure, sure," she said. Then: "You know the part I like the best? The costumes. I think that is a beautiful touch."

Then she started laughing like a horse or a hyena. And I got out of there. Maybe it wouldn't bother you like it did me, watching a really good-looking woman laughing and laughing at herself in the mirror.

Now then. Looking back on it with the full benefit of hindsight, I would say that mistakes were made and some things went seriously wrong. One mistake was to get Papa McDaniels involved in it. I talked him into letting me use his official car from the Sheriff's Department, just for a little while, in return for a fistful of tickets to the strip show. (Little did he know that I had the two best ones with me.) So we had a real police car, and when we were ready we could pull the guy over.

We located the car all right, parked at the revival meeting. We were just hanging around the tent, listening to the music and the preaching, waiting for the guy to come out. When I went back to check on the car it was gone, I mean *gone*. And somebody with a sense of humor had replaced it with a hearse which had funny things written all over it.

Oh shit, I thought. And I rounded up the two girls (who were really silly-looking in their carnival costumes) and we took

off in McDaniels' car cruising around looking for the Mercedes.
I wasn't worried ("He can run but he can't hide"), but I didn't
want to waste a lot of time on it anyway.

After a while we saw him headed back for town on the old
airport road. I put on the blinker and he pulled over as meek as
can be. I thought it would be a piece of cake.

Now I would say that two things went seriously wrong. First
off, this guy wasn't no fairy pipsqueak at all, the way the young
lady had described him to be. He was a big strong guy and he
fought like hell. He punched out the lights of poor old Faye.
Broke her big nose and chipped her front teeth. She looked
terrible for a couple of weeks after that. He knocked me flat on
my ass and was about to throw Cindy in the ditch when I used
the baseball bat on him. That quieted him down considerably.
I mean completely. That was when I had some trouble with
Cindy. She came up with this pair of heavy-duty garden shears
and something else in mind besides a joke. I had to wrestle with
her to get the shears away. She spit in my face and clawed at
my eyes. So there really wasn't any choice but to take the bat
to her, too.

Me and old Faye finished the job. Then we dragged Cindy
and put her in the back of the car like a sack of meal and we
got the hell out of there.

I tell you the whole thing was a mess. Faye had to dance
with her face like a mule had kicked her and Cindy had a big
bandage on her head.

Mr. Dillard, the boss, kicked me off of my job as the chief
talker for the dance show and moved me right back down to
hard manual labor where I had originally started out. That
turned out to be the toughest ninety dollars I ever earned. Naturally, the young lady never showed up with the rest that she
owed me. What with all the hell that broke loose around town,
I can't really blame her. She might possibly have come later, but
we didn't hang around. As soon as Mr. Dillard could get cleared
and okay with the county sheriff, we packed up (with me already

assigned to heavy work and loading) and moved on out of there right smartly.

I often wonder whatever became of that fella. If he got the message and the joke and all. One thing for sure, considering everything, we did a real nice job on him and his private parts. And Faye, good old Faye, she did the prettiest bow ribbon you ever saw. It was nothing else but artistic, if I do say so myself.

Here and Now

FALLING IN LOVE AGAIN

Dear Curly—

You may be surprised, maybe even *astonished* to get two letters in the same calendar year from me. But, lucky you, you are maybe the only person left in the whole world at this moment ("at this point in time," as they all say) to whom I could write to share some things which are more a matter of feelings than of any news or information or any attempt at persuasion. Hey, I couldn't con you even if I tried. I know. I have tried. And failed.

You are getting this letter because you are you and there is nobody else. The good news is that you do not have to answer. Truth is, you don't have to *read* this letter. I will never know the difference.

Under these circumstances I feel completely free to impose on you.

What I really want to tell you, old buddy, is that I think I may be in love again. For the first time in a long, long time. For the first time in memory. I must have been in love with Annie at some time, but I sure can't remember it now.

It's a librarian here in Paradise Springs. Looks a lot like Judy Davis in *My Brilliant Career*. Meaning, to be sure, that she is much too young for old Billy Boy.

But be that as it may, here we are now happily living together (in her house). And it's all good time.

It's a big old frame house, a classic nineteenth-century Florida house, set in the middle of three or four acres (I never asked) of overgrown land *right smack in the middle of town*. House and land go back to a time when there wasn't any town, merely a village crossroads with a store or two and a church and, of course, the sweet-water springs which gave the place a name and for a while (turn of the century) served as a kind of spa for well-to-do folks from elsewhere. The springs are a polluted trickle these days. People keep coming anyway. Not for the water.

Anyway. We share this big old white frame house with high ceilings, with sleeping porches upstairs (we sleep in one and it's like being in a tree house) and down, spacious and well-kept. It's really a kind of a showplace. Was owned by one family from the time that it was built until Eleanor—that's my librarian—bought it at a bargain price with her inheritance. They wouldn't sell it to just anybody. And she had to promise to maintain it much as it is and not under any circumstances to sell off the land around it in parcels. That was a personal promise, carrying next to no legal weight, if any. A point which a number of local developers have made in trying to persuade Eleanor to let them at some of it. To no avail.

It is shady and quiet and more or less concealed by the trees—tall pines, some oak and sweet gum, and a couple of magnolias. Which don't really do well this far south and in this sandy soil. But even if they are not as grand as the magnolias of the Carolinas and Virginia, they are glossy green and good to have around. Back of the house are a few citrus trees which have somehow or other endured and prevailed in spite of bad freezes and hard winters. They blossom and fill the air with sweetness and they bear fruit.

Way back, Curly, people tried to plant orange groves this far north and evidently got away with it for a while. There was a period of mild winters early in the century. More recently some gamblers have tried to grow oranges and grapefruit again. But now the land is getting too valuable, and winter is still a huge risk.

Eleanor keeps a lot of different plants around the house—azaleas of various colors and kinds, some classic poinsettia, oleander, camellias and even a clump of bamboo.

Hey, but this is supposed to be about love, about falling in love again, the flare of a match suddenly struck in a dark room.

I mean, you know me, Curly. I'm a material guy, right? But I am happy to report that I am no more immune than anybody else you can think of.

We have fun, you know? We go out to supper—she hates to cook after a hard day in the library. (I'm not sure she knows how to cook. Who cares?) We hunker down and watch the tube or a movie on the VCR. We watched *Persona* the other night. Remember? It's the one where Bergman puts Bibi Anderson and Liv Ullman out on one of his rocky islands and gradually they become each other. It was playing at the Rialto here during the weekend I am concerned with. We are trying to make some kind of connection, some sort of synchronicity between *Persona* and the story I am trying to tell. So far no luck. No *rational* connection.

Anyway. We watch movies and we listen to music, mostly classical. You know what, though? Like some other women I remember (all except Annie), Eleanor likes to make love with some music playing in the background. (Too many movies, I guess.) I remember one girl—the one who worked at Simon & Schuster, remember?—who could and would make love only to *Bolero* or *Rite of Spring*. Damn near killed me. Well, Eleanor is different. She likes *Chant,* that Gregorian chant disk that somehow ended up on the pop chart. Makes for a quiet, easygoing rhythm, more in keeping with my advanced years. Makes for plenty of slow and gentle foreplay.

Please disregard all of the above. I do not condone the game of kiss-and-tell. But I can't exactly ignore the fact that she is wonderful in bed. Just what the doctor ordered.

I like her, too, as a person. I enjoy just having a drink and talking with her. About this and that. About anything. Librarians are well-informed, Curly. And she is being very helpful with my research.

What I am saying is I like her a whole lot, quite aside from being in love with her. A lot of times the two don't go together.

Is there a downside? Well, we all have our bad habits. Hers is smoking too much, all the time actually. (I may end up smoking again, myself, just in self-defense.) And not just that. When she is finished with a cigarette (she usually smokes about half or two-thirds of one), she just flips it away. Anywhere. Or sets it down and forgets about it. Doesn't fool around with ashtrays. The floor, the rugs, and most of the furniture in the house, her house, are extensively covered with cigarette burns. One of these days she is going to burn the house down. With us in it.

But until that happens, I haven't got a whole lot to complain about.

I don't expect it to last very long. Nothing good lasts very long. Something will go wrong. More likely I'll do something or say something irredeemably wrong. And I hate and fear that. Because it will be hard, it will be lonesome without her. Is that what love is? The recognition that life will be less, that it will be a huge loss to be without the one you love? And maybe the knowledge that all the time before, the life you had before you fell in love, was wasted time. Love is a time of brightness bracketed by losses on both sides.

Advice and counsel for lovers and the lovelorn, from Billy Tone, Ph.D.

Thanks for listening, Curly. Next time you hear from me, please don't tear up the letter without checking the contents. Because next time there will be a check. A solemn promise.

Stay well. Hang by your thumbs and write if you get work.

Best—

Billy

P.S. If you run into Annie, don't tell her (*please!*) that I have found a little love and happiness. She will send me a pipe bomb

if she ever finds out. She likes to think my finest hours were
spent with her.

B

Here and Now

MORE **W. E. GARY**

Met at the Cosmos Health Club, where he works out on the
machines three days a week. Afterwards he took me out in the
country to the Black Baptist Barbecue, at an old country church
which had long since come into good times by cooking up some
of the best ribs in this part of the world.

Mixed group of customers, pepper-and-salt, all sitting together at long plank tables under oak trees and tall pines. Nothing served but ribs, slaw, Wonder Bread (in huge stacks of slices,
used for napkins; no silverware), soft drinks and beer.

His joke of the day: What do you say to a black man in a
three-piece suit? Answer: Will the defendant please rise?

Driving to and from the church and later as we sat in his car
(a brand-new Jaguar XKE) in the parking lot, motor and air
conditioner running, he tells me a story:

You may think that I am a black man who has swallowed
outrage and settled for cynicism. And I say that the true source
of cynicism *is* outrage. And I also say that it is precisely that
cynicism, born of outrage, that gives me the edge and allows me
to do so well in my chosen profession of the law.

And now, sir, here is a story to tell you who I am and why.
Why a story? Good question. Well, sir, I take this from the old
Judge, who may have been my father. God alone knows that
now. May or may not have been my father, but sure enough
was my teacher, my mentor, my role model in ways that nobody
else was or ever could be. And one of the things this old Judge
was forever and a day saying was that our stories are who we
are. Not that our stories *reveal* who we are in the fullest sense.

And not that our stories can be translated, like something in a foreign language, like a foreign film with subtitles, into the simple clarity of a simple statement. But that our stories are who and what we are, nothing more or less. And that we are nothing more or less than the sum and substance of our stories, whether these be jokes or tales of woe or a judicious mixture of the same, a little of both. It's not a matter of fact and fiction, he would say. In our stories, our true stories, fact and fiction are one and the same.

Right or wrong, he gave me something to think about. And here is a story out of my own childhood that the Judge himself loved to hear me tell. Which may be the chief reason the memory and the story have stayed with me. So far.

So. Once upon a time, when I was really no more than a barefooted child in short pants, my mother sent me away for a while to stay with my Aunt Odessa out in west Florida. I don't know why that happened. Didn't know then, don't know now. Knew only that I was put on a Greyhound bus (a seat in the back, even for a small child, in those Jim Crow days) and sent some hours north and west to be dropped off at a dusty, dirty little bus station where Aunt Odessa met me and drove me to her home in a shiny new automobile. It was, the way I see it now anyway, a long, gas-guzzling pink Cadillac, a classic pimp-mobile, what some white folks were wont to call in those days a "coon cage." Never mind. Best-looking vehicle in that crummy little town and that godforsaken, dry county.

(You've got to understand that we never owned a real car. My mother never even knew how to drive. They would come get her and take her home after work. And if, for any reason, they couldn't or wouldn't, why, she would walk all the way coming or going.)

Aunt Odessa was all dressed up and glittery with jewels. To go with the car, I reckon. She picked me up at the bus station and we went out to her place—a large, rambling, unpainted shack a way to hell and gone out in the deep piney woods. Her place was an overgrown field in the woods that used to be a farm. It had electricity and even a television. But no plumbing. Just a well with a pump and an outhouse.

All that was by choice, her choice, because Miz Odessa had plenty of money and she owned property, too, not only in the country, but some lots and houses downtown. I mean to tell you she was rich and getting richer all the time. It didn't serve her purpose to advertise her personal wealth. Except for the car. But you have to remember that black folks might not have paint on their houses in those days and might not have a pot to flush, but if they were living and breathing they would have a set of first-class wheels. You would see a shack without much more protection from the wind and the weather than a corn crib. And right smack in front of it would be parked a brand-new expensive automobile.

I can understand that attitude. I don't really *need* this classy Jaguar, do I? It probably doesn't help anything or improve my image around here. And in some places, still, in the benighted and Faulknerian South, it will get me pulled over and asked for my license and registration. No hard feelings. Nothing personal. Just that the po-lice (black ones, too; they're all the same) can't imagine that a black man could legitimately own a hundred-thousand-dollar car. Unless he is a dope dealer or something. So—is this perverse or what?—I take a certain pleasure in being pulled over and checked out. And proved to be a rich black man with a record as pure and blank as fresh fallen snow. (Even though it does not snow down here.) It makes them very polite and pissed off. And it gives me a wonderful opportunity to demonstrate my noblesse oblige.

Anyway.

All I'm saying is that her fine set of wheels didn't, in those days, fully indicate the extent of Miz Odessa's personal wealth. Which was considerable and then some. The few who knew about it were amused at her little game, and she flat-out fooled the rest of them.

Now, you are wondering (unless I am mistaken) what the *source* of her wealth might be. This was in the days before dope—a simpler, happier age. Odessa was a bootlegger. She didn't *make* the stuff. She left that chore and danger to crazy-ass white crackers in the deep woods. She purchased moonshine on a regular basis and retailed it to a wide variety of country customers, black and white—including some honky-tonks—and earned a considerable profit from her efforts.

For the most part the Law left her alone. First of all because she allowed them to share a modest portion of her profits. Which, if nothing else, sweetened their disposition. Second (and I'm sure you understand this), they figured that the vices of making and selling and drinking illegal booze had been around since the earliest days of the Republic, indeed *before* we were free from Britain, and, allowing for ups and downs and changes in taste and so forth, would still be with us until the end of time. As far as the local law enforcement was concerned, somebody was going to be selling bootleg whiskey, and it might as well be Aunt Odessa as anybody else. At least they knew her and she was reliable and generous.

Of course, every once in a while, for the sake of appearances, they would have to crack down and arrest a few people for violations of the code. When they were fixing to do that, they would always warn her so she wouldn't get caught. They would just clear out some of her competition. Keeping everybody honest, so to speak.

That summer when I went to visit Aunt Odessa was a time when the Law decided to crack down on bootlegging. But Aunt Odessa had plans of her own, as it turned out.

One hot day we were sitting around the house when the white man who made the whiskey and supplied her with it pulled up in the yard in his pickup. He tooted on his horn and sat there until we came out. That was part of the racial ritual. *We* go out to *them.*

"Aunty," he said. "I got whiskey. But I don't think you want any of it."

"Why not?"

"Well, Aunty, mainly on account of the Law is right behind me. They is parked right up the road yonder right now and they can see everything we do. Whenever I leave off whiskey, they will come in right behind me and make a bust. So I just thought, on account of we have been doing business for many years, that I would warn you that they are going to arrest you if they can."

"Oh, I don't think so," she said. "I don't think they will mind if I just buy a couple of gallons off you."

"Suit yourself," he said. "But don't say I didn't give you fair warning."

He draws off a couple of gallons in a bucket from his barrel of moonshine and he totes it inside.

"Where you want me to put it, Aunty?"

"Here," she says, producing a large old-fashioned china chamber pot.

"You sure?"

"Right in here."

He pours the bucket into the chamber pot and then takes off.

She is giggling about something.

I am wondering what in the world is going on.

She takes out her false teeth and puts them on the shelf. Then she sits down on the chamber pot and modestly spreads her skirt out around her. She is just sitting there when here they come pounding on the door.

"Open up, Odessa! It's the sheriff speaking."

"You go let the sheriff in," she tells me.

I open the door and in come the sheriff and a young deputy.

"Excuse me if I don't get up, Sheriff," she says, sounding funny without her teeth. "But I am having an attack in my kidneys and I just can't leave my pot."

"Where is that moonshine?" the sheriff asks.

"What moonshine?"

"Mind if I look around?"

"Not at all, Sheriff. Help yourself."

They search the whole place, looking over and under and around everything. And all the time she just sits there on the big old chamber pot, giggling to herself.

"All right, Aunty," the sheriff says. "We know you got moonshine in this house. We saw him bring it in. We know it's in here. So I'm going to have to ask you to get up and let us have a look in that there pot you are sitting on."

"Help yourself, Sheriff." She gets up and steps aside, smoothing her long skirt. The sheriff and his young deputy approach the chamber pot very carefully, like it had a bomb in it or maybe a snake that would jump out and bite them. They look down at the liquid in it and, of course, can't tell what it is.

The sheriff turns to the deputy with a kind of a sad expression.

"Okay," he tells him. "I've been the sheriff of this county for twenty-five years. You have been working for us for maybe a year and a half. The way I see it is I have got seniority on you. No question about that."

"No, sir, no question about that."

"So, all things considered, I think it's a fair request."

"What is?"

"I want you, Deputy, to determine if the liquid in that aforesaid chamber pot is moonshine or not."

"Do I have to?"

"Afraid so, Deputy."

At just that moment the crazy old cuckoo clock that Odessa had on the mantelpiece cut loose and announced the hour— *Cuckoo! Cuckoo! Cuckoo!* And all of us jumped.

A long pause while the two men look at each other. Then the deputy takes off his broad-brim hat and rolls up his right sleeve above the elbow. He hunkers down alongside of the chamber pot. Takes a breath and holds it and then reaches in and dips his fingers in the liquid. Slowly takes a sniff of his fingers. Then, even more slowly, a little taste.

Jumps up on his feet.

"It's moonshine! By God, Sheriff, it is sure enough moonshine!"

"Odessa," the sheriff says. "You damn near fooled us this time. And if I was all alone you would have got away with it, too. But we got the goods on you and you are under arrest."

Still giggling, she put her teeth back in.

"I'll be back in time to fix supper," she told me as she went outside with them, the deputy carrying the evidence.

Her trial came up about a month later. Came the morning of the trial she got up real early to go into town. When I asked her why, she explained to me that she was planning to walk all the way. This struck me as truly odd; she could have driven her own car or she could have caught a ride with any number of people who were going into town for the trial. And, in fact, she arranged for me to get a ride with some people coming in later on. She put on her worst clothes, tacky and raggedy and worn-out, took out and left behind her false teeth, mussed up her hair, and went barefoot. By first light she was already walking on the hot and dusty dirt road.

When we got to the courthouse and took our seats in the segregated balcony, they called her case. And Odessa came in. She looked terrible, all sweaty and dusty, ragged and barefooted. The young white lawyer who had been appointed to defend her looked very embarrassed, like he didn't want to get anywhere close to her.

Now, this was the first time Aunt Odessa had ever been tried for anything in the county court. Seemed to me, and to the others who knew her, that she would want to make a good impression on the judge. A lot we knew!

Before they even got under way good, the judge asked her to come forward and approach the bench. She got up giggling and went towards the judge. About halfway up to the bench she all of a sudden squatted down and took a leak on the floor of the courtroom. I was so ashamed and embarrassed that I shut my eyes and tried to pretend I was somewhere else.

Next thing you know the judge calls the sheriff and the county attorney and gives them a terrible tongue-lashing. How they have wasted his time and the county's resources, bringing in this poor, demented old colored woman and trying to claim that she is some kind of a big-shot bootlegger in the community. This woman is pathetic, he told them, but not as pathetic and inept as they were, trying to bring a case against her. The judge chewed them out really good and dismissed the charges against her, calling a recess while somebody (probably the young deputy) went and got a mop to clean up where she had peed on the floor. And then we all went back home. She insisted on walking home again and that suited me fine, because I did not want to be seen with her.

When she finally got home, she filled a washtub with well water and took a long bubble bath. Got herself all cleaned up and dressed up (laughing to herself the whole time) and then we got in her Cadillac and drove back towards town to the Dairy Queen to get some ice cream.

When I finally got up the nerve to ask her why in the world she had done what she did, she seemed a little surprised at my ignorance. But she told me anyway.

"Looka here, Willie," she said. "I could have paid a big fine, maybe even done some days in jail for that. This way it didn't cost me anything but time."

"But Miz Odessa, how come you let them catch you in the first place?"

"That was the whole idea."

And she went on to tell me how she wanted to teach the sheriff a lesson and to make an impression on the county judge.

"Well, ma'am, you sure succeeded in that. You made an impression all right."

"I should hope so."

She explained that thanks to her performance, she doubted that she would ever again have to appear in that court before that judge. He wouldn't hear of it. And, more to the point, she seriously doubted that the sheriff would ever arrest her for any

crime this side of first-degree, planned and premeditated murder. She would keep on selling moonshine and generously sharing her profits with the sheriff and we would all live happily ever
after.

And, as far as I know, that's how it happened. I only saw
her one more time. After I got my degree and started practicing
law, she asked me to draw up her will. And I did so. The old
woman had a pretty big estate. She had squirreled away most
everything. I charged her a fat fee—she could afford it. And,
you know, she wanted to give me something of hers, something
personal. I think she thought I would ask her for the cuckoo
clock I liked so much as a child. But I didn't. I asked her for
that chamber pot. And she still had it and gave it to me and I've
kept it ever since then. To remind me. Remind me of what?
Everything. Just everything. Know what I mean?

Then and There

DEBBY LANGLEY: PRECIOUS MEMORIES

If you really have to blame somebody, you can blame Professor Katz.

I do. As far as I am concerned, he is personally responsible
for most of my troubles and woe.

I hate Katz. Sometimes I think he has ruined my whole life.
Right at the beginning.

I did not intend for any bad things to happen. All I wanted
was to get those pictures back. That's all. And, well, it was worth
a try.

You can blame Katz to start with, because he was the first
one to tell me about Martin Pressy and all that. I had just written
this theme, my first written assignment, on the subject of "My
Expectations in Marriage." What happened was that I made the
mistake of putting down the way I really feel. That marriage is
a whole lot more than just legalized sex. That there is a whole

lot more to life than screwing, anyway. That, sure, sex is fun (even if it is not as much fun as it's supposed to be in books and movies). But there are many other things.

Katz was always telling us to be honest in our compositions. He said that honesty would be part of our grades. So I put it down the way it really is. I went ahead and pointed out that the Lord has gifted me with exceptional beauty. And that I was blessed not only with a pretty face, but also with a neat body that can drive men crazy. And so, I opined, the Lord must surely have intended me to use my gifts for something. Some good purpose.

I openly confessed that I did not want to be just another housewife. Especially a plain vanilla suburban housewife. My dream, as I put it in my theme, was to be and do like Jacqueline Kennedy. At the time I wrote this theme she had not yet fallen into the clutches of that old Greek man. But it's kind of spooky because I went on to say that I hoped to find a nice older man who might appreciate me more than dumb boys my own age.

(Okay. So I was "flirting" a little bit with Katz. He likes that. And I surely did not say I wanted to marry a professor or anything like that.)

I said that "women of substance," the wives of important men in the community, actually have a whole lot of power and can do a lot of good if they want to. But usually by the time they get there, they are so old and tired that they don't give a shit anymore. Or, anyway, words to that effect. I said that what is needed in this country is young wives for the rich and the powerful. They can keep the old guys happy real easy and without losing any sleep over it. And they can do a lot of good things in the community.

When I went to have my conference with Katz, he said that he had no choice but to give me a D-minus on account of all the little mistakes in grammar and punctuation. But he went on to say that my thoughts were really interesting. I wasn't doing them justice. He said, however, that if I worked hard, if we worked hard together, I would probably end up with a good grade, maybe even an A.

I really thought he meant it. I mean, there he is already about forty years old and too old for serious sex and things like that. The thought of that never entered my mind.

Now. When his friend, Martin Pressy, wanted me to pose for him, bare-ass and in the altogether (every guy with a camera wants that), I naturally refused. Katz told me I might be making a big mistake. He pointed out that Mr. Pressy isn't all that old. And how he is really rich and is looking after his poor old mother. And how lonesome he might be.

Well. I got to thinking about it. Sometimes when I went into town, I would go by and take a look at their big old house. And I would think about all the stuff that must be in it—silver and good china and crystal and jewelry and furniture—and what it would be like to live there. Then I would think about what it would be like to be able to go shopping any day I felt like it, knowing I could buy any pretty clothes I would want to. How it would be to have real respect from salesgirls and waitresses and other underlings like that.

I could even give scholarships in my name to the college and I would never have to take any crap from them again. I might even create an endowed chair for Katz if I felt like it.

And I could travel lots of places and always go first-class.

And, of course, I would do charity organizing and volunteer work, too.

And we would have lovely parties in that big old house.

I kept on thinking about it.

Finally I went ahead and agreed to go to Mr. Pressy's art studio and pose for him. What I was thinking . . . I mean, I might as well be as honest here and now as I would be in a class theme or something. What I was honestly thinking was that he would take one good look and find me irresistible. And one thing would lead to another and we would end up getting married. I had already heard from Katz that Mr. Pressy's mother was pushing him to get married and start having grandchildren before she passed on. So I thought I had a pretty good chance to hook him.

Only he wasn't all that much interested. He told me that I had a great body and would be a wonderful addition to his book. But it was clear that he was only interested in me in an *artistic* way.

(I don't know this for sure, but I am guessing that Mr. Pressy is queer. Maybe that's why some of his old friends call him Missy Prissy.)

Anyway. To make a long story short. When I didn't make any progress, when he just paid me off and said so long, I realized that my picture, pictures of me in the nude were going to be in Pressy's book and I wouldn't have a thing to show for it. Never mind that people, perfect strangers, could go into a bookshop and plunk down their money and take the book back to the privacy of their own homes. That would be plenty bad enough. But what if Mama and Daddy heard about it (which they *would*, because there are always lots of people to tell you news like that) or just accidentally ran across it in a bookstore? Not that they go to bookstores a lot. But there is nothing to stop them, is there? What if our preacher should get hold of a copy? Which seems possible. Because he collects stuff like that (I know for a fact from Charlee, his daughter) and keeps it in a box in the back of his closet. Even if I didn't get in trouble, it would be embarrassing.

But the worst thing of all would be that it might get in the way of the kind of successful marriage I have been dreaming of. The kind of people I would want to marry, the kinds of families I would like to marry into, won't be tickled pink to find out that the blushing bride has been a nude model.

I appealed to Mr. Pressy to let me have those pictures and negatives. He told me to go and peddle my papers. Because I had signed a model release form and a contract and that was that.

So I had to do something drastic.

I went to see Katz and tried to get him to help me. He wasn't any help at all. He said if I wanted to get married so bad, then maybe I should marry him. I thought he was just kidding. So I just laughed in his face and said I couldn't possibly make it on the money they paid an untenured teacher at Baptist College.

He said he had some other things going for him, never mind what. He said he wasn't so bad off as I might think. And then he stated to me, or at least he implied very strongly, that if I intended to make a good grade in his course maybe I had better be more friendly and affectionate.

"Do you mean put out?" I asked.

"You said it, I didn't," he replied.

God! Everything was turning out just awful. I didn't know what to do next. But then I decided that the Lord didn't give me the gift of a good mind for nothing. I decided that I would think my way out of this whole situation.

First, I had to get Katz off my case. And then I had to see if I couldn't get those pictures back from Pressy and maybe even get even at the same time.

Katz . . . Well, he had that waitress girlfriend, that cracker girl named Ruthe-Ann, and would sometimes shack up with her in that old house trailer behind the Hitching Post. Big deal. That wasn't enough to get him in any bad trouble. And, besides, even if she is common, I have always liked Ruthe-Ann. She has never done anything bad to me. Sometimes sisterhood is more important than selfishness.

Now. The only unusual or suspicious thing that I knew was that he was always typing in his office and sometimes late at night in his faculty apartment (when he wasn't shacked up in Ruthe-Ann's trailer). Typing and typing like a madman.

To make a long story short, I sneaked into his office and found out what it was he was typing—*porno!* Would you believe it? Mr. Katz was writing these sex books all the time, as fast as he could type them. Then they were published under other people's names. I have actually read some of them and they aren't too bad if you like that kind of thing—corny, you know, but pretty sexy.

But that's no way to get rich. He probably got less than a thou or two per book.

Maybe that's what was wrong with him. Writing and typing all those dirty books gave him a dirty mind.

Anyway, I got the proof on him, and then I fooled him good. I let him think I had thought things over and wanted to see him. I got all dressed up as sexy as possible and went over to his apartment and let him think he was finally going to score and get his jollies. Then I lowered the boom on the bastard.

I told him I knew what he was doing and could prove it. He would be canned so fast it wouldn't be funny if the administration ever found out. I said I fully expected an A in his composition course. And if I got A, *maybe,* just maybe I wouldn't blow the whistle on him. That's all I would promise.

I wasn't trying to be mean or anything. Honestly. But a girl has got to protect her virtue whenever she has a chance. That took care of Katz.

Or so I thought at the time.

Now then. As for Mr. Pressy. Please understand that I only intended to scare him. Nothing more than that. He is a very nervous and sensitive type.

So I went first to see Papa McDaniels of the Sheriff's Department. Papa has always had a crush on me, the dummy. I allowed as how I would be eternally grateful—and I would prove it, too—if he would do me a favor and help me to play a trick on this older man who was always harassing me and making my life miserable. I made it very clear that I did not want the older man in question to be hurt or anything like that. Just scared real good and maybe embarrassed. Just a trick. Something like the kind of tricks that fraternity boys pull on the pledges during initiation.

Papa said he could probably handle that okay.

I told him that the man in question would be driving at the wheel of a white Mercedes sports car.

"Wait a minute," Papa said. "That will be Missy Prissy. He's got the only one around here. I don't think I can do that."

I made a face.

"But," Papa said looking directly at my books, as if he was talking to them and not to me, "maybe I could, you know, *arrange* something. Maybe we could get a stranger to do it."

"How would we do that?"

Then Papa told me to go and see this man who works for the carnival, the Maupin Brothers Carnival, that was setting up to play over the weekend in town. He told me what to tell the man and to drop his name, Papa's I mean, and to say that he will be getting his detailed instructions from Papa.

That part was easy.

Then on Thursday night, the night of the tent revival, we learned that Pressy was going out to photograph the people there. Maybe he was expecting or hoping there would be some serpent-handling or something dramatic.

Anyway, Pressy took off for the fairgrounds. I broke into his studio to get my pictures back. I spent a long time in there looking for them everywhere. But I couldn't find them or any of the other ones for the *Magic Book*. Only weddings and baby pictures.

How Professor Katz got hold of them, my pictures and negatives, I do not know. He won't say.

All I know is that he got them, prints and negatives, my signed release and everything. And he says he is keeping them in a safety deposit box at People's Bank and Trust.

I offered to make a deal with him.

"It looks to me like a Mexican standoff, Professor Katz," I said. "As long as you have got the pictures, I can't tell on you for writing those porno books, can I?"

He laughed out loud right in my face.

Then he explained to me that he had just been awarded a federal government grant to study American porno and to write a serious book about it. And wasn't that a big joke? He couldn't care less who else knows about his harmless little hobby.

Then he suggested to me a deal, and not a very nice one, either, whereby I could earn back the prints and the negatives, one at a time, before the end of the semester.

"But, sir!" I exclaimed. "There must be twenty or thirty negatives of me!"

"I expect so," he said. "I haven't actually counted them yet."

At first I thought I would fool him by accepting his deal. An old guy like that. He would probably lose interest or die of a heart attack long before the end of the semester.

But, lucky for me, he was only kidding. Or maybe just testing. Because when I burst into tears (I had to do at least that much if only for good manners), he said he was only fooling. And he gave me his clean handkerchief so I could blow my nose. And he was very tender and sweet.

I say lucky for me because I guessed wrong about him. He is as hale and hearty as a grizzly bear. He doesn't smoke and doesn't drink much. And he *jogs* every day. I would never have been able to kill him just by screwing. And, you see, I forgot completely that he is a Jew. He is one even if he did convert to keep the job here at Baptist College. And, as all the world knows, Jews are more interested in sex than anybody else.

They are good at it, too. Better than Baptists. I can tell you that much without compromising myself or my reputation.

As for Martin Pressy and his fancy car. How could I know that somebody would steal it? How could I imagine that the guy from the carnival would do the trick on the wrong person and total the car in the process?

As for Mr. Pressy, I don't care about him one way or the other any more. He can publish his dumb stroke book any time he pleases.

Through thick and thin I have managed to keep my reputation. A good reputation is like gold. Like money in the bank. And I am not a quitter.

Come June and I will have earned an A in Katz's course.

Come June all Katz is going to have left is happy memories.
Memories and a quarter will buy you a cup of coffee.

Here and Now

CONVERSATION BY MOONLIGHT

You know what's really wrong with you, Billy Boy?
*No. But I am dying to know. And I know that if I keep very
quiet and very still you will tell me.*
I mean what's *really* wrong. Not counting the obvious little
things. Like your snoring when you are deep asleep.
Wait a minute. Do I snore? Nobody ever told me that.
Not counting your vain and boring obsession with age and
the decay of the body, your continual counting of a few gray
hairs.
Wait until you get some. See if you don't count.
Not counting your childish ignorance of and attitude towards women. Which—if I may speak briefly for the sisterhood—is flattering in its attribution of magical spiritual power
and glory and keen and sensitive intelligence to any woman with
a pretty face and a healthy youthful body. Not counting your
fond appetite for unhealthy junk food.
*Hey, if it's good enough for President Bubba, it's good enough
for me.*
Not counting your dumb jokes and your incredibly bad taste
in popular music. Not counting your completely simplistic ideas
about politics and the state of the nation. Not counting your
champagne tastes and profligate ways with your money or anybody else's. Not counting your absolutely predictable and un-
flinching procrastination on everything that matters. Not
counting your obvious inability to make a commitment to me
or to anyone else or to anything.

I knew it. I knew it was love all along. Why else would you put up with me?

I do love you, Billy, I *think*. But let's don't change the subject. What is really and truly wrong with you is that somewhere along the way you have stifled your lyrical impulse.

Hey, I never even pretended to be a poet. I can't stand the stuff, limping along down the middle of the page.

What I am trying to tell you is that you make me happy. And when I am happy, my whole self wants to sing and dance, to purr like a cat by the fire. And I feel bad for you because you can't feel the same way. I don't think you can ever be happy, Billy. And it makes me sad.

Well, babe, as long as I have you around to cheer me up, I'll be all right.

That makes us sound about like Sonny and Cher.

Who are they?

Then and There

ALPHA

I remember how we used to play in the attic. How it was always so hot and dusty up there. But we used to play and hide up there all the time anyway. We would try on different clothes from the trunks. And Penrose would take Daddy-and-Mama's love letters out of the tin tackle box and untie the bow ribbon and read them out loud. Not because he cared about them, really, or even understood what the words he was reading meant. But because he knew how much I have always disapproved of taking away or intruding upon somebody else's privacy. Privacy is so very precious. Even for dead people. Maybe especially for dead people.

Here and Now

INTERVIEW WITH **SHERIFF DALE LEWIS**

There is no escaping the moral climate of the modern world. It comes here, too, in all of its fury and madness. Maybe there was a time, long before my time, when we could sit here at a great distance from the heart of things and thank God for our blessings and our difference. Let the great Yankee cities drown in their own cesspools. We could sit right here in safety and virtue and point and say "I told you so." But not anymore. We have some big cesspool cities of our very own now—Atlanta, Miami, Birmingham, New Orleans (though New Orleans was *always* corrupt, from Spanish and French days; New Orleans was Third World before that was either a word or a concept). And all the plagues and diseases of our times have been visited upon us.

Lewis looks a little like Kevin Costner, if Costner had harder angles and edges and etched lines around the eyes that seem to come from a squinting vision of some terrible things. He's tall, fit, well-groomed, crisp in starched khaki and wears, I notice with some surprise when he puts his feet up on his desk and leans far back in this swivel office chair, a fairly new pair of black Nike cross-trainer shoes. His office is at the heart of a state-of-the-art labyrinth setting of computers, fax machines, copiers, scanners, radios, cellular phones, a busy staff. He seems proud of it when he shows me around the place.

If Dave Prince came in here, now, he wouldn't be able to believe it, he says. What he had to work with in 1968 was primitive compared with what we have now. We've got machines here that can do a whole day's work in less than five minutes. And guess what? He handled about as much business as I do and with at least as favorable an outcome by any standards.

Still, we do like our new toys.

Lewis tells me, in a canned version he must have used for VIPs or schoolkids, with slight changes in language, what they do and can do. Which, above and beyond, his basic duty as chief law enforcement officer of Quincy County, includes a network of cooperation with the town, the State of Florida, and a variety of federal police—F.B.I., Drug Enforcement, the Bureau of Alcohol, Tobacco and Firearms. . . .

He pauses at that point to comment on Waco:

A really major fuckup, he says. They could have served the search warrant on Koresh quite easily and without much trouble. You know he was playing in town, in Waco, two or three nights a week in a rock-and-roll band with his name on the marquee. He wasn't hiding out or anything. It looks to me like those boys at ATF wanted to put on flak jackets and steel helmets and play soldier boy.

I would guess, without being too cynical about it, that they were under a lot of pressure from somebody way up high, maybe as high as you can go, to do something dramatic and, as they say, *newsworthy*. Well, to that extent, you could call it a big success. They got on TV all right and stayed there until the end, when it looks like they got tired of playing the game and just killed all those people. It probably wouldn't happen like that here.

Can't be sure, though. Look at Waco. They had Texas Rangers there and the Rangers had already had dealings with Koresh and had actually served warrants on him. They knew the score. But the Feds paid no attention to the Rangers or anybody else. They probably wouldn't listen to me, either, if we ever had something like that here.

Lewis goes on to tell me that Quincy County has its full share of petty and serious crime:

We are part of the big picture. It's not as dangerous out here as it is in the inner cities. We've got criminals and lawbreakers of all kinds, from chicken-fuckers to murderers. But we don't have enough predators and terrorists to change the way people live. Nationally, we've got a bigger problem than anybody, at least in public, is willing to admit. In a year's time, statistically at least, it's probably safer to live in Sarajevo than in Washington, D.C. Somalia is a safer place to be than Detroit.

For the time being, Quincy County, Florida, is a fairly safe place to be, although I do think we are fighting a losing battle. Drugs and drug money have changed everything for the worse, especially here in Florida. It's a problem right here, too, though not as bad as it could be. I keep wondering why they aren't using the old airport to bring in drugs. It's ideal. And maybe they are, but I doubt it. We keep a pretty close watch. What does Jojo say? He owns the damn thing.

In his own office, door shut on the quietly glowing high-tech scene, he says: Let's talk a little bit, first, about Vietnam.

"I would just as soon not, if you don't mind."

Where were you?

"When?"

During the Nam years.

"That's a lot of years. Different places, Sheriff."

Okay, how about 1967 and 1968.

"Mostly stoned out of my gourd, as they say, or said, anyway. Moving around. Down home, both coasts . . . I turned into what they decided to call a hippie. I didn't actually dodge the draft, though. I even took my pre-induction physical. In beautiful San Francisco, as it happens. But I never got called up. And I don't know why."

What would you have done if you had been drafted?

"Hey, I don't know. I don't know what I might or might not have done. It just never happened."

Well, put it another way. What was your attitude? Were you against the war?

"Wasn't everybody?"

Not everybody. Not then or now.

"Everybody I knew was against the war. It was like being against sin. Only the honest-to-God truth is I didn't know anything much about it."

People in your family were in Nam. I know that for a fact.

"People in my family have been in all the wars, every fuckin' one of them, since the first white men hopped ashore off of their longboats and took aim at the first Indians they ran into. We have even had a couple of official and certified heroes over all those years."

Jojo Royle, he was an authentic hero.

"I had a first cousin, Denny was his name, who served three tours in Nam, got shot up a couple of times and earned himself some medals. Oh, we were there. As usual. But not me, personally. Can you dig it?"

For the first time I notice his big badge and his shiny belt and holster, carrying what looks to be a classic and conservative police .38 special. A sociopolitical statement? Why not? The Nike shoes are. The starch in his khakis is. Everything in America today is a sociopolitical statement of one kind or another.

Where were you in the summer of 1967?

"The Summer of Love?"

That's the one.

"San Francisco, man, where else? Bell-bottoms on my jeans and flowers in my hair. Looking to score drugs and get laid."

So what were you listening to?

"New stuff. Stuff from out there mostly. Nothing was quite national yet. Big Brother and the Holding Company."

God, I loved that Lady Janis!

"The Grateful Dead, the Byrds, the Doors, Mr. Jimi Hendrix, the Jefferson Airplane. . . ."

We got a lot of that stuff, too, when it was on tape or on Armed Forces Radio. We knew some of what was happening.

"That's more than I did. A lot of the time I didn't even know what day it was. I am your classic example of an addictive personality. The sixties were heaven or hell (take your choice) for somebody like me."

Lewis lowers his feet and fumbles in a desk drawer. After a moment he produces a book: *Red Thunder, Tropic Lightning: The World of a Combat Division in Vietnam*, by Eric M. Bergerud.

That's my old outfit, he says. I was in the Two Twenty-seventh, the Second Battalion of the Twenty-seventh Regiment, the old Wolfhounds, of the Twenty-fifth, Tropic Lightning Division. And that's where I was in 1967–68. We were mostly in the area around Tay Ninh and Cu Chi and Dau Tieng. Cu Chi was the big base camp for the division, and the evac hospital was there, too. We fought Charlie and pretty soon the NVA, too, all over the map around there. In the rice paddies, in the old rubber plantations.

Our outfit—you can read about it—was really in the thick of it during Tet. Which was when I got hit. Not too bad, but I was in the hospital by the end of March and early April when the things you are interested in happened.

He sits up and looks right at me, giving me a blue-eyed squint. Like he is trying to decide if I am human or not. Then for the first time he offers up his smile, a very sunny expression that suddenly makes him seem more boy than man. In an old movie he would have offered me a cigarette and held a light for me.

Hey, well, he says. We'll never agree on everything. Let's talk about your problems.

He rises, opens a closet door and pulls out a box.

Dave Prince was a born pack rat and so am I. So we got stuff here concerning the first weekend in April that should have been thrown away many years ago. But I suspect it was an obsession of Dave Prince, just trying his best to put together what in the hell had happened around here.

It was beyond him and anybody else, really. Even you. Although you're lucky. That can be part of your story—how it can never be really understood or all the questions answered.

Not surprising, though. Think about the King murder. That should be the simplest thing that you can imagine to solve and to understand. King and the shooter and one bullet. And all the brains of law enforcement in this country, and all the reporters and the writers, still can't come up with anything that absolutely makes sense.

This one here is a little bit more complicated. Plus you didn't have the world's greatest brain trust in law enforcement or the law either. Two people were actually tried and found guilty by a jury of their peers. But the trial was a travesty. A barrel of laughs for everybody except the accused and the victims.

"What became of Papp and the fat woman?"

Fat woman died in prison within a couple or three years. Congestive heart failure. Papp did his time and got out and disappeared. I would guess that he's dead and gone by now. Seems likely. But you'll have to find that out, won't you?

"If I can."

You know who might know? Penrose. For any number of good reasons.

At precisely this point, as if the mention of Penrose Weatherby served as a cue, the phone on the sheriff's desk rings, and in a moment he has to go to work. We agree to meet again when it is convenient.

I've been through most of the file, he tells me. And there's more to it than you have let on or, maybe, than you know.

Then and There

FAREWELL, **FATHER CLAXTON**

A letter came from her in yesterday's mail.

Almighty and most merciful Father;

Opened it today after carrying it around, stuffed in my back pocket. Written and dated more than a month ago, but postmarked from Titusville (going or coming along the East Coast) on the last day of March. A good guess, hopeful, that she has moved somewhere much closer to home. Maybe, who knows? She is on her way home, finally. Taking her sweet time.

The letter, at times undecipherable/unreadable, at times incomprehensible, is uniformly furious, angry beyond any good reason or good sense (has she inherited my temper?) and, I hon-

estly think, unfair. So? Did I honestly expect any wisdom, even
worldly wisdom, coming from a wounded adolescent?

Daughter, I was drunk. I meant you no harm. Did I do you
any harm?

But that isn't what she talks about in the letter. What she
asks more than once is this: Do I have any idea whatsoever what
it means, what it is like to be a minister's daughter? And, of
course, I do not and cannot know that, though I can easily
imagine it.

How about her? Can she imagine what it is like to be the
father, a minister, a priest, a preacher of the Gospel and yet at
the same time to be, fully aware of it, a failed father, a failed
husband, a failed priest?

Daughter, I acknowledge that I have hurt you, wounded you
gravely. I freely admit that much. What more can I do or say?

We have erred and strayed from Thy ways like lost sheep.

No. She can't imagine it. And should not, really. Her youth
and her good health and even her furious confusion serve to
protect her from knowing more things than she ought to know.
Her ignorance, her innocence, even her weakness, give me some
good reasons to live in spite of all my follies and failures. Which
are by now beyond counting and (most likely) beyond all forgiving.

*We have followed too much the devices and desires of our own
hearts.*

Well, then, the letter arrived yesterday and I opened it today.
A letter full of rage and blame and obscenity and, yes, nonsense.
But nevertheless something. I could argue, could take it that she
still cares enough to want to hurt me. Cares enough to want to
make me pay for my real and imaginary misdoings.

It might just as well have been a letter from her mother. (Though there has never been one of those. Not one! Not
since she cursed me and left me and left the child, too, and vanished into thin air.) So much alike. They are. Except that she
curses and blames her mother even more than she curses and
blames me.

Who can blame her?

I fear for her.

I feel a great and heavy sense of fear. I sweat and tremble if and when the phone rings, late or early, suddenly and unexpectedly. Afraid that it will be my own wild child. Or, worse, afraid that it will not be her voice, but some stranger's with bad news (anything, everything) about her. And I am always relieved—Lord, forgive me—when it is not my own child, but is somebody else, anybody else, in trouble, sorrow, need, sickness or any other adversity.

I would gladly heap sorrows on the heads of others, friends and strangers alike and equally, if I could spare my own daughter, though I know perfectly well that it's beyond my power to spare or to save her from anything.

Forgive me, daughter, when and if you can. I couldn't help myself.

We have offended against thy holy laws.

All day yesterday I carried the letter unopened. Today I carry it, crumpled and wrinkled and well read, like some kind of fetish or talisman. I am here now in my empty office, full of clutter and trash to be sure, but empty, empty, empty. Trying to think on and to prepare my Sunday sermon. Something or other to say for Palm Sunday, for the Sunday of the Passion. For Holy Week ahead of us.

Betty, of course, isn't here today. Not after last time, yesterday, when, as in some kind of a farce, I chased her around the desk, her desk, then the room, then in and around the parish house. Chased her with fully lustful and unlawful intentions. Until she simply outran me, outlasted me and left me panting and heart pounding. Lucky for me.

Now, as a result of this, my latest folly, there is nobody here to help with the typing or to answer the phone. Maybe she will come back to work again after a few days. She needs her job. So do I need mine.

Forgive me, Betty, I couldn't help myself.

Palm Sunday. Well, at least she finished cutting and pinning the crosses made of palm leaves. The children especially like them.

Palm Sunday.

The Gospel coming out of St. Matthew, telling the story of the trial and the crucifixion. Ending, as it must and must have, in darkness and terror. No light coming again until the stone is rolled away on Easter morning.

But there is also the story of Palm Sunday (in Mark 11, in Luke 19, in John 12)—the villages of Bethphage and Bethany ("the town of Mary and her sister Martha"), the colt for him to ride on, the garments and leaves and branches (only in John are they called palms) spread in his way to ride across and over, and finally the people saying: "Blessed be the King that cometh in the name of the Lord: peace in heaven and glory in the highest."

The entry of Christ into Jerusalem . . .

How to preach that moment with any sense of meaning to these my poised and comfortable congregation? These my sad and sorrowful sinners, one and all? The thin and shabby figure of Jesus, coming into the city from his brief time of teaching and preaching and healing, surrounded by his thin and shabby followers, himself tall and straight and ridiculous, feet dragging, on the little colt, ass, donkey (What was it really? Does it matter?), the shabby crowd cheering (jeering, too, surely) as if the great Herod had shown himself among them. Jesus coming into the great and ancient city in some kind of forlorn and foolish honor to live out his last few days and shortly to die in dishonor. Cursed by even common soldiers and thieves.

How can he love us? Why should he love us?

Yet, all said and done, who wouldn't give everything in the world to be among them, in the crowd, running to keep up with the tall, thin, shabby, beautiful man, soon to be called (and believed to be) the Son of God, ourselves running alongside or climbing a tree to see better like Zacchaeus in Jericho, ourselves shouting ourselves hoarse to see this strange sight, this absurd and foolish procession?

Something like that.

Something about how all our pomp and pride and circum-
stance and ceremony, all our forms of fame and celebrity, are
turned into nothing at all, nothing worth having or desiring by
this vision. . . .

Came then, as I was in the first sweat of my thinking, thinking that pretty soon I had better pull out my little Royal portable
manual typewriter and put some words (with two fingers) on a
blank page, words chasing words like dogs, came then a heavy-
fisted knocking on the back door of the parish house. So emphatic I thought, for no good reason, it must be the police.
Thought maybe my daughter had set them on me or, if not,
then maybe Betty, the secretary. Or her jealous husband—Barry.
Actually, it could have been any number of people, all kinds of
people on a slow Thursday afternoon, none of them (I was willing to venture) wishing me a whole lot of good.

One of these days a peephole in the back door to the parish
house. But not yet. It's either play dead or open it.

I opened it and faced three perfect strangers who might as
well have been angels or people from Mars for all the common
humanity they possessed and expressed: a midget or dwarf, a
tiny man, anyway, albino of color, his eyes pink as any rat or
rabbit (Do rats and rabbits have pink eyes? Check on that), wild
and heavy eyebrows and nostril hairs like a pair of tiny brooms;
next to him, towering over him, holding his tiny hand as you
might hold a small child's, the most enormous woman I have
ever been close to, made even larger (if you can believe it) by
the light and flowery dress she was wearing, which made her
seem like a gigantic package, wrapped in cheerful paper and
looking for a bow ribbon to finish the job, a naturally sweet-
smelling woman like many large and fat women, as gentle and
thoughtful as a cow; the third being an amazing black man, not
amazing in his skin and bones, in the flesh, except for the extraordinary blackness, almost blue-black of him, but in his costume—desert boots, kneesocks, starched khaki Bermuda shorts
and a khaki short-sleeved, military shirt with epaulets, all sur-

mounted by a classic old-timey explorer's pith helmet, and if he had been wearing a monocle and carrying a swagger stick it would have been appropriate, but he was in fact wearing a pair of glasses with those fashionable little round lenses; he was smoking (puffing is much more like it, like an old-time locomotive) a large and deep-bowled corncob pipe like General MacArthur's.

And how must I have looked to them? Myself caught barefooted, bare-chested (shirtless), wearing dirty khaki pants, my old Marine Corps logo and "Death Before Dishonor" tattooed on my chest, nipple to nipple?

The first of us to speak was the dwarf, his voice so childlike and pure that it made me instantly revise my initial impression.

"Would you, please, sir, inform the reverend that we are here?"

There was a moment for the truth. I could have told these people that, like it or not, I was the reverend whom they were seeking. But I let that moment pass, thinking that I would run and change into my proper clothes and clerical collar and then return and be unrecognizable to them as the same man who had just opened the door.

"And who shall I tell the reverend is calling on him?"

"I am Little David, the evangelist. These are Geneva and my man Raphael."

"Come in and make yourselves at home," I said. "I'll go and find the reverend."

I left them in my office and ran up to the sacristy. I decided to vest, to put on robes. I don't know why. It just seemed called for.

When I came back they reintroduced themselves either out of good manners or because they really and truly didn't recognize me in the robes.

We have left undone those things which we ought to have done;

"I see you've got a picture here of Brother Martin," the amazing black man said, gesturing at my framed photo of Martin Luther King, Jr.

"I think he's a great speaker," I said, "a great preacher. And he may even turn out to be a great man."

"Maybe so. He got a good thing going there, that's for sure."

"What can I do for you good people?" (Did I really say that?)

"Couple of things," the child-dwarf evangelist said. "First one is I want to receive your blessing. I want you to bless me."

"Why me?"

"Well, you know," he said, narrowing those pink eyes to slits, "I always ask around whenever I come to preach in a new place—new to me. Before I stand up there and profess and pretend to preach and to heal, I need to receive the blessing of someone who can be called holy."

"You have come to the wrong reverend. You have sure enough come to the wrong man in the wrong place."

"I'm not so sure. I asked around."

"Then somebody is joking. Somebody has pulled a trick on you."

"Why do you say that?"

"If people in Paradise Springs told you I was righteous and holy . . ."

"Oh, nobody said anything like that."

"Did they tell you that I drink too much? Not to put it nicely, I am a kind of a drunk."

The child-dwarf nodded as did the other two.

"In fact I may just help myself to a drink right now."

"I would rather that you didn't, at least until after we have left," Little David said.

"Did they tell you that I drove my poor wife crazy? And then when she got good and crazy she ran off with two Jewish comedians and that's the last any of us has ever heard of her? Did they tell you that?"

"That's not all," Little David said in that strange ghostly child's voice. "They also described you as an inveterate womanizer, a skirt chaser of the highest degree. And someone who subscribes to dirty magazines—*Playboy, Cavalier, Swank.*"

"I subscribe to *The New Republic,* too."

"Be that as it may . . ."

"There's some of them," the sweet-voiced fat woman said, "who hinted to us that you may have abused and taken advantage of your own beautiful daughter."

"Now, wait just a big minute!"

"I'm not saying that we would believe something like that, just that we heard some definite hints."

Myself (foolish in my full vestments and now dying for a drink): "Well, what if it's the truth, what then?"

"I don't think you understand what I am saying, what I am getting at, do you?" Little David said. "I know that Episcopalians are supposed to be pretty lighthearted and casual when it comes to religious things. I know that. But didn't they teach you no theology in school? Where did you go to school, anyway?"

"Sewanee."

"They teach some theology there. Some, anyway. You just probably didn't pay much attention."

"Where is all this leading us? I mean, even though I am almost a complete failure as a pastor, I still have some duties, some things I have to do."

Glance at my Timex wristwatch and continue. "In about half an hour I have got to go over to the hospital and call on some of my parishioners. So, anything you have to say . . ."

"It won't take that long," he said. "But I do want you to understand why I picked you out to give us your blessing."

"I would like to hear that."

And we have done those things which we ought not to have done;

"In the absence of a saint, of which I have not yet had the pleasure of seeing a live one," Little David continued, "I am forced to turn to someone who has truly suffered and has made other people suffer—which is often the same thing—someone who is a believer, but who is lost and troubled as I am lost and troubled.

"I am in the healing business, but I can't heal myself. And neither can you and you know that.

"What I'm saying is you aren't perfect, but you'll do."

"Do what?"

"Bless me and my enterprise. Give the three of us your blessing."

And there is no health in us.

"Do you really think it would help?"

"Do you think I would be here if I didn't?"

"I don't even know you people."

"You know us well enough, as well as you are going to. Hey, we might be three angels come calling."

"All right. How do you want it?"

"What do you mean?"

"Kneeling or standing."

"Me and Raphael will kneel. She won't, because if she does, she won't be able to get up again. And we won't be able to lift her."

But thou, O Lord, have mercy upon us, miserable offenders.

"Let me get my prayer book."

"Don't you know any by heart?"

"No. Not really."

"Okay."

I opened *The Book of Common Prayer* and stood before them, the midget and the black man kneeling, the woman hulking over me. I had to resist the impulse to kneel down in front of her. And I read: "Almighty and everlasting God, from whom cometh every good and perfect gift, send down upon the Clergy, and upon the congregations committed to their charge, the healthful spirit of thy grace; and that they may truly please thee, pour upon them the continual dew of thy blessing. Grant this, O Lord, for the honor of our Advocate and Mediator, Jesus Christ."

"*Amen!*" they said, and "*All right!*"

And then I put my hands on the heads of the two who were kneeling.

"The grace of our Lord Jesus Christ, and the love of God, and the fellowship of the Holy Ghost be with us all evermore."

"*Amen! All right!*"

They rose. The midget smiled a bright smile.

"I reckon that done it," he said. "I can feel it. I can feel the glory. You definitely got the touch."

"Anything else?"

"You said something about a drink. I could use one. So could Raphael. Geneva doesn't touch the stuff."

I took the bottle from my desk drawer. Poured out three belts in coffee cups.

"Here's looking at you, kid," the midget said, all good cheer now.

"Were you really in the Marines?" Raphael asked.

After they left, I got dressed and walked over to the hospital. Some of my people are dying over there. Maybe it was the drink (actually more than one), or maybe it was the strange fellowship I felt for and with these three freaks. But whatever it was, I felt better, enough so that I think I did some good service at bedside.

Spare thou those, O God, who confess their faults.

A couple more drinks just to keep the mood going. Maybe I can finish my sermon for Palm Sunday. Got to write it down just before I finish it. Got to type it. Maybe I should call up Betty at home and apologize sincerely, deeply and sincerely. And beg her to come back and help me get ready for Sunday. I could dictate to her. I could introduce her to the Reverend Doctor Dick. She already knows him pretty well. Too well. Shame upon you, Reverend Dick.

What if?

What if those three freaks were nothing more or less than figments? Creatures out of my somewhat askew imagination. Some kind of an hallucination.

Or what if they were angels? Came to wake me up and remind me of my bounden duty? What if that?

They told me there is a carnival in town, too. The two of them are sharing the old fairgrounds—the blinking lights and Ferris wheel of Babylon; the shouting and singing and sweaty prayers of Jerusalem.

Our Lord riding a donkey into the city of Jerusalem. Would the dwarf and the fat woman and the black man stand and clap their hands for Jesus passing by?

Would I?

Restore Thou those who are penitent; according to Thy promises declared unto mankind in Christ Jesus our Lord. And grant, O most merciful Father, for his sake, that we may hereafter live a godly, righteous and sober life. . . .

Lordy, I am drunk or, anyway, getting there. Here it is, the tag end of Lent. And I gave up booze for Lent. That lasted about twenty minutes on Ash Wednesday. I can't remember a day . . . Maybe I'll try A.A. Only trouble is that A.A. meets right here in this parish house of my own church. It wouldn't do at all. Would it? But I have to do something.

Confess and pray.

To the glory of thy holy name. Amen.

Sunset, a splendid, blaring (trumpets and trombones) Florida sunset in the windows. I return to the vestry and hang up my vestments. I dress again in my dark suit and clean, starched, clerical collar.

It is getting dark quickly now. What happened to today? I haven't written my sermon yet. Maybe tomorrow. First thing in the morning while I'm still fresh.

I leave the parish house, turning off all the lights (for once) and enter the dark rectory. I do not trouble to turn on lights. I climb the stairs all the way up to the attic. Here I need some light to see my way. I feel my way to the middle of the long, low-ceilinged room, still toasty warm from the risen heat of the day. Sweating. I feel for, find, and pull the string of the overhead light, a dull and naked bulb. Thirsty, I find I have (thoughtful fellow) brought the diminishing bottle with me. I take a swallow and turn to the cedar chest. My wife's cedar chest, full of her things. Things she left behind when she left me. Sharp, clean scent of cedar chips then the vague scent of her perfume.

I kneel by the chest and plunge my arms into the sweet and filmy clothing here as if I were bathing myself in water.

Much later I hear myself weeping. Like a child. Like a fool.

Now I hear something. Someone in the house. Someone on the stairs. One or maybe more than one. Maybe my freak angels have come back for me. Come back, beautiful creatures, come back and carry me away. Carry me home.

Here and Now

INTERVIEW AT WEATHERBY HOUSE

It would be funny if it weren't at once so surprising and so . . . *apt.*

"My grandfather built it. My daddy was born and grew up here and I was raised here, too," Penrose tells him.

A well-kept, recently painted, two-story frame house. Shady, well-tended yard. You could call it a lawn. Smack in the middle of which is the sign, so close in appearance to those historical markers placed at roadsides and at real historical sites that it is seriously indistinguishable from them. The text describes the house, the Weatherby house, as an early-twentieth-century Florida dwelling, lived in by several generations of Weatherbys, and birthplace and homeplace of the distinguished real estate developer (the word "visionary" is also casually used, and why not?) Penrose Weatherby.

"This is where we lived and where we were in 1968. Daddy still lives here even though it takes round-the-clock help. Costs me a bundle, but it's family, you know? And he wouldn't be happy at all at some place like the Canterbury. I keep the place up and I look after him. It's the least I can do."

They go up the walk to the wide front porch. There is a swing there which the ghost of a breeze has set in subtle motion. The yard has the green, sweet smell of old Florida.

"I'll get you squared away," he tells Billy. "He'll be glad to have somebody besides Leroy to talk to for a change. Don't tire him out too much, though. Daddy is, always has been a little bit crazy. He gets crazier when he is overstimulated and tired.

"First, though," he adds, "before we get Daddy involved, let's just slip upstairs and take a quick look at Alpha's room. We have kept it pretty much the way it was since the day she was murdered."

A neat, small world. Austere. Single brass bed. Seems more like the room of a young teenager than a grown woman. Teddy bears and stuffed animals. A calendar for 1968, still open to April. A few posters—Twiggy, looking forever sweet and daffy, an aerial view of San Francisco, Elvis and (oddly?) Che Guevara. A cheap plastic radio at bedside. He can't help wondering what kind of music she listened to. Some clothes, plain and colorful alike, but simple, hanging in a neat, sad row in the closet. A double row of shoes (flats and low heels) on the closet floor.

"She loved shoes," Penrose says. "It was her great weakness."

"Did she leave any letters or papers? A diary, maybe?"

"Daddy burned all that old stuff. He wouldn't have kept anything except Mama made him. By the time Mama died, he had gotten used to keeping this room in memory of her. But he never comes in here."

Billy Tone suddenly thinks that all over America there must surely be rooms, little shrines, preserved in honor of people, loved ones, who died young.

Except for being one-legged and, at the moment, sitting in a mechanized wheelchair, Jack Weatherby looks quite a lot like Dub Taylor (the father of C. W. Moss, remember?) in *Bonnie and Clyde*. Weatherby wears clean, loose trousers and a T-shirt decorated with a smiley face. A bedroom slipper on his foot.

Go ahead and ask me how I came to lose my leg.

The old man looks to be deadly serious. So Billy Tone asks him that question.

Follows then a confused story of a confused and troubling time. As in all authentic war stories, some of the details—dates and the names of places and unit designations, for example, are precise and authoritative. Other things are by now dimly remembered, dreamlike, perhaps long past the boundaries of factual truth.

Weatherby, a very young soldier (maybe even underage) was enjoying the easy life, only casually military, in the occupation of Japan.

He says:

We were stationed at SASEBO—Thirty-fourth Infantry Regiment of the Twenty-fourth Division. At any given time most of us had a hangover and maybe most of us had the clap. When, on a rainy, windy Sunday—June 25, 1950—the North Koreans attacked South Korea. I had never even heard of Korea, let alone the North and the South of it.

He explains that in a few days some understrength units, including the Thirty-fourth, were cobbled together and armed and equipped with whatever was available. Sent off to South Korea . . .

We all thought we were going to Taiwan. Didn't know where that was, either.

Sent off to fight a delaying action, a losing battle all the way down the rugged peninsula to the final perimeter, behind the Naktong River, at the port of Pusan. A rosary of strange names: *Taejon, Ansong, P'Yongt'aek, Osan, Suwon, Sojong, Ch'onan, Choch'won, Yongdong, Taegu, Hwanggan, Chirye, Kumch'on, Sangju* . . .

A few of the unlucky ones went by air and got themselves shot at first. We went over on a rusty, stinking ship. Which soon smelled sweet to us, at least in memory. The minute we landed at Pusan the whole fuckin' country smelled like a cesspool of human shit. World's biggest shithole. Sure, the Japs used human shit for fertilizer, but the whole country didn't stink of it.

Landed at Pusan. Then trucked to railroad. Boarded flatcars and headed north. Coming south, passing by them, were long trains of boxcars, packed with refugees, fleeing ROK (South Korean) soldiers, heaps and stacks of unattended wounded. . . .

The weather was terrible. Rained four or five times a day. And in between the rains it was hot as the unholy hinges of hell. Mud, mosquitoes, bugs everywhere. We were sweat soaked and always thirsty. Some guys wouldn't or couldn't wait for clean water. Drank from little creeks and ponds and ditches. And right away got the running shits and added their share to the stink and filth of the country. Daylight lasted until after nine o'clock, 2100, and that was all to the enemy's advantage.

In the almost treeless hills and the rice paddies of the valleys they soon found that their old World War II equipment was less than adequate:

We had our M-1s and our carbines, and they were okay. We had pretty good machine guns and some mortars—almost all the sixty-millimeters but not the eighty-ones. Our two-point-six bazookas and the seventy-five-millimeter recoilless rifles wouldn't do a thing, nothing against them big Russian T-34 tanks. They just kept coming and coming. Ran over and all around us. In the dark they infiltrated through us. In the daytime they got close, dressed up in white like refugee farmers, and then shot the hell out of us. And we were always running out of ammo and C-rations.

Everything in disorder. Radios not working. Wire communications broken and disrupted. No way to call in artillery or air strikes.

Our officers, the ones who didn't catch the bug-out fever, sent their messages the old way—by runner. You can imagine how that worked.

In about ten days units of the Twenty-fifth division began to arrive from Japan. And more units would be coming, were on the way from Japan and the States. By then the Twenty-fourth Division had lost 30 percent of its men. Was pulled back for rest and recuperation.

Listen to this. Listen here. On July twentieth the Twenty-fourth Infantry of the Twenty-fifth Division broke and bugged out at Yechon. The Twenty-fourth was an all-black unit. Broke and ran not just once, but again and again. They had to put roadblocks and MPs to catch the niggers and send them back to the front. So there went our chance, our one chance for a little R-and-R. Back we went, directly to the front again. And the first thing that happened was they blew most of my right leg off with a mortar round. I damn near died before they got me back to Japan. Might have been better if I had just been killed.

Anyway, I blame the niggers for it.

Now I know they are all busy rewriting and revising the history to make it look like the coons were nothing but a bunch of heroes. You saw that movie *Glory,* didn't you? What a crock of shit! Take it from me, they broke and ran in Korea. They ran like hell to save their black asses every time they had a chance. One thing a nigger can really do is run. And don't let anybody tell you otherwise.

So I have spent the rest of my life with one leg to show for it, a leg and a stump. And don't tell me that I owe the bastards anything.

But never mind all that. Let me tell you the craziest thing of all. When we left Japan for Korea they made us pack our Class A khaki uniforms in our duffel bags so we would have a dress uniform to wear in the victory parade. If they ever have a victory parade, I'll get Leroy to push me in my wheelchair.

Leroy nods impassively. Outside something, a cat most likely, has upset the blue jays and they are squawking. Weatherby looks up and out the window, then directly at Billy Tone.

Mr. Tone, do I know you? Who are your people?

"I'm kin to the Singletrees and the Royles."

Well, sir, the Judge, the Colonel as they called him, was a pompous old bastard. In '68 he would have been just about my age now, give or take. I never cared for him. And when he died, he left all that money to that nigger. Which I take to be a joke, the Judge's last laugh. Pissing all over Paradise Springs.

No, I never liked the Judge. Jojo, though, that's another story. He was an honest-to-God warrior and you have got to respect that. Oh, he never joined the Legion or the VFW or anything like that and never marched in a parade or anything, but he was the real thing. One of the truly brave.

Wonder what became of him.

"Well, sir, he has inherited the Judge's old place. And he's holed up there, living there."

Well, we all went and got old, didn't we? Then: Does he still own the nigger radio station—the soul music station?

"As far as I know."

That's one of the Judge's jokes too—got to give him credit for a powerful sense of humor. Maybe I could be funny, too, if I had enough money to fool around with. You can play plenty of good tricks and jokes if you are rich enough.

Do you know what I am talking about?

"Not exactly, sir. I'm not sure."

Well, it went like this. Judge Singletree, he put up the money in the late forties or early fifties to buy that radio station. He could see the future and see that the niggers were finally coming along and would pretty soon need a radio station of their own. So he bought it and set it up. Then he got Jojo hired to be a disc jockey, Mr. Jazzbo they called him. Jojo was so good at imitating and impersonating that the coons thought he was one of them. I never knew a white man of that age and generation who could sound so authentic and black. These days a lot of the kids can sound as black as can be, but it was a rare gift thirty years ago. And anyway, who would want to?

So Jojo, not knowing that the Judge actually owned the station behind the scenes, got himself a job as a disc jockey at WDFO and played a lot of shouting and screaming soul music (polluting the airwaves, in my humble opinion) and was a big hit around here with all the local spear chuckers. Who didn't even know he was white. It was a big secret. Might have stayed

one, too. Except Jojo was on the air when Martin Luther Coon
got himself wasted in Memphis. And old Jojo just lost it right
there on the air and started calling out the natives to rise up and
burn the town down. The station manager, his boss, a very respectable Negro, and an undertaker by trade, he came flying
down to the station and cut Jojo off the air before too much
harm was done.

Of course, when that circus tent out at the fairgrounds, the
revival where they killed my daughter, Alpha, when that tent
caught on fire, people looked up and saw the flames and figured
that the niggers had already started burning everything down. I
know *I* did. I had my M-1 rifle and a double-barreled shotgun
and I was ready for the bastards. But nobody came around.

And I'm still waiting . . . Where was I?

"Jojo and the radio station."

Yeah. Well, the way I heard it—and by the time things get
to me now they are usually somewhat distorted—way I heard it
was Jojo never knew who owned the radio station until the
Judge died and left it to him in his will.

Yes, sir, the Judge must be laughing his ass off in heaven or
hell (most likely the latter, if there's any justice left in the world).
He has created a hotshot nigger lawyer who can sound like an
Englishman when he wants to and, at the same time, he took
his closest and favorite kin and tied him in a knot with a black
radio station. Best part is that the station is making good money
these days. And why not? The airwaves are full of screaming
Ubangis, night and day. You can hardly hear anything else. And
if you turn on the tube, there they are, slam-dunking, shucking
and jiving.

Pause. Then: Hey, are you tape recording this conversation?
We better have some ground rules.

You are interviewing me for this book you say you are writing. Now then. I don't want to change anything, and I don't
want to go over your text or anything like that.

He produces a tape recorder of his own and turns it on.

I am taping our talk just like you are. Is that thing running?

Anyway. One rule. I am not going to use the word "nigger" during this entire interview. You may wonder why, especially since I am willing to say "nigger" any other time that I feel like it to anybody I feel like saying it to. Including my main man, Leroy, here. He don't care, do you, Leroy?

"Nosuh."

But be that as it may, some really strange things have been happening to our language, our American lingo. These days there is no four-letter word or dirty word that you can't cheerfully say in mixed company. Most of them are used all the time on television. You can go right ahead and say things like "cunt," "pussy," "prick," "asshole," "fart," "piss," "shit," "cocksucker" and so forth, even (thanks to the common usage of our dark-skinned brothers) "motherfucker." But you may not be so crude and insensitive as to say the word "nigger." You can publicly blaspheme and mock any known form of religion or religious group (except, of course, the Jews). You can put a crucifix in a bottle of urine and call it *Piss Christ* and get yourself paid for it and praised for it—by the United States Fuckin' Government, for Lord's sake! But, believe me, you better not say "nigger."

Well, I don't want to be so insensitive as to turn people off from the good sense of what I am saying just by the use of a loaded word. And, believe it or not, I don't want to hurt anybody's feelings, either. If some nigger or other should happen to read your book, it won't make me feel better to make him feel worse.

And even if I did go ahead and say the word "nigger," your New York City publisher will probably cut it out anyway. So what's the point?

And I've got one more good reason which may strike you as being completely cuckoo. Never mind. I seriously and sincerely want to try to preserve and maintain some standards. If I protest against the frequent and public use of words that offend me, words like "cocksucker" and "cuntlapper" and "motherfucker," then shouldn't I at least have the decency not to use the words that piss off other people? There is a distinct decline in the civility of American discourse these days, and I don't want to contribute to the trend, if you know what I mean.

So, I am going to use another word. Now, some people I know use words like "Ethiopian" and "Nubian" and "Ubangi." But I can't see where that is any different. I, myself, prefer to use the word "barbarian." Mainly because, in my best judgment, that is what they are, the overwhelming majority of them, anyway, barbarians. Alien and uncivilized. Spear chuckers. Jungle bunnies. "Barbarian" seems to say it best of all.

Sure, it doesn't cover all of them. There are plenty of them, I'll agree, that you and I could both learn a lot from. But you will also have to agree with me—there are a hundred, maybe a thousand Mike Tysons for every Ralph Bunche in the woodpile.

Anyway. If you decide to use any of this interview in your book (and I don't give a shit if you do or you don't), if you quote me on anything, please use the word "barbarian."

Now then. You have come here to my house to talk to me because I am the father of the victim—my daughter, Alpha. Well, I hate to disappoint you. But I am not going to have a whole lot to say about Alpha. I loved her a lot and I miss her and I am sorry she is gone. Some people thought (probably still do, if and when they think about her) that she was crazy. That she was clearly a schizophrenic who heard imaginary voices and was not responsible for her actions. I don't believe that. I think she was tuned in to the world in a different way from most people. She was very sensitive and very intelligent. And I wish I had been able to raise enough money to send her off to college where she could make something out of herself. Believe it or not, as mean and bitter as I am (*and have every right to be*), I wanted Alpha to be happy if she possibly could be so. I worried over her and came about as close to praying for her, praying over her, about as close to prayer as I could come since I gave up on God and on praying, too, in Korea. I never did anything for Penrose. I didn't have to. He turned out meaner than me and a whole lot slicker. He's been in God's hands all along. I don't know what that tells you about the nature of God—that He could put up with Penrose. Who knows why? Why do the ways of the wicked prosper?

I'll tell you something else. One thing I don't approve of at all is this modern-day habit of exploiting dead people to make money and whatever else (respect? reputation?) goes with writing a book. You might not believe this, because I am an uneducated man. But I am a one-legged man and I can read and even write. And I have spent a lot of the time sitting around this house reading all kinds of books—good ones and bad ones and mostly so-so ones. And lately, over the last few years especially, there have been all kinds of books exposing and exploiting the dead. Which is a goddamn cowardly and lowlife thing to do.

Now then. Mr. Tone, I ain't picking on you. As far as I know and can tell you aren't the worst of the lot. But I'm here to tell you right now that you will get no help from me in telling Alpha's story. Even if I really could help you. Which I can't. I am sure that Penrose will make up for my silence on the subject. I may talk a whole lot when I've got a captive listener like you, but that Penrose, he is positively loquacious. He will tell you all that you want to hear and then some. Only, Mr. Tone, I wouldn't trust him too much. You don't get as rich and successful as my boy Penrose by telling people the straight-up-and-down, unequivocal, unambiguous truth.

I hope we understand each other.

Now then. Another reason that you are here at my house today talking to me is that you will have heard, around and about, that I am an unreconstructed racist. That's another loaded word. It's very bad nowadays to be a racist, worse than to be a sodomite or a pedophile or even a draft dodger. Nevertheless, what you have heard is correct—I *am* a racist.

But before we go any further here, let me explain what that means and let me point out to you that you are one, too, whether you know it or not and whether you believe it or not. My source here is the federal government itself, the Kerner

Commission, appointed by LBJ in the wake of the inner-city riots in the summer of 1967 (and several summers before that). Ain't it a sketch how the barbarians won't come outside and riot in cold weather? That report was made public early in 1968, in plenty of time to serve as inspiration for the rioting in April of 1968. Never mind that Otto Kerner was a big crook who would shortly be convicted and sent off to cool his heels in the slammer. His ideas were and still are taken as gospel by half of the half-ass liberals in America. He said that *all* white people are racists by definition. And it was he who planted the seeds of an idea that is bearing its own poisonous fruit here and now—that a barbarian cannot be racist no matter what he thinks and says and does. Only white folks can be racist, and all white folks, even the good liberal ones, *are* racist.

If that is the case, then it's no big deal for me to confess that I am a racist. Because I already am a racist and I know one when I see one, I insist that these Black Muslims, people like this Khallid Abdul Muhammad, who are running around telling their people to go out and kill white people and to desecrate the corpses of the already dead white people, people like that are racists, too. By any definition. And I don't care what former Governor Otto Kerner said or what Professor Leonard Jeffries, Jr., is saying.

Because I am a racist, I recognize that we are in the big middle of a race war, right here and now in this country. That's what the barbarian said, the one who walked through the cars on the Long Island Railroad shooting all those white people. He knew exactly what it was—an act of terrorism in the undeclared war between the races. He knew what he was—a soldier in that war. Of course, it's pretty easy to be a soldier, a big-time terrorist, when the other side is unarmed and helpless. The government wants to keep it that way, too. They want us to be unarmed and helpless, totally dependent; and they are willing to sacrifice a considerable number of us to the enemy. Witness the recent (recent enough) Los Angeles riots. Even the cops, who were watching it on television in their stations, didn't get seriously concerned until about fifty people were killed. That seems to be the magic number—fifty. We let the barbarians have their way—"venting their rage," as the politicians call it—until the death toll rises above fifty. Then we try to calm them down a little.

If the Israelis thought and acted that way, they would have disappeared off the face of the earth long ago. Fuck with them and you get yourself punished. Somebody gets punished, anyway. And quick.

Kill fifty people and burn down a billion dollars worth of property and you will get yourself on television and you will get a government grant.

Of course, the government doesn't always act that way. They can be killers, too, on a grand scale. They killed more than eighty people, at least a quarter of them little children, in Waco. Trying to serve a search warrant. Don't fuck around with Miss Janet Reno and Bill Clinton. They will kill you and your wives and children too. And they sure won't lose any sleep over it. Eighty! That's a lot of people all in a day's work. Has anybody ever said they were truly ashamed or sorry about that massacre? Hell no! Those folks in Waco even had a barbarian lawyer. But a fat lot of good it did them.

You know, if you can kill eighty, you will just as soon kill six million. Get it?

Okay. We've got a war on. It's called the crime problem. That's code. There's no getting around the numbers. Roughly half, forty-seven percent, of all the violent crime committed in the United States is perpetrated by barbarians. Mostly by male barbarians between the ages of fifteen and thirty-five. Now consider this. Even if every barbarian alive, man, woman and child, was committing these crimes, that would still be a little less than twelve percent of the population committing roughly half of all the crimes. But since it's mostly males, teenage to middle-age, you have maybe five percent of the population at most committing half of the crimes in America. That means that if you should happen to encounter a male barbarian between the ages of fifteen and thirty-five, the statistical chances are very good, very high, that he is a criminal and is up to some criminal activity.

There are other interesting numbers. I have read several places that, at any given instant, one out of four barbarian males is either in jail or involved with the criminal justice system. And that doesn't even count the others who are out there at the same time actually committing crimes and getting away with it. You will read, from time to time, about sensitive and superior barbarian males who get very annoyed because people react suspiciously to them. Listen, with odds like that, a fellow has every right to be suspicious of anybody with a black face. With odds like that you would have to be nuts not to be extremely wary all the time. Should you go ahead and let yourself be robbed and crippled or killed just to prove that you are a nice liberal person? Only Christians can be asked to offer up their lives like that. And among Christians only saints are authorized to *throw away* their lives. Are we a nation of criminals and saints? We certainly aren't a nation of Christians, who are not even allowed to pray in public places.

One of the favorite liberal points about barbarian crime is that most of their crimes are committed against other barbarians. Is that supposed to make the rest of us shrug and feel a whole lot better? Does it prove anything at all except that the average barbarian criminal is too fuckin' lazy to go out of his own neighborhood in search of victims? For the life of me I can't figure out how, even in the tangled-up mind of the liberals, it can be a plus for the barbarians. Most likely it's another example of the liberals' relentless contempt for the common white folk of the country. Most likely they think we are stupid enough to be reassured by the news that barbarian predators prefer to feed on their own.

Anyway. Talk all you want to about the root causes, but nevertheless the barbarians, at home and abroad (look at Rwanda; look at Uganda, Somalia, the Sudan, Liberia, Nigeria, Haiti), have proved themselves to be a criminal people. Or, if you want to put it more honorably, they are terrorists in a world-wide war. . . .

Throughout all this the male nurse, Leroy, has been quietly dozing in an armchair, breathing deeply, just this side of snoring. No doubt, none of it is new to him. And he might as well catch forty winks as sit around and listen to insults.

All right, he continues without even a prodding question from Billy Tone. You have crime. Then you have the criminal system, the judicial system of the nation. It is built on the foundation of Anglo-Saxon law and the petit jury. (The grand jury is an excrescence.) As the petit jury goes, so goes the nation.

Now then, Mr. Tone, have you seriously followed the tribulations of the jury system over the past few years, particularly in places like Newark, Detroit, the District of Columbia, etc., where you are apt to get a barbarian jury? I doubt it. Point is that in most cases race is crucial, far more important than right or wrong or any consideration of the law.

Billy Tone, seeking to be a neutral listener, a visitor from outer space, cannot avoid at least a brief intrusion. "Well," he says. "We had maybe fifty years of the opposite situation. Where a black man couldn't look for equity or justice from a white jury."

Do two wrongs make a right?

"No, sir."

You may think that is a frivolous question. It is not. It is now the policy of the U.S. government to remedy past wrongs with other wrongs.

But we will only argue, and I'm not interested in your opinion. You came here to ask mine.

"Yes, sir."

So. After crime we have the problem of education. Look at the public schools these days. There has been a steady and relentless deterioration—I mean it is clearly quantifiable; you can *measure* it like body temperature—of American public education dating from the day of *Brown v. Board of Education. By their fruits ye shall know them!* The effects of integrating the schools

over thirty years have been disastrous. Hell, even the barbarians
admit it. They are doing their damnedest to get separate schools
and to get control over the schools. Meantime the test scores
and aptitude evaluations are steadily falling. The teachers are
underpaid and incompetent. And the schools are profoundly unsafe. You can't go safely to and from the bathroom if you are a
student. Great gobs of money have been spent trying to improve
the schools. And the schools have been steadily getting worse
and worse.

And thanks to the quota regulations that they insist on calling "affirmative action," incompetent barbarians are now being
placed in positions of management, responsibility and power.
Not just in government jobs, either. Consider the quality of
service we get from our affirmative-action Postal Service these
days. For whose benefit, do you suppose, are these nine-digit
zip codes? Not just filling the rolls of government with barbarians, but everywhere in the private sector as well.

Are things running any better? Are the barbarians really doing better or acting better? I ask you. And another perfectly
serious question is this: how many of these barbarians would be
able to make their own way in life *without* some kind of a special
deal or special tests or so-called affirmative action? Not many,
you have got to admit.

And what will be the result of all this tinkering and tamper-
ing with the lives of ordinary, loyal, white, law-abiding, hardworking citizens? Will we now live in a more peaceful and
orderly society? Or will it all get steadily worse and worse as
it is now? Besides banjo and singing and dancing and basketball, what are the actual accomplishments of the barbarians
among us?

They are always talking about the need for "role models."
Well, they damn sure need some and "role models" are few and
far between among the barbarians. You might think that the
various voting rights acts of the 1960s would have introduced
us to some barbarian leaders worthy of honor and emulation.
Name half a dozen. Name one. Consider the barbarian mayors

of the abandoned inner cities—Newark, Detroit, Birmingham, Los Angeles, Chicago, New York City—have any of them ever been free of the taint of scandal and corruption, even crime? You want a role model for barbarians? I'll give you Marion Barry.

Throughout recorded history (regardless of race or creed or color) barbarian peoples have been mainly involved in raping, robbery, murder, looting and pillage, and the overthrow of established order. Which is the one thing they do not and cannot understand. Why should we expect our own barbarians to be in any way different from and superior to Visigoths and Mongols and Huns?

And on and on and on he went, in a sincere and controlled fury.

(Later Billy Tone will run into Leroy out at the Baptist Barbecue, buying some ribs for supper for himself and old Jack Weatherby. And Leroy will tell him: "I hope you don't hold a lot of what was said against Mr. Jack. I mean, he's not a bad man, just very *opinionated*. I don't mind it. Truth is, I might even enjoy listening to him carry on if it wasn't so damn personal.")

When the old man runs out of breath and energy, Tone manages to ask him a question that has been playing along the edges of his mind. It popped into his head earlier, but now seems somehow important.

"Mr. Weatherby, how did you feel about Martin Luther King?"

When he died, the same evening that Alpha did, I took some comfort in the news. I thought he was a big-head, big-mouth troublemaker and that he had it coming. Spoiled rotten preacher's boy, the pet nigger of rich limousine liberal Yankees. And even some down here. Nothing like a little money and security to give people a social conscience.

If I hadn't been paralyzed by my own shock and grief over Alpha, I think I might have put on my artificial leg and gone out and danced in the street. Certainly I thought about it. And I have to say when I first heard the news on the radio I was happy. I poured myself a good stiff drink. I didn't know Alpha was dead or dying. Not yet. . . .

But, he goes on, a lot of time has passed and many things have changed, and I have changed with them. Compared with those who came after him, Martin Luther King looks good. Tell you the truth now, I think it was a great loss. That things got a lot worse after he was gone. No question. That maybe, because he had good sense and could count, we wouldn't have the race war we are fixing to have now, sooner or later.

Whenever I think about it, it puts me in mind of the words of David about the murder of Abner from the second book of *Samuel: And the king said unto his servants, know ye not that there is a prince and a great man fallen this day in Israel?*

Looking past Tone, out the window and across the squirrel-happy, jay-haunted lawn, the angry old man wipes his glasses with a handkerchief. Then the air conditioner cuts on with a noisy jolt and shudder. Leroy seems to be sound asleep at last, snoring like an old hound dog by the fire.

Mr. Tone?

"Sir?"

Would you like to hear my thoughts on the subject of the Jews?

"Another time. I have imposed on you enough for today."

Then and There

ALPHA

He is the Devil. Only no one knows it. No one but me.

It is a terrible thing to be the only one who knows something. Because then you are the only one who can do anything about it.

I received the definite proof in my dream. But when I asked the Angel what in the world I was supposed to do about it, he just disappeared, vanished as usual, and left it all up to me.

Why choose me when so many others stand more in the need of healing?

Why single out a young girl to beat the Devil?

Why me, unworthy and wishing most of all things to be left alone?

The Angel did not answer. He vanished into all that light and then the light was gone. And I woke up in the darkness, bathed in sweat, as if from a broken fever, troubled at heart and wondering.

Then and There

EXCERPT FROM TRANSCRIPT OF
*State of Florida v. Mary Lou Frond
and William Papp*

*[Direct examination of the witness Raphael McKenzie
by the prosecutor (Mr. Cooke)]*

EDWARD COOKE: Now then, Rastus, just a few questions . . .

RAPHAEL MCKENZIE: Raphael.

COOKE: What?

MCKENZIE: My name is Raphael.

COOKE: Like the angel?

MCKENZIE: I don't know anything about angels.

COOKE: How would you prefer that I should address you—as Mr. McKenzie?

MCKENZIE: I don't care what you call me. I just want to get this thing over and done with and get out of here.

COOKE: And the amenities don't matter?

MCKENZIE: Not to me, they don't.

JUDGE SPENCE: Excuse me for butting in, but what is all this, anyway, Ed? Some kind of a bad joke?

COOKE: Your Honor, I assure you that I have no intention of introducing any levity into these solemn proceedings. My concern with these trivial modes and manners of address is in part for the benefit of the out-of-state press here present, who tend to make too much of these matters. I want the record to demonstrate that the State has made every effort in good faith to maintain an appropriately serious and circumspect attitude and demeanor.

JUDGE SPENCE: You said a mouthful.

JOHN RIVERS: Doesn't he always?

JUDGE SPENCE: Yes, but does anybody have a clue what he is talking about?

MCKENZIE: Amenities.

COOKE: Would you like the clerk to read back my last question?

JUDGE SPENCE: Get serious.

COOKE: Yes, Your Honor. Now then, you say you don't care what you are called in this courtroom?

MCKENZIE: No, sir. I didn't say that exactly. . . .

COOKE: That as far as the amenities of civil intercourse are concerned, you are perfectly willing to throw yourself upon the discretion of the Court?

MCKENZIE: How did intercourse get into this?

JUDGE SPENCE: Order! This is my last warning to you people. And I include our Yankee visitors from the fourth estate.

COOKE: Very well. Please tell us in your own words, to the best of your recollection, what part you played in the actions and events of that fatal night in April.

MCKENZIE: I slept through most of it.

COOKE: You were asleep the whole time?

MCKENZIE: No, sir. I was sound asleep in the truck when the revival meeting started. But then I got waked up.

COOKE: What woke you up?

MCKENZIE: Not what. Who. He did, sir, that little old white boy over there.

COOKE: Let the record show that the witness has plainly indicated Penrose Weatherby. He woke you up. Why?

MCKENZIE: I don't rightly know, sir, unless it may be that he is just so naturally mean-natured that he wouldn't let a tired and wore-out colored man get any sleep.

COOKE: How did he wake you up?

MCKENZIE: Well, sir, you see, he took a kitchen match and put it in the sole of my shoe and then lit the far end of it.

COOKE: Is that what is popularly known as a hotfoot?

MCKENZIE: Some folks do call it that.

COOKE: After he gave you the hotfoot and you woke up, did he say anything to you?

MCKENZIE: Yes, sir, he did.

COOKE: Could you please tell us, to the best of your recollection, what he said to you?

MCKENZIE: When he stopped laughing about the hotfoot, he said something like "Hey, nigger! Goathead Papp is looking for you everywhere. He is as mad as hell and you better get your big black ass in high gear." That is exactly what he said. Or words to that effect.

COOKE: And did you say anything in reply?

MCKENZIE: No, sir, I did not. I was still about half asleep. I couldn't think of anything to say. I just jumped up and went looking for Mr. Papp.

COOKE: And did you find him?

MCKENZIE: Yes, sir, I sure did. He was by himself in the business trailer.

COOKE: And what was it he wanted you for?

MCKENZIE: I never did find out. Because, as quick as I came in the door—I was in a big hurry and I didn't bother to knock or anything—he jumped up from the desk he was sitting at and busted me right smack in the mouth. And then he pointed a pistol right at me and said he did not think he would kill me because I was not worth killing, anyway. And anyway, he said, this was not happening. He said I was still asleep in the back of the truck and dreaming all this.

COOKE: What happened next?

MCKENZIE: I just backed out of the business trailer real slow and easy with my eyes closed and making a snoring noise out of my nose.

COOKE: So he would think you really were asleep?

MCKENZIE: No, sir. So he will know that I got the message.

COOKE: You say that he jumped up and hit you in the face when you came into the trailer. What was he doing, what was he up to when you came in?

MCKENZIE: He was kind of hunched and hunkered down in front of the safe. And he was taking money out of the safe and putting it into a suitcase on the desk.

COOKE: Did that surprise you?

MCKENZIE: Sir, I have lived a good while. Nothing much surprises me any more.

COOKE: Very well, then. You say you backed out of the trailer with your eyes closed and making a snoring sound. Then what?

MCKENZIE: Somebody had removed the steps up to the trailer door. So I fell down and like to have busted my ass.

COOKE: Do you know who that somebody was?

MCKENZIE: No, sir, I do not. And far be it from me to point the finger of accusation at anyone . . .

COOKE: The finger of what?

MCKENZIE: Accusation.

COOKE: Go on.

MCKENZIE: I know this, though. After I fell down and then collected my wits and my senses, I heard what sounded a whole lot like that little old white boy, Penrose Weatherby, out there in the dark laughing at me.

COOKE: What did you do next?

MCKENZIE: Well, sir, I didn't mean any harm. But I figured that if I was going to get any sleep, I had better kind of scare him, or whoever it was, from tormenting me any further.

COOKE: And what did you do?

MCKENZIE: I picked up a couple of rocks, about the size of hen eggs or golf balls. And I chunked them out there in the dark where the laughing was coming from.

COOKE: And did this produce any result?

McKENZIE: The first one that I threw didn't. But after I threw the second one, I heard somebody out there holler out like he got caught by a pretty good lick.

COOKE: Then what?

McKENZIE: I went on back to the truck. I strung a little piece of wire across, with tin cans attached to it, so I could hear him coming if he tried to sneak up on me again. Then I rolled up in a blanket and went back to sleep.

COOKE: Before you fell asleep did you notice anything missing or rearranged?

McKENZIE: Not then, I didn't. But I did an hour or so later when the police arrived and woke me up. And the truth is, I didn't notice anything at that instant, right then, because of the misunderstanding.

COOKE: Misunderstanding?

McKENZIE: That's what it was. When the deputy climbed up on the truck, he must have tripped over the wire. Because what woke me up again was the cans rattling. And I had put—I forgot to mention—an old table leg where I could reach out and grab it. I did not mean to hurt anybody. I was just planning to use it to scare him, or whoever it might be, away.

COOKE: Of course.

McKENZIE: Well, sir, when I heard the cans rattle, I woke up quick and came up swinging that table leg. And more or less by accident I landed a pretty good lick upside the head of the deputy before I even knew he was one.

COOKE: And what did he do?

McKENZIE: Well, sir, naturally—and I don't blame him a bit, what else could he do?—he commenced to cuss me up one side and down the other. And he proceeded to drag me off the truck. And then he and the other one, the other deputy, began to beat on me pretty good with their billy clubs.

COOKE: Did you try to explain anything?

McKENZIE: No sir, I did not. I figured that I would try to

stay alive first and explain things later. I mean to say they were really laying into me. If I had been a tent peg, I would have been driven deep in the ground.

COOKE: Did you lose consciousness?

MCKENZIE: I went limp and played possum and hoped for the best.

COOKE: After this misunderstanding was finally cleared up, did you notice anything was missing?

MCKENZIE: Yes, sir, I did.

COOKE: And what would that be?

MCKENZIE: The crate that I keep the snakes in was gone.

COOKE: Did you find that same crate later on?

MCKENZIE: Yes, sir. Underneath of the window of the business trailer.

COOKE: Now, then, you have heard Penrose Weatherby testify that he stood upon a crate to watch and to observe what was going on inside the trailer.

MCKENZIE: That's what he said.

COOKE: Would you say that he stood on top of that crate?

MCKENZIE: I don't know what crate he stood on.

COOKE: Penrose Weatherby has testified under oath that he did not take a crate with snakes in it and that it was not he who released the snakes into the tent and tried to arouse them by fire, causing the tent to catch fire and that in turn causing the revival service to end abruptly and amidst some considerable confusion. What do you say to that?

MCKENZIE: The last thing in the world that I would ever want to do is to dispute the word of a little white gentleman like Penrose Weatherby. So let me say, and it is the God's truth, I do not know how that crate got out of the truck or how the snakes got loose in the tent. And, frankly, I don't believe it will do much good for me to speculate on things that I do not know and cannot know. If Penrose Weatherby says it was none of his doing, that's good enough for me.

COOKE: Thank you very much. Your witness, John.

Here and Now

POPULAR CULTURE:
MEMO FROM
ELEANOR LEALAND TO BILLY TONE

Dear Billy—

If you remember the sixties, you weren't there.

Here are some answers to some of your questions, about the best I can do with the materials at hand.

Maybe you think it's funny—I do, but, then I have an odd sense of humor—for me to be *writing* this to you in memo form. People don't usually send memos to the people they spend their nights and share a bed with. At least I believe that to be the case. How would I know for sure? Except for my own brief and unlucky marriage, I have never actually lived with a man before. That *is* what we are doing, isn't it, living together?

Anyway, it is easier just to write these things down than it would be to try to talk about them. We can talk later. And I confess that I hate to think of wasting the precious little time we have together with a whole lot of conversation about pop culture in the 1960s.

Also, to tell the truth, it's kind of fun to scout around the library and take some notes on all these things. It can be, fairly often, very quiet and very boring around here. There are (thank God) some people who still use the library regularly, and even more who use it some of the time. But it is awfully quiet. We try to attract more interest. We have all kinds of audiotapes and videotapes and computers and CDs for all those people who find the printed book to be too formidable to deal with or too irrelevant to matter. We have a lot of the first fruits of pop culture right here and now.

I have an idea, based on nothing more than imagination and pure speculation, that it was the 1960s, their peculiar context

and climate, that changed us from a place for storing and pre-
serving books to what we are now—"a learning resource center." God, the euphemisms of our own time are uniformly
repulsive, don't you think? I even have a few thoughts about
how this came to pass, but will save them for a bit later.

This has been fun for me in a way. A little jog down *your*
memory lane. Forgive me for mentioning it, especially since you
seem to be extremely sensitive about the difference in our ages,
but I was not quite three years old in 1968. Unless I am wrong
in my arithmetic, you were going on eighteen at that time. For
me there has been some sense of discovery; because even though
most of the cultural icons and artifacts of 1968, trash as well as
treasure, persistently, indeed relentlessly, continue to exist, and
not in an antiquarian sense either, even so, it is surprising to
contemplate a time when these things *began* and were new. Put
it another way. A child takes the world as it comes and is given
to him/her as utterly mysterious and yet always the same. *Item:*
I find it difficult to unlearn and to imagine a world in which
pop culture was not always at the very center of things. The
child in me, still active and demanding, assumes that the Beatles
were always with us from almost the beginning of time. First
the Big Bands, then Elvis and the Beatles. For you, though, they
date precisely from a particular time and maybe even recall a
particular place—*A Hard Day's Night* or maybe *The Ed Sullivan
Show*.

It's complicated. May I, to borrow from your usual habit,
resort to simple anecdote? A few weeks ago, not long before you
arrived here in Paradise Springs and first came calling at the
library, a bright young boy, a regular after-school browser, came
up to my desk, alive with the excitement of knowledge that he
just had to share.

"Miz Lealand," he said. "Did you know that Paul McCart-
ney was in another band before Wings?"

Weigh that, Billy guy. Above and beyond the sudden sense
of being old, old, old in a young world, it says something or
other about pop culture.

I am not sure how useful any of this may prove to be for your project, for the book you are trying to write, except, perhaps, to waken and to stimulate your own personal memories of the times. If that is what you want. Pop culture is, to be sure, a shared and common currency for those who were aware of it and experienced it at the time (or even subsequently, like myself). So in that sense it ought to be valuable in an allusive fashion to establish a rapport with the reader, most acutely with readers of roughly your own age and background. Your generation. But for all the other readers (if any), older and younger, these things may not mean quite the same thing and almost certainly will evoke a different set of personal memories and responses.

Which, I suppose, is why "generations," by which I really mean that peculiarly American distinction—*decades*—can be easily and casually distinguished from each other. Can even be set against each other. Can be manipulated as consuming units.

The latter comment will tip you off, Billy, as to where I come from and come down. Being a bookish person, a *librarian* for Lord's sake, I have to be suspicious of the ways in which things are defined and marketed to us, including the whole concept of the artificial distinction between decades (is there really, seriously, a generation X out there, unattached to all the rest?) Pop culture is designed and manufactured; then it is marketed and merchandised. Nothing spontaneous about it. It's a commodity, as poor old pale-faced Andy Warhol figured out all by himself. The truth said to be at the center of it all may not even be there.

Pop culture is mostly expendable, indeed *created* to be so, burns bright and hot and quick and then is gone. That is the whole business and essence of it. To be presented (like a fast-food meal), consumed and then . . . *eliminated*.

But, ironically, it doesn't really work out that way, does it? Because there is always a lot of connection and overlapping between the "real" generations. The language (slang) and the pop culture (local and regional) of my parents' time continue to exist in and through me whether I like it or not. And, of course, they in turn have picked up and discarded bits and pieces of the pop culture of my time as it may have affected me and impinged on them.

So, Billy, it is all much more complex than either the pedants and students of pop culture (and they are many, more and more all the time) and its purveyors can realize or would admit if they could.

And then there is a larger problem, another kind of complexity. Pop culture, at least throughout our own lifetime and maybe throughout this whole century, is created and reaches us *not* in response to any taste or demand on our part, but instead from what other people, people in the profitable, if risky, business of creating and disseminating pop culture come to think we *ought to* like and need. We only get to pick and choose from among the strictly limited choices they offer us. Thus any examination of the "taste" of a particular time in America in this century can only really tell us about the "taste" of the makers and purveyors of pop culture.

Then, too, and don't forget it, you really have to consider the character (and history) of any particular place in the larger scene. Paradise Springs, like a whole lot of other isolated, godforsaken little Southern towns of the time, urgently wanted *not* to feel so distantly parochial and provincial. Nobody here really wanted to be viewed (as, of course, they most certainly were) as a bunch of remote and unsophisticated hicks and primitives. Pop culture offered a quick and easy way to establish themselves as members in good standing of the vast herds and flocks of sadly hopeful consumers, nationwide.

God, I wish I were Susan Sontag or somebody like that so I could explain it all with brilliance and authority. Are you intimidated by her, too? I bet I am better and more fun in bed. What do you think?

Enough already.

Let's get to it.

TELEVISION: Keep in mind that locally we only had CBS in those days. It was possible to pick up NBC and ABC if you had all the latest equipment. Remember, this was before people had satellite dishes, etc. Now we have cable and pretty much everything. Also please bear in mind that the overwhelming majority of TV sets in Paradise Springs would still have been black-and-white in 1968.

Anyhoo . . .

Fourteen of the twenty-five top-rated TV shows in 1968 were CBS programs (in order of ratings): *The Andy Griffith Show; The Lucy Show; Gomer Pyle, U.S.M.C.; Gunsmoke; Family Affair; The Red Skelton Show; The Jackie Gleason Show; The Beverly Hillbillies; The Ed Sullivan Show; My Three Sons; Green Acres; The Smothers Brothers Comedy Hour; Gentle Ben;* and the *Thursday Night Movie.*

Imagine watching all that kind of stuff during the worldwide anarchy of 1968!

And who was paying for all this crapola?

The top TV advertiser of the year was Procter and Gamble. They coughed up $181,924,200 for commercials. Tobacco was still big-time and big bucks (though not for long): R. J. Reynolds, $57,092,000; American Tobacco, $52,703,500; Philip Morris, $36,474,600; British-American Tobacco, $30,603,000. The Marlboro Man commercial was one of the most popular ads on the air. And there were others, from the early sixties, that seem to have lasted and made as much impression on people as anything else, real or imaginary—Charley the Tuna (around since 1961); Colonel Sanders (hustling all the way from 1964 to 1980); Mr. Whipple of "Please don't squeeze the Charmin" fame; Gunilla Knutson saying "Take it off. Take it all off," in a Swedish accent, on behalf of Noxema; old Dinah Shore singing "See the U.S.A. in your Chevrolet." It may yet prove to have been a great age for the commercial.

Other commercials? Best I can do for you, at least for now, is a book—*Best TV and Radio Commercials,* edited by Wallace A. Ross (New York: Hastings House, 1968). The editor tells us

(p. 6): "A total of 1938 American television commercials, 589 radio, and 439 international cinema and television commercials were entered in the 1967 competition. Approximately ten percent of the 2966 total were selected as finalists and were awarded certificates." About the coming of color he tells us (p. 6): "Approximately 79% of the entries were produced in color, as opposed to 47% in 1966, 15% in 1964, and an expected 90% in 1968."

There is a professor over at Gainesville—Robinson, I think his name is—who dates all kinds of major changes in the American psyche from the advent of color in films and especially television. I heard him give a dazzling lecture about *The Night They Raided Minsky's*. Certainly it was happening fast in '68. He also says that the generation of the sixties, raised on the *Howdy Doody* show, with plenty of noise and violence, is almost completely different from the next group, who were brought up by gentle *Captain Kangaroo*. If you are interested, I can look up some of this stuff. And maybe he's still alive to talk to.

Ross tells us that the advertising industry was changing quickly at that time (p. 7): "To a great extent the look in commercials comes from a new breed of young creative minds—copywriters and art directors who detest the conventional, seek individuality and believe that advertising must reflect the environment and the times . . . not a gilded promise of utopia."

Think about that for a minute or a minute and a half, Billy Boy. The guys ("young creative minds") making the commercials seriously believing that their odd and expensive little art form should represent reality, "reflect the environment and the times." In short, commercials become (at least in the minds, if any, of their makers) a form of *reporting* just at the same moment that TV news programs, themselves firmly supported by a foundation of commercial advertising, become vehicles of advocacy, i.e., political and social commercials. No wonder people couldn't tell the difference. It was not just a matter of context, I would argue—the direct cut from the war in Vietnam to the problems of bad breath and body odor (savage surrealism) and back again. But at least the two elements, news and advertising, would seem to be much the same thing, equally believable or equally incredible.

As long as we are talking about television, here are the "sweethearts" of TV (on basis of ratings etc.) in 1968: Mary Tyler Moore, Judy Carne, Goldie Hawn; Sally Field in *The Flying Nun;* Marlo Thomas in *That Girl;* Eva Gabor in *Green Acres;* Elizabeth Montgomery in *Bewitched;* Barbara Eden in *I Dream of Jeannie;* and (ah yes!) Diana Rigg as Mrs. Emma Knight Peel in *The Avengers.* 1968 witnessed the beginning of *Laugh-In* (January 22nd) and the end of *Batman* (March 14th). Surely all you late-adolescent males were still missing Julie Newmar ("Catwoman," five feet ten inches tall, weighing in at 145 pounds and measuring 38-23-38, if you can believe official measurements) in early April.

But what can you *do* with all this in your book? You can, of course, find ways and means to list their names (or others), hoping to invoke the spirit of the time. Ideally you could have some sort of collage—a page of photographs or drawings of these perky women of the sixties. Even that, though, would not be fully allusive. You would need the sound and sense of them. I'm sure this could be accomplished if, instead of a book, your form for this creation were, say, a CD-ROM. No doubt the technology for it already exists. You could have your text interspersed with selected sights and sounds of the sixties. But what good will that do you? Will the story be more credible and accessible? I wonder.

Anyway. It isn't a CD-ROM or anything. Just words on the page.

You ask about movies. And therein lies a tale. You may or may not remember that we still had the drive-in, out on what was the edge of town, in those days. (Where the new Wal-Mart is now.) Double features, horror movies and what passed for B-grade flicks in those days. Most people didn't care what was playing at the drive-in. The whole thing was a lot more social than aesthetic. Or so they say. What was playing at the Moonlite

Drive-In Theater in the first days of April 1968? *Cool Hand Luke,* which had already played downtown in 1967, back by popular demand, I guess; *The Good, the Bad and the Ugly,* which was new. The Saturday night late show, a twin bill of horror flicks, one of which (according to my sources) has become a cult favorite (guess which one)—*The Horror at Party Beach* and *The Curse of the Living Corpse.* Downtown the *Paramount* was showing *The Graduate* some time after its initial appearance in 1967. The Rialto . . . well, now, the Rialto is a kind of special case.

Martin Pressy owned the Rialto then. Still does, as far as I know. It's the oldest of the theaters around here, the only one with a full stage and dressing rooms. Where they could do plays, honest-to-God theater, from time to time, and where they had vaudeville shows—they were on the regular circuit—during the Depression. As late as the sixties, after Pressy bought it and refurbished it and fixed things up to suit himself, they were doing concerts and stage shows of one kind or another there. They still use it, even now, for things like the annual Junior League musical show. Back then in 1968, Pressy had turned it into an art theater for foreign films (you could subscribe to a whole season) and for occasional stage shows. First week in April the film was, as you know, *Persona* by Ingmar Bergman. That weekend they were supposed to be featuring a mostly female rock group, a band called the Honeybees. The paper has an interview with the only two males in the group—identical twins just out of the Air Force, the bass guitar and the rhythm guitar/lead singer—written by your cousin Jojo. He used to do occasional pop culture pieces for the paper then. Did you know that? Anyway, he interviewed the twins who played with the Honeybees. Only thing I don't know, can't seem to find out, Billy, is whether they actually performed that weekend or not. After all that happened here and then the King murder and the wild weekend of burning and looting and rioting nationwide, they may have cancelled out. There weren't any real riots here. But who would leave the big show on television news to go downtown and listen to a little-known rock group?

More? The week *before* April the feature at the Paramount was *Planet of the Apes.* Pressy's Rialto was showing *Closely Watched Trains.* I bet Professor Katz went to that one.

POP MUSIC: Your best bet on this is probably Jojo. If he can and will remember. He was still working as a DJ then.

Here, for what it's worth, are some of the artists with albums on the pop charts between December 1967 and April 1968 (Kind of a lively time, if you ask me. Which you didn't): Herb Alpert, Ed Ames, the Beach Boys, the Beatles (*Sgt. Pepper's Lonely Hearts Club Band* and *Magical Mystery Tour*), the Bee Gees, James Brown, the Byrds, Glen Campbell, Petula Clark, Cream, Donovan, the Doors, Bob Dylan, the Four Tops, Aretha Franklin, Jimi Hendrix, Engelbert Humperdinck, Jefferson Airplane, the Lettermen, Claudine Longet, the Lovin' Spoonful, the Mamas and the Papas, Dean Martin, Sergio Mendes, the Mills Brothers, Smokey Robinson and the Miracles, the Monkees, Hugo Montenegro, Peter, Paul and Mary, Wilson Pickett, Elvis Presley (*Clambake*), Gary Puckett and the Union Gap, the Rascals, Otis Redding, the Righteous Brothers, the Rolling Stones, Simon and Garfunkel, Frank Sinatra (Nancy, too!), Sonny and Cher, Strawberry Alarm Clock, Barbara Streisand, the Supremes, the Temptations, the Turtles, Vanilla Fudge, Dionne Warwick, Andy Williams, the Mothers of Invention (Frank Zappa).

Of course the April cutoff date arbitrarily eliminates a whole lot of things that soon enough became part of the 1968 (and ever after) cultural context. Take Janis Joplin, now seen by everybody as the very *symbol* of the sixties and of that particular year. She would soon be a huge hit at the Newport Folk Festival that summer. And her album with the group Big Brother and the Holding Company, *Cheap Thrills,* was going to be a huge commercial success. The Stones had two big singles—"Jumpin' Jack Flash" and "Street Fighting Man." The Grateful Dead was bringing out their second album, *Anthem of the Sun.* The Doors had all kinds of hits, singles and the album *Waiting for the Sun,* that year. The Who had two albums—*The Who Sell Out* and *Magic Bus.* Bob Dylan was back on the scene with *John Wesley Harding.* Joan Baez had a couple of albums, got married and published a book (*Daybreak:* which we don't have in the library and never did). Joni Mitchell was just getting going on her own that year. . . .

It goes on and on, Billy.

Busy time, huh? Think of all that *stuff,* all those *people*—and remember these are only the best-sellers—coming out, filling the airwaves over a four-month period. Nationwide. Same stuff being played all over—in Moscow, Idaho, and Tallahassee, Florida, and Augusta, Maine. Linking (handcuffing?) the whole country together like it or not. Think of all the *money,* the millions upon millions of dollars, coming out of pockets and wallets and pocketbooks and checkbooks to pay and pay to keep this pop culture industry running, humming its synthetic tunes like a mass of electric prayer wheels turning and turning.

Do I sound a little bitter? Well, I am a librarian and we have to live on the dust and chaff of this glittering pop culture harvest. And if everyone who bought at least one record album in 1968 had also (at roughly the same price then) bought at least one hardcover book, *any* book, everything, the whole publishing and literary scene, would have been, would now be radically different. Still, I have to admit I am as guilty as the next one. In 1968 (or even now) if I had to choose between Updike's famous *Couples* and *Sgt. Pepper's Lonely Hearts Club Band,* it would sure enough be *arrivederci,* Updike.

Maybe you should listen to a whole lot of this music while you are writing your book. Maybe there ought to be a sound track for the book, all the golden oldies, just like *The Big Chill.* Maybe you should put together a tape cassette of your interviews.

So, what does all this add up to, Billy? What will you do with it? One thing that I can see much more clearly now than when I first started browsing around the old library for you is how much of this stuff has *lasted,* how much of it is still with us. It could be argued not by me, but somebody, maybe one of those supersmart, assertive, aggressive, abrasive New York women (are they more fun to be with, Billy?), that between television and the huge impact of pop music and pop culture in general there was no longer any place left for traditional culture in either its elite forms or its old-fashioned simple and folksy regional shapes; indeed no place for different regions anymore. No more North and South, except for differences in climate (and this modified by central heating and air-conditioning) and the inescapable facts of geography. Accents, dialects, idioms, all the differences and distinctions which serve to make us truly various (and, yes, *diverse*), are all but gone and were quietly disappearing then.

Did anybody in 1968 sense this and feel threatened? I wonder.

FASHION: Here I better warn you. Consider the source. As you may well have noticed, Billy Boy, except for my underwear (which did surprise you a little bit, didn't it?), I am not really with it. Why bother? My taste isn't to be trusted. Also, except once in a great while, in the Luxuria Beauty Parlor, I have never had much time for or interest in women's fashion magazines. Ask Moe Katz. He *cares.*

Nevertheless a few obvious observations about the 1960s scene. Skirts very tight and very short. Everything above the knees. Lots of stripes, vertical and horizontal, or bold geometric patterns. Shoes with buckles. Turtlenecks. Flouncy blouses. Wigs and hairpieces very big. But that's all "high fashion" stuff. What were the kids into? Headbands and flower garlands for their hair. Tights and ponchos. Leather jackets. Afros. False eyelashes. Buttons—smile buttons, political and social statement buttons ("Fellatio Is Fun!"), peace buttons. Beads. Hey, and don't forget high hippie fashion ("a touch of velvet, glimpse of satin in a smash of red, clash of blues, whispering voiles and brocades helter skelter everywhere, boleros, headdresses, trousers and capes." Thank you, *Vogue* magazine).

Who were some of the big-time models? Again, you better ask Moe Katz. And—here's another change in the American scene that was already beginning—models, that is, people who simply strike poses for photographs, were beginning to be taken seriously. At least in their public roles. Their "reality" was unknown and irrelevant. All that was "real" was the image. Soon, Billy Boy, everyone in the world would be a *model* of something. Everyone in the world would be striking poses. Jean Shrimpton, captured then forever as thin and pale and altogether beautiful, is now in fact a plump middle-aged British lady who owns a small hotel in Cornwall, according to a librarian friend of mine who has actually stayed there.

It is truly strange to think of these people and others from other worlds (Jackie, after all, married her Greek tycoon in fall of 1968) going about their secular, worldly business while Paradise Springs had a tent revival meeting and a double murder.

There's a change for you. Tent revival meetings. They were already rare, I think, by the 1960s, already old-fashioned. Something that had endured in rural America for a century or more. And like everything else, they never died out completely. There are still, I am told, a few, a very few, old-fashioned revivalists and traveling tent revival meetings. But television has taken over for them. Tent revivals have gone the way of the medicine show.

But, then and there, at the tag end of the 1960s, tag end (if you are right, and I'm not at all sure that you are) of the old South, there was one here in Paradise Springs, an old-fashioned tent revival that managed to attract a fairly large crowd of people on a certain Thursday evening in April. Strange. Truly strange, also, that a quarter of a century later I should be studying that time on behalf of someone who was there, anyway.

This may not be a whole lot of help. But don't you say that I never did anything for you.

Love,
Eleanor
XXX OOO

P.S. Sometimes you can get lucky. I was going through some old files, hidden away in a storeroom, when I found the enclosed document.

For the record, Miss Jane Eversoe, who prepared the document, was a legendary figure in our library. Maybe you even remember her—thin and straight as a broom handle, gray hair, mouth like a zipper, granny glasses, a caricature, a self-parody. The wicked witch in *The Wizard of Oz*. But she did her job.

I don't know how this happened to be saved all these years. Maybe because it was a capital case.

No sign of what may or may not have become of the books in question.

A CHECKLIST OF THE BOOKS TAKEN
AND IMPOUNDED BY THE SHERIFF'S OFFICE
FROM THE TRAILER OF WILLIAM PAPP
Prepared by Jane Eversoe, County Librarian

Allen, Casey. *New Concepts in Nude Photography*. South Brunswick, N.J.: A. S. Barnes and Co., 1966.

Basch, Peter. *Peter Basch's Guide to Figure Photography*. Text by Jack Rey. New York: Amphoto, 1961.

Dienes, Andre de. *Best Nudes*. London: The Bodley Head, 1962.

———. *The Glory of de Dienes Women*. Los Angeles: Elysium Inc., 1967.

———. *Natural Nudes*. New York: Amphoto, 1966.

———. *Nude Pattern*. London: The Bodley Head, 1966.

———. *Sun-Warmed Nudes*. Los Angeles: Elysium, Inc., 1965.

Haskins, Samuel. *Cowboy Kate and Other Stories*. New York: Crown, 1965.

———. *Five Girls*. New York: Crown, 1962.

————. *November Girl*. New York: Madison Square Press, 1967.

Henle, Fritz. *Fritz Henle's Figure Studies*. Introduction by Jacqueline Judge. New York: Bonanza Books, 1962.

Rawlings, John. *The Photographer and His Model*. New York: Viking, 1966.

Rittlinger, Herbert. *The Photographer and the Nude*. New York: Focal Press, 1961.

The Shameless Nude. [No author or editor listed.] Los Angeles: Elysium, 1963.

Tulchiz, Lewis. *Creative Figure Photography*. New York: A. S. Barnes, 1967.

————. *The Photography of Women*. New York. A. S. Barnes, 1964.

Wooley, A. L. *35 mm Nudes*. New York: Amphoto, 1966.

Yeager, Bunny. *Camera in Jamaica*. New York: A. S. Barnes, 1967.

————. *How I Photograph Myself*. New York: A. S. Barnes, 1964.

————. *How I Photograph Nudes*. New York: A. S. Barnes, 1963.

————. *100 Girls: New Concepts in Glamour Photography*. New York: A. S. Barnes, 1965.

Also miscellaneous copies of naughty magazines: *Cavalier, Evergreen Review, Playboy, Saga, Swank*, etc.

(Guess what Mr. Papp had on his *mind. What's on your mind, Billy?)*   *E . . .*

P.P.S. You want to know about soul music in 1968? Ask your cousin Jojo. You want to know about sex and skin in '68? Ask Moe Katz. If he hasn't forgotten about it, he can tell you a thing or two.   E L

P.P.S. (again). I just talked on the phone to Professor Katz
and he said not to forget about country music. True, there
wasn't any country station nearby. But chances are you could
get country music on a good radio, and there were plenty of
jukeboxes with country tunes to play. Katz says to remind
you that the Grand Ole Opry in Nashville had not yet moved
out to Opryland. That it was the time of Tammy Wynette (she
had several big hits; he isn't sure whether or not "Stand By
Your Man," that archetype, was released early or late in 1968)
and Johnny Cash. Cash had the only "outlaw" image. Willie
Nelson was not yet on the big scene. Katz says country music
was just about to explode into big time and big bucks. But
not quite yet. Unless you count Elvis as (partly anyway)
country.

Here and Now

MOE KATZ ADDS A FEW WORDS
ABOUT POP CULTURE

Do you realize that Kim Novak was still a sexpot in 1968?

Well, now. You know how I feel about the supermodels and
how I am also usually about fifteen minutes ahead of my time.
Maybe a little more than that here in Paradise Springs. Anyway,
looking at it retroactively, you can very quickly find out the
names that would have been considered worthy.

Of course, Twiggy was and always will be *numera una*. Nobody was ever more cheerfully skinny. At least in all of her pictures. And (see, Billy?) that was a thing that was happening in
the sixties that had not really happened like that before. The
distinctions between "image" and "reality" finally broke down.
All of a sudden there was no reality except in the image. In
movie terms, nothing existed outside of the frame. And every-

thing was two-dimensional. No core, hidden or visible. People became symbols of themselves and the "real" self was irrelevant. Many public figures became symbols not of any self at all, but instead of ideas, of positive and negative stereotypes. Bull Connor of Birmingham came to represent Instant Evil. Martin Luther King, Jr., was the walking and talking (oh my, he could *talk*) embodiment of Goodness. Just so with JFK and Tricky Dick. The press told us (still does as far as I know) that the 1960 presidential election was determined by the "five o'clock shadow" on Nixon's face. (Years later Don Johnson in *Miami Vice* would make stubble fashionable.) The quality of makeup could make all the difference. Even the candidates came to believe it. JFK's image was of youth and vigor and what they now call "family values." Yet he was in fact, it turns out, the most fragile and unhealthy President we have had since Woodrow Wilson *after* Wilson had suffered his stroke. And JFK was an inveterate, insatiable lecher. A wild womanizer. In his case, none of these things made any difference because the image was the "truth" and the facts were neither true nor false. Merely irrelevant details. Is not Bubba Bill Clinton in a similar situation? He is much loved and much hated. And in both cases it is his image that is loved and/or hated. Nobody is seriously interested (not even Clinton) in the hard facts of his life.

Lucky for him.

If I may add one more brief Katzian observation.

Ever since the sixties, celebrities and public figures (increasingly the same thing) have not, for the most part, been held responsible for anything. How can an *image,* true or false, assigned or earned, do good or commit evil? Tricky Dick had a legitimate beef when, after he had won the election overwhelmingly in '72, *The Washington Post* got on his case and kept on it until they ran him out of office. What did truth and falsehood have to do with anything? An image is neither true nor false. It simply is. And seen in that light, the Supreme Court decisions, beginning with *New York Times Co. v. Sullivan*, make impeccable good sense. *Pace* Anthony Lewis, last liberal leaf on the tree, it wasn't really about the First Amendment. It was simply the judicial acceptance of the fact that it is absolutely impossible to libel a public figure. *There is nobody there to libel.*

Anyway. Back to the present and the purest examples of the culture of the image—my wonderful models. About whose "reality" we know nothing and care even less. About whose beautiful images we are almost theological.

Well, Billy, here is how *Vogue* (incandescent, slick and shiny bible of the irredeemably ephemeral) described the face of the sixties: "Bony, pale-skinned, big-eyed, vulnerable, lacquered with a stony stare of arrogance."

But there are other images of the times: the cuddly, goofy, androgynous camp of Penelope Tree, her odd, perhaps perverse charm enhanced by the knowledge that she came from such a serious and prominent family; something of the same thing in the case of that beautiful image of utter emptiness, the original airhead, Marisa Berenson; and never to forget, not able to, the Lucky Tiger Jack-Off Queen, whose lithe, painted body danced in the daydreams of many more or less refined creatures of both genders and a variety of in-betweens—Verushka!

Add to this note the notion that we in Paradise Springs (or Nome, Alaska, or Arab, Alabama) were made aware of this. We could not escape from the impact of the culture of images even if we had wanted to. Only a hermit or a cloistered nun could have been free of at least most of it. And we cannot now escape from any of it. The only difference is that here and now some of us, at least some, have painfully learned how to live in and among these ghostly images.

And, Billy, pray also consider the depth of contempt that public figures and images share in their views of us. We are poor gullible fools! Miserable, ridiculous, utterly contemptible consumers of whatever it is they choose to sell to us.

Meanwhile, my lad, they constantly adjure us against cynicism. They warn us against allowing ourselves to become cynical as if it were the eighth deadly sin. And in one sense they are right to worry about it. Because to be a cynic implies that there is some standard of truth (however camouflaged and hidden) against which the validity and viability of images might be tried and tested. To believe that there is anything, any core, behind and within the superficial appearance of a given image is, de facto, a confession of folly.

I don't know. It may turn out to be a good thing after all. But no matter, good or bad, ruin or redemption, it's the world we have had to live in. At least ever since the sixties.

Then and There

PICTURES: THE SAWMILL

Under what appears to be a high tin-roofed shed, the shadowy space dominated by the huge circular saw blade, half a dozen men and boys, black and white, stand solemnly, awkwardly, looking at the camera. At least one of the boys is barefoot. The clothing of any one of them would have done well to outfit a scarecrow in an open field. A little to the right, in the open, sits a tall, straight-backed, bearded horseman, well mounted on a large and handsome riding horse. This man, wearing a dark suit and a broad-brimmed hat with a feather of some kind stuck in the hatband, is smiling brightly, whitely, not so much at the camera as at the invisible photographer. And with a complete sense of well-earned pride.

You do not need to be told, as the note affixed to the back of the print tells, that the sawmill with its high woodpiles and stacks of cut lumber belongs to him. Just as the half dozen men and boys work for him.

He is Henry Singletree (father of the late Judge), who in due course made a kind of fortune from the sawmill and from turpentine. Less than a generation earlier he would—indeed, he and others hereabouts may well have done so—have used slaves for these things. Later, before the century turns, he will for a time depend on convict labor until that practice is successfully challenged. For now, though, he has this small and serious group of men and boys who tote and fetch and dance in almost frantic attendance on the huge singing saw blade.

Sooner or later the barefooted boy will lose his right arm and thus his life to the blade. He has no vision of that now. Truth is, looking more closely you notice he alone among them is sly and somehow lively even as he stands rigidly like the others. It may be the mere ghost of a smile which, ghost or flesh, seems to tell you that he knows a thing or two, a hawk from a handsaw, and will not have to go barefoot for long. And (it tries to tell you) he will not be here forever, either, among these dumb others who are standing, patient and enigmatic as beasts in a barnyard. He has a plan of one kind or another. He knows that he has some talent or gift that will save him. It will not save him from the leap of the saw.

The foreman, name of Blaze (Darlene's great-grandfather), a large man, tall and stout in overalls and wearing boots, is farthest back from the camera. He is hatless, but wild-haired and bushy bearded. In the picture you cannot see his eyes. Can't see, either, the scars on his face from the wounds he took and survived at the battle of Lookout Mountain. When he was a boy no older than the doomed and barefooted one. Might have been barefoot then, himself, as were many of the young soldiers of the South then and there. He is a stern taskmaster and places not much weight or value in the expression of emotion. Which he calls womanly. But when the boy dies from the saw the foreman will weep like a woman for the loss of all that unspent life and unquenched hope.

For now, in this print of an old photograph made by an unremembered photographer, he stands guard over his little group, uncertain of everything except his own knowledge, skill, and courage and certain that all three of these virtues will be tested continually for as long as he may live.

The handsome man on the handsome horse will not weep

over the boy. Nevertheless, though he will never show it, he will be stricken with sorrow. For he, too, was once (and remembers it well) a barefoot boy, gifted and sly, aiming to do something more than merely to endure. The difference, he believes, is and has been luck. Nothing more and nothing less. He would have been happy to share his luck with the poor boy or anybody else. But it was never his to do with as he pleased. And his luck could leave him here and now or any time to come.

Here and Now

JOJO ROYLE, HIS VERSION

There is this story about Jojo. No. There are *stories*, a cloud of them, about old Jojo. Some true, some false, many unverifiable. He attracts stories as a magnet gathers together iron filings. Take an identified and certified hero. A hero with credentials. A rare being, after all, since most heroes, the authors of truly heroic actions, here and now or then and there or ever, are not named and known and believed in. Medals go to real heroes only accidentally; and, anyway, are given on behalf of all the unknown and unsung heroes. Take an identified and certified, much decorated hero like Jojo, and you will quickly discover that stories cling to his comings and goings like sandspurs and stickaburrs on your pants leg. Acts of extraordinary heroism may very well be true, the unadorned, unvarnished factual truth. But beyond that, the stories that come along afterwards are mostly understood to be a matter of myth. And the truth of myth is not only, if at all, factual.

This story is not, of course, circulated or confirmed by him, but is referred to by a number of people who choose to accept or confirm it. And it's something that sounds so much like Jojo in those days.

How a few days, three or four only, after D day, on a blustery afternoon with low cloud cover, a P-51 Mustang suddenly came

out of the clouds and made a low-level pass directly over Omaha
Beach. How an antiaircraft battery, under strict orders to fire on
any and all aircraft coming in below a thousand feet, opened up
on the Mustang and hit it.

Shuddering, smoking, the P-51 struggled to climb high
enough for the pilot to bail out. Which is exactly what happened. Pilot managed to bail out over the water (wind blew him
back to the beach) moments before the P-51 exploded in flame
in midair.

How the American pilot landed, safe and sound, on the
beach. Safe and sound and furious.

How this pilot was wearing a class A (dress) uniform and was
holding in one hand an unopened bottle of bourbon that he
had scavenged ("liberated") somewhere and had taken great
care to salvage even as he was desperately trying to save his life.

How now the pilot was absolutely furious not because they
had shot him down and damn near killed him while doing it,
but because he had a date with a beautiful Limey lady in London
and now he would have to miss it.

"All I had to do was to make one quick little pass over the
fuckin' beach and then head home," he told the gunners. "But
you sorry-ass guys had to go and shoot me down. You all ought
to be ashamed of yourselves."

But he cracked open the bourbon anyway, and they had a
little party before he found a ship to carry him back to England.

Well, it sure sounds like Jojo. So I like to believe it happened.

In the summer of 1940 Jojo was sixteen and looked a year
or two older than that. He was spending the summer with the
Singletrees in Paradise Springs and learning to fly a Piper Cub
out at the airfield. Before the summer was over, armed with a
false birth certificate, he ran away to Canada and joined the
RCAF. By 1943 he was flying the brand new Mustangs in
Squadron no. 414, the Sarnia Imperials. Short and wiry, Jojo
was just the right size for the cramped cockpit of the Mustang,
even though he had to stand up to taxi because of the high
angle of the nose. His first combat mission with the Canadians

was at Dieppe. Later on he transferred into the USAAF, flying the new and improved Merlin Mustang, with its elegant Rolls-Royce engine. He was with the 354th, escorting B-17s over Germany. Before the war was over and done with and before he was even old enough to vote (in those days), he was a much decorated ace, only a kill or two behind the greatest of the Mustang flyers like Dan Gentile and John Godfrey.

"I was lucky, very lucky," Jojo said later, safe at home. "But you know, I think I burned up, used up most of my luck over there, a lifetime's worth. I haven't had a lot of luck since then."

Not quite true.

The Judge's only son, Richard, was killed with the 82nd Airborne in Sicily. So when the war was over and Jojo came home, the Judge took him on as a kind of surrogate son. Found him jobs. Let him live in the old house anytime he wanted to even as he helped Jojo find a place of his own. And when he died, the Judge left Jojo the house, the radio station, and some pieces of real estate, including the little airport, and some money, too; though the bulk of the money went to Willie Gary.

All this Moe Katz tells me by way of preparation, in case I don't know it already. Biggest single problem for Jojo, Katz says, is that he has never had any formal education beyond his own experience. After the war, it soon became a world where you have to have a college degree to get any kind of a good job. Jojo had never even finished high school. Smart guy. Could have gone to school because he had plenty of GI Bill coming. But that never even occurred to him.

Katz says: "What you have got now is a seventy-year-old cousin with the mind and soul of a teenager. Which is why he was a great disc jockey without even trying. But something stopped or was anyway frozen in place in the war. Truth is, he is your classic walking-wounded case. Country is full of them from all of our wars. I expect there are a lot of them around. More than you could guess or imagine. If you are into the habit of images and symbols, then he is a man of and for his times."

Then there is the other thing, another kind of a wound.

Nothing would ever equal the excitement he had known. He came home a hero and has been one ever since. And has experienced nothing that matters as much. The rest of his life has been, *must* have been, tedious.

Jojo, hugely fat these days, obese really, an unlit cigar clenched in his teeth, himself barefooted and dressed in a stained and slightly ragged terry-cloth bathrobe, greets me at the door with a big warm bear hug.

Took your sweet time getting here, boy, he says. I thought you had gone and forgotten all about your family.

"I didn't want to bother you."

Sure. (Wave of hand to include the cluttered living room.) You can see how busy I am all the time. Well, come on in and let's have a drink.

He shouts something in the direction of the kitchen door. And in a moment it opens for a tall, skinny woman, early forties most likely, a country woman, a cracker, who could, a generation earlier, have stepped right out of a Dorothea Lange photograph. She brings bourbon and a dented, tarnished silver pitcher of branch water. A couple of Jefferson cups.

Fuckin' refrigerator is on the fritz again, he says. No ice. Ruins the taste of good whiskey anyway. Switch on some lights around here so we can see each other.

Then in afterthought: This here is my girlfriend, Emily.

She does not smile, but nods as she moves to turn on some lamps.

"I'm Billy Tone," I say.

She knows who you are. She keeps up with what happens around here. If anything happens, old Emily knows about it. Right?

"Right," she says softly.

In a moment she returns to the kitchen. She, this Emily, will be from the deep boonies where, oh, twenty or thirty years ago, the women kept to the kitchen even at mealtime.

Thanks, Jojo calls after her.

"You're very welcome," she says over her shoulder in a flat, soft voice.

In a moment I can hear faintly, vaguely, a radio playing country music in the kitchen. Jojo doesn't seem to notice. That explains his loud voice, too. Jojo is now about half deaf. That doesn't stop him from talking:

Lord, it's no fun getting old. But what the hell do you know, Billy? Nothing much. Not yet. Sure, you have probably slowed down a little. You probably have to watch your weight and maybe even take some medication to control your blood pressure and cholesterol level. And maybe you get depressed off and on. You may even take something for that. Lots of people do these days. You have occasional twinges of pain in the joints. And if you stay up late and drink too much, you end up with a bad hangover. You tire easier and you recover your energy more slowly. But, on the whole, you are still at home in your body and there are good times and bad. There is no reason to believe you won't be feeling better tomorrow or the next day than you are today. Maybe that's the big enormous difference between your state, not being young anymore, and mine—being old and getting older. You know all the time that things (yourself) are not going to get better. The best you can hope for is that they will get worse slowly. Nothing works right anymore. But I can still get it up once in a while and I do like the company of a woman. Over the years, I have tried all kinds. And nothing can beat a born and bred cracker girl. For fidelity, anyway. Better than having a hound dog around. Of course, you have got to watch yourself, watch your back a lot of the time. Because if you cheat on a cracker girl or do her any real harm, she will kill you for it.

Anyhow, Cousin Billy, let us raise a glass and drink to long life, good health and at least the hope of a little good loving.

Takes a deep swallow. Then: Are you fixing to marry that librarian?

"I'm too old for her, Jojo."

Perish the thought. Leave that judgment up to them. What happened to your first wife?

"Annie?"

Was there another one?

"Annie was basically a crazy. It took me a while, too long really, to figure that out. Now she's happily married. To her psychiatrist."

Well, she was a Yankee girl. But rich, Billy, very rich. Seems like a man could put up with a little run-of-the-mill insanity for the sake of some financial security.

"I've thought about it. I've wondered."

That's another difference as you get older. Money gets more and more important. Center stage. You know, when I was your age and younger, I wanted to know who was fucking whom, that kind of thing. Nowadays all I want to know is how much money somebody's got, and where and how did they get it.

Now that we finally have cable I watch a lot of television. I like sports and the cop shows. I like *Hard Copy* and *Oprah* (I *hate Geraldo!*) and C-Span. I watch VH1 and E! and A&E. My favorite commercial is the Energizer Bunny. I enjoyed the Swedish Bikini Team, but the Feminazis got rid of that one.

It's enough to keep an old guy, this one anyway, from any serious self-scrutiny. Which would be a sad process.

It also spares me having to listen to National Public Radio—all those hoarse-voiced, middle-aged, prissy women and all those prissy, faggy, smart-ass guys.

Ain't civilization just wonderful?

How the hell did we get along all those years without television? They sure took their sweet time inventing it.

Somebody else I like—Dennis Miller, the comedian.

You know what Emily wants—a satellite dish. Cable doesn't offer enough for her. And I expect maybe she's right.

It is the oldest house still standing in Paradise Springs, the main part, modified and added to, dating from just before the War. (Which is what a few people hereabouts, not without affectation, of course, call the Civil War or the War Between the

States, just as their grandparents did.) Like the Pressy house . . .
which was later, postwar, late 1870s. The Pressys were carpet-
baggers, Jojo will always say, even though they moved here from
Alabama. Like the Pressy house, the old Singletree place is surrounded by the town now. The driveway into the jungle of trees
and overgrown shrubs and bushes cuts between a filling station/
convenience store and a one-story walk-in medical clinic. The
house is almost concealed from view. Behind it, at a dusty distance, are the railroad tracks. Rumble and whistle of freight
trains and the Amtrak passenger trains headed for the Florida
Gold Coast. House could use some paint and repairs. The old
carriage barn is still more or less standing, but barely. Jojo has
a dead pickup and a lively Porsche stored there. I can live pretty
cheap and I don't even mind it, he says. But when it comes to
cars, I'm just like a nigger. I can't endure without a nice set of
wheels.

About now Jojo notices the soft sound of the radio from the
kitchen.

Shouts: Hey, Emily honey, turn that radio down, will you?
I can't hear myself think.

Then to me, more softly: There have been times, boy, when
I was so lonesome in this big old house that I played the radio
loud night and day just for the sound of human voices.

But you aren't here to talk about my problems and follies.
You're here to talk about the first week in April of 1968. And
why not? It was a lively and confusing time. Brought out the
best and worst in a lot of us.

Turn on your tape recorder and let's get down to it.

Edited Transcript of Conversation
and Interview with JOJO ROYLE

What I remember first of all is the morning and the interview
I did with the rock musicians down at the Rialto Theater. That
would be the morning of Thursday, April fourth, 1968. Not a
bad day at the beginning of it as I remember. Check the weather
report in the *Trumpet* for that day. Nice enough day as I recall

it, but I also recall I was (not unusual at all in those days) dealing with an almost terminal hangover.

Anyway, sometime around nine or nine-thirty I went into the Rialto, coffee mug (about half bourbon) in one hand and my clumsy old reel-to-reel recorder in the other, camera hanging from my neck. All ready to do whatever I could with this all-female rock-and-roll group, the Honeybees, that Pressy had booked in. They had a record out and around, I think, and looked to be right on the edge of breaking through, making it.

Funny, I never heard of the Honeybees again after that day. Disappeared, I reckon. Happens all the time. Then and now. The whole thing about American pop culture (maybe "high" culture, too, for all I know) is that there is such tremendous waste involved and created. Know what I mean? I don't know how many failures it takes to make one success, what the ratio is. But it's extravagant. A cruel mathematics working against a lot of talented people.

So. The Honeybees. A bunch of long-legged, big-haired, tough-talking girls with a dream of making it big like the Beatles or somebody. And my memory, from listening to them rehearse that morning, my memory is that they had put together a pretty nice sound. Outwardly angry, kind of premature punk. Inwardly kind of cute. Twenty years later they might have made a little splash like the Bangles or Heart. Who knows?

But what interested me most that morning was the two guys they had just hired on. They were just out of the Air Force—a few days before that, really. I think the lead singer, whose name escapes me if I ever knew it, was in love with one or both of these guys. I say both because they were identical twins and looked exactly alike in every way. Played different instruments—one was lead guitar, replacing some woman who had quit the band; the other played bass guitar. Or maybe (nobody but the two of them could tell the difference) they switched around on the instruments if they wanted to. Seems to me their name was Bush. Maybe Bash. I don't know.

They were a pair, though. Couple of characters. With their

close-cut, sidewall Air Force haircuts and still wearing their Air Force gray trousers and shiny black shoes. They could hit some good licks, too. Pretty good musicians for the time. Guitar playing was fixing to change forever in just a few months when Jimi Hendrix came on. But they didn't know that yet. Neither did I, though I ought to have. Working as a DJ for a black station, I would surely have heard something about Hendrix. But if I did, it didn't register.

Anyway, I was mostly an impulsive, shoot-from-the-hip journalist. (Goes without saying that was the character of my disc jockeying.) Minute I walked in and drank my potent coffee and heard them play a set, I had made up my mind to do something on these Bash brothers. *Identical twins join all-girl band.* I took some pictures of the band and the girls to keep them happy. And then interviewed the guys. Aiming to get double mileage out of it. A print piece, a feature, for the *Trumpet* and something for my evening show at the station.

They were a pretty funny pair, I remember that. Very scatological. And I wondered how to edit that and how much to use. The black man who owned WDFO—at least I *thought* he owned it at the time; I never dreamed that the Judge owned it and he was working for the Judge—this black man, Roy Pickens, the undertaker, was hopelessly bourgeois and proper. He was forever complaining about the kind of language I used on my show. I remember thinking that I might just run one of their full-strength scatological jokes and blow his mind. If he happened to hear it or hear about it.

We had a pretty good talk, all in all, and I invited them to come out to the airport in the morning and I would give them (one at a time) a ride in my Mustang.

I still had a '51 in those days and maintained it, too. Remember?

"Yes. You took me up a couple of times."

I thought so.

Anyway. Just at the end of the interview a very spooky thing happened. At least it turned out that way later. One of the twins said he had had a weird dream the night before. Said it was in some place like Washington. A lot of big white monumental buildings around, though in fact he didn't recognize any of them. Memorials to unknown Presidents and the like. He was in a great crowd of people, mostly if not all (he could not remember), *predominantly* a great crowd of white people. All these people were weeping. They were crying out loud. He wondered what they were crying about and if maybe he wasn't supposed to be crying too. Then he asked someone nearby what was going on.

"Don't you know? Martin Luther King is dead."

Next thing he—not King, but this guitar player—was standing high on a platform above this crowd, saying: "Free at last! Free at last! Thank God Almighty, I'm free at last!"

The kid could do a pretty good impersonation of King's voice and oratorical style. I remember that we all laughed. Except him. He seemed concerned.

"He's all right, isn't he? I mean, nothing has happened to King, has it?"

"As far as I know, he's just fine and dandy," I said.

"Yeah. Well, it was a strange dream."

I went over to the *Trumpet* and typed up my feature piece. Dudley liked it all right and ran it on Saturday.

I was doing my show, early evening, and playing the interview with the Bash brothers when the news came in about the murder of King in Memphis. Well. You will have heard what happened, what I did. You will know more than I do about it. Because I just lost it completely. I cut the music and started yelling and screaming on the air. The black engineer should have cut me off. But he didn't. Because I was a white man. And because maybe he knew who really owned the station. I don't know. But he called Pickens, and Pickens came flying down to the station and pulled the plug.

After that my memories are mostly fragments. I remember being out at the airport and seeing the lights all on and the Cessna that some stranger had landed there and nobody else around. I was going to take the Mustang up for a look at things. But I was so strung out I knew I couldn't do it.

Next thing I knew, I was in the emergency room. Where there was already a lot of excitement. A bunch of people with minor burns from the tent revival. When they got around to me, I couldn't make any sense, and they put me in the psychiatric ward for a few days.

When I got out and went home to the Judge's everything was fairly calm. Like nothing had happened. Only everything had happened and everything was different.

You know I keep thinking about what you're doing here and how things have been. I have a great nostalgia for the old days. Which I think of as the days of the Judge. He was a better man than we are, Billy. Maybe his whole generation was better. Paternalistic? Sure. Limited, too, by habits and prejudices and what they now call "mind-set." But they *believed in things*. Believed in the country and its future. Believed in the essential goodness and decency of . . . each other. They were willing to sacrifice for their beliefs. To give up. To do without. To be patient when they had to.

But if they were better men (women too), it's a better world now than even they could have imagined. In many ways. Of course, it's a whole lot worse in other ways—crime and coarseness, the absence of manners and amenities, the constant, unrelenting vulgarity of the culture and so forth and so on.

So my feelings are mixed, Billy Boy. Mixed up.

They were mixed and mixed up back then, too, that weekend in April of 1968. When the news of the murder of King came in, I had that screaming tantrum on the air. I lost my little job.

You know what I was thinking to do with myself? I mean, if you can call the rough and rudimentary workings of my mind *thinking*. I got it in my head to take my plane, the *Dead Mule Two*, and to sign on with the Carnival. Go with them. With the rides and games and sideshow freaks and over-the-hill stripteasers. I would take people for rides in my plane and be part of the Carnival.

I was serious about it. And first thing in the morning, I pulled myself together enough to go out there and try to talk to somebody. But there wasn't anybody. There wasn't anything left of them to prove they had been there except trash and the marks and places where their tents and booths had been.

The minute all the things happened over at Little David's revival, the carnies packed up and hauled ass in the night. And, as far as I know, nobody missed them much.

With them gone I had no alternative but to continue to drink myself crazy. Next thing I know I was in the hospital.

"Anything else?"

Well, one thing. While I was wandering around, before I took myself to the hospital, I would swear that I saw Verna Claxton. I would bet my life I saw her, but I wasn't a reliable witness. I mean, nobody would believe me, then or now. But there she was. Mad as a March hare but just as beautiful as ever. Her daddy was my friend. I always wondered if he had really killed himself or somebody else did it.

"You're not the only one."

I guess not. But it was a sad story. At least he didn't live long enough to have to deal with the new prayer books. That might have killed him anyway if nothing else did.

As for all the rest of it, I don't know any more than you do—probably not as much. I did go to some of the trial. But I don't know what came out of all that. Not truth, that's for sure. Not justice.

Sometimes I think—hey, I know it's not true, but sometimes I think it anyway—that Penrose is to blame for everything. But he was only a kid then. You know, he's been after me for a good while to sell him this place. And, of course, he really wants the airport. I'm not going to sell him either one unless I have to. One of these days (and I don't think it will be too long, either) this town's going to need a commercial field for commuter flights. And there it is—just waiting. Like I am.

Oh, yes. You wanted something else from me—some of the

stuff I was playing at the station about that time. Well, it's been a while, Billy Boy, and I sure as hell can't remember everything.

But I do remember we were playing stuff by Otis Redding ("Dock of the Bay," maybe) and Dionne Warwick. And James Brown and Aretha Franklin, Smokey Robinson and the Miracles. There was a "Best of" album by Wilson Pickett. The Supremes and the Temptations had a string of hits. And all kinds of stuff. I remember playing comedy, too. Stuff like Flip Wilson's *Cowboys and Colored People*. Sometimes some blues, old and new. It was fairly tame, even for that time. But it was the beginning of something. White people were beginning to see the potential of black Americans as yet another market, a new crowd of consumers. Maybe that's an improvement. Time will tell.

Meantime money is the great American equalizer. Not a bad place to be if you've got a little. A hard time if you're down and out.

And now, pouring out some more whiskey, Jojo seems to be done with the subject.

I seem to remember you have some children, Billy.

"Two. Annie got custody, but I still see them every once in a while."

That's good. Sometimes I wish I had children. And grandchildren. But then I always come to my senses. I would worry too much about the world they have to live in.

When I am ready to leave, Jojo asks me to stay a while longer.

Stay for supper, he says. We can send out for Chinese or maybe a pizza. I mean, we are just like everybody else. Hell, worst-case scenario: I can ask Emily to fry us up some chicken. She's not the world's greatest gourmet cook. But she can at least fry chicken. And that's a start.

At the door he puts his arm around my shoulders.

You want to know the craziest thing? I got a call the other day from Martin Pressy, old Missy Prissy. I don't know where he was calling from—Rome, Athens, maybe Prague. Anyway he tells me he is running around photographing fat people in the altogether. He's fixing to do a whole big book of nude fat people.

And you know what he said? He said he heard I had put on a lot of weight the last few years and would I consider posing for him. And, you know, he didn't mean any harm, not really. He really thinks I ought to be in his book. He said he would fly down and do the job right here if I wanted.

"What did you say?"

I told him to send me a round-trip, first-class ticket to wherever he is—London, Athens, Prague, East Timor—and I'll come to him. Which is a safe bet. Because Missy may be rich, but he's as tight as my old uniforms.

Then: Change your mind, *please*. Let's send out for Chinese.

I can't refuse him.

Late, late in the night (early morning, close to daylight in fact), remains of Chinese dinner spoiling and stinking on the cluttered coffee table, the bourbon down to its last finger or two, Emily having long since slipped off to bed somewhere in the old house, Jojo finds himself doing what he has almost never done in my presence—telling war stories. Nothing much about himself or what he may have done or what may have happened to him, though he is sometimes introduced as a witness or an observer to give an anecdote the weight of veracity. Most, as I recall (tape recorder having played out hours ago), being little *fabliaux*. Mostly funny, though sometimes involving death and disaster as inevitable consequences. Gallows humor, then. Laughter of the condemned. Chewing on ironies, some of them bitter, like a plug of chewing tobacco.

I must have, at some point, ventured some fatuous remarks about "the good war." Which amused him more than it angered him.

Which then somehow leads him to tell about the time in '44 when he was hit by flak while escorting B-17s over Germany:

Didn't know it at first though my ship—the *Dead Mule* I

named it, after that nigger honky-tonk right here in Paradise Springs—wasn't performing well. Something wrong, though. But I thought maybe I could make it back. Sure didn't want to bail out and get picked up by the Krauts. Managed, luck as much as anything else, to get the *Mule* back to Belgium before it gave out on me. I could bail out or maybe set down somewhere. There was a landing strip which had been a Kraut field. We had been briefed that it was probably in our hands now.

I thought I would take a chance on that and maybe save the old *Mule* at the same time.

Was losing altitude, coming down pretty quick, but found the field and had a chance for a look. What it looked like was there were a couple or three Kraut aircraft looking inoperable and some of ours, too, just parked by the runway.

Decided to try it. Got lucky and brought the *Mule* in more or less in one piece. Myself too. Came to rest in a field beyond the landing strip. *Mule* tipped up high but didn't go over. Not enough gas left to burn, so the biggest problem would be getting out and down unless somebody came and helped me.

Which they did. Some of our guys. Not real happy to see me or the *Mule,* either. More trouble for them. And one guy said (perfectly straight, like you would make small talk about the weather) he had been hoping I was dead or at least unconscious. So he could have my leather flight jacket. He had been wanting one. I said he could have mine if he paid me enough for it. But he didn't have the money.

There was the crew of a B-17 waiting at the field, too. They had bailed out a couple of miles away. One was wounded and one, the navigator I think, broke his leg in the jump. But the rest of them—me too—had nothing to do until somebody figured out how to get us back to our outfits.

We decided to take a walk into the nearest village, a fair-size town, really, and not much damaged or shot up. Full of folks celebrating and carrying on. They had been liberated a day or two earlier and been drunk and slaphappy ever since. They broke out wine and cognac and beer that they had stashed away and pretty soon we were as cockeyed drunk as they were. They shared their food—and they didn't have much.

I remember we were in this low-ceilinged basement place with big heavy tables and a lot of people crowding around. When we finally came out the daylight was beginning to fade and a chill was coming on. I was glad I hadn't sold my flight jacket.

About then we heard some noise—music was what it was supposed to be, a drum, a fife, and some kind of a brass horn toot-tooting like a hunting horn. And everybody came running to see what it was.

A kind of a parade. The three musicians, if you could call them that. Then a whole bunch of guys with pitchforks and axes, a few with hunting rifles and shotguns. What they had on display was a couple of German prisoners they had flushed out and caught somewhere in the neighborhood. These guys, the Krauts, were low-ranking soldiers and had been hiding out. Deserters probably. Probably planning to surrender to the rear-echelon Americans or the Limeys or whoever moved into the area now that the main line of resistance, the front, had moved east of there.

We aren't talking war criminals, Billy, just a couple of young guys of absolutely no importance who, as they say, ended up in the wrong place at the wrong time. For the sins of their country they paid a price. The Belgians had cut off their dicks and put them in their mouths and then sewed their lips together. A sight to behold!

Of course they were both in shock and probably didn't really know what was happening to them. Didn't have long to live anyway. But, sweet Jesus, that was a terrible thing to see. I didn't continue to see it. But I do remember it. Can't forget it. And I flash on it sometimes when people start talking about "the good war." War is no fuckin' good, boy. No such of a thing. . . .

Sure, worse things happened to people on both sides. And I saw worse things than that. But that one stays so clear.

Jojo finishes the last of the bourbon straight from the bottle, drops the bottle on the floor. Closes his eyes and settles more deeply into the armchair. In a moment he is snoring, deeply and steady as an old dog.

I tiptoe out into the new day.

Here and Now

JOJO ON THE SUBJECT
OF SOME OF THE OTHERS

ALPHA: She sure was a pretty little thing. In a boyish kind of a way. And at times there was something really radiant about her, an overflowing of inner light. Troubled? No question about that. But not, it seemed to me then and still does, troubled with the mundane problems and trivial concerns of most of us earthlings. Her troubles were purely and simply cosmic. Like those of Little David. Like Father Claxton.

Isn't that something else? The only three mystics in the history of Paradise Springs, and all of them wasted on the very same day.

I took Alpha for a spin once in the *Dead Mule*. My original and obvious goal with her was to fuck her. What else? Her androgyny and intensity were a challenge. This was, after all, the swinging sixties when everybody was busy fucking (or trying to) anybody else who would hold still long enough. Our idea of a mystic was Hugh Hefner. But anyway, when I saw all that childish excitement in her eyes and that unquenchable radiance while we were up there high above the earth, as if she had wings herself, and had been up there before, if only in dreams, I couldn't continue to think of her that way. She seemed to be a pure spirit. Aflame. Dangerous as wildfire, too. Something told me then and there to be afraid of her. And I was. And I was right.

DARLENE: My oh my. She was really and truly something else. A walking and talking wet dream. If they had ever had a Miss Wet Dream title, statewide or national, I believe she would have won it easily. She kept half of the peckers in Quincy County in a state of erection just in honor of the fact that she existed. And I'm willing to bet you that a whole lot of tired old guys can still get it up, standing tall, just remembering her.

Her biggest secret, her secret asset, was that she was not one bit stupid. Gifted with such a body, with such fabulous flesh and bones to inhabit, she didn't seem to need a mind to go with it. Mind was not required. So nobody ever really credited her with having one. In the long run this—being underrated—has proved to be a distinct advantage to her. She and Alpha were more than friends. They were more like a team.

PENROSE: Well, he is the man of the hour. Sometimes I find myself thinking that he is the man of the future, too. It's true (isn't it?) that we are rapidly turning into a nation and a people without any real and serious principles. A people without any core. Led, at the moment, by a President who suits us (we *deserve* him) perfectly. A man without a core or even a shadow.

Anyway. In our world Penrose is a kind of hero. A truly representative man. Mark my words, one of these days, one fine day, Penrose will rise up and run for political office. Governor or senator or something. And if there is any justice in the way things work out (which, thank you Jesus, there is not), he will run and win and we will get more of what we deserve.

W. E. GARY: A lot of people around here mistakenly assume that I must hate Willie for taking the bulk of the Judge's estate. And maybe I should at least envy him, but I don't. First because I made out just fine, thank you. I mean, the Judge didn't owe me a thing, nothing. And he did owe Willie Ed plenty. Seems to me that he has the legitimate claim. He became the dutiful and only son. I was blood kin, true (and so are you, Billy, like it or not). And the Judge always liked me and was generous to me. And generously left me more than I had any right to expect or hope for, more than I deserved.

Willie has gone on to great things around here. And he hasn't peaked yet. People—the ones who matter, anyway—like him and they like to see him succeed. It makes them feel better about the past.

As for him. You might wonder—I sometimes do—how deep and how painful his hidden resentments are. Frankly, I don't have a clue. But I'll tell you something else. I don't think he does, either. At least part of him is a mystery to himself.

And, of course, he has to be careful. Things are a lot better these days. But the race problem is far from over. It's just kind of well disguised now. So Willie can never know, not with any certainty, if—and if so, how much—he is really accepted. Maybe his children will and maybe not. But he won't.

Meantime I get a big kick thinking about the whole thing. How the very existence of Willie must drive old Penrose to distraction! Although you have to keep in mind that, Penrose being Penrose, he will sooner or later figure out a way to turn his own resentments and pains (maybe Willie's too) into profit.

Then and There

MLK PICTURE

A black-and-white photograph attributed to Bob Fitch. An airport waiting room, sterile, with rows of plastic chairs. In one chair, end of the first row of chairs, more or less center frame, is Martin Luther King, Jr. Eyes closed, head lowered as if asleep or, anyway, half-asleep. Right leg crossed over the left. Left hand lightly, almost idly, touching his left ankle. His right hand holds a burning cigarette.

Only photograph I have ever seen with King smoking. Did he (like JFK) smoke a lot, smoke all the time? But (like JFK) not, if possible, in any photographs.

I wonder what brand he smoked.

He is wearing a dark overcoat, unbuttoned, a single-breasted suit of a lighter shade, white shirt, dark tie, dark socks, and very shiny shoes (patent leather or spit shined?) with high and thick heels. Did he often wear heels and elevator shoes on public occasions?

Sitting nearby, the only other person in the frame, in another row of chairs set at right angles to King's left is a young and slender Andrew Young. Also in a white shirt with a dark tie, dark suit. His shoes (loafers?) are thin and scruffy, could use a shine.

What we have, then, is these two black preachers caught in the numbing and antiseptic glare of a public waiting room.

King (as noted) looks asleep or on the edge of sleep. Young looks pensive but alert. Aware of the photographer and whoever or whatever is outside the world of the frame. Young has removed his overcoat and laid it across a chair. King looks too tired to take the trouble. At this moment of overwhelming fatigue, hot and cold don't matter much.

The caption states that the waiting room is in Chicago (Midway? or O'Hare?). But it could be anywhere and anytime during the days of MLK's public mission. From 1957 when he returned from Montgomery to Atlanta to act as president of the newly formed Southern Christian Leadership Conference and as pastor of the Ebenezer Baptist Church until his sudden death in 1968, he was almost continually (except for a few vacations and a few very brief times behind bars) in motion. Giving speeches, attending conferences and seminars, leading demonstrations, preaching, fund-raising. Day after day passing through airports. The biographies carefully trace the astounding facts. For example, that in 1957, his first year in the whirlwind, he made more than two hundred speeches and logged thousands of miles. It was like that from first to last. Take the last half-month of his life. He was in Memphis, in Mississippi, New York, the Catskills, Memphis again, Atlanta, Washington, D.C., and, finally, Memphis.

What else do we know (are we told by the biographers)

about his travels? That he greatly feared flying in small, single-engine planes. That when (March 1957) he was a member of the American delegation to the independence ceremonies of Ghana, he was invited to the cockpit and allowed to sit briefly at the controls. That the plane from Atlanta to Memphis on April 3, 1968, was delayed at takeoff because of a bomb threat. That he was forever arriving, being met at airports and departing, a genuine celebrity in the fashion of the times, never altogether alone.

So. This picture is taken (and one of the few in which he seems wholly unaware of the camera) in the appropriate place.

The weariness is real and true, bone deep. He was tired for years.

The vanity—the elevator shoes, the well-cut clothes, the crisp white shirt—is real also. And had always been a part of his life and style. MLK had always been a natty dresser. In college his nickname was "Tweed."

The attentive—even anxious—Andrew Young is, up to a point, a chip off the old block, modeled on his master. MLK preferred his younger supporters to be well dressed, exemplary, in their public appearances with him. Except, of course, in some of the marches and demonstrations. Where most of them, like King himself, wore their blue jeans and gray workshirts like costumes or uniforms. Most of the young in the more rebellious organizations—SNCC, CORE, the Panthers—affected the proletarian style. Even his own Jesse Jackson refused to conform. On the next to last day of King's life, on the balcony at the Lorraine Motel, King and his old friend Ralph Abernathy are in coats and ties; Jesse stands in blue jeans, rolled up at the cuff, an unzipped windbreaker and what looks to be a striped T-shirt or sweater.

It appears from the biographies that King did not like Jesse Jackson very much or trust him either. Andrew Young, faithful and concerned, could (in MLK's view) be completely trusted.

MLK dozes in the photograph, a lit cigarette in his right hand. Confident that Young is on duty, on guard.

Then and There

BILLY PAPP'S VERSION

Now that it has all come out in the open, I want to put down exactly what happened as far as I was concerned. I am fixing to tell the truth, the whole truth, and nothing but the truth, no fooling and so help me God.

If I told any little white lies in court during the trial, it was only in order to protect others and because, being innocent, I did not realize the gravity of the situation. I did not have the slightest idea that I would end up behind bars like this. (I guess I am lucky that the Supreme Court has outlawed the *hot seat* or I would be in it, too.) I am a born optimist who believes that every cloud has got a silver lining.

That may be one reason why I am in the mess I'm in right now.

Look here, if I was even one-half as slick an operator as they say, I wouldn't be here. I would never have been working for Little David in the first place. There wasn't no money in it to speak of, not for me, except what I could arrange to pad onto expenses. He may well have been a very spiritual man. I wouldn't know about that. One thing for damn sure, though. That Little David had a pretty fair and accurate idea of the fluctuating value of a dollar. And when he felt like it, he could add and subtract like a machine.

I was a pure fool to ever fall in with him and the rest of that bunch. Now, don't that go a long way to prove my innocence?

I don't want to go so far as to pretend I am some kind of an angel or something. I have my faults. And I would like to take the opportunity right here and now to sincerely apologize for some of the things I said to the reporters after the jury brought in the verdict. I was in a state of complete shock and not responsible for what I was saying. I know that my trial was not a "joke" and a "frame-up." No man in his right mind would ever call the Honorable Judge Spence a "half-wit" or a "dirty old man." I am especially ashamed of referring to my attorney, Mr. John Rivers, Esq., as "a drunken bum who couldn't piss in a boot, let alone try a law case." He done the best he could, all things considered. Like I said, every cloud has got a silver lining, and now that I have come to my senses, I can see that my trial was a very worthwhile and educational experience. I have learned my lesson. And I am going to prove it, too, by sticking to the facts and telling exactly what I did and saw and heard. I am not going to put down any opinions and hearsay evidence.

Let's go back to the beginning.

I left Little David and the rest of them outside of Waycross, Georgia. Me and Geneva caught the Greyhound bus and came on down to Paradise Springs a week ahead of time. That's because it takes at least a week of careful planning and arranging to build up a proper interest in the show. It is a lot tougher than it used to be. Tent revival meetings have got all kinds of strenuous competition nowadays. Most people prefer to go to drive-in theaters or watch the tube or maybe go and soak up a few beers somewhere. So you gotta get their attention. What I usually do is hit a place early, slap up a whole lot of posters around town, get acquainted and get in good with the local Law and the merchants, meet folks, get around town and present the right kind of image. It's all part of the business.

The reason why I went almost every night to the White Turkey is that it is widely known to be the most high-class honky-tonk in the county, and you have got to go and be seen where the best people go. And that is the exact same reason that I would drop by and shoot a few games at the Paradise Springs Billiards Parlor. I wasn't shooting pool for the fun of it. Some got up in court and testified as to how I was a hustler. That is not so. I can shoot a pretty good game sometimes, but those people were just sore losers. You know the kind that I mean.

Usually when I'm advance man I work alone. But this time

Little David sent Geneva along with me, "to keep me honest," as he put it. I told him he didn't understand shit about the high cost of living and the inflation. He said he would send Geneva along then to see about all that. I replied that that was no way to reduce overhead. He answered me that it was an old saying that two can live as cheaply as one.

That was the reason that Geneva and me registered as man and wife in the motel—to save money. There wasn't nothing between us, no kind of hanky-panky. If I was fixing to shack up with somebody, Geneva would be the absolute last on my list. No offense intended to her. It's just that I don't even think of Geneva in that way. As for why we registered as "Mr. and Mrs. Hoss Cartwright," that was not for the purpose of fooling or deceiving anyone. Who would be fooled? We had both had a few cans of beer at the last rest stop before Paradise Springs and we were feeling pretty good. Besides, we had to make up *something* and put it on the register or it wouldn't look respectable.

Well . . . I was in town for one week. I put up the posters the first day. After that, I spent the daytime either keeping appointments downtown or shooting pool. And at night we would go out to the White Turkey and maybe have a few beers and mingle around.

Now, this here Penrose Weatherby, the little brother of the unfortunate dead girl, he testified that he knew me well from the poolroom. That may be so, but I did not know him from Adam. That is to say, he was just a skinny, pimply kid that was hanging around, the kind you send out to get you some cigarettes or coffee or something. I did not pay him no mind one way or the other. And I certainly did not know his name.

I was shocked and surprised when he showed up to testify in court.

And now, before going ahead with what happened on that fateful night, I would like to clear up once and for all any misunderstandings about my relationship with Miss Darlene Blaze. I would never say anything to hurt a young lady's precious reputation. I would die with my lips sealed if I thought it would do any good. But so much has already come out in public during the trial that the only decent thing for all concerned is for me to tell the truth.

Yes, we did become acquainted at the White Turkey. As it happened, Miss Blaze was without an escort at the time, her date, by the name of Buddy Joynes, to the best of my memory and recollection, having passed out cold in the parking lot where he had gone to take a pee. I happened to be nearby, myself, for the same purpose, when he fell out. She asked me would I help her put him in the back seat of his car so he could sleep it off for a while. And I gladly did so. After that, she thanked me and offered to buy me a beer, which is how we began to become acquainted.

When we came and sat down at the table, Geneva, who was feeling no pain at the time, started being a bad-mouth and a party poop. And this attitude of hers was preventing me from becoming decently acquainted with Miss Blaze. I did not know what Geneva might do or say next. I began to be worried about the public image of Little David Enterprises Inc. and what might transpire if there was a bad scene. And that is the one and only reason why I put a few drops of medicine—what the prosecutor insisted on calling a "Mickey," but what was actually a very mild sedative—into Geneva's beer while she was off in the ladies' room. Shortly thereafter when she had come back to our table and killed her beer, she said she felt a little dizzy and needed to get some fresh air. And that was the last we seen of her that night.

Miss Blaze observed me when I put the stuff in Geneva's beer, and she did not utter nor register any known form of disapproval.

I was not lying when I told Miss Blaze that I was in show business. I admit that I was exaggerating when I implied that I was a bona fide talent scout. However, my days working with the carnival taught me how to recognize and to appreciate real talent.

I offered her the audition sincerely and I honestly thought that she took the offer in the spirit which I intended.

So I was very surprised at what she said about this on the witness stand.

It went something like this:

MR. RIVERS: Now, then, Miss Blaze, how long did you and Mr. Papp remain at the White Turkey?

MISS BLAZE: Until they threw us out.

MR. RIVERS: Approximately what time was that?

MISS BLAZE: Shortly after two o'clock in the morning. They stop serving at two.

MR. RIVERS: And what did you do then, after, as you have said, they threw you out?

MISS BLAZE: I cannot recollect too clearly. I mean there I was and I had been drinking beer pretty steady since a little after five o'clock. I guess you could say that I was a little bit high.

MR. RIVERS: Do you mean drunk?

MISS BLAZE: I said high. I was staggering a little but I still knew who I was.

MR. RIVERS: Miss Blaze, have you ever heard of the Hitching Post Motel?

MISS BLAZE: Yes, sir.

MR. RIVERS: At that point, even if you were, as you say, "high," did you feel that you were acquainted with Mr. Papp?

MISS BLAZE: More or less . . .

MR. RIVERS: Which is it—more or less?

MR. EDWARD COOKE: Your Honor, Mr. Rivers is justly proud of his Ivy League education and the fact that he received his law degree from fair Harvard . . .

MR. RIVERS: Wait just a minute!

MR. COOKE: But I must object to his trying to flex his expensive educational muscles for the sole purpose of browbeating this good and simple country girl. And I must object.

MR. RIVERS: And I object to counsel's insinuation that I am . . .

JUDGE SPENCE: Gentlemen!

MR. COOKE: I worked my way through college.

JUDGE SPENCE: Shut up, Ed, will you please? Mr. Rivers, you may proceed with your cross-examination. But please frame your questions with more clarity.

MR. RIVERS: Thank you, Your Honor. Let's see . . .

MR. COOKE: You were just getting to the good part, John. They were on the way to the motel.

JUDGE SPENCE: Order! Order in the court.

MR. RIVERS: Miss Blaze, isn't it a fact that, upon leaving the White Turkey, you and Mr. Papp did go directly to the Hitching Post Motel and that you did then proceed to spend the night with him in his motel room?

MISS BLAZE: No, sir.

MR. RIVERS: Are you denying it?

MISS BLAZE: Well, not exactly. Not all of it. Actually, see, we did not go into his motel room. He suggested that, but I refused to do so.

MR. RIVERS: I caution you that you are under a solemn oath.

MISS BLAZE: Oh, well, you probably know all about it or you wouldn't be asking anyway. It's the truth though. I refused to enter the room that he had already bought and paid for and was living in. I insisted that Mr. Papp rent another room and he did so. We picked room 113 because 13 is my lucky number.

MR. RIVERS: Why did you go into a motel room with Mr. Papp?

MISS BLAZE: He was planning to give me an audition.

JUDGE SPENCE: Order in the court!

MISS BLAZE: He stated to me that he could help me get to the top in show business. I stated to him that I had already had a bellyful of that when I was the singer with the band at the Mickey Mouse Club before it was closed down for liquor law violations. And he stated to me that he was not talking about anything small-time like that, or words to that effect.

MR. RIVERS: Did you honestly believe that Mr. Papp

intended to hold an authentic audition in room number 113 of the Hitching Post Motel?

MISS BLAZE: I had my doubts.

MR. RIVERS: But you went with him anyway.

MISS BLAZE: I didn't have anything else to do at the time.

MR. RIVERS: And did Mr. Papp actually give you an audition?

MISS BLAZE: Well, we got inside and he stated to me that it was probably a little too late for a singing audition and that it would be a shame to wake up the neighbors. So we discussed the situation awhile. Then he suggested that I could do, like, a hootchy-kootchy dance.

MR. RIVERS: A hootchy-kootchy dance?

MR. COOKE: They don't teach that at Harvard.

JUDGE SPENCE: Shut up, Ed.

MR. RIVERS: Will you, please, tell us what you mean. Explain it for the members of the jury and the others, excepting of course, counsel for the prosecution, who may not be familiar with the term.

MR. COOKE: Objection!

JUDGE SPENCE: Listen, you two. This is a first-degree murder trial. And I would appreciate it if you would try and be serious, at least in the courtroom. You hear?

(Counsels nod affirmatively.)

JUDGE SPENCE: You may answer, Miss Blaze.

MISS BLAZE: I forgot the question.

JUDGE SPENCE: He wants you to tell what a hootchy-kootchy dance is.

MISS BLAZE: You know, it's just that you kind of shake and dance around a little without too many clothes on.

MR. RIVERS: Would you call that a legitimate audition of your talent for show business?

MISS BLAZE: Well, sir, some girls can do it and some can't.

MR. RIVERS: Did you execute this performance to music?

MISS BLAZE: It was too late for the radio or the TV, so Mr. Papp, he put some cellophane over his pocket comb and hummed a tune through it.

MR. COOKE: Ask her the name of the tune, John.

JUDGE SPENCE: One more time, Ed, one more smart-ass remark, Ed, and I'll have to hold you in contempt.

MR. RIVERS: May I continue, Your Honor?

JUDGE SPENCE: Suit yourself.

MR. RIVERS: Well, then, after this so-called audition, why didn't you get dressed and go home?

MISS BLAZE: I figured as long as I had gone that far I might as well spend the night.

MR. RIVERS: Did you and Mr. Papp sleep together?

MISS BLAZE: There was only the one big double bed. And I wasn't about to sleep on the floor for no man.

Etc., etc., etc.

Miss Darlene Blaze made me look pretty bad in the courtroom. And everybody had some good laughs at my expense.

Mr. Rivers cleverly trapped her into admitting that she accepted a gratuity of money from me the following morning. But she even turned that around so as to prejudice my case.

He asked her if she realized that by accepting the money from me she was behaving like a common prostitute.

"Well, I am *not* a prostitute," she said. "And I have never done anything common in my whole life."

"But you asked him for money. Why?"

"I hardly knew Mr. Papp. He was new around here, a stranger in town, and I wanted to impress upon him that he couldn't take liberties with local girls just for the fun of it."

"So you were thinking of his own good and the good of the community?"

"That is correct, sir. That is exactly what I had in mind."

Well, anyway, that morning at the Hitching Post was the last time I saw Miss Blaze until the night of the revival, when she suddenly showed up knocking on the door of my trailer.

It is true that I phoned her up a few times, but that was only common courtesy.

Now, then, we get to the night the murders actually took place.

Here is exactly what happened as far as I witnessed it.

We had a very big crowd show up. I had hired three off-duty sheriff's deputies to handle the traffic and the parking and in case of any rough stuff. And also because the sheriff himself had suggested it was the right thing to do. Even before the service began I paid them off, in cash and with a bonus, not so that they would leave early, but just in case they had any reason to.

I was feeling good because I could tell we were going to get a big collection. I would be up half the night counting the money. But I do not mind losing a little sleep under those circumstances.

I started to go off to my trailer, planning to settle down with a pint of vodka and an art book until the service was over.

About my art books that were seized by the police and entered in evidence against me: I have got no apologies. I am a lover of art and beauty. And I will tell you what I told the sheriff at the time: "If *Bunny Yeager's ABC of Figure Photography* isn't art, I will kiss your ass."

Anyway, I am on the way to the trailer when I run into this kid, that Penrose Weatherby, who is waiting for me. He says he has come all the way out here under false pretenses. He wants me to give him some money because there aren't going to be any snakes like is advertised on the poster. I explain to him patiently that it is against the law in this state to play with snakes. He states to me that if I don't give him some money quick, he's going to find a cop and claim I was trying to "molest" him.

This Penrose is some bad kid when he wants to be.

"Aren't you even a Christian, kid?"

"Don't give me that crap," he replied. "I walked all the way out here just to see the snakes you advertised."

I took a good look around. It was dark and nobody was near us. Now, I wanted to be fair to the kid. But, at the same time, I knew he needed to learn a lesson or two before he got himself into real trouble.

"Well, son, I guess you have got a point," I said, fishing in my pocket.

The greedy little runt came right up close to me with his hand out and a grin all over his face. All I did was reach out and wipe that grin off with the back of my free hand. But he fell down and rolled in the dirt and commenced hollering and carrying on. Naturally, I was concerned. If somebody came along, there could easily be a misunderstanding.

So I gave him a quarter to shut him up.

"It was an accident," I said. "I didn't mean to hit you a hard lick like that."

"Don't flatter yourself," he said. "My sister hits harder than you do."

And then he took off in the dark before I had a chance to grab him and get the quarter back.

Later, when the collection was all in, I took the money from the tent over to David's trailer. Then it occurred to me that with such a big collection—the most we had gotten in months—there might be some danger of robbery. And that is the reason I took the whole safe over to my trailer. I figured it would be safer there.

And that was the only reason I had a loaded gun with me.

About the nigger . . .

Raphael has been with us for quite a while. But I would be lying if I did not admit that he can get on my nerves. When we work with a nigger crowd or else an integrated congregation, we can use him as a valuable part of the program. He has some education and he can preach if he has to. Other times, such as in Paradise Springs, he just hangs around and helps us with the equipment.

As it happens, he is supposed to keep an eye on the big crate containing the snakes.

I do not have any prejudice at all. A nigger is as good as a white man as far as I'm concerned. But I did not get along personally with Raphael. He was paid too much money, more than he deserved, because of all the things he *could* do, including to preach in a pinch. I may not have a whole lot of education in school to speak of, but I could have preached all right, too, if they had ever given me half a chance. The one time I got called upon was on short notice, and that was a bad and rowdy bunch of rednecks. They were there looking for trouble and I don't think they would have listened to the Lord Himself. Nevertheless, David blamed me for the damages to the chairs and lights and tent, and he took it out of my so-called salary too.

Personally I just couldn't get along with Raphael. I will admit it was kind of silly for me to call him Rastus all the time. I would call him Mr. Rastus Coon, trying to provoke him so I would have a good excuse to whip his black ass. But that guy is some slick operator, very cool. He would keep on smiling and just ignore me. He tried to get back at me in little ways he knew would aggravate me. Like wearing those Bermuda shorts and kneesocks and a pith helmet. The very sight of him strutting around in those Bermuda shorts and that pith helmet would outrage any man. It was like he *wanted* to make me have a racial prejudice.

To top it off, sometimes he smoked with this long cigarette holder.

Well, there I was in the trailer, my trailer. I had the safe wide open and the gun in plain sight. And I was transferring the money from the safe into my suitcase because I figured that if anybody tried to rob us they might not think to look there. And *wham-bam!* in comes Rastus Coon without knocking or anything.

It was my honest impression that he thought I was trying to rob the money and that he was planning to be cut in for a share. Which is why—and the only reason—I pointed my pistol at him and urged him to get the hell out of there. I had no intention of shooting anyone, not even him. But knowing that they scare easy, I thought it would save a whole lot of useless conversation.

Which it did. Because he turned around and took off running like a big-ass bird.

Well, I had just about finished up transferring the money to the safety of my suitcase when in came Miss Darlene Blaze. She seemed to be all upset about something. The best I could make of what she told me was that her best friend (who later turned out to be the unfortunate Alpha Weatherby) had lost her mind in the excitement of the revival. And she had given away a lot of money that she shouldn't have, that wasn't hers.

Miss Blaze said she would do most anything to get it back.

I suggested that we could meet over at the Hitching Post later on that night and discuss the situation.

She said that would be all right with her.

I gave her a drink out of my pint and we talked a few minutes. I was only kidding with her, sort of *testing* so to speak, when I suggested that she should carry my suitcase over to the Hitching Post, for luggage, and wait for me there. A lot has been made of this suggestion on my part. But I wanted to see if Miss Blaze was really serious about her friend. I did not think that Miss Blaze would become involved in any way in what even *looked like* a crime unless she was serious and her friend was in real trouble.

But my best point was never even raised in court. Suppose, let's just pretend, I really planned on taking that money. Do you think I would have really trusted anyone to keep the suitcase for me?

There was still plenty of time before the end of the service, so I suggested to her that as long as she didn't have anything else to do, maybe she could do me another little dance like the last time.

She said she didn't have but about five minutes because she had to get back and look after her friend.

I said that five minutes was fine. I turned on the transistor radio so she could have some real music to move to this time.

"I don't know why I bother to get dressed at all," she said, jumping out of her dress and shoes and starting to dance around.

Well, with the radio playing and the air conditioner going and me concentrating on Miss Blaze's dancing, I wasn't paying any attention to what might be going on outside of the trailer. Next (and first) thing I know, Geneva Lasoeur comes barging into the trailer.

She takes one look at Miss Blaze and makes a wisecrack about the hot weather and ways to beat the heat.

I make some sarcasm like what did she think my trailer was—a public bus station? But Geneva wasn't interested in arguments.

"Give me your gun, quick!" she said.

"Anything wrong?"

"Let's see," she said. "The snakes got loose in the tent and the tent is on fire and David has gone crazy and is fixing to kill somebody if they don't kill him first. That's all."

And Geneva was gone.

Miss Blaze had grabbed up her clothes and vanished.

I ran after Geneva to help her, trying to do my duty in the emergency.

I do not know why I had the radio with me. I do not even remember that. I must have just grabbed it to have something in my hand.

People were running around, rushing hither and yon, yelling at each other. I was delayed getting through the crowd and the smoke. By the time I got to David's trailer Geneva was already in there and the other two were laying on the floor deader than a couple of catfish. Geneva handed me the gun back.

Then the police busted in and they didn't give anybody a chance to explain anything.

"Turn off that radio, you son of a bitch!" they told me. "You're under arrest."

Now, of course I realize that Miss Blaze sat upon the witness stand and denied outright that she ever did any kind of a dance, even a quick one, in my trailer that night. And I realize there is no real proof that she was ever there. Except my word of honor. I don't want to contradict a lady. I try and be a gentleman and I wouldn't even mention these details if a lot didn't depend on it.

About the money . . . All I know is that it was all there, safe in my suitcase, when I left the trailer. So somebody had to take it. It wasn't me and it couldn't have been Geneva or Miss Blaze. She was out there in the dark somewhere trying to get dressed. If she had been running around in the crowd in her red underwear, she would probably have been seen and noticed by somebody.

That leaves only one other person, one person who *knew* about the money. Yes, sir, that leaves you-know-who, Mr. Rastus Coon. And I have got more than just idle suspicions. For one thing, there is the matter of the dime. A normal human being would take all of the money or, if they was in a hurry, they would probably leave some bills and change scattered around. But Rastus Coon would leave one dime behind in the suitcase for a joke.

He is a very mean one and smart, too. Remember how he acted at the trial? He showed up wearing bib overalls. And he never wore overalls before that time in his whole life. And all that "yassuh" and "nosuh." Pully-woolly and "I reckon this ole shine don't rightly recollect."

The jury loved him. They actually took his word against mine.

Whoever wants to find that missing money will have to find Mr. Rastus Coon first. Just go to someplace like Paris, France, and look for a nigger in Bermuda shorts and kneesocks, wearing a pith helmet and carrying a long cigarette holder. He is probably there right this minute, drinking champagne and high-price wine, screwing white women and laughing his head off.

He better laugh while he can. Because as soon as I get things straightened out, I am coming after him. And I'll find him, too, wherever he is.

I only hope he hasn't spent it all already. But you know how they are about money—here today and gone tomorrow.

Here and Now

THE POET:

NOTES ON THE LIFE AND TIMES OF MLK

• Born in Atlanta 15 January 1929. Killed in Memphis 4 April 1968.

• Child of the Great Depression. All his childhood and youth spent, played out against that grim background. Depression and World War II.

• But in many ways, much more than most people, he was secure and sheltered in the storm. He, who would in all due time, soon enough, make history himself, was spared the worst of his times at the beginning. Safe and comfortable in that very fine (in fact elegant for the place and the times) two-story, twelve-room, gray-and-white house at 501 Auburn Avenue. They would move to a bigger and better house in 1941. His father, like his maternal grandfather before them, was safe, too, in reliable respectability as the pastor of the very large and popular Ebenezer Baptist Church. The whole family was busily engaged and involved in the life of the Church. MLK singing solos at an early age while his grandmother played the organ.

• True enough, it was not possible for him to be spared *all* of the routine indignities and humiliations that accompanied being black in that place and in those times. But no question or doubt that he was at least spared the routine indignities and humiliations of being poor. While most people in the South and the nation, white and black, were poor by any kind of standard or measurement. He had not only hopes and goals (rare enough) but every expectation of achieving them.

• The various and sundry biographers (except those for children) do not come up with much in the way of drama or trauma during his childhood and youth. Insofar as children and adolescents can be happy at all, he must be said to have enjoyed a happy and uneventful childhood. Atlanta's Negro middle class was much like the white middle class in blackface. A kind of a minstrel show maybe, but nevertheless sharing most of the same values. More like each other than like the aggrieved and suffering poor. And for that reason, among others, MLK must have been potentially more sensitive to insult and injury and injustice than the vast majority who took these things for granted and could not allow themselves to imagine the world to be any different or better than it seemed to be. MLK more vulnerable, then. Yet already, as his birthright, granted the power not to be seriously hurt. Living, growing up with a strong sense of safety and respectability and potential, perhaps (why not?) a strong, unchallenged sense of his own superiority. Certainly never, early or late, good times or bad, was MLK the victim of an inadequate or diminished self-esteem.

• But the truth is—and his biographers have to accept this and do—that his story does not really even begin until he and Coretta are settled in at his first church—the Dexter Avenue Baptist Church in Montgomery. Story begins then and there in 1954 and continues until 1968. A short time, almost all of it in the spotlight.

• Begins in earnest in early December of 1955 (a little more than a year since he was officially "installed" at Dexter Avenue) with the arrest of NAACP secretary Rosa Parks on a city bus for refusal to give up her seat. A few days later the bus boycott begins. And as the youngest (twenty-six) and newest preacher on the scene, MLK finds himself nominated (by his new friend Ralph Abernathy) and then quickly elected president of the newly formed Montgomery Improvement Association. The risks, including the risk of complete failure, were high at the outset. Did the older and wiser preachers and black community leaders choose him out of fear for themselves? Was MLK the potential (and classic) *fall guy*? Probably. Most likely. At least that was a large part of their general thinking. Let young MLK be highly visible and up-front and let's just see what happens.

Then two things happen, neither really imaginable to MLK

and the others involved. First (not easily but implacably) the boycott succeeds. A clear-cut victory. Second, MLK almost instantly becomes, for many reasons, the darling of the press, a worthy and admirable hero whose basic message of nonviolence and love suits the needs and assuages the fears of the white establishment. Encouraged, rewarded, supported. By February 18, 1957, he was on the cover of *Time*. By August he and others had founded the Southern Christian Leadership Conference.

• Point of fact, then. From the moment he was chosen to be the leader of the Montgomery boycott until the very instant of his violent death, he was a public man. There are private sides of his public life, but there is no private life separate or distinct from the public life.

• Not a new story there. What is new and special about MLK's public life is something a long time coming but, even so, surprising in its abrupt arrival—how a public life in our time is made or unmade, created or destroyed, by the press. MLK early on sees that he and his cause (causes, plural, as it goes along) stand or fall by and through the public perception. Which may or may not, at any given moment, coincide with any "reality." MLK seems to have sensed from the beginning, uneasily to be sure, that in public life all gestures are symbolic; that whether something is true or false matters far less than how it is taken to be.

• From the beginning to the end you have MLK asking first and foremost how the press is treating his story. How stunned he must have been (what could it *mean?*) to find himself, so quickly following the successful boycott in Montgomery, first a national figure, then, soon after, an international person, one who was presumed to possess powers commensurate with his prestige. Someone who was believed and believed in. Supported. Near the end when the March 28th (1968) march in Memphis went bad, ended in violence, looting, a death and many injuries, many arrests, his first thought and concern was how it would be viewed by the press. Rightly so. For this time the coverage was almost wholly negative.

• There is a generational thing at work here. Remember that former President Harry Truman (when asked) called the famous march from Selma to Montgomery (March 21–25, 1965) a "publicity stunt." By which he meant that it served no more purpose than publicity. By which he meant to say that it was not "real," not "really true." By which he meant to express moral contempt for all those who trade in symbolic acts and gestures. But Truman was from the last generation of American public figures to make a distinction between appearance and reality and to favor the latter. By MLK's time (and he was one of the first to realize the magic of this, even before JFK discovered it for himself) the distinction was already without meaning. The next generation of American public figures has by consensus agreed that there is no "reality" separate from "appearance" and that the latter can be altered, transformed, edited, colored, camouflaged, concealed, revealed by what is now crudely called the "media" to take and to fit any protean shape at all. Orwell knew it in 1948 ("Freedom is slavery"). Victories can be defeats and vice versa. Whole wars in the late twentieth century are symbolic gestures, publicity stunts in which real blood is shed and real lives are lost in an otherwise meaningless context. No, *not* meaningless. It can mean anything and everything. Only the (real) lives and (real) blood are meaningless.

• In a sense, seriously, the murder of MLK was a symbolic gesture, a publicity stunt. The murderer—James Earl Ray or whoever else it may someday turn out to have been—had no personal enmity, knew next to nothing (except what he read in the papers, saw and heard on TV) about MLK, most likely couldn't care less about the private life, if any, of MLK. MLK was killed for whatever he had come to symbolize to the murderer. Or, more likely, simply because he *was* a symbol, a public figure. How can you take life away from a symbol? MLK bled and died and was buried. But as symbol he has risen from the dead. With a switch and a button his image and rich memorable voice can be summoned up, seen and heard as if alive, at least in his public speeches in public places.

• Consider his funeral. He considered it, planned it long in advance. Asked for a humble mule and wagon to carry his body home to earth. A mule and a wagon, only symbols, a symbol of and from a life he had never known (nor anyone in his family for three full generations) except in imagination. Nevertheless how apt. As for "reality," he might as well have asked for a Viking burial in a flaming ship.

• Because, by the end, the private life and the private man were without meaning or "reality"; nobody took his private sins and problems seriously. In that sense LBJ and J. Edgar and the FBI (good name for a punk rock band—"J. Edgar and the FBI"?) were a full generation out of touch. Tape recordings of MLK's bedroom exploits and conversations could not hurt him or even be used as blackmail against him, because, for all practical purposes, the private man did not exist. Only the public man could be injured and certainly not by and for any private behavior.

• Do you doubt me? Take a look at old Bubba Bill. He knows the score.

• MLK was a master, then, of the art of the public life and the symbolic gesture, from the days in Montgomery to those final few days in Memphis. Point of fact, that can be taken as his whole life, the dozen or so years between those two cities. Thus the photographic book, called "a documentary," *Martin Luther King, Jr.: Montgomery to Memphis* (Norton, 1976) makes good sense. It is a life of fluttering images like a magician's shuffled deck of cards. Constant (if not perpetual) motion: hundreds of speeches and meetings, fund-raising, sermons at his (again in 1960) Atlanta church, and a staggering number of demonstrations, marches and campaigns: Montgomery, Washington, Atlanta, Albany (Georgia), St. Augustine, Birmingham, Selma, Chicago, Memphis. Speaking and writing and witnessing. In and out of courthouses, in and out of jails. Win some and lose some. Sooner or later meeting with each President—Eisenhower, Kennedy, Johnson. Heads of state. An audience in Rome with the Pope. Not even the gifted and lucky child could have dreamed these things. A fairy tale all the sweeter for its constant danger.

• How can all this be appropriately dealt with in the context of fiction? It seems to me obviously false and misleading to try to invent a private life for a public figure who (well before the end) had none. Seems to me that MLK, or some fictional surrogate, no matter, can only be known and seen as that mysterious, ghostly being, the public figure. Mysterious maybe because a public figure is not only a person without a private life, but also a being without a core. A shadow who can cast no shadow. (Cf. President Bill. Coreless.)

• How can MLK (or any other ghostly public figure) be known and defined, then? And by whom? By the people, the characters, real or imaginary, who at least have dimensions, all around him. For or against him. Lesser heroes and villains. Even the murderer. Maybe especially the murderer. Who can create a character for MLK by whatever he takes MLK to be.

• An odd thing. MLK is, finally, deeply mysterious to us. But the murderer (no matter who it was), about whom we really know not much, maybe not even wanting to know very much, the murderer is not such a mystery to us in this murderous age. Easy to picture. Easy to imagine. Easy to understand (What is there to understand?). Easy enough—and don't bother denying it—to identify with.

• Begin with the shooting, from the killer's point of view, as planned. Send the killer away in flight and then flash back to the beginning of the Memphis troubles. The hot day of the first disastrous march. MLK not wanting to be there in the first place. Urgently busy trying to plan and organize his latest and most ambitious march on Washington—the Poor People's Campaign. Which is scheduled for April 22nd. MLK's mind and thoughts are elsewhere. Has let himself be talked into a gesture. An ordinary march to show solidarity with the striking sanitation workers. Arrival (late) from New York at the airport, accompanied by Ralph Abernathy. Chaotic beginning of the march. Riot begins. King and Abernathy flee to the Holiday Inn. Watch events on television. Is that ironic or what?

• From there we will move inexorably toward April 4th. Final scene (for MLK, anyway; I may cut back to the killer for the ending) to be on the windy, rainy night (tornado warnings) in Memphis. When he made his final "Mountaintop" speech at Mason Temple. MLK had not planned or wanted to go. Had other plans (personal, social) for his evening at the Lorraine. Sent Abernathy in his place. Abernathy calls and pleads with MLK to get dressed and to come and speak at the temple. Big crowd there. (They had feared the weather would keep the crowd embarrassingly small.) Major press coverage. (In his new distrustful mood MLK had feared the press would make much of a small turnout.)

• MLK agrees and goes. Gives his talk, sweat shining on his round face. We have it all on video. Because of what will happen on the next day that talk now has a valedictory tone, seems shadowed with premonition. In fact, Abernathy and Young and the others (was Jesse Jackson there at the Mason Temple? Check that) have heard it all before more than one time. It's a quilt of snippets. A chamber of echoes of many other speeches. Boilerplate. Yet, maybe for that reason, more profoundly moving than it might have been. In that sense much like the famous March on Washington speech. Where MLK was not able in fact to deliver the speech he had labored over and so was forced to fall back on tried and true, familiar fragments.

• How appropriate (symbolic?) for a contemporary public man. That his last public words, those words which retain the power to move a listener to tears to this day, should have been uttered out of a great weariness and out of habit, not thought or even the awareness of any inspiration. Though surely the breath of God blew through him that night whether he knew it or not.

Here and Now

CHANGE

W. E. GARY

Well, of course, for me the great change—already well under
way by 1968, but still a problem at the time—is the end of *de
jure,* outward and visible segregation. To put it simply, my life,
such as it is, would not have been possible, not even as an imag-
inative paradigm, a generation earlier. A generation later it is
hard to remember how things were. In my sunnier moods I
think I am feeling the subtle, tectonic shifting of inward and
spiritual things. For the better. Other days and I think that
maybe the only real change is the removal of signs and symbols—the "Colored" drinking fountains, the "Whites Only"
rest room.

Even so, my world (like yours, too, Billy Tone) is not as
narrow as all that. The only person I know of (oh, there must
be plenty of others, but I don't happen to know them well
enough to judge and say), the only person I know whose life
and vision are almost totally dominated by the facts of color and
race is old Jack Weatherby. Maybe his son, too; but if so, he
hides that along with everything else. Penrose is, after all, a
prime candidate for the Florida Tomb of the Heroic Real Estate
Developer. Meanwhile he is whatever he has to be to buy and
sell.

Anyway. Good changes and bad changes. The look of things
and the feel of things have changed a lot in my lifetime. By the
end of the sixties a lot of these changes were well under way,
but they are clearer, easier to see now.

One big change is what you are doing right now. You are
running around this town soliciting and accumulating opinions.
And here I am, holding still long enough to express some of
mine. The stereotypical journalistic stance of give-and-take. I

don't think that back then we could have done this. Don't think we would have. Nobody was really interested in our opinions about anything. What's more—and here's a point I would really like to make—I don't think we really had any opinions on a whole lot of subjects that were outside of our personal and local concerns, that were fairly remote from the quotidian facts of our lives. The year 1968 was one of the big years of protest about the Vietnam War. But the truth is, I think, no, I really *believe* that most people in the country didn't know where they stood on that subject. The protestors were being taken very seriously, not precisely because of their numbers and power and influence (though, at this late stage, I tend to believe they at least influenced the North Vietnamese to keep the war going), but because they actually held an opinion. The others, all the rest of us, didn't realize that we had the right, that we were entitled to an opinion about a lot of things we didn't know anything about.

In any case, that has all changed now. You can go ask anybody in Paradise Springs their opinions about almost anything—Bosnia, Rwanda, health care, sexual harassment, gun control, AIDS, abortion, you name it—and they will have and express an opinion, sometimes even a passionate one, untroubled by whether they happen to know anything about the subject or not. They will have a strong opinion on, say, Bosnia, even if they can't find it on a map.

If you follow the drift of my argument, I'm saying that in this new world, where so much has changed and everything is perceived as changing, we have a wealth of opinions where we used to have very few. But I'm not sure they matter very much, if at all. Partly this is because everything has become politicized. You end up making a political statement, like it or not, with everything you say and do and . . . think. So, all pollsters to the contrary, it has become impossible to know if an opinion or an idea is serious or just a reflexive tic.

All of which means, I'm afraid, that we are at the mercy of the *opinion-makers*.

Nevertheless everyone thinks he is entitled to an opinion and entitled to be listened to.

PENROSE WEATHERBY

Well, if lawyer Gary believes that, he is full of bull. I think he knows it, too. He was just dodging your question. Making smoke.

It's a tough question any way you look at it. Because so much has changed around here—and everywhere else. So much is changing right here and now even as we talk about it.

But if you asked me (and you just did) what the biggest single change in the life and times of these parts—I mean Paradise Springs and Quincy County and even the state of Florida—I would have to say *mobility*.

By which I mean the ease and the freedom of people, the American people, to move and to live wherever they please. Sure, they wouldn't have come here, halfway between the coasts, if we didn't have the goddamn sandflies and the mosquitoes more or less under control and if we didn't have air-conditioning. But nothing would have changed for the better around here without mobility. Like a lot of little towns, coast-to-coast nationally, we would have just dried up and died out as all the young people wandered off to the big cities. A lot of our youngsters still go off to try to make it in the cities. We lose a lot of them. A lot of them come back, too, as soon as they grow up enough to figure out that they have been fooled and that, anyway, the life-style here is better and a lot easier.

About the only person from Paradise Springs to make it big in New York City is Martin Pressy ("Missy Prissy" we used to call him even before he turned out to be gay). He's had plenty of success with his photography. But it wouldn't make any difference, anyway, because Pressy has a shitpot of money ever since his mother died. Talk about mobility—he could live anywhere he wanted to in the whole world. You can bet he won't wind up in Paradise Springs. Practically *gave* his house away. But

I don't want to bad-mouth him. He still contributes a lot to local charity and we owe him a lot.

Meantime, though, we have all these new people coming in from all over the country. Looking for the sun and for a slower, gentler pace, and, yes, sir, for some personal safety. We are especially attractive around here because things are cheaper than on the east coast or the west coast. Less crowded, too. And, anyway, they can live here and go to and from either coast whenever they feel like it.

Not to mention the people coming from all over the world. Along with every other kind of ethnic American you can think of, we have some Cambodians and Vietnamese and Koreans (not many, thank God, but some) and they are hardworking people and fit in pretty well. We also have a few Cubans and South Americans, a spillover from south Florida. Just enough of these folks to add a little spice to our lives. Not enough to create problems. Yet.

So the local Crackers, people like myself with deep roots in the community, still basically run things. The old Florida families, ones like your people, the Singletrees and the Royles, are still around, but kind of out of the real action now. They really didn't want to deal with change. The way things were suited them fine. And why not?

Mobility changed all that. Change came on four wheels, rolling down an interstate highway. And people like yours truly welcomed it and embraced the future. We did a lot with a little. And we could do more, too, if the goddamn pinko environmentalists would just get off of our backs!

JACK WEATHERBY

If Penrose believes all that, he is in for a big surprise. In his pretty picture you'll notice he doesn't mention a couple of things—drugs and the Jews. Ever since we've had the flow of drugs—*that's* something that began in the sixties and has just got steadily worse—and now especially with crack cocaine, we have had serious crime even in nice places like little old Paradise

Springs. There looks to be no end to it. Not in sight, anyway. Not as long as people like that Janet Reno make our policy. Hell, she's from south Florida. I wouldn't be surprised if she was in the drug business herself. Partners with Ron Brown and Mike Espey and that woman Elders *(Where do you suppose her son got the drugs he was selling in the first place?)*, with Big Bubba himself, taking a fat cut right off the top.

Hey, don't get me started! There is a drugs and Whitewater connection as sure as God made green apples.

As for the Jews. Well, I've got nothing against them personally. We've always had a few Jews around here. Some of them were my good friends growing up. But now we have plenty of them. Too many. They started coming in force soon after World War II. (Which they either dodged or served in rear-echelon outfits like Quartermaster Corps, counting socks and shirts while other people got their asses shot off. Same thing in Korea, and, I'll bet you, in Vietnam.)

Anyway, they commenced to come down here after the war killed off the Depression. Which was a sure sign that things were going to get better, economically at least. They come buzzing like flies wherever the honey pot is at. Now we have got a big temple and a rabbi and a whole community of them—doctors and lawyers and entrepreneurs. And everything is all copacetic. Except that bit by bit they have got a piece of everything that is worth anything around here. They are pretty secure and sure of themselves. They are already fussing and carrying on about the Christmas scene we have always put up in the park by the courthouse. And they raised holy hell about the prayers we used to have at the high school football games.

Oh, they are here all right and likely to stay. In a way that's a good sign. When they pack up and leave a place, it's done for.

But I'll tell you one thing. Penrose, he better be careful. He thinks he can run with them and at least be equal if not outsmart them. He may be in for a rude awakening. One of these days they will pick him clean. He will be as poor as Job's turkey. And I would laugh, too, if it didn't directly affect my own well-being.

The only group that Penrose hasn't had to come to terms with so far is the towel-headed A-rabs. And that's only because they haven't stumbled on Paradise Springs yet. But they will, and soon enough. They are already buying up stuff and wheeling and dealing in Georgia and South Carolina. It's only a matter of time. The Japs, too, they are bound to come. Penrose better watch his back, cover his ass.

Here I am rooting for Penrose, wishing him the very best, out of the urgent hope that I can die quietly and comfortably in my own house and not some stinking nursing home. Like poor old Dave Prince. Know what I mean?

LLOYD MACINTYRE

That's a sloppy question. Best it can do for you is to get somebody to talking. But in that sense it probably works for you. When there are all these major changes, no one thing can stand by itself. It's a lot more complicated than that. Nevertheless people have ideas and will try to answer you. And so will I.

The really extraordinary thing to an outsider, somebody like myself, is the retirement population. All these retired people, geriatrics, coming to live and die here. It really changes everything. Brings in all kinds of money and at the same time creates all kinds of new and different jobs. I read a study which estimates that it takes four or five new jobs in the service area just to take care of the needs of each old-timer.

But it changes everything else, too—medicine, law, public safety and, above all, politics. These old folks vote and are a powerful block. More so, I think, than a lot of politicians realize or will admit.

Of course, the whole country, indeed the developed world, has an older population. But this is a special situation with all these elders coming like pilgrims to live here and live out the last part of their lives. It's bound to change the character of the place drastically.

Or will it? They come here because they like it. They may become the biggest conservative force to keep it the way they found it and like it. That's a typical contemporary dilemma, wouldn't you say? They come because of the climate and certain qualities they admire and desire. But their act of coming is the greatest force for change. Kind of like the Heisenberg principle. Do I have that right? Anyway, it is changing right before our eyes.

Look. Even though it was an early and committed part of the Confederacy, and suffered on account of that during the War and Reconstruction, Florida was never truly part of the South or even, originally, of the nation. Was Tory, fought for the British during the Revolution. Was Spanish (for the second time) after that. Was a raw frontier place until the early years of this century.

What I'm trying to say is that we never really belonged. And with this large geriatric population we still don't and won't.

Where all this is going, I don't have a clue and neither does anybody else as far as I can determine. But you better believe it's causing changes in everything. It's destroying the old identity of the region. But at the same time it's creating a new regional culture—a culture of and for the old. Didn't Jonathan Swift write something about that?

MOE KATZ

A lovely dumb question, Billy Boy.

You probably expect me to come up with something aesthetic. How, thanks to the miracle of television, thanks to all these new high-tech, electronic links to the larger culture (Public Radio and videos and CDs and computers and E-mail and fax machines) we are at last able to share in the national, even the international culture. Almost as immediately as anyone else. And only at the expense of our own particular and peculiar culture—of which there wasn't much, if any, anyway. Now I can sit in my grungy trailer and be almost as up-to-date as most of the people in New York City. Maybe more so, in a way. Because while they are busily working away at fabricating the culture, working at it for a living, that is, I am busily consuming it, and

I have more time and leisure to consider it, to think about it, than they do. If I want to. I can turn it all off with a button or a switch any time. In a serious way that makes me more powerful, more *free,* anyway, than they are. Because they can't stop cranking it out whether I'm paying attention or not.

I could make a good case, my lad. But I won't. And I'll tell you why. Everything I was just talking about is just engineering. Consumer engineering, to be sure. It's changing all the time. Tape and CDs replace the old vinyl LPs, just as vinyl replaced the old 78 records which in turn replaced piano rolls and so forth. And new things are on the drawing board. But, don't you see, those are just *things,* ephemeral things. The essential thing is and was there—the sound of music and human voices. We have technically developed new ways to hear and appreciate them. But even if we are hearing them better, what we are hearing is essentially the same.

No. What I want to think about is something else. Food.

When I first came down here in the early sixties, they still served a salad with sliced fruit and little marshmallows. You couldn't get a glass of decent wine this side of Jacksonville. Garlic was something you used in a necklace around your dog's neck to keep off the fleas. Except for the Baptist Barbecue, you couldn't buy anything really interesting to eat in the whole county. If you happened to be a good hunter or maybe a patient and adroit fisherman (and I would never claim to be either one) you could furnish your own dining room table with some very good things—quail and dove and duck, wild turkey, venison, black bass, catfish, mullet, shrimp and crab, crayfish and so forth. Makes me salivate like a Pavlovian dog just naming them.

But let's face it, the food for most everybody was bland and boring. People who could, people like Martin Pressy, went away as much to get something good to eat as anything else.

Now then, Billy. Take yourself down to the malls and check out our supermarkets. All the usual chains. I'm not talking health foods and not little gourmet places (we have a couple) with fancy coffee beans and herbal teas and little cheeses from all over the world. I'm talking your standard supermarket with looming aisles and piped music and electronic checkout counters. Plain vanilla. Purely American.

Take a good look at what we have there, day after day, the spoils of the nation, of the world. We've got Irish and English and Dutch and German beer. *Somebody* is buying it. We have French wines and Italian and Alsatian and Australian. *Somebody* is drinking it. We have goat cheese and grape leaves from Greece and ginger beer from Britain. We have everything.

Walk down the meat counter, as long as a city block, and just consider all the kinds and cuts and the high quality of it all. Sure, your basic snobs (I sometimes count myself among them) complain that all this stuff *looks* a lot better than it really is. Maybe so. But not all that long ago there wasn't much choice. Lamb chops were few and far between.

And produce. Linger there and study the lettuce and the tomatoes, the fruit, the vegetables. Squeeze a little. Look at the herbs and spices they offer up in sure and certain trust that they will be bought and used in local cooking.

Listen. Nero in all his power and glory never had anything like this. It would stagger him. It would stun a world-class trencherman like Henry the Eighth.

You want to see the change? The triumph of the American empire. Go look at the photographs from the thirties and forties—Walker Evans, Dorothea Lange, Margaret Bourke-White. The American proletariat and the poor are gaunt, thin as shadows. Now the same people, their children, anyway, the proles, the poor, even the homeless, are fat, fat, fat. It's a different kind of misery from a different kind of diet. It's the rich who are gaunt these days. They can afford the luxury of eating right and the leisure of keeping fit.

Our whole underclass is like a middleweight fighter—Jake LaMotta or Roberto Duran, say—who quits and suddenly doesn't have to make the weight anymore. Who has been hungry for a long time.

So. You asked me. I'll tell you. The greatest change has been food—supermarkets and fat people. Tomorrow ask me again and I'll tell you something else.

SHERIFF DALE LEWIS

I'm not even going to try to answer that question. Because it is too obvious and really doesn't mean anything. Any answer would be equally inadequate and incomplete.

You look at Florida, even this backwater part of the state, you look at it for a generation, for a decade, for a year or a season, and what you see is change. Everything changing all the time. New people, new faces, even new flora and fauna down in south Florida around Miami. New plants and animals (and probably viruses) from South America, Africa, India.

If you look at Florida it's changing right before your eyes. Like time-lapse photography of corn growing. In that sense maybe it's just an exaggerated version of the whole country. The United States busily (and without regrets) reinventing itself every decade at the least.

Anyway. You look at Florida, you look around yourself at Paradise Springs, and everything you see seems to be changing. You perceive change. And the American mind-set (at least for the time being) is that perception is everything. Not what you see is what you get, but what you see is all there is. And, like God after Creation, we surmise that all this changing is good.

What interests me more than that is what *isn't* changing and *hasn't* changed. I would rather consider what we have in common, the living and the dead, all the generations of us. What holds us together and has not changed.

And you know what I'm thinking about? Warfare and invasion. Violent fighting in all its forms that has haunted this place and its people (whoever they were) since time beyond record or remembering, since the days when the earliest tribes and clans—the prehistoric ones without names who have left us here and there, even here in Quincy County, their enigmatic burial mounds; and the days of the Timucuans, the Tocobega, the Apalachee, the Tequesta and all the others. They were smashing each other's skulls with their clubs and stone axes.

Along came the Spaniards, the French, the Limeys, fighting each other and the Indians all over and across this cursed peninsula. Came the Americans, finally, and took on the Seminoles for years and years. There were even some fights, skirmishes, in the swampy hammocks of the southern part of this county. And then the Civil War. Out of this rough, raw, thinly populated frontier country we furnished more than our fair share of men to the Confederacy. Most of them went elsewhere to fight, mostly to the bloody West. But boys and old men fought the Yankees and died here.

You want to see an image for the period? Take a good look at the pictures of young Lewis Payne, who was hanged for his part in the John Wilkes Booth conspiracy. He grew up not too far from here. Must have passed more than once through the little village settlement of Paradise Springs. Some of your people, Billy, may well have known him by sight. He was somebody to know, I reckon.

Then with the next war, the Spanish-American one, where we were the base for the invasion of Cuba, we enter into the century of war.

What else can you call it? Has there been a single day, even one, of peace on the globe for a hundred years?

What we have in common, the people you have been talking to, is the wars—the Judge in the Great War, from which, no matter what his real rank was, he earned the honorary rank of Colonel; Jojo, the Mustang ace in World War II; old Jack Weatherby, who left his leg in shit-stinking Korea; myself and many others from around here who left parts of ourselves in Vietnam.

Where is all this going? What am I trying to argue? Just that we, this place and the people in it, can't begin to be known or understood except as a haunted place, a home for old warriors, ghosts and in the flesh, all the same.

Florida is a pretty place, a postcard place, filling up, day after day, with strangers. But then, that was always so.

Even the Seminoles, the oldest people among us, were strangers. What does it mean, "Seminole," in Creek language —"runaway"? "outcast"? We are all runaways and outcasts.

JOJO ROYLE

Well, Billy Boy, you sure opened a can of worms with your question. The inquiring reporter gets an earful. And, when you think about it, everybody, the whole gang, predictable, if a little surprising.

Moe Katz, all that stuff about the new age of fat, he surprised me a little until I remembered that he is writing the preface for Martin Pressy's new book. Which is going to be about fat people.

Ever wonder how the old wheezing billygoat gets so turned on (obsessed might be the better word for it) by those sleek young, glittering, and incredibly skinny supermodels? Take a good look at Pressy's book when it comes out. It may be sick, but it is an experience. You will be alone in a world of human fat and human ugliness. It becomes the only world there is. Consider that Moe has to concentrate on that, to study it, in order to write his introduction. I think it's a little game ole Missy Prissy plays with Moe, trying to mess up his head. After all, Moe Katz was always the one man that he respected as being as crazy as himself.

And Dale Lewis surprised me a little. I hadn't imagined or expected he would be so, well . . . *historical*. He doesn't seem the type. But, what the hell, maybe Dale has been reading some books about Florida in his spare time. Ask Eleanor if he's been checking stuff out of the library.

As for me? Well, permit me to be equally predictable. We all perceive the world and reimagine it to fit what has happened to us from the first moment somebody spanked us into life and breath.

The greatest change in Paradise Springs in my lifetime is the old airport.

Of course there was always some kind of an airport here, as long as I can remember. I learned to fly a Piper Cub out there when I was a kid.

But came World War II and this whole state became one big airfield. The world's largest aircraft carrier. Tampa and Orlando had the huge bases (not counting Pensacola, which had always been big). But they came here, too, and laid out all those long runways and built the control tower and the hangars and the barracks and several thousand men to fill them up and to double this county overnight.

And then they abandoned it, closed it down at the end of the war. By the time I got home from overseas they had all left.

Some of them were already coming back to live here. But they left the airfield just as it is now. Not much real use to anybody, to be sure, except for some private pilots and some sky divers and such. And maybe some kids looking for a place to drag race and a quiet place to get laid. I still keep my plane out there even though I haven't flown it in a long, long time.

Everybody wanted it in the worst way—the developers. A prime piece of land just begging to be used. A fella like Penrose would still probably give a lot, top dollar, to own it.

You know who owns the old airport. I do. I'm the one. The Judge bought it, cheap, from the government right after the war. And just let it be, let it sit there. Which is how it came to me. And I have let it sit there, too.

What am I getting at? I'm giving you the symbol of change from my perspective. The war came along. And suddenly the big world was here in the middle of our little one with all its power and technology. And then, just as suddenly, the world was gone on about its business, leaving this thing, this sign behind like the huge footprint of a giant. And inch by inch (with a long way to go) the weather and the land are reclaiming it.

Every once in a while something happens out there. Back in

April of 1968, during all that, we had some excitement. But I guess you know all about that already.

Here and Now

CHANGE, CONTINUED:
BILLY TONE HAS AN OPINION, TOO

Memory is confused and confusing and, like the past, most often simultaneous. In spite of chronology, the distinction between early and later memories (and thus with all the changes that have taken place gradually or suddenly) is blurred and vague.

It's hard for me, then, to say for sure when a great many now-familiar things were new and strange.

Sometimes very slight changes can prove to be enormously significant.

For example, the *New York Times.* Now you can buy today's *Times* (and the *Wall Street Journal,* if that's your pleasure, or even *U.S.A. Today*) at the drugstore and even in those curbside vending boxes. If you have enough quarters in your purse or pocket. You can also get home delivery. So you don't need to wait a couple of days to catch up and find out what's happening out there in the big world. (Or, anyway, what the *Times says* is happening out in the big world; no real problem there—people still tend, more or less, to trust the *Times.*) You can easily have the *Trumpet* and the *Times* side by side on the breakfast table.

This is a very slight change; because you could always read the *New York Times* if you didn't mind waiting a few days for it. I can still remember as a child piling into the Judge's big car, together with the Judge and Richard and sometimes Jojo, and riding over to the Atlantic Coast Line depot to pick up the Sunday *Times* on the following Monday or Tuesday. We thought it was a great treat. But the *Times* might as well have come to us from the moon, albeit a glittering and glamorous one. The fact that we were not part of the world of the *Times* was neither surprising or disturbing. Just so, what happened hereabouts surely meant next to nothing to people in New York. And, by the same token, it seemed that what happened to them or what they made happen impinged directly upon us no more or no less than we allowed.

Now, like it or not, thanks to many changes great and small, we are part and parcel of the same national scene. And we are no longer spared by time, distance, or even ignorance. Where once we were a region, in and of itself, we are now merely a distant province. We, ourselves, are by definition provincials, even in our own place. And whatever happens to them, those others at the bright center of things, bears down relentlessly and directly upon our lives. Measured against these things, our daily lives seem to be trivial and insignificant. Our thoughts and hopes and wishes do not matter much, if at all. Linked by the new federalism of constant news and information—in print, on television, by E-mail, fax and Internet—we are some way diminished, losing the strength and virtue of our identity and our pride in it. For the first time, really, we can see ourselves, not darkly but clearly, in the eyes of distant strangers. What we see of ourselves from their point of view is not at all likely to enhance our self-esteem. We have become small and ridiculous. Like the Lilliputians. We are, from this point of view, here to be managed, manipulated, exploited. We are nothing more than the pitiful consumers of whatever they wish us to consume.

By the same (probably fallacious) act of the imagination, we can also see them, those others, our betters and our managers, if not in fact our owners (in my case my publisher), as sly and shifty, ruthless and wholly self-serving, clever and cunning, utterly without the inhibition of any principles, and almost always in all things hypocritical.

Lately many nationally prominent people (read: *celebrities*) profess to be at once baffled and concerned by our new and expansive American cynicism. Panels and councils, committees and commissions are busy everywhere studying the ways and means by which they may yet be able to restore us to our proper trusting and trustworthy condition in the grand scheme of things.

They should know, somebody should tell them (not I, not I, Lord, let this cup pass) that, looked at from *our* standpoint, the choice is not between skepticism and bland idealism, but between cynicism and revolution. Maybe old Jefferson was right that regular bloody revolutions are the necessary price of liberty.

And something else. Something Katz has said to me more than once, and some of the others, too: By constant and regular exposure to the worst the world has to offer, we have become hardened and almost immune to atrocity. No terrible thing happening to others elsewhere has any meaning beyond a reflexive raising of the eyebrows, a knowing shrug. Although we do profess (tell me who does *not*) our generous compassion, we have, in fact and in truth, next to none for any pains and suffering beyond our own. This is the simple truth of this, our most merciless age. Join this condition with our indifference to the prevalence of vulgarity in all its shapes and forms, and you will have some sense of who we really are.

These are things I think of when I face myself in the shaving mirror.

To all of which sweet (and relentlessly naive) Eleanor says: "It sounds to me like you need to take a little vacation."

Well, she is probably (once again) right.

Here and Now

SHERIFF DALE LEWIS AGAIN

We meet late in the afternoon in a small dark bar just off of Orange Avenue. We sit in a booth, both nursing a beer, drinking from the bottle, ignoring the frosted steins. I can tell in a minute that he has been a heavy drinker, too, in his day. Must have whipped it. But, the way he sips at his beer, still afraid of it. Country music playing softly from a glowing jukebox in the far corner.

There is more to it than you seem to realize, Lewis is telling me. There is the whole thing about the pilot who landed at the airfield by mistake.

"I don't know anything about that."

Dave Prince got a complaint from the guy, Lewis replies. He wasn't looking for anything. Just wanted someone to know his story—if it's true. Then there is the death of the Reverend Claxton, the Episcopal minister at St. Luke's.

"I thought that was a suicide."

Well, that's how they disposed of it. They called it suicide and moved on. That's understandable. They didn't have any serious reason to think otherwise. It's a strange one, though. Odd things and loose ends. They might not be so quick nowadays.

"Like what?"

Like a lot of things. Look at the file. They find the guy dead, very dead, been dead since Thursday and they didn't miss him until he didn't show up for early service on Palm Sunday. Dead in the attic of the rectory. He's got his pants and undershorts pulled down around his ankles and he's got a cum-splattered *Playboy* on the floor in front of him and he's got a pistol, an old .32 caliber Smith and Wesson in his right hand and that's odd.

"I've heard about teenagers hanging themselves at the moment of orgasm."

Doing it with a gun, though, is odd. Different anyway. Especially since this Reverend Claxton was apparently left-handed. And no note or anything. It's all in the file. See for yourself.

"You think there was more to it? A man in spiritual crisis. A man whose wife has just left him. A man whose only child, his daughter, is nothing but trouble."

You knew Verna Claxton, didn't you?

"So did everybody else around here."

True enough. But you were kind of close, weren't you? Especially close. Story went around that you were even thinking about marrying her.

"We were kids, Sheriff."

Call me Dale. This ain't official business. This is nothing but idle speculation.

"We were nothing but kids, though it's hard to believe that Verna was ever a child."

She was a wild child, that's for sure. You know, in Dave Prince's notes there were some witnesses who claim they saw her here in town at that time. A couple of people said they actually saw her at Little David's tent revival. That would be an odd connection, wouldn't it?

"Yes, if it happened."

She was said to be with some guy. Nobody that anybody knew. One witness (you'll see all this in the file) said later that it was Wayne Starkey. But he was not a reliable witness in any case. He was always seeing celebrities around Paradise Springs. But let's say it was Starkey. . . .

"Why?"

Just for the sake of argument.

"All right."

Then that means Starkey met up with Verna Claxton long before the official version. They were supposed to have met in New Orleans in the summer of '68. That was when Starkey started wasting people.

"They were caught in Arizona in August, as I recall."

I expect you would remember that much if you had been in love with the girl.

"Love? I don't know. I thought I was in love. But the truth is I was obsessed."

I can understand that. You do see what this may mean, though, don't you?

"Not exactly."

Look, Billy. If they were together, if Wayne Starkey and Verna Claxton were already a couple in early April of 1968, then there's no reason not to think that they didn't start stealing cars and robbing and killing people just about the same time. Never mind finding a string of unsolved crimes all over the Deep South, though. Stick to right here. Somebody took Pressy's fancy sports car and wrecked it. Somebody swiped a Baptist College station wagon that was found a week later in a parking lot at Pensacola. Maybe somebody killed Father Claxton and made it look like a suicide. Who knows?

"Not I."

You were here in town at the same time, weren't you, Billy?

"I had my mother's old Oldsmobile and was headed west, hoping to make San Francisco. I spent Thursday night here and then drove on in the morning. I remember the fire at the fairgrounds, but that's about all."

If you had seen Verna Claxton, alone or with somebody, a stranger like Starkey, you would most likely have remembered it.

"Most likely."

But you didn't.

"Not that I recollect." Then: "You don't think Wayne Starkey killed Father Claxton, do you?"

I don't think anything, Billy. I am just interested in the possibility. It would go a long way towards explaining some things.

"But I guess we'll never know."

Probably not.

"Dale, would it bother you if I had a real drink? I mean, the sun is over the yardarm and I could use a little belt."

Why would it bother me?

"I don't know. I was just wondering."

Then and There

LOG OF THE STRANGER WHO FLEW THE TWIN CESSNA

1. Let us keep it short and sweet and to the point.

2. If you think I am going to give you my name and address, you are crazy.

3. Flying alone in own plane. Flight plan from Woodrum Field, Roanoke, Virginia, to Kissimmee, Florida.

4. Purpose of trip: vacation and recreation. Plan to meet wife and kids there.

5. Trouble with oil pump north of Atlanta. Delay of several hours. Night flying necessary.

6. Navigation not my bag. Especially night navigation. Some instruments on blink. Radio not in good shape.

7. Lost over north Florida somewhere. Looking around for airport or landing strip.

8. Observed large fire burning near unidentified town. Came in low to look at fire and search for landing strip.

9. Suddenly many runway lights turn on. Big field all lit up. Figured somebody down there saw me.

10. Couldn't raise anybody on my crummy radio. Got into landing pattern to come in.

11. Touching down almost collided with white Mercedes coming wide open down middle of runway. Landed with knees shaking and cold sweat.

12. Found field closed and mostly locked up tight. Hangar, equipment and storage shacks. A few airplanes parked and tied down. Including a vintage Mustang. Couldn't locate a phone. Must have been one but couldn't find it.

13. Car still sitting on runway. Doors open, motor running, lights on. People inside ran away into nearby woods. Nobody else in sight.

14. Taxied back near to car.

15. Borrowed fancy heap (must be stolen in first place). Idea: drive to town and get oriented. Maybe get good stiff drink too.

16. Headed up highway toward glow of fire.

17. Police car came out of dark. Lights flashing. Pulled me over.

18. Got out quickly. Said something like: "Boy, am I glad to see you, Officer."

19. Not a cop. Big monstro guy in ragged jeans and dirty T-shirt punches me in mouth. I bust him right back.

20. Two others, big girls in crazy hootchy-kootchy costumes, jump all over me.

21. I fight back.

22. Guy clobbers me with baseball bat. Groggy. Everything in slow motion like a dream.

23. They pull down my pants and take them.

24. They carefully paint my crotch, cock and balls, red, white and blue.

25. Crazy thing. They put a combination bicycle lock (kid's trick) down there.

26. Big monstro guy: "Now. You leave that nice lady alone. You hear?"

27. They drive off.

28. Plan. Get back to plane quick as I can. And go. Go anywhere.

29. Problem: How to fly plane with bicycle lock still on me. No way.

30. Problem. Driving car back to field. Tricky to drive with lock. Lose control and wreck car in ditch.

31. Self not hurt. Anyway no worse.

32. Find nothing in glove compartment. Trunk contains one brown manila envelope and locked metal carrying case.

33. Took stuff with me. One step at a time back to airfield.

34. Couldn't open carrying case. Brown envelope contained prints and negatives of good-looking naked girl. Great tits.

35. Can you beat that.

36. Found file in own toolbox. Very carefully filed lock off. Slow work.

37. Found shack unlocked (somebody shot the lock) and cut off runway lights.

38. What if somebody comes along and asks me to explain everything?

39. Dozed in airplane.

40. Woke with dawn coming. Revved up engines and took off.

41. Taking metal carrying case and brown envelope with me.

42. Climbing and circling over field and then over campus and buildings of college or school campus.

43. Flying over golf course. See a naked lunatic with piece of blanket for covering stagger out of woods onto fairway. Staggering in circles.

44. Figure he ran into same folks I did.

45. Buzzed old bum several times. Grass high. Herded him back and forth. Bum a pretty good runner when scared.

46. Why buzz bum? Seemed like good idea, thing to do, at the time.

47. Bum on hands and knees. Shaking fist at me and plane.

48. Felt bad. My problems not his fault.

49. One more low pass. Bombed him with brown envelope.

50. Envelope busts open. Contents blowing all over fairway.

51. Possible headline: PILOT BOMBS BUM WITH PRURIENT PHOTOS.

52. Make something out of that.

53. Climbing I watch bum chasing and collecting pictures.

54. Toss carrying case into middle of pond. Nice splash.

55. Fly due south.

56. Arrive safe in Kissimmee.

57. Wife laughs at my new paint job. But believes nothing of my story.

58. Study map after fact to see where I have been. Draw big circle around it.

59. *Never ever land a plane at Paradise Springs, Florida!*

Here and Now

MUD IN YOUR EYE

MOE KATZ

It's truly strange and strangely apt how things work out.

There you have old Jack Weatherby. Bitter and mean as a snake. But principled. A man of values and principles. Albeit all the wrong ones. At least for this day and age.

The cross he has to bear is, of course, Penrose. A cheerful man with no principles or values at all. A man perfectly in sync, perfectly in keeping with this day and age.

But, Billy Boy, there is more.

Part—though not all by any means—of the irony is that no-body else will tell you about this. You could poke around forever and not find out unless and until you stepped right in it. Or stumbled over it. Because nobody will tell you this, not freely. Even Penrose's worst enemies around here (and there are a few) would not mention it until you asked the right question in the right tone of voice. And that's because no matter how much this place has grown and changed, is growing and changing, at heart it is still not even a small town but a crossroads village. Gossip may grow like kudzu and be the main pastime, more popular than bridge or bowling, around here. But when it is an outsider, they will rally around one of their own and offer nothing at all except bland smiles and meaningless shrugs.

Of course, there is an irony at the heart of this situation, too. Because, in fact, you are not really an outsider at all. You are directly connected to, descended from the earliest people of the crossroads village. But they, the defenders of the myth, if not the faith, are too new—one generation out of Alabama or even

Ohio or New Jersey—to know you as anything else but a stranger from outside.

"What the fuck are you talking about, Katz?"

Penrose. His problems. His cross to bear.

"Like what?"

Exactly. You don't know because you never asked. Some kind of a reporter you are!

"Asked what?"

About Penrose's son and heir.

"He's got some little kids."

Yes. But he also has an older one. Penrose is thirty-eight years old, right? He was twelve, just old enough to be a Boy Scout, in 1968. Well. When he was twenty, give or take, he knocked up a country girl and there was a brief marriage. And the child of that union, a lad named Widmark in honor of his mother's favorite movie star, has made something of a name for himself, although it isn't the Weatherby name he uses, but his mother's name—Shifflet. You have never heard of Widdy Shifflet?

"No. But there are lots of people I never heard of. I never heard of Kurt Cobain until he was gone to rock and roll heaven. I try to keep up, but I can't."

Back in the early days of his rise to power and glory Penrose was part owner of a place called the Hi Hat. A topless bar way out in the boonies towards Gainesville. He figured that if Hugh Hefner (most likely his original role model) could turn tits and ass not only into dollars and cents, but also into a philosophy and a way of life, why not Penrose? Why not, indeed? Well. He was a wee bit premature. Quincy County wasn't really ready for topless entertainment even at that late date. But mud wrestling was another matter.

"Mud wrestling?"

Girls and girls, guys and guys. Sometimes girls and guys. Sometimes guys against alligators. There was a brief season of success. And the kid, Widmark, loved it. He couldn't get enough of it. And when he grew up (sort of) and ran away from home, he surfaced as, I kid you not and swear upon everything holy and sanctified, as a performance artist. A master of an art called "mudding." He gets naked and smears mud all over himself and on some other naked people from the audience. He is pretty well known now. By most people except you, Billy. He has been pictured, mud-covered, in *Newsweek*. The National Endowment for the Arts has given him a couple of grants. Senator Jesse Helms has named him as a minor public enemy.

And, of course, poor old Penrose is mortified. He lives in constant apprehension that the kid will decide to come home to Paradise Springs. Or, worst-case scenario, that he will let the world know who his daddy is. Which really doesn't matter because everybody around here knows already that Penrose is the sire of Widdy Shifflet.

"Are you kidding me, Katz?"

What's more, they—by which I mean everybody else—they think it is perfect. That the kid is, seriously, a chip off the old block. That it is meet and right that the eldest son of Penrose Weatherby should be a master of mudding.

And since I am spilling the beans, Billy, I will tell you something else. You may or may not have noticed that it is very hard for an avant-garde artist to make a good living in America. I mean, there is probably more money in the long run from kite flying than there is for mudding. So how can the kid live a life between performances?

"Beats me."

He is sponsored and supported by Martin Pressy. Pressy knows that there is something there he can use.

"Maybe he can take pictures of the kid mudding fat people."

No. No. I think Pressy likes the idea that Penrose's dreams of grandeur have come to this. I think he likes the idea that an off-the-wall performance artist could come out of his town, Paradise Springs. I think he probably sees some validity and value in the art of mudding. At the very least Martin sees it as a perfect symbol for the life and art of our age.

"What do you think?"

I try not to think about it.

Then and There

MARTIN PRESSY

Praise is rare and blame is everywhere. And so, if I were to blame anyone (which I would much rather not), I suppose I would have to blame Mother and Moses Katz. About equally.

Actually, truth be known, the whole subject is more than a little distasteful to me. I must admit that I was terribly upset, at least at first, as much or more by the bad things that happened at the tent revival meeting as by the barbarous destruction of my beautiful automobile and the simultaneous loss of my materials for *The Magic Book of Woman*. It was an altogether traumatic experience. Make no mistake about that.

But, nevertheless, already I have begun to see it in a different light. Even my losses have proved to be gains. I think of it as a learning experience.

It is true that I was (still am) a photographer by craft and trade. At the time in question I was limiting myself almost exclusively to commercial things—portraits, especially of children, and wedding photographs and the like. I also did most of the work for the yearbook of Sidney Lanier High School and Baptist College. But, prior to that time and those events, I never had any interest in doing work for the county. And I had next to no interest in doing press photography.

To be perfectly candid, I didn't need the money. Still don't, thank the Lord. You could call it all a hobby at that point.

Sometimes, to be sure, I have imagined myself as an artist with a capital *A*. And like many a romantic, I always considered Art and Commerce to be strange and hostile bedfellows. I only opened up a studio and became involved in that modest sort of photography because I had to be here in Paradise Springs anyway. I came home to be here for an indefinite time after Mother suffered a debilitating stroke. I had to look after her affairs and to supervise her care and rehabilitation. And it pleased Mother, bless her heart, that I had a real office, some kind of a business I could go to like a real grown-up. Pleased her, too, that I was at least vaguely involved in this community. She always loved Paradise Springs. She grew up here. It is the center of the universe for her.

Believe me, I am not trying to sound superior or condescending. It is quite true that I would prefer Paris or Rome or Venice or Tangier, some exotic and decently civilized place. But my own tastes and preferences don't matter that much. Mother is a great woman, a great lady, really; and she can live as fully and as brightly here, even confined to her favorite rocking chair, as anywhere else under the sun. And where Mother lives, there you shall find me. For as long as she lives. And may it be long. She is frail and fragile physically, but she has pure fire in her spirit. It seems entirely possible that she will outlast us one and all.

When I came back home to look after her (Father being long since dead and gone), she was concerned that I would settle for a reclusive life, staying here in the house, tending to her needs, playing cards with her, reading to her, and so forth and so on.

"I do not wish ever to be a burden to you, Martin," she told me. "But, by the same token, I do not wish to be bored by you. You must be my spy. You must go out into the world and see what's happening. Then we shall have some interesting things to talk about in the evening."

Of course she was right. She always is.

Now then. *The Magic Book.* That was a phase, a stage I had to pass through, I suppose. It made some sense at the time. And I don't regret it. Nothing to be ashamed of. An artist has nothing to be ashamed of, really, except the neglect of talent.

Partly it is Mother's fault. Her lighthearted teasing troubled me more than it should have. When I would bring back the bridal photos or the prints of some wedding I had covered, she would always look at them with great interest and ask a lot of questions about all the details—what everyone wore, who was there, what brand of champagne (if any, in this benighted community), who sang, what music was played.

"That's what I miss most," she said. "Weddings."

"Why don't you attend some of them with me? I'll help you. We can tuck you into your wheelchair and go together."

"I prefer to look at your beautiful pictures and to hear you talking about it and to imagine it all. It's ever so much more amusing than the real thing. I have always wept at weddings, even when I was just a little girl. It's supremely foolish, I know, just an old woman's vanity, but I hope and pray I shall never cry in public again. Except of course at your wedding, Martin. Oh, on that happy day, I shall cry like Hecuba."

"That day may never come, Mother."

"Rubbish! Don't say that. Don't even think that. Of course you will marry. You will marry some big, fine, healthy girl who can have lots of children."

"Oh, Mother!"

"You will do it for me, Martin, so that I can play the part of a cranky and eccentric mother-in-law. So that I can be a beloved grandmother."

"The only reason I would ever get married is so that you will come to the wedding and weep copiously in front of everyone in Paradise Springs."

It was just a game, I think. No, I know it was. I know that if I had come home then—or if I were to come home today—with a blushing bride-to-be, Mother would have a superb and theatrical final stroke and die on the spot.

All of her arguments were specious. Take the family name. Pressy. It is my late father's name, and she certainly has no serious interest or intention in giving that name the least touch of immortality. Or her feeble social arguments. For example, that as the most eligible bachelor in this town, I owe some kind of debt to the community, like a young prince in a fairy tale, a debt to be paid by my choosing one girl to be the brightest flower in our garden before they all wither away into weeds and nettles from neglect and shame.

I suppose she really believes that. She did not (does not) think of it as an expeditious means of redistributing wealth in Paradise Springs. True, we happen to be, by a good deal, the wealthiest family in the community. And in that sense I imagine I can be considered highly eligible. But I should be a great deal less than candid with you if I did not openly and cheerfully admit that I am not exactly well equipped—mentally, spiritually and, yes, even physically—for the prolonged rigors of conventional domestic life. No doubt, I could find someone willing to take the risks, to undertake the burden, to make the sacrifice of marrying me and living with me . . . and Mother. In exchange for considerable material comfort and security. And, indeed, there have been, from time to time, signs and portents—even, shall we say, the preliminaries of interest and opportunity.

But marriage, as far as I am concerned, is out of the question.

It remains a game with us. Sometimes a third party may be involved. *Item:* Our late lamented Episcopal minister, the Reverend Lee Claxton. Aptly named. A sweet fruitcake, that poor fellow! For his own reasons he called upon Mother regularly, as often as possible. And it was she who brought him into the game. Always eager to please her (and why not?), he joined in with enthusiasm. Together they tried to tease me into the most memorable Episcopalian wedding ever performed and held in Paradise Springs, Florida.

It is entirely possible (why not imagine the worst?) that Claxton may have hoped, sooner or later and somehow, to arrange for the eventual sacrificial bride of Martin Pressy to be none other than his one and only, dreadful teenaged daughter, the desperately wicked Verna. I was at least spared that.

None of this is, to be sure, directly pertinent to anything except in the sense that all this teasing and fooling and discussion, Mother's little game, planted some careless seeds which survived and grew roots.

I was forced to think about, to come to some kind of negotiated terms with my own sexuality. And I also began to think seriously about women—no no, I mean Woman, almost

infinitely mysterious in all of her guises and forms. Woman became the secret and ambiguous subject of my art.

Moe Katz bears responsibility for that. It was, I see now,
basically his idea, not mine; though, superb Socratic teacher that
he is (when he is sober), he led me to imagine that I came to
it all by myself.

Katz was reputed to be, to have been, anyway, a first-rate
scholar. A very bright, very young man with a brilliant future
before him, teaching at a top-flight Ivy League university. But
by the time I first came to know him, he was a prematurely
"dirty old man," having run out of chances and options, having
come to the end of the line (and lucky to have that much left),
teaching the empty-headed girls and boys of Central Florida
Baptist College. He is maybe the oldest living assistant professor
in the business. Doing the best he can to stay out of public
trouble, to hold on to his shabby job and modest salary. Hoping
that someday, with a little luck, he might manage to sail into an
adequate retirement. Between the halls of ivy and the red-brick,
decayed gentility of Baptist College lay a wilderness of booze,
pills, drugs, good and bad women, and a whole lot of half-assed
philosophy. I hate to put it so crudely, but that is the case, the
simple story.

Nevertheless, Moe Katz is a fascinating fraud. When I came
back to Paradise Springs he proved to be someone I could talk
with. No, more accurately, somebody I could listen to.

We first met in the steam bath of the brand-new Cosmos
Club. I was there, as ever, in my ceaseless effort to fight the
metabolic tendency to fat that I have inherited from Mother.
He, fat and indifferent to it, was there fighting his continual
hangover. We often ran into each other there at the Cosmos and
soon were friends.

Katz worked on me with his fashionable and heavy talk about
the dark goddesses of pre-Christian culture, witchcraft, the oc-
cult, the female principle of the universe, the magic and mysteries of Woman, etc., etc., etc.

Now it all sounds too sad and silly for words, but then I was

more or less susceptible. A couple of guys up to no good. Well,
I was looking for something to do with my skills with a camera.
And it was not difficult to imagine that we had been misled in
our image of God. God was much more like Mother, for example, than any man I had ever known.

Thus the idea for *The Magic Book* began in the sweaty con-
fines of the Cosmos Club.

For the next year or so it became a sort of obsession with
me, urgent yet desperately furtive. For obvious reasons.

The greatest single difficulty I faced (as you may imagine)
was getting the subjects for my art. None of them really wanted
to. That is, they did not volunteer (with one notable exception,
to be duly noted). Indeed, each in her own way was reluctant,
to say the least, requiring the most careful and subtle persuasion—one might almost say, metaphorically, seduction. Thus,
the very act of seeking out and persuading each of these seem-
ingly reluctant subjects, while it might seem a shamefully dis-
honest enterprise on one level and did, in fact, cause me some
grief and guilt, was nevertheless an important experience for me.
And it has become, ironically, and in ways I could not have
imagined, a significant part of my development as an artist. Psy-
chology, empathy, sensitivity to the needs, the strengths and
weaknesses of each subject, were demanded of me. Some measure of real understanding, an identification with the subject, bor-
dering upon genuine compassion, were also required, though
not to the extent of inhibiting me from my purpose. From all
of this—call it a "confidence game," if you insist—has come a
better, deeper intuitive understanding of myself and my real purposes as artist.

Which is to say that gradually, as slowly yet inexorably as if
the process had been a chemical one taking place in my own
studio darkroom, the outlines of my design began to take shape
and form. The design had always been there, I surmised, waiting
to be discovered, but I could not have dreamed it before then.
Yet, through blind and perhaps commonplace impulse, out of
visceral and glandular gnawings, through a rich variety of

rationalized whims, I staggered, clownlike, until I literally seemed to stumble upon a design of some grandeur, a statement which, I hoped, would contain beauty and truth.

I had never given much credence to concepts of fate, predetermination, predestination, etc. I had never considered Man (myself) as a puppet, created by the accidents of heredity and environment, the victim or hero of his own unconscious or of some vague and vast Collective Unconscious. I thought of myself, for better or worse, as Martin Pressy, free spirit, wide-awake and conscious, thinking and being, one who saw the dim outline of a pattern or structure and at that moment exercised freely the choice to seize upon it or reject it outright.

I was, I thought, responsible for the whole of it. And I allowed myself a certain pride of achievement even though, in an undeniable way, my chief accomplishment was merely to make a choice.

In short, I was a damn fool. But then, it took all that and more for me to come to this much wisdom.

We learn so little and so painfully.

Item: After all that intense effort at the art of persuading reluctant subjects to cooperate (the effort itself, as indicated, an education to me), I came to understand that money would almost always do the trick. The only real trick was determining the price. Of course, the fact that it was all for Art, that it would all be legal and correct, and that there would be no hanky-panky on the job, etc., made it easier to find suitable subjects. But (I can see it now) cash was always the key.

And now I must try to speak more directly about the tent revival meeting and the dreadful events of that night as far as they concerned me.

First the real reason why I went to the meeting. True, I had plans to photograph the revival, and I had paid Little David Enterprises some money, a decent fee, for the privilege. But the real reason I went there was in the hope that I might have an opportunity to talk to Alpha Weatherby. Darlene Blaze, a jolly and statuesque earth girl and one of the best subjects I had for

The Magic Book (no trouble at all persuading her; no false modesty there), had called me and suggested that, following the revival, I might be able to pick up Alpha and herself and to drive them home in my car. This would give me a chance to talk to Alpha and to see if I could persuade her to pose for me again.

Alpha had posed for me just once. And the photographs had been exceptionally good and suitable, almost perfect for my purposes. Though slender and almost boyish in figure, she seemed to convey not an androgynous sensuality, but an intense and fiery sort of spirituality which added a new, unexpected and wonderful dimension to my book's structure.

She posed once, then refused to pose for me again. Now that I understood her place in my scheme, I needed at least one more session with her.

"She won't do it again. I'm pretty sure of that," Darlene told me. "Maybe I can line up somebody else for you."

I tried to explain to Darlene that nobody else would do. I tried my best to explain and express the particular qualities that Alpha had as a subject, the unique spiritual dimension that Alpha could add to *The Magic Book of Woman*.

"Oh, I get it!" Darlene said. "You're looking for a real tall, skinny girl without much boobs."

"Well, there's more to it than that. But, yes, that's the basic idea."

It was Darlene's suggestion and stratagem that I should arrange to "cover" the revival meeting photographically. That I should then "happen to bump into them." That I should offer them a ride home.

It seemed feasible and plausible.

So I packed up all the prints and negatives and releases, the entire file of *The Magic Book,* in my metal fireproof carrying case. Locked it. Then put it in the locked trunk of my car. You see, there had been a burglary at the studio and I didn't want to lose all these things.

I was just closing up the studio and preparing to drive out to the fairgrounds when the phone rang.

It was Debby Langley. One of Moe Katz's students out at the college and the only one of my subjects who had managed to give and to cause me any real trouble.

A word of explanation. Moe had strongly suggested Debby Langley as a natural subject for my book. But when I approached her she was not only reluctant, but apparently incensed by the very idea. Though she had a marvelous figure and even some experience in modeling, she was absolute in her refusal. So be it. Except that much later, very late at night, she telephoned the house. The first I knew of it was when Mother woke me.

"Someone," she said sternly, "a young woman who says her name is 'Gypsy,' insists on speaking to you, Martin."

"I swear I don't know anyone named Gypsy."

"Well, I think you'd better talk to her if either of us is going to get any sleep. She has already called three times and will probably keep calling until you talk to her."

It was, of course, Debby. She sounded somewhat intoxicated. She said she wanted to pose for me now, tonight, and that this would be my one chance. Now or never!

In my state of mind I took this as a kind of sign, a message from the muses that could not be ignored. I agreed to come out and pick her up outside the college in a few minutes.

I hurriedly got dressed.

"Martin," Mother called. "Have you gotten some little slut into trouble?"

"Oh, God no, Mother. Believe me, everything is perfectly all right. Nothing like that. I do have to go out for a while, but I promise you that everything is all right.

"Just don't catch any horrid, unmentionable diseases," she called after me as I was leaving.

The whole session was unfortunate. I think she would have been a fine model, really, but she was drunk (or, anyway, pretending to be drunk). And all the shots I got were flawed by a certain excessive, plastic sexuality. They might have been appropriate for some second-rate skin magazine. But not for the pages of my *Magic Book.*

I am sorry to have to report that she threw herself at me. It should be (you understand, surely) a scene from a farce. As we trip and dodge and hurry, myself and the ripely naked young woman, round and round my studio, crashing into this and that. And once I fell and she sat powerfully astraddle of me. But nothing more. Left me panting and deep-breathing on the floor, like the body of a drowned man tossed up on the beach, while, sweaty and dainty (and suddenly sober), she tiptoed to the sink and vomited like a sick dog.

By the time I got her safely back to the college, to the place where she could slip under the chain-link fence and back to her dorm room in the dark, she was quietly talking of marriage. As if we had, in fact, made the beast with two backs together.

Evidently she was not being facetious. A painful series of phone calls followed this clumsy episode. When I made it abundantly clear that, for the well-being and best interests of the both of us, marriage was completely out of the question, she then demanded the prints and negatives back.

And I might have been glad to give them to her (especially since they did not fit into my book) if she had not tried to threaten me. Now angry myself, I reminded her that she had signed a release, accepted a check in full payment and subsequently cashed it. I told her that I had no intention of returning the prints or negatives. I suggested to her that if she continued to make phone calls and threats, I would be forced to "take some kind of action." I suggested two possibilities. One was to sell them to one of the skin magazines, something I could legally and ethically do. The other, perhaps less kind, was to mail them in a plain brown wrapper to the dean of students at the college. . . .

"You wouldn't! You wouldn't dare!"

"Oh, yes, I would," I told her. "And I will, too, unless you stop bothering me."

"That's blackmail," she said.

"Not exactly," I said. "But you can think of it that way if you want to."

Sobbing, she hung up. And I did not hear of her or from her until the night of the revival.

She began by professing great shame and apologizing for her earlier behavior.

She wanted to "make it up in some way," to "prove we were still good friends." Couldn't we meet and talk about it?

I told her, as politely as possible, that there was really nothing to talk about, but that I would be pleased to meet her some other time. I explained that I had to cover the revival meeting, professionally, and could not continue the conversation at this time.

"Maybe later," she said. "At the studio . . ."

"I won't be coming back to the studio tonight," I said. "Call me some other time."

"Oh, you won't be coming back to the studio tonight?" she asked, oddly I thought. "Well, then, yes, I'll call another time."

Hung up.

Suspicious ever since the burglary, I took the prints and negatives of Debby Langley out of the files, put them in an envelope and locked it in the trunk together with my fireproof carrying case of *The Magic Book*.

Then I drove out to the fairgrounds and tried to busy myself pretending to take pictures.

In the confusion after the snakes got loose and the tent caught on fire, I ran back to my car. It was gone! In the precise place where I had parked it was a large black hearse, all decorated with crude paintings of flowers and the peace sign, graffiti and slogans. I peered inside. There was a note—written on a shirt cardboard, in crayon—on the dashboard. DRIVE ON DUMMY, it exclaimed. HELL AIN'T HALF FULL YET.

Stunned at the loss of my beautiful (and very expensive) car and everything in it, I ran about, pushing my way through the crowd, trying to find a policeman. I found Sheriff Prince and attempted to explain my situation to him. He was not interested. Or, anyway, he was preoccupied with problems of his own.

"You got any film in those cameras, Missy Prissy?" he demanded.

I nodded, and then he seized me and propelled me towards one of the trailers parked at a little distance from the blazing tent.

"Do something worthwhile for once in your life," he told me. "Go in there and photograph the dead bodies."

At first I thought I might vomit in simple reaction to the blood (clots and gouts of it) of the wounds and the dead bodies. But my craft saved me. I took a careful check and then began snapping pictures of the corpses from a variety of angles.

Which is how Alpha Weatherby posed for me one last time, together with the tiny body of the midget evangelist. Both of them as naked and bald as stones. The simple mechanical matters of taking the pictures calmed and wholly engrossed me.

That set of pictures is, in my opinion, among the best photographs I have ever made. I knew, even as I took them, that there was more truth in them than in the entire lost portfolio of *The Magic Book*. At that moment I believed that the portfolio (thus my book) was lost forever. My extravagant and lovely sports car was even then being mistreated, if not wrecked, by a person or persons unknown. But none of that matters anymore.

The pictures turned out to be excellent.

Today I continue living at home with Mother. And I keep my studio and photograph children and portraits, weddings and social events. But my real life, my real art, begins when the phone rings and it is Sheriff Prince or maybe one of his men.

"Pressy," he'll tell me, "there's been an accident, a terrible two-car accident out on U.S. 17, just north of Lake Copeland (or wherever). Can you get out there right away and make me some pictures?"

"Sure," I say. "I'm on my way."

One more thing. *The Magic Book* portfolio.

Early the next morning I received a phone call from young

Penrose Weatherby. He very politely informed me that he believed he had located something of mine. And he would be
happy to see that it was properly returned to me, all safe and
sound, in return for a modest reward for his efforts and good
will. We haggled a bit over the price, but in the end I gave him
as much as he wanted.

Later I discovered that he had removed and kept a couple
of the best prints of Darlene Blaze, but not the negatives.

Then and There

THE SECRET BOOK OF **PENROSE WEATHERBY**

Some time later, maybe after the trial, Penrose wrote some
notes in his *Secret Book,* a loose-leaf, three-ring notebook with
"School Days" cheerfully and boldly printed on the cover, a
notebook which he had swiped from a fat and nearsighted girl
during lunchtime at school. Its hiding place was an old trunk in
the low attic of the house, close beside the great blades of the
attic fan, which did the best it could to pull hot air up and out
and to keep a breeze flowing in the days before everybody had
central air-conditioning. For Penrose that fact, air-conditioning,
represents the demarcation of old Florida and new Florida. You
had to be tough to get through the long hot months without
wilting and with no more help than fans. Once there was easy
air-conditioning and the mosquito had been more or less neu-
tralized if not controlled, strangers and outsiders came pouring,
overflowing into the state to live there. New population and a
new Florida.

In the trunk, concealed by old clothes and Halloween costumes and near the ribbon-wrapped packet of love letters that
he enjoyed reading so much, Penrose kept the *Secret Book.* It
was divided into four parts. Part one was labeled "The World in
Which We Live In." This section was reserved for newspaper
and magazine clippings that had especially pleased Penrose. At

least once a week, sometimes more often, Penrose would go to the library to look through old and new magazines and news-papers, searching for suitable material among the accounts of natural disasters, murders, rapes, robberies, outlandish crimes and errors, incredible strokes of bad luck and misfortune. Pen-rose had no idea what a tabloid was, though he was clearly cre-ating a personal one; and to this day, a quarter of a century later, he finds himself without knowing or, indeed, even wondering why, buying a tabloid paper at the checkout counter of the su-permarket. Penrose was extremely selective, a strict editor, for he discovered early that news of these things was plentiful. After he found a clipping that pleased him, that seemed worthy and right, he would wait, perhaps as long as several weeks, allowing it to ferment, thinking about it, rereading it if and when he could, trying to imagine it first as an event, entirely in and of itself, and then as something in relation to the other clippings already a part of the *Secret Book*.

When something endured, passed his skeptical scrutiny, he would go ahead and cut it out, swiftly and discreetly with a single-edged Gem razor blade. (This latter, tool and weapon, more or less safely carried, stuck in a large fishing cork in his pocket). As a next stage the liberated clipping would be placed in a bureau drawer, under his shirts or shorts, for further study, for what he called "aging." Only a few of these clippings were fully "distilled" and ended up taped or pasted into the pages of the *Secret Book*.

Part two of the book was labeled "Corny Sex." Penrose had decided that he was just naturally hornier than most other people. This horniness could easily become a serious problem if he allowed it to get the best of him. And so, in order to free his restless mind and to stay healthy, he created a kind of game or discipline to master what otherwise might have become cha-otic self-indulgence. "Corny Sex" was exclusively devoted to photographs of women—nude, in bathing suits, in their under-wear. These were the women, or, to be more accurate, the two-dimensional, representative images of the women, in his life who had been (in his words) "retired from active duty." Which category was composed, first of all, of those female figures who had exercised a remarkable power by arousing at once his imagination and his natural instincts on at least ten occasions over an indefinite time period. Next placed in "semiretirement," these pictures were given the severe test of pure imagination. If their inherent mystery and witchery could do its work on the basis of memory alone, they were then cut out of all context and neatly pasted on an individual page in the *Secret Book* and soon forgotten. Penrose was not then (or now) of a nostalgic nature, as he would have gladly explained had anyone asked him. Other people could press flowers in the pages of books. He, on the other hand, was, in a very real sense, liquidating these powerful sources of solitary joy. In one sense "Corny Sex" might be conceived of as a kind of commemorative album. In another it was a kind of morgue.

The third section of the *Secret Book* was entitled "Epistles." Here Penrose kept carefully written letters, none of them intended ever to be mailed, addressed to real and imaginary persons, dead or alive.

The final section of the *Secret Book* was called "Conversations With My Friend." These pages were, in plain fact, notes and monologues offering the essence of his views on a variety of subjects and events, random in order and importance. Penrose was, from an early age, fully aware that, things of this world being as they are, it was highly unlikely that he would often have a chance for a sustained and serious conversation with another human being. He was cheerfully resigned to the fact that it was highly unlikely he would ever have a real friend.

In the hot, stale (smelling of dust and sorrow), low-ceilinged attic where the light from small windows was pale and faint, and dust whirled and danced like a swarm of dervishes, where some insect, bee or dirt-dauber, buzzed forlornly among the shadows, Penrose opened the trunk and took out the *Secret Book*. He opened it to the "Conversations" section. Then he took out his special, gold-plated ballpoint pen, picked mainly for the sake of the initials engraved on it—R A T, for Robert A. Thorpe, principal of the Sidney Lanier High School. On a particularly good and lucky day, Penrose had managed to acquire the pen off the principal's desk even as the aforesaid principal, Rat Twerp, was himself busily engaged in swinging an emphatic wooden paddle across Penrose's upraised backside.

Penrose turned pages until he found a clean sheet of paper and wrote as follows:

1. You may be wondering what really did happen that night (April 4th) out at the tent revival meeting.

2. So do I.

3. I surely did not learn a whole hell of a lot in the courtroom during the trial. And I tried not to let on all the things I *did* know because it didn't seem the right time and place to do so.

4. The best I can do at this stage is to put down the things I was aware of and to put it down the way it seemed to me.

5. Quick as we got there, I left Darlene and Alpha and slipped out of the tent. Figuring they never would miss me anyway.

6. Which guess proved to be correct.

7. I went in search of Goathead Papp intending to con some money out of him. Which I did.

8. Next I went to Bill Wright's Texaco Station, roughly one-half mile north of the fairgrounds. Had myself a king-size Dr. Pepper and a bag of peanuts for my supper. Stole a box of kitchen matches. From the station there was a good view of the carnival going on at the other end of the fairgrounds, the lit-up Ferris wheel turning. Other things moving. Figured I would try to see the freak show and maybe the strip show at some point of the evening.

9. Leaving Texaco station, I paused long enough to loosen up the radiator draincock on a Ford station wagon with a lot of luggage and out-of-state (Yankee) license plates. Chances good that draincock would fall out a few miles down the road.

10. Walked back up the highway in direction of the tent

revival. Stopped only once to drop trousers and throw a bare-ass moon at a slow-moving schoolbus full of old ladies with hats on.

11. Messed and milled around for a little while to no special purpose.

12. Decided to go on expedition and to determine where they were keeping the snakes.

13. While doing so I jumped up and down in front of lighted trailer window long enough to see Papp taking money out of the safe and putting it in suitcase. Pretty big bunch of money.

14. Located lazy nigger asleep in back of truck. Woke him up and sent him off to report to Papp.

15. Next discovered crate with snakes in it on back of truck and removed same.

16. Nigger hit me with rock the size of golf ball in the pitch-dark. Must always remember to keep moving while laughing out loud at someone in the dark. Otherwise a sitting target. Knot upside my head.

17. Then saw Darlene go inside of Papp's trailer.

18. Dragged snake crate over to trailer window so I wouldn't have to jump up and down to see in.

19. What I saw was Darlene with most of her clothes off doing hootchy-kootchy for Papp.

20. Pretty good show, but got tired of watching it.

21. Dragged crate over close to tent. Opened it up and dumped out snakes. Snakes very groggy and lazy.

22. Moved empty crate back to trailer window, guessing Papp would find it and think that the nigger had been spying on him.

23. Went back to see about snakes. Snakes still very groggy. Shoved them close to tent, pointing inside. Found two posters. Lit same. Applied to snakes. Snakes more lively. Crawled under edge of tent.

24. Tent began to catch fire where I had lit posters. Some kind of solvent on canvas. Sorry.

25. Quick hid out in dark to observe the commotion.

26. Saw Little David go into his trailer. Was just about to go get crate and spy on him when I saw Alpha go into same trailer.

27. Ran to highway to deputy sheriff directing traffic. Told him Little David's trailer was on fire. He run off in that direction.

28. Rolled in the dirt and tore my shirt and started crying.

29. Found other deputy. Told him Papp had grabbed my sister and taken her into trailer. Deputy run off in that direction blowing his brass whistle.

30. Very soon heard sounds of gunshots. Figured it must be one of the deputies.

31. Sneaked back around to Papp's trailer and stood on crate. Nobody home. Darlene's silver cross on the floor.

32. Went inside to get it for her. Saw suitcase packed full of money. Bills of many denominations, large and small. Took that with me, too.

33. Went into pine woods to edge of old Seminole Golf Course close by Baptist College. Buried money in good place near to small pond at edge of fairway.

34. Took empty suitcase back to trailer.

35. By now much excitement in and around revival. Fire Department on scene, hosing down everything in sight. People running around in every which direction yelling and carrying on. Across the wide fairgrounds field carnival lights blooming in dark. Ferris wheel turning quietly.

36. Inside Papp's trailer. Nobody home.

37. Left suitcase where I found it. Plus a dime left over from his quarter. Plus some pennies.

38. Ran home and climbed up mulberry tree and sneaked into my room. Slept a few hours.

39. Just before daylight took a pillowcase and went back for the buried money. Was stuffing money in pillowcase when I saw: Katz, naked except for a piece of a blanket, sneaking across the golf course towards the college. Then a plane, twin-engine Cessna I think, came out of nowhere and took to buzzing poor

old Katz. Who was running back and forth like a huge cock-roach.

40. Plane bombed him with papers. Then flew low over the pond and dropped a metal case (really looked like a bomb) in the pond practically right in front of where I was hidden in trees. Kissed my ass goodbye and waited for explosion. None. Took a peek. Metal case floating in shallow pond.

41. Waded out and retrieved it. Didn't (yet) know what was in it but saw MP initials and assumed (rightly) it was property of Martin Pressy. Not the Military Police.

42. Buried it. Planning to sell it back to Missy Prissy in due course.

43. Sneaked back home and into my room. Driveway full of blinking police cars. Cops all over the place. But nobody saw me or was looking for me.

44. Put on pajamas and came downstairs. Mom and Dad crying and all. Found out then that poor Alpha was dead and gone. Wasted by Papp and the Fat Woman.

45. And that is positively all that I know about anything that happened. Which is next to nothing.

Finishing these notes, Penrose carefully signed his name and the date.

Then he put the *Secret Book* back in its safe hiding place.

Then and There

VERNA CLAXTON TELLS HER TALE

I don't give a hoot what everyone else in the rest of the world thinks. Let them think what they please. Let them scoff as may. This is addressed to the only three people I really care about—me, myself and I.

First off, I had positively next to nothing to do with anything that may have taken place at Little David's World Famous Tent

Revival Meeting on the evening of April the fourth, 1968, in Paradise Springs, Florida. Keep that in mind.

And always remember that the widely publicized hearing concerning me and Wayne Starkey took place at a much later date and in the state of Arizona. And all it was about was only certain things that they alleged to have happened within that state and nothing else.

As for all the serious stuff that took place in Paradise Springs, me and Wayne were already long gone, highballing it away from there. Sure we stole a car, but we were not responsible for any of the rest of it. No matter what others may choose to think or say.

I know all about how bad people are. ("Natural depravity" was what my poor daddy used to talk about. And he ought to have known.) I know that once you have slipped up and have actually done one or two bad things, after that they will lay all the bad things that have ever happened right on your doorstep. They know that Wayne is a terrible person. Just because I went along with him and happened to be present when some of the things they have blamed on him took place, they think I am a terrible person, too. Well, I don't care what they may think. It's no skin off of my sweet ass. As far as I am concerned they can go right ahead believing whatever they want to in their low-down dirty minds.

I will let the record speak for itself. Let the whole world take note that nothing, not a blessed thing, has ever been *proved* on me. We have yet to stand trial. I used the correct word, "hearing," to describe that joke in Tucson. They never *tried* us for anything. We got arrested and charged with all kinds of terrible stuff, that is true. And it is likewise the case that Wayne signed all kinds of statements about some of the things we are supposed to have done. That is because, deep down, underneath all the tough-guy, macho, smart-ass attitude, Wayne is a weakling and a coward and a pussy.

Naturally all the bad stuff got in the papers and in a couple of magazines also. But before they could even get the trial cranked up and started, they had to have a hearing to determine if we were really sane enough to stand trial. And, as I guess everybody in the world knows, we both flunked that test. They had real psychiatrists and hotshot expert witnesses and all, but none of that was really necessary. Because they put Wayne on the stand and just let him talk. Once he started talking, it was all over but the medication and the straitjackets. We were both (separately) bughouse bound. Sanity has never been one of Wayne Starkey's strong points. He is smart and sometimes he can be funny. But he is also completely spaced-out. That's his main charm. So (it was bound to happen) five minutes after he started answering questions at the hearing, they were already making room for him at the funny farm.

Fair enough. But why, how come they had to put me there, too? At first I blamed everything on old Wayne for dragging me along with him. That was exactly what they wanted me to do—to rat on Wayne. But in the end I outfoxed them, anyhow. I got over being mad at crazy Wayne and only remembered and thought about the good times we had together. Of which there were some. Mostly when we were having good sex together. Anyway, I have come to understand the real reason that I am salted away here with all of these real nuts. They didn't try us in court (and never will, either), because they knew damn well that they would have a very hard time convicting us. Since they were smart enough to figure it out for themselves that Wayne is a weakling and a lunatic, they got him to sign all that crap. Then, before he had a chance to change his mind and his story, they had us both locked up in their snake pit. The only one who could have cleared both of us was me. I could have given them some real problems. But all they had to do was to get some of their shrinks to testify that I am crazy too.

Naturally I reacted very strongly to all their derogatory re-marks at the hearing. Who wouldn't have? And don't forget I was shocked, deeply disturbed by all that Wayne had said and done there.

I only wish that Daddy would have been alive to see it. I can picture it, how Daddy, all phony and spiffy in his clerical collar, would have got up there and cried and carried on and agreed with them. Daddy was so stupid and so incredibly square. They probably wouldn't have had to pay him, either, for his testimony. Not one penny for his testimony or his tears either. He would fly all the way out to Arizona and back at his own expense.

Probably all they would have had to do was to suggest to him all the bad publicity that was sure to come out of a full-scale trial. Daddy was always terrified of having his good name hurt. Which makes the way he died almost funny if you stop and think about it. Except *I* didn't plan it that way. It was all Wayne's idea on the spur of the moment.

Anyway, I know that Daddy, that dirty rat, would have been crying and telling them all how I had been crazy all along and how it was really all his fault because he should have put me away long ago.

Crap! Bullshit! Baloney! That's what I would have said and that is what I say now.

Only, Daddy, I miss you a lot sometimes. And I am very sorry what Wayne did to you and your reputation. And you were right, too, that I would have been better off if I had stuck with Billy Tone, or even that flaming faggot—Martin Pressy. Billy wasn't as exciting as Wayne, but at least he appreciated a lot of things about me.

Well, if the joke was on poor Daddy, the joke is on them, too. On the whole dumb, crummy state of Arizona and also on the stupid FBI who got themselves into the act because of all the alleged kidnappings and car stealings and so forth.

Ho-ho-ho!

So they put me and Wayne in the squirrel cage. And then they closed the books on the whole shebazz. Which, when you think about it, is really and truly superdumb. Because if we did not do all of the things that they claimed and never proved, why then, somebody else did, right? Weigh that. What it means is that there is probably a young couple still out there somewhere, knocking over gas stations and liquor stores, stealing good cars, and kidnapping people and giving them a bad time and sometimes even killing them.

The people of Arizona probably think they are safe because me and Wayne are locked up.

Well. The real joke is that we are safe and the state of Arizona isn't. Because those criminals are probably out there right this minute, barreling down the highway in a hot car, looking for kicks and laughing their asses off.

So if that's the way Arizona wants it, they can have it. I would not leave here now if they begged me to on bended knees. I just hope that that terrifying, murderous young couple comes down on Arizona like a dose of the plague and that I get to read about it in the papers.

They will be plenty sorry then, but it will be too late.

So I have got the last laugh coming. All that I have to do is to keep still and to be patient.

But I started out to tell about that night in Paradise Springs and how me and Wayne didn't have anything to do with any of it.

It is true that I was directly and personally acquainted with some of the people involved. So fuckin' what? That means nothing. Paradise Springs is a pretty small town. Everybody knows everybody, practically.

After we went to the rectory and caught Daddy jerking off in the attic and all that (Wayne did it. I didn't.) the plan was for me and Wayne to start out for San Francisco that very same night. We would go to the place, the big field, where people were parked for the tent revival and the carnival, and we would try to find a worthwhile car to steal. I was scouting around on my own when Wayne came wheeling up in this crazy-ass old hearse, all painted up with psychedelic signs and graffiti, that belonged to some fraternity boys from over in Gainesville. It was a wild-looking thing.

"Hey, let's go to Frisco and do something fun," he said.

"Not in that heap," I told him.

"Maybe we should go back and take your old man's car."

"Are you kidding? All he's got is a ten-year-old Plymouth and it won't even get us as far as Georgia. And it won't outrun a motor scooter."

We wandered around for a while, window-shopping for a half-decent set of wheels. Pretty soon we found Martin Pressy's white Mercedes. It was love at first sight. So we parked the crazy hearse in its place and then took off. Nobody even saw us.

We went and had a few beers at the White Turkey. And Wayne had some speed. After a while Wayne got it in his head that he wanted to test-drive the thing, to really open up Pressy's Mercedes and see what it could do. So we took it out to the old air base. Which is almost abandoned except that they still keep some private planes out there.

We tried it out on the runway. But Wayne said it was too dark for him to really enjoy it. I knew there were some lights out there if we could just figure out a way to turn them on.

Wayne shot the lock off of the power shack and then started pulling switches. All these lights on the runway came on. And a big rotating light on the old control tower. Turning like a lighthouse. It was really beautiful.

Then we jumped in the car and really opened it up. Back and forth we went. We had it all the way up to 120 when a crazy twin-engined airplane came in low out of the dark and almost crashed into us, landing.

That really blew Wayne's mind. He was profoundly pissed and more than a little scared. Quick as he could, he got us slowed down and stopped and then jumped out and ran for the woods. He probably thought it was somebody coming after him. But I was the only one doing that.

I ran after him and then we just ran together on through the woods and a swamp too. We ran and we ran, panting and sweating, until we finally came to a dirt road. We walked along it in the general direction of the lights of town, laughing now. After a while there was a parked car at the side of the road. It was a station wagon belonging to Baptist College. Way out there all alone. We tiptoed and sneaked up on it. We peeped in the back. There was this couple, naked on a blanket in the back, going at it, humping like dogs in heat. They were sort of all fat and middle-aged and ugly from what we could see.

Wayne gave me the pistol to hold. Then we went around to the front. He pointed to me that the keys were there in the ignition and he winked. Then we jumped in the front seat from both sides simultaneously and he started it up and drove off fast down the road.

The folks in the back started yelling and sat up, trying to cover themselves with the blanket. I pointed the pistol at them and they shut up.

"Hey, don't stop anything on our account," Wayne told them. "We like company and we're planning to take a long ride."

"Where are you planning to take us?" the man finally said. He sounded more than a little drunk (by now I could smell whiskey along with the fishy sweat smell) and thick-tongued.

Then I could see that it was Professor Katz. I could tell him by his voice and his big nose and his big old circumcised dick. (During my brief time at Baptist College I took a course from him—I forget what it was about—and earned an *A plus*.) I didn't know who the naked lady was at first. I mean, I didn't recognize her, bare-ass in the altogether with her hair all messed up.

"San Francisco," Wayne said. "Ever been there before?"

The woman went into instant hysteria, gasping and crying and generally losing control. It was then that I recognized her. She was Mary Faith, the dean of women at Baptist College. She is the one who finally expelled me from there and called me a slut. Now she was saying how if her husband ever found out about this he would probably kill her. She said Katz must have put some kind of a love potion in her Coca-Cola.

I told her to shut the fuck up or Wayne would kill her.

"What about you?" Wayne said to Katz, looking at him in the rearview mirror. "What's your excuse?"

"Tenure," Katz said. "I'm trying to get tenure."

Then the woman started sobbing again and cussing and praying, too, all at the same time. That bugged Wayne (he hated loud noises and too much emotion). So he told me to go ahead and shoot her if she didn't shut up right now. And I was ready to do it, too (*she called me a slut*) but the bitch just stopped like she had flipped a switch or something.

As soon as we got onto a paved road, Wayne pulled over and parked and told them to get out of the car right now.

"Naked?" Katz said. "At least let us put our shoes on."

"Naked you come into this world and you'll be going out of it the same way unless you do what I tell you," Wayne said. Then: "You can keep the blanket."

He produced his Swiss Army knife and cut the blanket more or less in half. They started off in opposite directions. We watched until their big white asses disappeared in the dark. Then Wayne scratched out fast, peeling rubber and blowing the horn.

I looked around and noticed that we were headed generally southeast. Which certainly is not the right direction to go if you plan to end up in San Francisco, California. Wayne had a terribly defective sense of direction, as I was to learn long before we ever got to Arizona. Now that I think about it, that's probably why the cops had trouble catching us. They thought we knew where we were going and how to get there. But, anyway, at that moment I did not care. Just as long as we were moving, going somewhere.

"That was very rude about the shoes," I told Wayne.

"How about that old fart!" Wayne said. "He'll do anything to get tenure. Except rent a motel room. He's too tight for that."

"I guess we are too late for the Summer of Love," I said.

"That was just a bullshit hippie thing, a publicity stunt," Wayne said.

"You're so cynical."

"And you're so cute."

Then and There

EXCERPT FROM TRANSCRIPT OF
State of Florida v. Mary Lou Frond
and William Papp

[*Continuing direct examination of witness Darlene Blaze*
by Edward Cooke, county attorney]

COOKE: Now, then, Darlene, honey, I know it is difficult for you, but I want you to try to control yourself and to finish up answering my questions.

BLAZE: But we have already been over it over and over again. I have been answering all your questions and I am sick to death of it. How many times do I have to continue to go over this stuff?

JUDGE SPENCE: The witness is directed to answer.

COOKE: It's all right, Your Honor. I fully appreciate how Miss Blaze feels. Darlene, this is the time that it really counts—in court. After this, I don't expect you will have to answer a lot more questions—unless the newspaper people get hold of you.

BLAZE: Yes, sir. Thank you, sir. I will try my best.

COOKE: Now, then, if we can get back to the subject of the money. At what point did you realize that Alpha Weatherby had all that money with her?

BLAZE: Well, I would guess during the collection. I mean, when they came around passing the collection plate, I saw her reach in her purse and put a fifty-dollar bill—the one with Grant on it—in the plate. And when she did that, I like to have fell out of my folding chair.

COOKE: Did you say anything to her?

BLAZE: Yes, sir, I certainly did. I told her that she had made a serious mistake by putting a fifty-dollar bill in there. I was still holding on to the plate and wouldn't let go of it.

COOKE: And what was her reaction? What did she do?

BLAZE: She told me to shut my big mouth and to mind my own business. Then she said she didn't mean to be rude, but not to worry, that she had plenty more where that came from. And she allowed me to take a peek in her pocketbook. And I could see that it was cram-full of money.

COOKE: I see. Now, then, if you don't mind, Darlene, I am fixing to ask you certain questions in a certain order. I want you to try to answer me directly and succinctly.

BLAZE: Okay, I will try.

COOKE: What were you doing at this time?

BLAZE: I was still holding on to the collection plate like I told you. I wasn't about to let go.

COOKE: Just answer this next question yes or no, please. Was somebody trying to take the plate away from you?

BLAZE: Yes, sir.

COOKE: And you didn't want to let go.

BLAZE: I didn't, either, until Alpha told me to.

COOKE: Just yes or no, honey.

BLAZE: Yes. Yes, sir.

COOKE: Someone was trying to take the plate away from you. Was that person the same one who was passing the plate?

BLAZE: Yes, sir.

COOKE: The one who was taking up the collection?

BLAZE: Yes, sir, on our side of the tent, anyway.

COOKE: Briefly, please: Where were you sitting?

BLAZE: In the back on the left. We were right smack on the far left.

COOKE: Where were you sitting on the row?

BLAZE: I was sitting in the aisle seat. And Alpha was right next to me.

JUDGE SPENCE: Mr. Cooke, I do hope that all these details are relevant.

COOKE: Oh, indeed they are, Your Honor, indeed they are.

They are entirely relevant. If Your Honor will permit me to proceed with my examination . . .

JUDGE SPENCE: By all means proceed. But try to get to the point.

COOKE: To resume, Darlene. You were sitting on the aisle, tugging on the collection plate against the person who was taking up the collection on your side?

BLAZE: Yes, sir, exactly like I just told you.

COOKE: Did this person, who was taking up the collection and tugging on the plate, say anything to you?

BLAZE: Yes, sir. She did.

COOKE: Do you recall what she said?

BLAZE: Yes, sir, I recollect it exactly.

COOKE: What was it?

BLAZE: This person said to me: "Turn loose of the plate, you dumb bitch!"

COOKE: Is that all?

BLAZE: No, sir. After Alpha had showed me all that money in her purse and had stated to me that everything was all right, copacetic, the person said to me: "Why don't you mind your own fuckin' business?"

COOKE: What did you do next?

BLAZE: I turned loose of the plate. But I only did so because Alpha told me to.

COOKE: And did you continue discussing this matter with Alpha Weatherby?

BLAZE: Yes, sir, I did. I whispered in her ear how she must be out of her mind. And she whispered back at me that she knew what she was doing and everything was all right.

COOKE: Why did you react so strongly to Alpha Weatherby's fifty-dollar offering?

BLAZE: Well, sir, I . . . Now I want to put this right, so please let me take my time.

COOKE: Take all the time you need.

BLAZE: Well, sir, to the best of my knowledge and recollection, as they say, Alpha did not have fifty dollars to her name.

So naturally I was surprised. And I was curious as to how she happened to come by it. But that wasn't the main thing, just part of it. I had another feeling also. Alpha was what you would define as a very religious person. And she had not . . . well, you know, been around and about as much as me.

COOKE: You felt responsible for her?

BLAZE: Yes, sir. She was my friend. And in my considered opinion and to the best of my knowledge, she was a sweet, clean, good, innocent . . .

JOHN RIVERS: Objection! I object, your honor.

JUDGE SPENCE: Sustained. Ed, do you mind telling me where in the hell you are going?

COOKE: Your Honor, the point I am trying to arrive at and make is crucial to our case. All of this is completely relevant and important, pertinent to my point.

JUDGE SPENCE: I sure hope so.

RIVERS: It appears to me that counsel for the prosecution is indulging in his justly celebrated flair for the dramatic.

COOKE: Aw, Jack, you are the only honest-to-god Thespian around here.

JUDGE SPENCE: Order! Order! Mr. Cooke, I am asking you to proceed expeditiously.

COOKE: And so I am, Your Honor, so I am.

JUDGE SPENCE: Get on with it.

COOKE: Darlene Blaze, what were you worried about when you discovered that Alpha Weatherby had what appeared to be a considerable sum of money on her person?

BLAZE: I was scared—and I told her so—that something bad might happen to her and to me, too. That we might get hurt or something.

COOKE: Why?

BLAZE: Because I considered it a dangerous and unsavory place for a young lady to flash a lot of money.

RIVERS: Objection!

COOKE: And did you say that to her?

JUDGE SPENCE: Objection overruled.

BLAZE: Yes, sir, or words to that effect.

COOKE: Now, then, let's get back to the person who took up the collection on your side of the tent.

BLAZE: Yes, sir.

COOKE: After, as you said, you let go of the plate, did you observe what this person did next?

BLAZE: Yes, sir, I did. The person went straight directly back to the front of the tent and showed the plate to Little David. Then he stood up—he was up there kneeling on the stage— and he and the person looked over in our direction. And then the person pointed right at us.

COOKE: I see. Now, then, tell me, Darlene, did you ever see that money in Alpha's purse again?

BLAZE: Yes, sir, I did. When we went back for the private healing part.

COOKE: Could you elucidate, could you explain that a little more clearly—the "healing part"?

BLAZE: Well, after the collection and the sermon, they had a healing session for the sick people.

COOKE: Where people go in hope of getting cured of real or imaginary ailments?

BLAZE: Where they go and pray with the preacher and hope for the best.

COOKE: Go ahead with your account.

BLAZE: Well, they announced a healing session. And to my surprise Alpha said that we should go. I replied to the effect that there wasn't anything wrong with me, at least nothing that that little half-pint of a preacher could cure.

JUDGE SPENCE: Order! I will clear the courtroom if this noise continues.

COOKE: Go ahead, Darlene.

BLAZE: Alpha told me that she wasn't feeling too good and that she would like to see if he could help her feel better.

COOKE: Did she mention any specific symptoms or complaint?

BLAZE: No, sir. She just allowed that she wasn't feeling too good.

COOKE: Did you try to persuade her not to attend the healing session?

BLAZE: No, sir. I figured that if Alpha had already made up her mind, there was no stopping her.

COOKE: What did you do then?

BLAZE: I got up and went with her.

COOKE: Why?

RIVERS: Objection!

COOKE: Witness has not even answered yet.

BLAZE: Because she asked me to.

COOKE: Now, as I understand it, this so-called healing session was held in a separate tent or enclosure attached to the main tent. Is that correct?

BLAZE: That's right. We lined up outside and went in a few at a time.

COOKE: And you went in with Alpha Weatherby?

BLAZE: Yes, sir. I went in and kneeled down right beside her. I was next to her when he came along. He put his hands on both of our heads at the same time.

COOKE: Would you repeat for us, to the best of your recollection, what was said at that time? And what happened.

BLAZE: We kneeled there in a row, and he came along. He said to Alpha: "Bless you my daughter, what is wrong with you?" And she said it was something very serious and very special. He asked her what that could be. She said it was not a medical illness. She said that she was possessed by a demon and that she had come here, walking a good long way, because she had seen his picture and realized that he was the only one who could cure her. She said that he could easily get rid of the demon and if he did, she would offer up all her worldly possessions and dedicate her life to the service of the Lord.

COOKE: Please try to control yourself. I am almost done.

BLAZE: I am trying. I really am trying.

COOKE: What did Little David say?

BLAZE: I heard him tell her that it was a very special situation, but he would do the best he could. He told her to come back to his trailer after the service was over and done with and he would see if he could help her.

COOKE: Now, then, let's jump ahead in time. After this public, so-called healing session where did you go?

BLAZE: We went out the back flap of the tent so we could go around and get our same seats again.

COOKE: As you came outside of the tent what happened?

BLAZE: There was somebody right there at the exit with a collection plate, collecting for the healing.

COOKE: And did you recognize this person?

BLAZE: I did. It was the very same one that had been taking up the collection before.

COOKE: Did you make any offering?

BLAZE: I didn't but Alpha did.

COOKE: Do you recall what kind of an offering she made?

BLAZE: She pulled another fifty-dollar bill and some ones and fives and loose change out of her pocket and put it all in the plate.

COOKE: Now, then, Darlene. I want you to be sure, very sure, that you can answer my next question truthfully and definitely. Or not at all. Could you recognize that person with the collection plate if you should happen to see that person again?

BLAZE: I could. I would recognize that person anywhere.

COOKE: Is that person in this courtroom now?

JUDGE SPENCE: Speak up a little bit, Mr. Cooke.

COOKE: Is that person in the courtroom here and now?

BLAZE: Yes, sir.

COOKE: Would you please indicate that person?

BLAZE: There! There she is. (*Indicates the defendant, Mary Lou Frond.*) That hideous, slimy tub of guts and lard! Right there!

JUDGE SPENCE: Order! I will have order in this court! Do you-all hear me?

Then and There

MLK PICTURE

It is a close shot, head and shoulders, black-and-white, of the two men together. Between them, just over Malcolm X's shoulder, we see part of the round face of another black man, light-skinned cheeks shaped in what must be a fixed smile, wearing heavy, hornrimmed glasses. Malcolm X is light-skinned and he wears glasses, too. Behind MLK's head is only the ear of another close witness, evidently a white ear.

The caption of the photograph, credited to the Library of Congress, informs us that this picture was taken on the one and only occasion that MLK and Malcolm X actually met—March 26, 1964, at the Capitol while the Senate was debating LBJ's civil rights bill.

Malcolm X, facing the camera, though not looking at it, looking at MLK instead, is a good deal taller and thinner. MLK is standing or moving at right angles to Malcolm X, not (here anyway) making eye contact. Both men are smiling, Malcolm X the more so. Both men are wearing crisp white shirts with thin, dark neckties. Both have on dark jackets. MLK's looks at a glance (and a glance is all we are given) to be the better fit and quality. Malcolm X has on a coat that, even in this glossy photo, seems to be of a coarse-textured knit wool, like a sweater. Maybe it is more fashionable.

The two men spoke to each other. MLK first: "Well, Malcolm, good to see you." To which Malcolm X is reported to have replied: "Good to see you." Then they spoke to each other briefly in low voices; were watched as they walked together, but not overheard. They might have met again and spoken together in Selma, Alabama, on February 4, 1965, at the outset of the Selma demonstrations and march. Makcolm X arrived on the scene suddenly (did the SNCC boys put him up to it?) and spoke to MLK's people at Brown Chapel. But MLK was in jail at the time. Coretta brought MLK the news of Malcolm X's visit and his words to her—"I want Dr. King to know I didn't come to Selma to make his job difficult."

On February 21, less than three full weeks after that flying visit, Malcolm X was killed by Muslim gunmen at the Audubon Ballroom in Harlem.

Much has been written by scholars and biographers about the deep differences between the two men, about their radically different backgrounds, their religions and philosophies, about the sharp differences in their goals and objectives, tactics and strategy. How Malcolm X often publicly ridiculed MLK as a classic Uncle Tom, once calling him "a black mouse on a white elephant." How even so, though they were bound to be far from friendly, there was a certain kind of fellowship between them. How each came, finally, to a violent, sudden death. How death has joined them together.

In "My Last Letter to Martin," a sermon he preached on April 7, 1968, MLK's old friend and new successor, Ralph Abernathy, summoned up a list of biblical and historical figures, saints and heroes, and, as well, martyrs of the civil rights movement, all of whom MLK could now meet and talk to in heaven. One of them, the last named, somewhat defensively to be sure, was Malcolm X.

Here and Now

A PRIVATE STATEMENT BY **BILLY TONE**
(MADE ON HIS M-425 SONY MICROCASSETTE-CORDER)

Testing: one, two, three, four.

This is Billy Tone speaking to himself.

My purpose at this point in time is to put in order (to the best of my recollection) my memories and thoughts concerning Verna Claxton, Father Claxton, Wayne Starkey and myself during the first week in April 1968. This does not constitute a confession of any kind; and even in the unlikely event that this tape should fall into the hands of others, it remains in large part deniable and unprovable, at least in any American court of law. In part, much of it, like the rest of my life so far, is chaotic—which is to say always disorderly and at times incoherent. Often riddled (and thus changed) by regret.

Nevertheless it behooves me to try to report on some of these things to relieve my confusion, if not my conscience.

Begin with Verna. Blond from head to toe, blue-eyed, she of the sweet skin impeccable, the breasts impossible, the body trim and lithe, incomparable. It was she who first taught me the oldest dance for two in Creation. And in fairness to the memory of her, I have to say that it/she was so good, so breathtakingly satisfactory, that it has almost spoiled me for any other kind of human connection. I used to think it was too bad that this marvelous creature was also endowed with a vicious character (in every sense of vicious—i.e., *vice-ridden*), for otherwise she would have been too perfect. But now I sometimes think I am the luckiest man in the world, lucky not that her character repelled me, but that because of her character she had no serious interest in me one way or the other. I thought it was love for sure. I would gladly have died for her and, less gladly, but without any hesitation or delay, would probably have killed for her as well.

Wayne did both. And I have always wondered who influenced the other one the most, whether he was a match for her and more so or whether he was more like myself than I ever imagined at the time and, in fact, lived out the brief and savage life that might as well have been mine.

Begins with Verna and me. Coming north from south Florida, where my mother had moved after the death of my father (heart attack). Coming north towards Paradise Springs in my mother's '64 Oldsmobile, warm early-evening air blowing in the open windows; rock and roll from the radio blaring out to warn the wide world of our coming and going. Both of us stoned and (at least I can speak for myself) myself being about as happy as I had ever been or could imagine being.

Going where? San Francisco, where else? Only going to stop by Paradise Springs and the rectory of St. Paul's so Verna could pick up some of her things.

Verna had told me more than once and with a strange, light-hearted good cheer that she hated her father's guts. That he was a phony and a hypocrite and a creep. That it was no wonder that his wife (her mother) had left him (her too) and, as far as anyone knew, had vanished off the face of the earth. That it was uncertain exactly how her mother, after some years of being a good and dutiful clergyman's wife, had run away. Only stories. One that she left with a minor rock-and-roll musician who had played at the Rialto, a little fellow who wore boots stuffed with flattened tin cans to make himself taller. That she fled in the company of two second-rate comedians who had briefly per-formed at the White Turkey. That she joined a carnival as a stripper and had been later seen and identified in Columbus, Georgia, and Montgomery, Alabama. This latter was the version that Verna preferred to believe. One fantasy she liked to spin out was how she would one day soon join a carnival as a strip-teaser, herself, and how, sooner or later, she and her mother would meet and work on the same stage.

I should mention one thing more. Which at the time seemed not exactly insignificant, but not really important either. One of the things I had with me, in the glove compartment as it hap-pened, was my mother's old .32 caliber Smith and Wesson re-volver and a box of shells. Why? I don't know for sure. It pleased Verna that I had it. And anything that seemed to please her was all right with me. But the *reason* why I had it (at some risk, because it was an illegal and concealed weapon and would take a policeman about ten seconds to discover if we got stopped for speeding or anything else) was the road could be something of a wild and dangerous place in those days. Or so it seemed. I really thought I needed something for protection. There had been some bad scenes here and there the year before, the first time I drove out to the Coast, and I thought the pistol would be a help. Symbolic more than anything else. I really never imagined using it except in desperate self-defense.

Boy, girl, car and pistol, hauling down the highway at an unsafe speed. Out in the middle of nowhere, suddenly popping up out of a ditch, there stands a wild-looking young guy, red hair and freckles, jeans and boots and a leather jacket, waving both hands as if for help.

"Stop and see what's happening," Verna said.

I have already driven past him. Have to stop and back up on the shoulder carefully so as not to drive into the ditch. In the rearview mirror I can see that he isn't moving towards us, just standing and waiting for me. I can also see now that there is a motorcycle in the ditch.

"Want some help?"

"No, I just want a ride."

"What about your bike?"

"Fuck it," he says, grinning. He has an impish kind of a smile. "It's no good. It ran me off the road."

"We can drive you to a garage," I say.

"I don't want to *fix* the fuckin' thing. I want to leave it behind."

"Hop in," says Verna without so much as a look at me.

"It isn't mine, anyway," he says, settling into the back seat. "I took it out of a parking lot in Titusville."

"Well, don't get any ideas about taking this car," she says, laughing.

And I see that she has opened up the glove compartment and produced the pistol and pointed it right at him.

"Hey, be careful!" I say to Verna.

In the mirror I see he has raised both hands and is hiding behind that impish grin.

"How far are you and your husband going?" he asks.

I start to say Paradise Springs, figuring we can put up with him for a couple or three hours. Figuring (correctly as it turns out) that he will entertain Verna for a while. But Verna beats me to it.

"He's not my husband."

"Oh, yeah?"

"He's not even my boyfriend. We just fucked a few times and now he thinks he owns me."

"Cut it out, Verna," I say.

"So where are you headed?"

"San Francisco," she says. "You want to come?"

"Why not?"

"What's your name?"

"Wayne."

"I'm Verna and sourpuss there is Billy."

"Pleased to meet you."

"Good," she says. "I'm glad all that is settled."

A little later we pull into a town just south of Daytona. May have been New Smyrna Beach or maybe Port Orange. At least that is what I guess now from the map. At the time I didn't know and couldn't care less.

We pass through the town, and on the highway on the other side I stop at a filling station for some gas and a pit stop.

While I am standing at the clogged and stinking urinal in the men's room I hear what sounds to me like a shot, the flat crack of that little pistol. And I come running back towards the car zipping up my fly on the run. There by the car, pistol in hand, grinning, is Wayne. Then Verna comes running, too, giggling and giddy, out of the station carrying a whole lot of loose money and some candy bars in both hands. The attendant, a young black guy in a clean white shirt, is nowhere in sight.

"Jesus," I say.

"Grab the wheel and let's haul ass!" Wayne orders.

"Do it, Billy!" Verna says.

They both jump in the back seat. To tell the truth, I don't think anything at all at first. I am in something like shock. I scratch out of the station and floor it, headed north. For a while, however long or short it is, I don't think of or about anything except putting miles and miles between us and that filling station. I don't even wonder why they are both in the back seat until finally the noise, their grunts and groans and Verna's familiar and exciting whinny, tells me what's going on right behind me.

I sneak a glance back, see the white flash of her flesh and he, Wayne, on top of her pumping away like a man doing calisthenics. He twists around slightly and points the pistol, now in his left hand, directly at my head.

"Drive or die, shithead," he says.

"You can watch, Billy," Verna calls out sweetly. "But not while you're driving."

"Here, have a candy bar," Wayne says.

Stoned and confused as I am, I am fully aware that we are in deep shit. There is a boy, somebody my age or younger, a black kid, maybe hurt, maybe dead back there. Shot with my pistol. We are fleeing the scene in my car. The filling station has been robbed. And I am as much involved and culpable as if I had pulled the trigger.

Rationalize as I will and do, there is no denying it. I can argue that I was forced to do what I did. Outside of my own hometown and a jury of my family and friends, who would want to believe my story?

But . . .

Be honest, tell the truth after all these years.

But even as I am racked by fear and guilt and self-contempt, what is really troubling me at that moment (and troubles me more now because it troubled me then) is Verna. I would rather be dead than lose her. I think this even as I guess—no, I *know*—that if I do not lose her, I will surely die, and soon. Because she is hurrying to die and not all alone. And I realize, know full well, even at that age, that danger is at the heart of the excitement of being with her. That to stay and to be with her is a form of suicide, fast or slow, orgasmic and deeply satisfying.

I have followed too much the devices and desires of my own heart and there is no health in me.

(I can't help wondering now if my fascination with the story of Alpha Weatherby, who was moving steadily towards her own death at almost exactly the same time that I was indulging myself in these thoughts, I wonder if the appeal of Alpha's story, thus of herself, still arousing my attention and bemusement after all these years, if Alpha is not another version of Verna, just as deadly but this time fueled not by vice but by an equally savage virtue.)

Never mind. Return to the car where, spent from sex, they are now thirsty and want me to stop again for soft drinks.

"I want a cool Grapette," Verna says. "It goes good with Mary Jane."

"Dr. Pepper for me," Wayne says.

I get out of the car at a country filling station and buy three soft drinks from an elderly man in overalls. The bottles are very cold and beaded, coming not out of machines but out of a large ice bucket crammed with big chips of ice. I can hardly hold the bottles, they are so cold.

I could speak to the old man. I could tell him. But I do not. I pay him and nod, and I take the three cold bottles of soda pop back to the car.

"What the hell is the matter with you?" Verna says to me.

"What do you mean?"

"Why are you crying?"

"I don't know."

I climb in the car behind the wheel and drive on.

Thinking about it here and now I believe that Verna saved my life. At least she cared that much.

Before we came to Paradise Springs she went to work on Wayne.

"Wayne, we are going to need a new car. I can't ride all the way across the country in this heap. We can do better."

"Yeah?"

"I've got just the car in mind. It's a sports car that will carry two of us."

"What do we do with your old buddy here?"

"I guess we leave him behind, Wayne."

"That may not be very smart. He's a witness."

"No. He's a perpetrator, just like us."

"I don't want to take any chances."

"Oh, Wayne, Wayne, that's what I love about you. You're a man who will take a chance, any chance."

"Yeah, but . . ."

"Don't disappoint me."

Then to me: "Don't you disappoint me, either, Billy."

At that moment I felt completely betrayed, though it would never have occurred to me to betray Verna.

We drove into Paradise Springs and Verna asked me to drop them off at the rectory of St. Paul's.

"I think I'll keep this, if you don't mind," Wayne said, showing me my pistol, then stuffing it under his belt.

Verna came around to the window on the driver's side, leaned in and kissed me on the cheek. She whispered some things in my ear. What I took her to be telling me: *You never saw anything happen at that filling station. You were in the bathroom. You don't know what happened. So whatever happened is not your fault. Remember that. And remember something else, Billy. You owe me your life. He would kill you in one minute and without thinking about it. You owe your life to me and you owe me something.*

I sat there gripping the wheel. I watched and waited as the two of them approached the old house. There was a light from way up in the little attic windows. That's all. I guess Verna had a key because in a moment they disappeared into the house and I drove away.

I crashed and spent the night at a cheap motel on the other side of town.

In the morning it all seemed unreal. A bad dream. She was right. I didn't in fact see anything happen. I went to the men's room and heard a sound I took to be a shot. But I didn't see anything. Later I could and would imagine (as if in memory) the body of the black boy lying there on the floor of the station like a huge roadkill. Maybe so. I could imagine and even remember it, but I never saw it. And I could also imagine (and I did) that after we drove off, peeling rubber, he got up and dusted himself off, laughing, and then lived out the rest of his allotted days without harm.

Who knows?

I know better.

I knew better then, but found the ways and means to deny it.

In the morning I got up refreshed. Smoked some dope and swallowed a little speed and started driving west. I know I must have stopped any number of times at any number of places before I made it to San Francisco. But I have no memory of any of that. Only of driving and driving and driving across this vast country, radio roaring and the road dancing ahead of me.

It was a long time, months, before I learned that Father Claxton had killed himself on or about the same time I passed through Paradise Springs. Later still, I heard the old rumors and gossip. I always assumed that the pistol was my mother's .32 Smith and Wesson. I always feared that Wayne killed him. Maybe it happened not long after I let them out of the car.

I was not surprised a few months later when there was a couple of killers, a young man and a young woman, who were wasting road people in considerable numbers. I knew long before the Law did that it had to be Verna and Wayne. Real serial killers before that term was even being used to describe what they were up to. And when they finally got caught I was not surprised, not even pleased to have my inferential guesswork confirmed. I was a little surprised at the way Verna presented herself to press and public after they were caught. But then she was always reinventing herself.

Not a lot surprises me. Except that sometimes on the shore and edge of sleep, an image, a picture appears briefly and fades. The filling station, an old and old-fashioned one. Lonely as if imagined by Hopper. That blue Oldsmobile at the pump. Nobody in it. A tall young man, a black boy in jeans and wearing a clean, crisp, short-sleeved white shirt, is standing by the pump filling the car. His face is smooth, pleasant, content. His mind is elsewhere. Something he has done, some place he has been. Or neither. Something that (he imagines) is going to happen. He is whistling a little tune. I can't quite hear it. It seems terribly important to know, but I do not know the little tune he is whistling.

And then the light begins to fade.

And then he is gone.

And then it is all gone into the dark.

Here and Now

THE POET: MLK, THE NEGATIVES

Frederick Buechner writes (and maybe I will use this as my epigraph unless I find something better): "I've been interested in the notion of a saint as a human being who's just as much clay-footed and full of shadows as the rest of us, but who is used nonetheless by God for His own purposes, in His own way."

MLK not a saint. Repeat *not*. No kind of. At least not to start with.

Plenty, a full measure, of flaws and foibles.

Incessant and insatiable womanizing. No doubt about it. Evidence overwhelming. And not just the J. Edgar Hoover tapes and then LBJ late at night in the White House laughing his big Texas ass off while listening to creaks and squeaks, grunts and groans of MLK and whatever woman of whatever evening . . . or morning . . . or afternoon.

The Reverend Doctor Superstud, Ph.D.

According to Abernathy's book he was busy making the beast with two backs on the last days of his life.

And we really don't know anything much about his finances. Except that it's clear he never lost or risked any money of his own. And ended up much better off (swimming pool and all) than when he started. An upwardly mobile saint.

So? Irrelevant. Being MLK paid off in dollars and cents as well as in prizes, awards, grants, fame and the love of women. At least some of whom had to be beautiful. Relevance? Only this: that there was no serious self-sacrifice involved. No sacrifice at all, really, until the final and ultimate sacrifice in Memphis. Which was none of his doing except to be standing in the right place at the right time for the assassin.

It is not as if he gave up much of anything to assume the public role of MLK.

Where else would he be?

What else would he be doing?

Even the big thing, nonviolent resistance, not being what it was thought to be then or now. Nothing much like Gandhi's.

More than once MLK spoke of the pure and simple practicality of it. They outnumber us ten to one, he noted. They outgun us even more. In violence we stand to lose big. Nonviolence is safer and gives us the moral high ground. All the more so while the nation is torn apart and fighting that war in Vietnam.

Man of peace (after all, he got the Nobel Peace Prize) and nonviolence not only stands better chance of success, but also comforts and reassures the constituency of white liberals.

Meantime you have Muslims and (later) the Panthers talking blood and guts, fire and brimstone. Liberal whites scared shitless. No excuse for not giving MLK whatever, large or small, he wants.

MLK couldn't have asked for a better scenario. If Muslims and Panthers hadn't come along he would have had to invent them.

Little things also.

The whole plagiarism business seems now to be real. No denying it. Can't even suppress it. Oh, they can and do argue (unpersuasively) that a different sense of *ownership* of words and ideas and arguments is involved. Old African customs and traditions, etc. Talking drums, etc. Bullshit!

Hypocrisy?

Probably. A very high level thereof.

Anything else?

Plenty.

People around him, close, involved and engaged in commonplace extortion and tough-guy stuff. MLK's disciples not a bunch of saints either.

And the racists have a solid point, too, when they argue that up to the very instant of his death it was mostly an almost riskless enterprise. Directly protected by Presidents. Most of the time in jail (to dismay of the young men of SNCC) he had special meals and special treatment. Not often in real danger. Bombs in Montgomery, but nobody hurt. More good than harm. (PR stunt?) Rocks in Chicago. But seldom, if ever, in real danger. Yes, crazy woman in Harlem stabbed him with letter opener and almost killed him. A sneeze away from death.

Did that make him feel immortal?

How could he lose, no matter what the apparent odds, with whole government of U.S., all three branches of same (except, of course, the FBI), committed to care and support of him, defending his actions if not all of his ideas.

The one time MLK and his whole Southern Christian Leadership gang were really in deep trouble was that libel case— *Sullivan v. New York Times*. No sweat. Supreme Court, for better or worse, completely rewrote the ancient and honorable laws of libel for sole and express purpose of saving MLK's black ass. If SCLC went under, who the hell would they be dealing with next—H. Rap Brown? Stokely Carmichael? Malcolm X?

No. Not a saint. A contemporary public figure, hustler, hypocrite and leader. No way saintly.

And yet . . .

And yet . . .

Everlasting irony of God.

By his death (the supreme sacrifice, the than-which-nothing-more) he paid off, once and for all, "a full, perfect, and sufficient sacrifice." All these petty debts and trespasses erased. Becoming in fact and memory the man he professed and pretended to be. Purged and purified, he became an emblem, a model of and for virtue. Became a monument. Became an avenue. A *boulevard* in many places. Became a schoolhouse. Became, finally, a holiday. Saint's day. Like it or not.

Became a figure so towering and transcendent and so widely and deeply admired that all these things, faults and flaws, and many others are now overturned and effaced. He is elected to a kind of sainthood in spite of himself. What was purely *image* or only partly true becomes the Truth. A transformation so marvelous (and maybe ironic, too, I'll concede that), maybe a kind of cosmic joke, that it belongs to a fairy tale. Hard facts (like straw) become bricks of gold.

What a classic American story!

Yet (*layers of irony*) it is, of course, almost beyond telling. At least the whole of it and truly. Except, perhaps by guileful and extreme indirection. We can tell this tale truly only by means of a sly duplicity. It will remain for others—aliens, strangers, descendants—to view it without blinking or winking.

What moves me most here and now is this one thing. I have read in several places (how else?) that maybe the last living thing he did in his motel room, just before he walked out onto the balcony and stood still a moment and was killed by a single well-placed gunshot, the very last thing he did in this world before entering the next one was to engage in a lively pillow fight with some of the younger members of his group, including (they say) Andrew Young. A pillow fight in a motel room! Followed by sudden death and immortality.

Well.

Except you become as a little child . . .

Here and Now

PRESENCES

"You may find some of this hard to believe," Darlene tells him.

"Go ahead. Try me."

They are sitting at the round oak table in the dining room of her house. Sipping herbal tea. Periodically, trucks hauling it east or west on the highway cause cups and saucers to rattle. Little spoons make bell sounds. Otherwise, though, they might as well be in the deep woods in a fairy-tale cottage. There is a soft sighing of breeze in the tall pines. Occasionally the squawk of a blue jay, the sniggle and chitter of squirrels, or sourceless birdsong. Sun filtering into the room through half-open venetian blinds. Dust motes dance in the light. There is the odor of incense in the room.

At what point did incense become available and become a conventional part of the bag of tricks of a working fortune-teller in this part of the world? Probably in the sixties along with everything else, only relatively late. As late as 1968, when he was in San Francisco, it was still vaguely exotic.

He is sitting at the large table, just himself and Darlene Blaze, who is acting in her professional capacity as Sister Cassandra. SISTER CASSANDRA/PALM READINGS/FORTUNE-TELLING is what the sign boldly announces at the edge of the gravel driveway.

He would never have found her. Would never even have found out that she is very much alive and still living in Quincy County (albeit at least a dozen miles from town on the old Gainesville Highway) if Moe Katz hadn't told him. Mostly by accident. Billy hadn't asked. He was taking Katz, wheelchair and oxygen and all, to the dentist (Katz: "I love to go to the dentist these days. The girl that works there, the hygienist—if you'll pardon the expression—is fresh from Germany, has a heavy accent and looks kind of like Ursula Andress in her prime. Gives me a huge boner every time she flosses and cleans my teeth.") and Billy had mentioned that, ideally, if he had time and any good reason to do this book right, really right, there were so many people he ought to track down and talk to. But couldn't. People like Billy Papp and Raphael McKenzie and Darlene Blaze.

Katz laughed and wheezed a little.

"I can't help you with the other two," he said. "But if you really want to talk to Darlene Blaze, it's easy as pie." Adding: "She doesn't call herself that anymore, though."

Billy did not tell her about the project or his purpose. Just looked in the yellow pages, called her number and made an appointment for a palm reading. Drove out there, following her directions, and found the place easily enough. Nice white frame cottage set back a ways from the highway. Somehow he expected another trailer or a mobile home. Get back in the country, only a little ways, and that's what you will usually find.

He pulled in and parked his rented Ford close by a big old Chevrolet pickup, dirty and rust-ridden, a bolt-action deer rifle on the gun rack, some cut firewood in the back. As he walked toward the front door he heard, from back in the woods, maybe a hundred yards or so from the house, somebody crank up a loud chainsaw and go to work on something.

Billy pushed the doorbell. It had a muted chime *ding-dong* like something in deep suburbia. He was surprised, expecting some exotic tintinnabulation or at least something more appropriate for the fortune-teller scam.

What would be the right kind of doorbell for a fortune-teller?

Pretty soon here came this large woman, tall and ample without being fat, dressed up in some kind of a down-home gypsy costume. Multicolored long skirt like a portable quilt. Some large and glittering costume jewelry. An incongruous Aunt Jemima bandanna on her head. Blue eyes, a gap-toothed bright smile (Hey, if it's good enough for Lauren Hutton it will do for Darlene Blaze), good posture and fine figure. Soft, husky voice and a pleasant greeting as if he were more guest than customer. Ushered him into the incense-smelling dining room where she half-closed the blinds and lowered the overhead light with a rheostat.

She took his right hand in hers, turned it palm up, then looked at the lines with a magnifying glass, beginning with a routine, singsongy explanation of her art and craft.

Then abruptly dropped his hand. Pushed back her chair and stood up. Lit herself a cigarette with a kitchen match, struck under the table, and puffed deeply.

"Is something the matter?" he said.

You don't really want your palm read, do you?

"Now that you ask me, no."

You have come here about something else."

"True. True enough. But as long as I'm here, I may as well have my palm read or something."

Why? It's all bullshit. Why waste your time and mine?

"That's the whole point. I want to waste a little of your time. But I am willing to pay for it."

And, she added, you are a little confused about what you want.

" 'Conflicted' would be the word for it."

You are completely skeptical about fortune-telling but you would still like to sneak a peek at your future.

"So would everyone else."

Well, she said, and so would I. But I can't help you.

"Actually you can."

Billy told her about the book he was working on and asked if she minded talking to him about those days.

Let me fix us a cup of tea and then we can talk awhile.

He has just now asked her about her general memory of the time. She has replied that her memory is okay and clear enough, but that it's much more than memory with her.

"What do you mean?"

I mean I am in touch with most of the people involved.

"Papp?"

No. He's alive somewhere—or else I would have heard. But, alive or dead, Papp is irrelevant.

"So who do you keep up with?"

Well, Alpha, of course, and Geneva and sometimes even Little David.

"Excuse me, but they are all dead."

They're in the spirit world, to be sure. But that doesn't mean they have ceased to be. It's not that simple.

"I guess not."

She stubs out her cigarette in an ashtray and blows a stream of smoke from her nostrils.

You may find some of this hard to believe.

"Go ahead. Try me."

I can't really tell fortunes. Nobody can, as far as I can tell, except some simple and obvious things and a little guesswork.

But I do have a certain gift which somebody might call extrasensory or psychic. I didn't always have this gift. Or if I did, I wasn't aware of it until later in my life. My young years were too physical for me to be conscious of much else but my body and my self inside of it. It took a while. I had to begin to lose my looks before I could begin to hear the voices within me.

It was a slow awareness. But as soon as I realized what was happening to me, how I was gifted, I began to cultivate that gift.

It works in two fairly distinct ways. Very often, even with perfect strangers, I can't exactly read their minds (though sometimes I can if the hunger and desire are strong enough), but I can often get a sense of what secret things are troubling them. I get some kind of a visual image, as in a dream—it's almost like dreaming it—and then I can see, in a flash like a photograph, what is heaviest, deepest-rooted in their minds. Usually something troublesome, some great trouble. But not always. Sometimes it's a happy vision. Sometimes. But not often.

I think this may be a fairly common gift. Maybe it's just a strong sensitivity to others. Who knows?

The other one isn't so common, though I have read and heard about other people who have it one way or another. It comes and goes and I usually can't control it. But, anyway, I am very conscious of some presences in the spirit world. Most of the time it's people from out of my own life, like Alpha. But sometimes it can be strangers. Who are haunting the thoughts and feelings of others—like people who come here for a palm reading or to have their fortune told in cards. Sometimes I can hear the voices of spirits and translate that for them.

It's not even a trick or anything. It just happens.

And once in a great while it's the voice of a complete stranger, someone lost among the other spirits. Someone without anybody else to talk to. It's weird and sad. Sometimes the voice comes in a foreign language and I can't understand what it is the spirit is trying to say.

But most of all the presences come out of my own life and experience. Alpha was the first spirit voice I ever heard and she has continued to come to me.

I understand her better than I ever did when she was still alive. And I think she understands herself and what happened better now too. She is mostly at peace. She says that it is very calm and peaceful in the spirit world. She says that everyone seems to be much the same as they were in life. Except that somehow each and everyone is touched with the light of a kind of beauty.

Geneva says the same thing to me. She tells me that she is still who she was, an enormously fat woman. But that it doesn't matter or have any meaning anymore except as a kind of sign of her presence: *There is nothing here in the spirit world that is not beautiful. So I am beautiful too. All things are bright and beautiful.*

It seems like maybe there are higher stages they will grow into. Seems like they are in a dimension where they can calmly consider their lives and worldly troubles and try to make some sense out of them. Sometimes this troubles them where they are now. Alpha worries about all the trouble she caused in the lives of others, especially in her own family. She does not blame her-self for the voices she heard that led her to do what she did. She says they were false spirits and they can fool anyone except the wisest of people. It worries her that Geneva, who did her no harm and intended none, was convicted of her murder.

Geneva is not troubled by that at all. *The thing is, there is no injustice in the spirit world. I am completely innocent here and I don't have to prove it or anything else.*

It seems that what happened in our world is unimportant except for the true crimes people have committed. They have to think about those things. But so many other things don't matter anymore. These spirits—at least the ones I know about—are very forgiving. They don't interfere in the lives of people still in our world, whether they loved or hated them. They watch them and forgive them and wish them well. They *watch over* us but without the power to do us good or evil.

Little David says, *I was right about one thing. Healing is the work of the Lord and I am glad I could do some. But you have to die to truly heal and be healed.*

You will be wondering—almost everybody does wonder—if they are aware of each other in the spirit world. And the best I can tell you is, yes, they are. And they have good feelings for each other. But it's not the same, either. The Scripture is right where it says there are no marriages in heaven. It seems like they are all together and yet they are all alone. At least at this stage.

"Tell me something," Billy says to her. "Have you ever been in touch with Father Claxton—you know, the Episcopal minister at St. Paul's who shot himself?"

He didn't shoot himself. Someone else shot him, but it looked like a suicide.

"Are you sure about that?"

What do I know except what he told me?

"Can you remember what he said to you?"

He said, *I forgive them, the ones who murdered me. They gave me a foolish death. But that folly opened the door to this dimension. I should be thankful.*

Billy notices that the afternoon light has begun to fade. He has been here a long time talking to this crazy woman. The last of the tea is cold in the bottom of his cup. He has heard the pickup start up and drive away. (That's my husband, Michael, she tells him. He's in the firewood business. He is a sweet, nice man but he can't read and write.) The ashtray in front of Darlene Blaze/Sister Cassandra is crowded with cigarette butts.

He stands up and stretches.

"I appreciate all the time you gave me," he says. He puts a twenty-dollar bill on the table. She ignores it, stands up herself and removes the bandanna from her head. Blond hair bursts free. It is as full, as bright and shiny as any model's on a TV shampoo commercial. He would like to touch it, to stroke it.

I am reading something on your mind, she says.

But it is not at all what he expects.

I see, she continues, a body, the body of a young black man in a white shirt lying facedown on the floor of a small room. He is not dead yet, but he is dying, bleeding from a bullet wound. He raises his head for a moment and we can see his face. Only now it is not the same face on the same young man. It is someone else. It is Martin Luther King and then he is dead.

Deeply troubled, Billy Tone drives back to town too fast and earns himself a speeding ticket.

A Little Later

MOE KATZ
PREFACE TO *FAT FAT FAT*:
PHOTOGRAPHS BY MARTIN PRESSY (1999)

So much has happened since, thirty years ago, Martin Pressy first came upon the scene with *The Magic Book of Woman*. The world has changed greatly—just *think* of the rush and swirl of changes since the 1960s! And as the world turns and changes, so has Martin Pressy; and as Martin Pressy has changed and grown in wisdom and stature, so has his art.

For one thing—not an unimportant development—Pressy has earned his stripes, paid his dues, and acquired an enviable national and international reputation as an artist. Shows in some of the nation's most influential museums testify to that, as do such honors as a MacArthur "genius" award. But the most significant witness to the power of his art is the art itself. His work speaks for itself, and the books he has brought out—*The Magic Book of Woman, Wounds and Scars* (1971), *Flesh* (1989) and now *FAT FAT FAT*—demonstrate the development of his art and can enhance our appreciation and understanding by helping us to come to terms with his major themes and obsessions, the chief of which is the perilous, quarrelsome marriage of body and soul. His principal subject clearly has been for all of these years the gradual and steady decay, disintegration and death of the body (outward and visible) and its implacable unfastening of itself from the (inward and spiritual) soul.

This was not easily evident at first. *The Magic Book of Woman*, celebrating, as it does, beauty of the youthful female form, might well have been misconstrued. It would have been easy to misperceive Pressy's artistic goals, by consigning his work to the general label of "glamour."

Changes in Pressy's life and his work allow us to see things differently. The biographical is often of no value whatsoever in coming to an understanding of an artist's work. But in Pressy's case some things, widely known now thanks to full-length pieces about him and his work in places like *People, Vanity Fair, GQ,* and *The New York Times Magazine,* are relevant. First that, shortly after finishing up *The Magic Book of Woman,* he became a photographer for the police in the (then) small Southern town of Paradise Springs. Out of this period in his life came the extraordinary photographs of corpses and terribly injured human beings which he deftly juxtaposed against photographs of ruined and wrecked automobiles and the rusting acres of automobile junkyards. *Wounds and Scars* was his "breakthrough" as an artist, giving rise to a serious reputation and a fiercely dedicated cult of admirers. During the same period while Pressy was working for the police, his beloved mother died. And Pressy, as he has indicated with some honest pride in several interviews, recognized that he is gay and came out of the closet. This latter liberation, of course, radically changed our sense of the meaning and implications of *The Magic Book of Woman*. Which may now be perceived as more satirical than it was originally taken to be.

Shortly after the publication of *Wounds and Scars* (which, by the way, Pressy had originally titled *Roadkills and Other Traumas*), Pressy moved to New York and created his studio there. For a good many years—eighteen to be exact—except for occasional forays into the world of high fashion, Pressy devoted himself to the work which ultimately appeared in a number of shows throughout the country and then in the book *Flesh*. These photographs are extreme closeups of fingers, knuckles, toes, hands and feet, unidentifiable except as being body parts and flesh, at once grotesque and beautiful, the body, skin and bones, abstracted from itself. There is a curious eroticism here, for all the curves and shapes of flesh seem to imply an entire body, exposed and easily accessible.

It was with the gallery shows and then the publication of the book based on them that Pressy received the accolade that only first-rate artists can earn, namely severe negative criticism from some (not all) of the prominent critics. They do not bother attacking the work of artists who are less than threatening to the status quo.

Never one to be deterred from his goals by critical praise or blame, Martin Pressy was already working on the subjects which are dominant in *FAT FAT FAT*. In his search for the spiritual essence of humankind, Pressy has here explored the grotesque excesses of the flesh in the forms of men and women of all ages, having in common only the enormity of their obesity. They are here portrayed in frame-filling nudity staring directly and solemnly at the camera/world-of-the-viewer. They are neither ridiculed (not a hint of Diane Arbus here) nor presented as possible objects of desire. Instead, beyond comedy or tragedy, they are presented as hugely vulnerable creatures. Like elephants or other rare and endangered beasts. They stand, facing the lens, altogether naked and yet somehow clothed in layers, wrappings, folds of flesh. Somehow their souls shine through the richness and ruin of their bodies. Jesse Helms or Jerry Falwell might not ever see it, but there is something purely spiritual and refined in these great, sad, harmless human beings. They suffer, yet they rejoice.

As in Pressy's other work, there is an implied sociopolitical statement in *FAT FAT FAT*. Elsewhere, particularly in the tormented Third World, poverty and hunger go together, and the victims of both conditions are as thin as skeletons. Here in America it is the rich, the beautiful, the lucky who are able to cultivate the luxury of being extremely skinny. The supermodels celebrate this curious American dream, being reduced to no more than bones and nerves and hanks of hair. But our poor, victims as much of the abundance of food as of the absence of money and status, are often incorrigibly obese. A cheap diet, overwhelming in its starch and fats, has rendered them unable to imagine themselves as beautiful.

And that is where the artist arrives. Studying Pressy's photos, accepting these people (in a total context of obesity), we come, first, to see ourselves, the fat person within ourselves, the heavy bear of self. But we also come to recognize the spirit of each of these beings, and of ourselves. And in the end, because the spirit is beautiful (or would be beautiful if we could only behold it), we see these freakish creatures as beautiful also, as worthy of admiration as of compassion.

The true artist is, among other things, a magician and, as such, more than a master of sleight of hand. The true magician is also dedicated to changing things, shapes, forms before our astonished eyes. With *FAT FAT FAT* Pressy has changed the world. After the experience of these photographs the world will look different and, perhaps, more wonderful.

Where will Pressy go next in his ceaseless quest for spirit and essence as revealed in flesh? God knows. But whatever Pressy does next, his work will be, as all his work has been, character-ized by visionary integrity, by technical expertise, and by a mind-set that, even at its bleakest and darkest moments, is never without a measure of irrepressible hope.   Moses Katz

Katz, you are getting more and more dotty as the years go by. But I love you like a brother for saying all these nice things.

Martin

Here and Now

THE POET: *How It Happened*

The man sits listening to country music playing softly on his portable radio. He sits awkwardly on a straight chair, hardly more than a stool, by the window. To his left a small dresser with a framed, adjustable mirror. Tilted so he doesn't have to see himself. Behind him the iron bedstead, a single bed with a soft, time-worn mattress. Holding the shape of him. Linoleum floor. He sips, mois-tens his tongue—no more—from a can of beer, opened a good while ago and nursed and already tepid, already tasting flat to him. The window he looks out of has no screen. He has raised the window about halfway and there is a chill in the air as evening comes on and he wonders if it is worth the trouble of lighting the gas stove in the fireplace. Wonders if, rusty and stained as it looks, the stove will even work. Meantime there's the radio, soft noise (it might as well be static), the odors of food cooking, rising from the bar and grill below on the street level and from the room just down the hall, a "light housekeeping" room with a kitchenette. The man who lives there, a middle-aged wino who has some kind of connection or relation to the landlady (he guesses), is frying up some meat on his stove.

The man in the chair by the open window is really not hungry

or thirsty, hot or cold, comfortable or uncomfortable. He is simply patient, relaxed like an athlete waiting for a whistle, a gong, a buzzer, an event to begin. His fingers rest lightly on the cracked layers of paint on the windowsill. He has pushed back the shabby curtains and raised the cloudy glass above his point of view.

The room behind him means nothing to him. Would not mean anything if he were forced to spend the rest of his life in it. Truth is, he has been in far worse places and spaces and, with his luck, he is likely to be there, in bad places, again.

He is not even thinking about that. He is thinking how calm he is. And that's a pleasure, a genuine source of pride. Because you never know, not for sure, how your body is going to behave. Your body can betray you. But he has trained and taught his body and his body has learned lessons. He raises both hands just above the windowsill, palms down, fingers together and extended. Not a quiver or a tremor. His breathing is even and steady.

He is also thinking that very soon, any minute now maybe, he is going to have to make a quick and an irrevocable decision. Either way it will work or not work. But he must decide which way to do it, one way or the other, not both.

What he can see from his window and see better from the bathroom down the hall is the pool and the parking lot of the motel across the street from where he is. He looks across the cluttered, brushy back lot behind his room, with a clear view of part of the motel and of the parking lot. The view is better, wider, from the bathroom window; and, just in case, he has already knocked the screen loose back there and dropped it into the bushes below. He has tested, raised and lowered the window also. The bathroom has some problems. For one thing, he will have to stand in the bathtub to have the best view out the window. The bathroom is also almost directly across the hall from the wino's kitchenette. A couple or three steps and the wino is in the bathroom. On the other hand the bathroom is right at the top of a flight of stairs going down. An easy exit compared to this room, 5-B, in the middle of the hallway.

Maybe he won't have to make up his mind. The wino or else the other guy in 5-A may be in there taking a pee or something.

A bath even, though that isn't likely. It doesn't look like anybody has used that old tub in a good long time.

He looks at his wristwatch. The time is getting close to six. The light is good, starting to turn, but not yet really fading.

Across the way a couple of cars turn into the lot and pull up and park in front of the motel. People are coming out of the rooms to the second-floor balcony.

He switches off the portable radio. Notices in the sudden quiet that the man next door isn't cooking anymore. Maybe he's eating now.

And now he is moving, smooth and unhurried, as if he were demonstrating how something like this is supposed to be done. By the numbers: Rises and turns to the bed and opens a large cardboard box there. It is a commercial carrying box for a Browning shotgun. But what he takes out of the box is not a shotgun, but a rifle, a Remington Gamemaster .30-06 pump-action rifle, model 760, with an attached seven-power telescopic sight. Moving already toward the bathroom (his feet have decided for him), he pulls from his pants pocket one of several penny-colored .30-06 cartridges. Pumps open the chamber and puts the cartridge directly in it, then pumps the chamber shut. Click-load-click. *A very satisfactory action. It is, after all, a brand-new rifle.*

He is in the bathroom, steps up and over, into the tub. Crouches slightly and places the muzzle on the windowsill. Looks through the sight and focuses. Even without the scope, just using the built-in iron sights, it ought to be an easy shot. Only a little more than two hundred feet.

He looks, studies. He can hear some banter between the men on the balcony and the men, the drivers, with their cars. Somebody says something and there is general laughter.

He ignores it. He is looking directly at a room number on a door: 306. *The door opens and the Target appears, steps to the balcony railing. One of the drivers hollers something to him.*

The man in the bathroom has stopped breathing, holds his breath. He takes up the slack on the trigger as the Target looks back toward room 306 again, then forward, his round, familiar, public, chocolate moonface filling the vision of the man in the bathroom as he tightens the trigger and then his ears are suddenly ringing from the explosion in the small room. And then the face pops like a balloon and vanishes.

The Poet then adds this note:

He had bullets, nine of them, they say now, in his pocket. But no clip. The rifle has a five-round clip. Why didn't he use the clip? Of course he didn't need it if there was only going to be one shot. But if he had missed the first time, he would have had to single-load another shot.

Doesn't prove anything. Just odd. And they never found the clip. Found everything else but not that.

Not necessary in any case. An easy shot, really. Think of that round head and face as bull's-eye. He could hardly miss it even though the shot was a little low and to the left.

Here and Now

CONVERSATION AT DAYLIGHT

Good news or bad news?
Do I get a choice?
Why not?
Bad news. Save the good for last.
Sure?
Go ahead and get it over with.

He tells her the truth as gently as he can. How his publisher has just been bought by an international communications company. How his contract has abruptly been canceled. How the Paradise Springs book won't come to pass. How—is this the good news?—his agent has lined up something else for him. Something out on the Coast. How—worst news—he has to leave and go out there right away. Immediately.

There is a mockingbird trilling and singing a rich repertoire, half a dozen different songs. Sounds so close that he could sit up in bed and reach and touch it.

Next to him she is crying softly into her pillow.

Don't be that way. Please.

What way?

This isn't really the end of anything. I'll be coming back for you as soon as I can. Or else I'll send for you.

How long have you known about this?

I don't know where or how. But I know we'll be together.

You could have told me before this.

I didn't want to spoil things.

It's not just that you are a liar, Billy, even though you do lie about almost everything. Even to yourself.

Come on. Get serious.

It's that you can't love anybody and you won't let anybody love you.

Even if that's true—which it isn't—people change. All the time.

You'll never change, Billy. I guess that's the main part of your charm.

Charm?

I didn't say you are not a nice guy.

Listen . . . I wish that mockingbird would shut the fuck up. Listen, Eleanor, I'll be anything you want me to be.

You're too old for me.

I knew it. I told you so.

Yes, you did. Well, I had to find out for myself.

I guess the whole thing was some kind of a learning experience for you.

It was fun while it lasted.

This is beginning to sound like some movie I saw.

She lights a cigarette.

Tell me all about Hollywood.

Hollywood is a place where everybody wants to be like Fellini only without doing a lick of work or taking any chances.

You can do better than that.

Okay. So there are these two guys, both of them producers, lost in the desert, dying of thirst. Suddenly they come upon a bubbling spring of clear water. Clear, clean, cold, wonderful water. Thank God, one of them says, and kneels down to drink. Wait a minute, the other one says, let me piss in it first.

I don't get it.

Maybe you had to be there.

Listen to that mockingbird.

(Smoke rings . . .)

Here and Now

ONE MORE LETTER TO CURLY

Dear Curly,

This has got to be a quick one.

If you are looking for a check (I know, I *promised*), forget it, old buddy. Sorry about that.

The deal on this book just fell through. But all is not lost. I'm off and running and will be in Los Angeles by the time you get this.

For reasons at once too banal and complicated to get into, I have got a good shot at doing a screenplay. It's supposed to be a comedy about a magic credit card. A vehicle for Tom Hanks or Tom Cruise or some Tom or other. I doubt very much that this thing will go very far. But if those guys are willing to pay me, I'll play any game they want me to. Whore that I am.

And if I get the job and get paid, just think, so will you. So wish me luck and not what you think I deserve.

Sure, I am more than a little sad the way things turned out. For a while, a few good minutes there, I was actually, seriously considering happiness as (as they say) a viable option.

Speaking of which, if you run into Annie, do me a favor, please. Please don't tell her any of this. It's not good for her to be proved right all the time.

I will be in touch with you once I get more or less settled out there in Cuckoo Land.

All best wishes to you.

Sincerely,
Billy

Then and There

FROM A LETTER OF GENEVA LASOEUR
(MARY LOU FROND)
ADDRESSED TO THE GOVERNOR

I know you are a very busy person and have troubles of your own. So I will try my best to be brief.

But I don't really know where to begin.

Well, one thing. I am sure that I got a fair trial, and the judge and the jury done what they thought was the right thing to do.

I know that I have committed a crime and that I have to be punished for it. But still I swear before God and man alike that I was not guilty of conspiring with Billy Papp to rob and kill the girl and Little David.

A lot came up at the trial that I didn't know anything about. A whole lot of it was news to me. And there were plenty of things to laugh at also. I do not blame the people for laughing at me. I have been laughed at before. A huge fat woman is usually a joke, any way you look at her. When they laugh, I do not blame them because it is so hard not to laugh sometimes even when you don't want to.

I am used to it now.

I am at peace with myself and with God. And I do not mind

their laughing anymore. Laughter is God's gift to humankind. If it wasn't for that gift, we would most likely all be crying all the time.

That was the truth that Little David taught me and it truly changed my life.

One time I had been all healthy and good-looking. Many men thought I was beautiful and they desired me in that sense. Then I got this thing, this *condition*. The doctors couldn't agree on the name for it, but I surely got it, name or no name, and I just blew up in size like a big gas balloon.

Being a woman and even a beautiful one once, I was very hurt and confused. I cussed everything and everybody and most of all I hated myself.

More than one time I tried to kill myself. But I was always too scared of the pain to do a good job of it.

I was a lost soul.

Then one time I went to a revival where they claimed to have healing. Because I would try anything. When I kneeled down, Little David put his hands on my head. And he whispered to me that there was no way he could make me young and thin and beautiful again, but he could *heal* me nevertheless.

I was very mistrustful and suspicious. But I went to him again later, privately, and he talked me into joining up with him and his group. The way it worked with me was very slow and gradual. I saw all kinds of suffering and tribulation all the time. And I saw how he suffered too, and always had, being so little and sickly and all. And after a while I came to realize that I did not care all that much about myself anymore. Not enough to hate myself. Little by little, I stopped worrying about me, myself and I all the time.

And that is how I came to love him. I stopped hating me and started loving him. And he loved me, too. And then it was a true glory, for I was truly healed.

We became common-law man and wife together and we shared one bed. I know that people would not want to believe this, and even if they did it would just make them laugh to imagine the two of us together. That is because they could not fully understand. I have been, as my record plainly proves, a prostitute and a hard-living woman in my time. I know all about sex and what can be done. And I know from experience that love and sex are not exactly the same thing. I had plenty of experience both good and bad.

Nobody has a right to know what went on between us privately. All I can say without being ashamed is that I loved him and he loved me and it was glory. There were times when I felt as light and frail as a little girl again and when he was a giant as big as a mountain.

Now I want to explain how things happened that night. I have seen and known many crazy things in my lifetime. And many times I have had to wonder if I wasn't crazy myself. But I have never seen anything to beat that night.

It is true that I did notice that young woman, the late Alpha Weatherby, because when I was first passing the collection plate, she reached in her pocket and produced a big fistful of bills and just plunked it in the plate, *deposited* it so to speak, like maybe an old candy wrapper or something.

A thing like that would be enough to make anybody take notice. And she and her friend had an argument about her giving away all that money. Her friend wanted to snatch it back, but Miss Alpha Weatherby wouldn't let her.

Naturally I pointed her out to Little David as soon as I had a chance.

Later on in the service she came up front to witness and to be saved. And her friend wasn't with her. She put another wad of cash in my plate up there. Then she spoke to me and asked me if she could see David in private later.

She did not seem crazy. She was very soft-spoken and she looked sincere to me at the time. And anyway she had already put so much money in the plate that I couldn't just refuse her.

That seemed to suit her, so I took her out the back of the tent and over to our trailer.

I better admit to something since it can't do any harm anyway now. That wasn't the first time I ever took a woman to our trailer like that. In our line of work we depend a good deal on people who get moved by the spirit and end up giving away a lot of cash as an offering. We never went out of our way to discourage them. That may have been wrong in a way, but we had to keep alive and keep going. And then, naturally, Little David had a way of attracting various kinds of women to him and his cause. Some of these women could be weird. So I would keep my eyes open and be available in case anything went wrong.

If I had ever suspected that Alpha Weatherby was crazy, I would never have led her to our trailer in a million years. But she appeared to be a sincere and deeply religious person and I guess that fooled me.

We went inside the trailer and I turned on all the lights and started the air-conditioning to make it comfortable. While I was doing that, she emptied her pockets on the bunk. I saw the pile of money and I also saw the pistol. And I knew then that there was trouble. But I didn't want to let on that I had noticed anything strange.

"Are you comfortable?" I said to her. "The air-conditioning will have it nice and cool in a few minutes."

"I'm fine," she said. "But I think I'll just slip out of this raincoat if you don't mind."

And I said to myself, Geneva, this is a crazy world and maybe you are crazy, too, from living in it. But this girl takes the all-time prize and you better get your ass in gear and warn David what is waiting for him in the trailer.

I excused myself politely and started back to tell David.

Only by that time the snakes had got loose in the tent, and then the tent was catching fire.

In the confusion I couldn't even find him.

Everything was all going on at the same time. It is a wonder I just didn't keel over dead with a stroke. I tried to catch my breath and think. I remembered that Billy Papp owned a pistol.

I thought I had better go borrow it quick before that girl had a chance to do anything with hers.

When I came bursting into Papp's trailer, there was her friend, the other one, dancing around. I tell you, I thought the end of the world was upon us. But I got Papp's gun and I remember *running* back to our trailer. I hardly ever run if I can help it because it is so hard on my heart. But at that time I didn't even think of that. I just started running. People were all milling around and I had to push and shove my way through them. I guess it did look wild, a great big fat woman, waving a pistol in her hand, and trying to run. It was not a sight you would forget right away. I wasn't surprised when they testified about how I looked and acted.

When I got inside the trailer, everything stopped dead. It looked like a movie or a photograph instead of something real. There she was with all of her hair cut off, standing with the hair all around her bare feet. She had David's straight razor in her hand, testing the sharpness of it with her thumb.

I knew she was going to kill him. I knew that she was going to kill him and cut off his head. I could tell it all in her eyes. And I could tell that he did not know it, either.

I did the only thing I could do. I started shooting with the pistol. I did not intend to hit anyone. I was not aiming at anybody. Just shooting to stop everything from happening.

I must have accidentally hit him first because he fell over by the bunk. Then she came towards me with the razor. And so I didn't see him grab her pistol. I was now pointing my pistol at her, in self-defense, and pulling the trigger. But it was not stopping her, and I realized that my pistol was empty and just going *click, click, click.* Then there was a loud noise again only it was her pistol this time, and she fell flat right in front of me. I saw her eyes go blank and dead as she fell. And I saw his eyes fading too as he fell off the bunk.

Papp came into the trailer and snatched his pistol back from me.

Right behind him came the police.

It all happened real fast and just the way I told it. And nobody had said a word to each other. The first ones to say anything were the police.

I still do not understand some parts of it. I know I was not trying to shoot David. That was an accident. But something else I am pretty sure of now. It was also an accident when David shot the girl. He intended to hit me, but his aim wasn't steady and she stepped right into the line of fire. What he must have thought was that I was out of my mind, going berserk out of jealousy. I know that's what he must have thought. And if he thought that, then he thought I had shot him on purpose.

I am sorry I never had a chance to explain to him.

I am sorry he is dead and I am sorry for the girl too.

And I am sorry for Billy Papp. Because he didn't really have anything to do with it. Knowing him as well as I do, I expect he probably was going to steal our money and take off. But then, there is no proof that we ever collected all that money anyway. There is only what was left of the girl's money in the trailer.

Your Honor, I know I am guilty. But I am not guilty of the whole thing that they said. It is not true that me and Billy conspired together with David to kill that girl. All I can say is I know how it was because I was there.

But I have no real complaints against anyone.

I have to ask your mercy because I am afraid of jail and I don't want to die in there.

If you can find some way to let me off, I will be grateful with all my heart.

But if you cannot find a reason or a way, I won't blame you.

If I have to stay in jail, I will surely die there. I cannot promise to be brave about all this, but I will do the best I can. For I believe that Almighty God, who has always loved me, will be kind to me in my misery. And one day I will shed my weary flesh and bones like old clothes and then my heart will be light again. I will be so light I can float on the air.

I am sorry about all the trouble I have caused you and the State of Florida.

There is only one more trouble I want to cause anybody. I have a married sister in Fort Worth, Texas. She is happily married to a chiropractor there. She feels bad and guilty about me, because I put her through school and everything but she was always ashamed of me. She has never done anything for me or had a chance to. When I die, I hope you will send my body to her so she can see that it gets buried properly. That will give her a chance to make up for what she hasn't done and to feel better about herself.

Don't we all need a chance for something like that?

Yours truly,
Geneva Lasoeur

Here and Now

A FEW WORDS OF FAREWELL

Making his manners, Billy Tone bids farewell to some of the people of Paradise Springs who have been helping him to create the book that was not to be.

LLOYD MACINTYRE

This time we had lunch at the Palmetto Club. Lloyd's treat. Included a pretty fair bottle of wine. So we could raise a toast or two to the perilous profession.

Billy, I'm sorry to see you go. Mainly because I have gradually, by fits and starts, found myself more and more interested in the year your untold story happened.

Guess who won the Heisman Trophy that year—O. J. Simpson.

But, all historical irony aside, it was a wild year, one of a series of wild and troubled years all across the globe.

Here's one for you. When did the massacre at My Lai take place? Give up? March 16, 1968. Somehow, even though it was reported, it was not "known," as they say, until 1970. But My Lai was part of the atmosphere. Just as, I suspect, down the road a bit we may well see that Idaho shootout and the Waco affair (can we call it a massacre?) were symbolic parts of something that went wrong between the American people and their government in our time.

I have to give the conservatives that much. Judging by those events, it really does look sometimes like Jack Weatherby's paranoid fantasies have some basis in fact—this government, this administration will kill you dead (in Idaho, in Texas, in Somalia) if you get in the way of their policies and programs and public relations.

Maybe that was always true. Maybe it was true in 1968.

Maybe I am just a burned-out newspaperman. Funny, isn't it? Prosperity has finally come to Paradise Springs. We are a growing city. My circulation is growing by leaps and bounds. The paper is making more and more money. Things are looking up. So why do I feel so vulnerable and threatened? Why do I feel like we are getting close to the tag end of things? Why do I fantasize that some crazy towelhead in Iraq or Iran is going to cause more trouble than you can imagine? Why am I not looking forward to the elections in November? Why is my most habitual gesture these days a great big shrug?

Well, here's to it, then, Billy. A toast to the great American shrug.

PENROSE WEATHERBY

Finally went out to see his big new house by the lake. A genuine manse (shades of a high-tech Tara!), just as you might have guessed, set on a couple of acres of grass as smooth and well-tended as a putting green. (P. took me for a spin on his John Deere lawnmower.) Met the lovely wife, Linda. A big-haired blonde originally from Wisconsin, wearing linen slacks, a cute T-shirt and sandals (beautiful feet and painted toenails). Met their two children, too—Jennifer and (what else) Ronald. Resisted a strong urge to ask him about the older, other son— Widdy.

Well, sir, of course I wouldn't wish you, or anybody else, any bad luck. I mean, there's plenty of bad luck to go around without looking for it. But I have to tell you that I am relieved you aren't going ahead with your book. Nothing personal. It's just that we have come such a long way since then. I mean, we were just a quiet little town, a backwater place, in those days. Going nowhere in particular and not in much of a hurry, either. Now look at us. We are part of the present, part of the action. And we have got a real future. You can bet on that. You can count on it.

What's the point of digging up the past, anyway? Nothing but ghosts and bones in the past anyway. Nothing but old news and sad stories.

Still and all, it might have been some fun to walk through the events with you. I mean, I don't have any special knowledge about what took place. But I was a bright and eager kid, around and about and with my eyes wide open. I might have been able to help you.

Sometimes I wonder what our lives would have been like if Alpha hadn't been murdered. Sometimes I wonder what might have become of her.

But mostly I try to live as fully as I can in the present and to keep my eyes on the future. I want Jenny and Ron to have a better life. I want to leave this world a little better place than I found it.

Isn't that the American way?

JACK WEATHERBY
I'll tell you something about the future. Do you see this piece of shit?

He hands me a booklet put out by Baptist College (not Baptist Barbecue): "Teaching a Diverse Student Body: Practical Strategies for Enhancing Our Students' Learning."

Now. Take a look at page two—"The Face of America in the Twenty-first Century." This is the key to their whole argument that we have to change the whole system and be multicultural. Why we have to have our children learn barbarian studies.

According to their own figures (assuming they are right) in a hundred years the white majority will have dropped from seventy-five percent to about fifty-three percent. Big deal! Look at the positive side. A whole hundred years from now we'll still be in the majority. And in a democracy (if that's what we are), that is what matters.

Unless they do what that Lani Guinier person wants to and give every barbarian two or three votes or whatever.

Anyway, I can't see any good reason why little white kids like my grandchildren should have to learn to talk Swahili or how to do Yoruba arithmetic or study grass-hut architecture.

Hey, why don't you sit down and write a book that tells it like it really is? I could help you a lot.

Or maybe you could help me. I've been working on one myself. I call it *Notes on the Niggerization of America*. I don't pull any punches, either.

Can you recommend a good publisher for a book like that? Will I need to have an agent?

SHERIFF DALE LEWIS

Win a few, lose a few.

Tell you the truth, I think you'll be a whole lot better off out in Hollywood writing about magic credit cards and shit like that.

Of course, I have to admit I was kind of hoping that with all your digging around, if you dug deep enough and long enough, you might come up with some answers about that Claxton case.

I say "case." But it isn't. Long since closed, over and done with. It's just a case in my mind. For no particular reason.

Loose ends. That's what life, real life is, Billy, a bundle, a crazy circuit of loose ends. Everybody looking for the pattern and there isn't any. Or if there is one, then only God can see it.

But we keep trying.

You keep trying, too, you hear?

See if you can hit it big out there in Dreamland. Then come on back and let's go bone-fishing down in the Keys.

DEBBY LANGLEY

Well, I am sorry about things, Mr. Tone. I was looking forward to reading your book and finding out what really happened back then.

Here I was, living the insulated life of a college student, far from the madding crowd (as they say), and all kinds of wild stuff was happening that I didn't know the first thing about.

I was so dumb in those days. Dumb but beautiful, if I do say so myself.

Now I'm not a whole lot smarter and I am sure not better-looking. But I like to think I am a little wiser. And I know I am happier.

When I was young and dumb and beautiful, I didn't even know what happy was. It was something I read about in school. Something every American had a constitutional obligation to pursue. But I didn't have a clue what it was or might be.

Happiness is helping other people, Mr. Tone. I have dedicated my life to helping Benjamin to pull his life together. To stop drinking and to start writing again. He is a wonderful writer. And he is going to get tenure next year or I'll know the reason why.

We have a lot of fun together, too. I don't mean only in *that* way. Though I am not ashamed to say we really click together in that way, too. But we have a lot of mutual interests. Like classical music and golden oldies and NBA basketball. He doesn't like to watch tennis as much as I do. But I reckon I can live without it.

Once Ben gets tenure, I expect we'll tie the knot and live happily ever after. He hasn't said anything definite, but I know it's what he wants to do. And so do I.

I wish the same to you, Mr. Tone. It's too bad that things didn't work out for you and Eleanor. But maybe they will. I mean, it isn't over until the fat lady sings, as they say.

I have to admit I never really understood that old saying. What fat lady? And what song is she supposed to sing?

Well, never mind.

Have a nice life.

RUTHE-ANN COOMBS

The trailer doesn't look much different than it did before. More books and magazines everywhere, if that's possible. More dirty dishes and glasses. Light shining through the Kate Moss lampshade. A morning talk show playing silently on the TV. Ugly people shouting at each other but not a sound. (I see the sense of it.) Katz in the little bathroom. Ruthe-Ann in housecoat and bedroom slippers.

I often think about how it was for us back then. The big obvious difference is that we were a whole lot younger. Or, at least, he wasn't *old* yet. I was still a teenager even if I had already been married a couple of times.

My trailer wasn't anywhere near as big and comfortable as this one is. But it was a whole lot neater. We didn't have all these books and clutter in those days. He still had an office out at the college. And it was like we were still getting acquainted. He was trying to make a good impression and would pick up after himself.

He would listen, too. I did a lot more talking than I do now. And he liked to listen to me jabber on for some reason.

Truth is, Mr. Tone, we had some good times. We had some fun. And, you know something? We still do. Sure, he is getting pretty old and sick. I reckon I could lose him anytime, though I hope not, even if I am the beneficiary of his life insurance policy. Because we get along. We like each other. Which is a whole lot more than a lot of couples I know of.

I'll tell you something else while I'm at it. One thing I really appreciate about old Moe Katz is he never tried to change me. Or to educate me. I have learned a lot of things from being around him and listening to him. But I did it on my own. He never tried to teach at me. If you know what I mean.

I mean, I am not an educated woman. It didn't work out that way. But he never was ashamed of me. Never. And he always respected me for my intelligence. "You got aplenty of native intelligence, Ruthe-Ann," he would say. "Not to mention good common sense. And I admire you for it."

Hey, we have had a pretty good life together. And I know I'll miss him when he's gone.

MOSES KATZ

Pretty soon here comes Katz out of the toilet in his wheelchair ready for some serious talking. Ruthe-Ann gets him a Diet Dr. Pepper and fixes me an iced tea. And I present Moe with a farewell gift. A copy, hot off the press (and at thirty-five bucks a throw), of *Arthur Elgort's Models Manual,* a big fat book with all the supermodels in it. He flips a few pages and begins:

It's a beauty. Worth whatever you had to pay for it. Probably too much. Worth every penny if only for the sake of this picture of Linda Evangelista playing the accordion. Oh, my, the amazing nostrils on that girl!

You probably already heard the Cindy Crawford joke. These days jokes are a little late getting to me now that I'm housebound.

Anyway. A guy is shipwrecked on a desert island. Settles in, all alone like Robinson Crusoe before Friday came along, and gradually has a pretty good life. Lonely, lonesome, but not without its comforts.

For a long time he sees not a sign of any ships or even jet trails. Like rescue is pretty much out of the question.

And then one day Cindy Crawford, half-conscious and about half-dead, comes drifting into shore, clinging to a big piece of driftwood. The sole survivor of another shipwreck. She is starving and terribly sunburned, suffering from dehydration and exposure.

Patiently, slowly, gently he nurses her back to health. And eventually she is as good as new.

One thing leads to another. As soon as she realizes that they are not going to be rescued right away, she settles down and becomes a good companion. They start sleeping together. Everything is just fine and dandy.

Then one day he says to her: "Cindy, we know each other pretty well now and all, I wonder if I could ask you to do something special for me?"

"Anything within reason," she says. "You saved my life."

"Well," he says, "this may sound a little crazy. But would you mind painting a mustache over your upper lip?"

A long pause. Then: "I guess I could do that if it pleases you."

"One other thing."

"What's that?"

"Could I call you Dave sometimes?"

A longer, brow-wrinkled pause. Then: "Oh, all right, I guess so."

"Great!" he says. Then: "Hey, Dave, guess who *I'm* fucking."

"I don't get it," Ruthe-Ann says.

It's a male thing, Moe says. Don't worry about it.

I see that he has been reading the *Times Literary Supplement* for March 11, 1994. For the sake, evidently, of the headlined lead article—"What Destroyed Weimar?"

The books keep coming out faster than I can read them. But I am going to keep at it. It's a big project.

And I have other good reasons for living. I can't wait to see Altman's *Prêt à Porter*. Which is bound to come along one of

these days. I really like his stuff. Back when I first saw *Nashville,*
I thought he was a smart-ass who hated all of us. And maybe
he is and maybe he does. But that's not what comes across,
finally. Another thing. I was confused by thinking that he is a
subtle filmmaker. He isn't. Farce is his genre, and the big broad
stroke.

You know, Billy, he could almost do a job with our little
Paradise Springs 1968 story. A whole bunch of people on separate, often parallel tracks. Like a big railroad yard. Full of noise
and activity. And what would he end up with? God knows. We
never will.

Well, I wish you the best of luck out there. Swimming with
the sharks. But who knows? Maybe we are ready for a credit-
card myth.

JOJO ROYLE

We met out at the airport. He showed up astraddle a big
hog (Harley Davidson) of a motorcycle. He puts me in mind of
Marlon Brando.

Am I too old for Hell's Angels? Maybe they have a senior
chapter.

Like it? I just got it from a biker almost as old as I am.

I'll tell you what else is new. I told Penrose Weatherby I am
finally willing to cut a deal and sell him this airport if he makes
me a good enough offer. Did he tell you that? No, I wouldn't
think he would.

Truth is, I could use the money. I'm getting too old to live
on the edge. Next thing you know I'll be one of these homeless
old farts, lugging everything I own in a plastic trash bag.

You know, I've been thinking ever since you came back, and
especially since we sat up all night drinking and talking like a
couple of kids. Thinking how we are just about the end of the
line for our kind, our people.

I'm not sad or pissed off about it. Everything burns out and
comes to an end. It's our turn now. But we had a good run.

We had some good fun while it lasted. Kicked a little ass, too, while we were at it. They can't take that away from us.

You know, Billy, I think if World War Two came along now, we wouldn't be able to win it. Not anymore. Can you picture Clinton—or any of them, *anybody* else, for that matter—leading us to victory against the Nazis and the Japs?

But there I go. There I am, just like all the rest of the family, living in the past.

I'll tell you, though, when the time comes, I'll be ready for it. There isn't a lot that I would miss. Letting go will be easy as can be.

Not just yet, though. Hop on the back of this hog, Billy, and let's open it up and see what it will do.

W. E. GARY

He came over to my place, Eleanor's house, to say goodbye. Jeans and jogging shoes and a very expensive leather jacket. Very courteous. Besides, I think he may have wanted to take a peek at the place. Place where Martin Pressy lived. See how it's faring. I expect his firm represents Pressy. Who else? If he had ever been inside before, he didn't let on.

He begins with the latest lawyer joke:

What's the difference between a lawyer and a catfish? Well, one is a nasty, bottom-feeding, shit-eating mudsucker. And the other is just a fish.

You know, one thing I am truly grateful to you for is that you never asked me what my thoughts, if any, were concerning Raphael McKenzie. I was waiting for that. Figured that sooner or later you would have to give in to the conventional theory (credited by liberals and conservatives alike) that it takes one to know one.

You want a little irony to chew on? Consider how many of our black writers have built whole careers depending on that stereotypical principle.

But there is more to it. Another turn of the screw. Precisely because you never asked me about the man (and, as time went on, seemed unlikely to) I began to think about him more than I might have otherwise. I wanted to come up with some kind of an answer, if only for myself.

Easier said than done. I don't have a clue. Or, to put it another way and more accurately, I have just a whole lot of clues, most of them inconsistent or downright contradictory.

I have studied his picture. To put it in your terms, Billy, he looks a lot like maybe a brother or a cousin of James Earl Jones. Which thought, right away, makes you wonder about his voice. Did he have a big, baritone, "Ol' Man River" voice? Maybe so. We know for a fact that he often led the singing whenever there was an integrated or a black congregation.

What else do we really know? Not much. He was a snake handler. No mean feat. He seems to have been reasonably trustworthy. He was deemed so, anyway, by Little David, and the rest of the group. A reliable kind of a person.

And not without a certain wit. The best photograph, the one they used several times in the paper, shows him standing posed against the assertively sixtyish psychedelic background of a Little David Enterprises truck covered with biblical illustrations. They are crudely drawn but brightly colored. They look almost like certain Haitian paintings.

Do you suppose he painted them himself?

Anyway, there he stands posing with the truck in the background. He is jaunty and more than a little silly in his pith helmet, his starched Bermuda shorts and his neat kneesocks. His desert boots. His General Douglas MacArthur corncob pipe at a bold angle.

I swear to God, Billy, I never saw a black man dress up like that. Not even as a joke or a costume.

Raphael McKenzie, if that is really and truly his name, comes here with this down-at-the-heels, nomadic little gospel troupe. While here he is only peripherally involved in their activities. And he is in no way, except as a witness for the State, involved in their crimes. He does his bit. He testifies in court. And then he

goes on his merry way, leaving not a trace as far as I can determine.

Who was he?

What did he think and know?

What became of him?

I am at a loss. Left with a web of questions.

And I owe it all to you—for not asking me. If you had asked,
I would probably have come up with something and then forgotten the fellow forthwith and forever.

As it is, I am likely to remember him for the rest of my life,
imagining a life, a series of alternative lives, for him. If I am not
very careful, Raphael McKenzie could become the scholar gypsy
of my own life.

As for Brother Martin Luther King, Jr. . . .

I appreciate the fact that you never once asked me my views
or my feelings about King. Everybody else does sooner or later.
That fuckin' one-eyed poet calls me up in the big middle of the
night.

But you didn't, Billy. And for that reason I am going to tell
you a couple of things. How I felt at the time. And one or two
things about the here and now.

When King was killed in Memphis, the same day we had the
tent revival murders here, I wasn't surprised at all. It confirmed
what I believed about white folks and what we called in those
days "the power structure." (Remember that?)

I was a kid. I didn't really approve of King. Oh, of course,
I took pride in seeing him, a black man, in the papers and on
TV, and it tickled me to see him moving with hotshots—the
President, governors, mayors. Like he was part and parcel of the
power structure himself. And I guess he was, when you think
about it.

Well now. I have to admit that I am part of the power structure myself. And I understand him better than I did then. I'm
not a kid anymore.

Back then I thought of King as a kind of an Uncle Tom in
a coat and tie. My secret heroes were guys like Rap Brown, with

his bandolier of bullets (and nothing to put them in), and Stokely Carmichael. While King was running around shooting his mouth off about this and that and the other, the young guys were *doing* things. Stokely had been to Hanoi and back. Rap Brown was under arrest by February of '68.

What I thought and felt that Thursday night, that weekend and for some time after, was that what happened to King was absolute proof of what happens when you play the white man's game by the white man's rules. When you get in their way, they will kill you.

All those riots (in more than a hundred different cities) in the days and nights that followed? Serves them right, I thought. Serves *him* right, King I meant, too, for all that mealymouthed, phony preaching about nonviolence.

But at the very same moment I felt a great sense of loss. Like somebody close and dear in the family had died.

Talk about mixed feelings. Contradictions. And there I was devoting my time and energy to looking after the Judge. And not even seeing or sensing any contradiction. It was like "real" life—me and Mama and the Judge—was completely separate from everything else.

Anyway. Time has changed everything. I won't say I was wrong. But I don't have the same views anymore. I think of Rap Brown and Stokely and (later) Huey Newton and that whole crowd as basically silly. They accomplished next to nothing. Nothing good came from them.

I think I understand King now. He wasn't a saint and a lot of his actions and achievements were smoke and mirrors. But he accomplished a lot. Not denying that. We owe him, you and I.

And one more thing, Billy. Something I have been thinking about for quite a while.

Let me put it this way. The biographers sweat and strain to make something, some kind of a story, out of his childhood. They huff and they puff. But there's nothing there except the privileged life of a spoiled preacher's son. The best they can come up with is a couple of very slight racial incidents—buying a pair of shoes one time and the clerk was rude; sitting in the back of the bus when everybody else had to anyway. And there is the death of his grandmother. And a couple of times he jumped out of his window in that big fine house he grew up in. They like to hint that he was suicidal. But, Billy, the window he jumped out of was like six or eight feet off the soft ground. Whatever else, young or old, King wasn't dumb. Nobody ever accused him of being dumb. I figure he was just making a quick and unobtrusive exit when he chose to go out the window.

What you can't deny is that he had a good, safe childhood and youth, not more than normally troubled. Protected. I mean, the Depression was going on and it seems never to have touched him or his family. When he was old enough, his daddy gave him a brand-new car. (That would be in the late forties.) Not such a big deal these days—I see kids from this little Baptist College tooling around in *BMWs,* and I even saw one kid at the wheel of a Range Rover. But in those days there were damn few kids whose folks bought them a car, new or old.

And so forth and so on.

Point I'm trying to make is that, by luck, by chance (call it what you will), by destiny, he was lifted to leadership from an almost completely safe and protected background. So utterly and completely different from the rest of us.

You might think that this form of innocence would be a great weakness. And in a sense it was. It was his greatest weakness. But at the same time it was his greatest strength. He had no reason at any time to imagine that things would go badly for him. Not the least idea of failure. And for quite a while, most of his life and career, all things seemed to confirm his expectations. You did good work and you succeeded and you were properly rewarded for it. Danger? What danger? Nothing happened to him. And I am not forgetting the time he was stabbed in the chest by that crazy woman in Harlem. That moment when he was a sneeze away from death. Point is he *didn't* die. Instead of making him afraid, it must have made him feel he was immortal. Certainly that (and everything else) made him feel he was chosen. That he really was like old Moses leading the people to the Promised Land. And in a very real and true sense he was.

And when he went out, when it was over, it was not (as it very well might have been) in a gradual series of failures and disappointments and losses. It came instantly—*whamo!* Blew his brains out before he had a chance to discover what I knew from about the time I knew my own name and long before I knew how to spell it. That life is all about losing. That nothing I do or leave undone, no success and no failure can change that. It's in the terms of the equation.

Martin Luther King, Jr. was spared that knowledge. But he paid the price for it. In the end it cost him his life.

You know what they say. You want proof that God has a sense of humor? Make a plan and see what happens.

REV. PETER WHEELRIGHT
Fulfill now, O Lord, the desires and petitions of thy servants as may be best for us; granting us in this world knowledge of thy truth, and in the world to come life everlasting. Amen.

DARLENE BLAZE/SISTER CASSANDRA
She called and asked me to come out and see her before I left town. "There's something I have to tell you about," she said. "No charge."

We talked in her dining room again. Incense burning. Country music playing softly in the kitchen or somewhere.

None of this may mean anything to you. I don't know. I have no way of knowing. And I do know that you are cynical and skeptical about communications from the spirit world. So are most people. And if I didn't know better, I might be that way, too.

Nevertheless, I have a message from the spirit world to you. I repeat it because it is my bounden duty to do so.

This message seems to be from the ghost of a black teenager who seems to be named Leroy Bethune of Port Orange, Florida.

He says he was shot and killed in 1968 during the robbery of a filling station where he was working.

According to him you were present at that time but did not actually see it happen. The people who shot him, a man and a woman, had no regrets or remorse at the time or even later on. Regret was not a part of their nature.

He says, though, that you have been deeply troubled and uncertain and guilt-ridden ever since then. Often to your own disadvantage and also to the disadvantage of other people close to you.

He does not think you should forget the event. That will be impossible, anyway, until the time comes when your memory fails you completely. Not to forget, then, but at least not to continue to indulge yourself in pointless self-scrutiny and guilt. The truth is that it had nothing much to do with you. You probably could not have stopped it from happening even if you had known in advance that it was going to happen:

Tell the man I forgive him. Where I am—and where he will be when the time comes—forgiveness is easy as pie. Tell the man I appreciate being remembered. But it is a big waste of time to be guilty about crimes and sins you didn't commit. There are enough bad things you have done and will do to worry about.

Mr. Tone, I am only like a messenger in this matter. I don't have the slightest idea (and, frankly, I couldn't care less) if this ghost is telling the truth. In this business there are always some evil spirits and bad angels who will tell lies and try to mislead people.

But, anyway, that's what this ghost told me to pass on to you.

The rest is up to you.

ELEANOR LEALAND

These words not spoken out loud, though how could I fail to hear her voice as I read them? Written on some nice (proper?) notepaper from the Frick Museum. Good little print of Whistler's *Harmony in Pink and Gray* (1881), portrait of young and proudly good-looking (beneath a splendid hat) Valerie, Lady Meux. Eleanor has highlighted one sentence in the brief accompanying text: "A colorful figure in society, she once created a sensation by appearing at a hunt riding an elephant."

I know real things in real life don't often have happy endings. Maybe never. Even so I'm sorry that things didn't work out for you, Billy. And I'm even sorrier, truth be told, that things didn't work out for us together. It's not cosmic. In the grand scheme of things it's worth maybe a sigh and a shrug as we go on about the muddle, what we euphemistically like to call the *business* of our lives.

Sigh. Shrug.

Listen, Billy, the truth is I'm going to miss you a lot. A whole lot. You're too old for me; we agreed on that. And we both have plenty of wounds and problems and bad habits. (So? So did Adam and Eve.) But, hey, we had some good times, some happy times to remember. To remember without regret. And I'm grateful to you for that.

It was a good thing to be in love again. While it lasted.

Good luck to you in Hollywood. Who knows? Maybe you'll have a little luck for a change. Whether you do or not, you can maybe take some comfort in the idea that I am (and always will be) rooting for you, wishing you well.

Then and There

ALPHA

He is just now beginning to shave my head clean and smooth
When lo and behold THE ANGEL OF THE LORD doth appear
How grand how bright how radiant all clothed in the light
The Devil does now his shiny blade put down and in fear does he grovel and crawl

Who knows that he cannot with Angels converse in words

Who knows not that words are the dupe and bane of poor mankind and are only dust to Angels

Who knows not that Angels speak only in the language of eyes oh eyes speaking as swift as sight and light

Who poor himself now though once upon a time an Angel himself and more shining than most and O so sadly fallen

Who has long since forgotten the radiance and has lost the immemorial language of the eyes

And so I speak to the Angel with eyes bright and blue as summer sky

Saying tarry a moment with me and wait until I am done and my bounden duty is discharged

Turn then from the Angel to the other there to see the straightedged shiny blade of his doom and all my joy

Taking then the straight and shiny blade of joy and doom

And now the Angel moves to take me home on wings of fire

Amen

BE WITH US, MERCIFUL ANGELS, NOW AND FOREVER